大学英语 **6** 级考试

听力必备

主　编：王长喜

副主编：曾利娟

　　　　郑成功

《长喜英语》图书编委会 编

中国和平音像电子出版社

前　言

今年，六级考试结束后，我们对北京、西安、上海、武汉十几所高校的考生做了一次深层访谈，很多人反映，听力部分很头痛。

首先，听音很被动。播音一开始，自己就被牵着走，不知道该注意哪儿、记录哪儿，稀里糊涂听完了，一看题，脑子里空空的。

其次，做题没节奏。播音听完了，一做题，往往一片空白，急着回忆刚听过的内容，下面又开始了，常常手忙脚乱，信心全无。

这么多考生对听力感到头痛，四、六级考试委员会一项内部阅卷统计也印证了这一点——考生听力部分平均得分不超过 130 分。

我们的分析

我们分析认为，很多考生之所以对听力不适应、得分低，主要由下面几个原因所致：

1、题型不熟悉　不同的听力题型有不同的考查倾向、不同的设题方式、不同的练习重点、不同的做题方法，对各个题型不熟悉、不理解，就不能针对练习、针对做题，导致复习盲目。

2、基础不扎实　听力最基本的语音能力、词汇能力、语法能力、特殊表达等不能扎实掌握，就很难在听力练习和听力考试中游刃有余。少了最基本的听力基础，别的什么都谈不上。

3、技巧没掌握　听力考试中，需要一定的、针对性的做题技巧，实用的听音技巧、推测技巧、做题技巧，可以让您在考试中从容自信、最佳发挥。好的技巧，可以给能力锦上添花。

4、练习不充分　归根到底，听力能力的提高最终还是要多练习，多听、多练，这是一条铁律。没有充分的练习量，技巧讲得再多、规律分析得再透彻，都只是帮衬，多听才是根本。

5、复习没定性　听力复习不是零碎进行、一蹴而就的，它需要一个计划、一个安排。很多考生听力复习三天打鱼、两天晒网，没有系统、没有计划，导致复习效率低、效果不明显。

本书的对策

为了帮助广大考生科学攻克听力难关、切实提高听力成绩，我们在对新题型听力潜心研究的基础上，编写了这本书，希望她能带您一起扎实基础、熟悉题型、掌握技巧、充分训练，循序渐进中必备知识全面掌握，步步为营中听力水平稳步提高。打好基础、各个击破、讲练一体、一气呵成，考场之上直取高分。

1、循序渐进 稳扎稳打 全书将基础讲解、题型分析、技巧提高、充分练习、整合模拟各个环节内容循序列出、科学安排，带着您有计划、有效率地一步一步踏踏实实攻克听力所有问题、所有难关。

2、基础能力 系统扎实 全书首先将语音、词汇、语法、特殊表达等听力考试中必备的基础能力和基础知识进行了系统温习和巩固，同时设计了针对性的练习，让您在进入各个题型的复习前，先把基础打好，从而一好百好、迅速提高。另外，这些基础能力在后面内容中也同步渗透。

3、题型规律 透彻熟悉 我们对短对话、长对话、短文理解、短文听写四种题型的题型特征、设题规律、做题方法进行了全面进解，并设计了大量有针对性的练习，让您对新题型听力全面谙熟、充分练习，从而到了考场上不再感觉不适应、不熟悉，每种题型都驾轻就熟、胸有成竹。

4、做题技巧 全面掌握 我们通过真题举例、过程模拟、实战练习，让您对各种做题技巧全面掌握，让您可以做到，不用听就知道问什么，没听完就知道考哪里，听不懂也能猜对答案，甚至还没听就知道答案，真正让您在提高听力水平的基础上，在听力考试中如鱼得水、如沐春风。

5、充分练习 整合模拟 我们在题型讲解、技巧讲解、基础巩固中，都给出了充分的练习题目，彻底杜绝光讲不练、光看不听的现象，让您熟悉了，还要能用上；让您理解了，还要做对题。最后给出 8 套新题型听力模拟试题，让您在前面各个突破的基础上最后全面模拟、整合提升。

6、边听边记 实战体验 为了给大家创造实战的感觉，也为了培养大家边听边记的良好习惯，我们在所有练习题目旁边都留出了作笔记的空间，双栏笔记、个性设计，最大化贴心呵护、创意服务。

7、分栏排版 对照解析 练习题解析中，我们采取了清楚直观的分栏排版、对照解析模式，通过这种分栏对照，方便您直观掌握我们在讲解中点拨的做题技巧和解题思路。独到设计，清新感受。

提示 本书共 16 套练习，由于磁带容量有限，第六篇 Model Test 5-8 的录音请登录 www. sinoexam.cn 免费下载。

目　录

第二篇　短对话高分必备

第三篇　长对话高分必备

第四篇　短文理解高分必备

第五篇　短文听写高分必备

基础知识必备

本篇主要涉及六级听力考试中常见的语音、语调以及基础的词汇和语法知识，并介绍了如何培养良好的基本听音素质和能力，旨在帮助考生迅速有效地解决听力基本功问题，为后面进入各个题型复习及最终高分模拟打好基础。

Chapter 1 第一章 语音语调

听力理解技巧是建立在听力理解能力基础上的,而语音、语调则是提高听力理解能力的基础。

但是,考生若想要在短期内对语音语调基础知识有一个系统全面的掌握,是不太可能实现的。因此,本章所涉及的语音语调知识只是六级听力考试中最常见的,其目的是帮助考生迅速有效地解决听力基本功问题,从而在短期内提高六级听力考试的分数。

一、语音速成

语音方面的能力主要涉及考生对易混音、连读、同化、重读、弱读、失爆等现象的辨别能力。交际中的任何一方不能熟练地运用语音或发音不准确、对语音变化不敏感都可能会造成双方的误解。因此,考生应具备正确的发音技巧和辨音能力,注意连读、弱读、同化、失爆等语音现象。

一 易混音

受汉语发音的影响,考生在英语语音辨别方面存在三大问题:一是由于汉语没有长短音的区别,导致考生容易忽视英语中长短音的区别;二是由于汉语中没有类似英语某些音标的音节,所以考生难以区分某些近似音标,或发不出某些音标;三是汉语中一些方言导致考生分不清楚英语中的某些发音。

下表收集了六级听力考试中造成考生失分较多的几个发音难点和易混淆音节:

iː	I	如:peek – pick; deed – did; lead – lid
iː	eɪ	如:wheat – weight/wait; bee – bay; bleed – blade
æ	e	如:mass – mess; bad – bed; dad – dead
ɑː	ʌ	如:staff – stuff; march – much; sharper – supper
aɪ	æ	如:fight – fat; bike – back; side – sad
v	w	如:veil – whale; vest – west; vet – wet
s	ʃ	如:same – shame; sign – shine; sigh – shy
s	z	如:course – cause; fuss – fuzz; house (n.) – house(v.)
s	θ	如:thing – sing; path – pass; think – sink
n	η	如:thin – thing; sin – sing; ban – bang
n	l	如:need – lead; night – light; nine – line
r	l	如:race – lace; correct – collect; right – light

【例1】 (99-6-S1)

President Clinton later today joins (S1) <u>former</u> presidents Ford，Carter and Bush at "the president's summit for America's future"…(former[ˈfɔː(r)mə(r)]很容易听成 formal[ˈfɔː(r)məl])

【例2】 (05-6-2)

M: Jenny，remember this: a job **worth** doing at all is **worth** doing well.

W: Oh，yes! I certainly won't forget it. But don't expect me to stick to the job just because it pays a few more bucks. A life of continuous exploration is a life **worth** living.

Q: What can be inferred about the woman from the conversation?

(worth[wɜː(r)θ]很容易听成 worse[wɜː(r)s])

易混音问题对策

1. 首先解决"说"的问题。

　　考生应反复练习这些易混音的发音,直到可以准确发出它们为止。只有掌握了这些音在发音上的区别,才能在听音时准确地将其辨认出来。

2. 然后解决"听"的问题。

　　在备考阶段,如遇到分不清的音,应反复聆听,尽最大努力在听觉上将其分辨出来。

Exercise 1　　　Read after me

请按音标朗读下列单词,注意区分易混音。

1. lighter[ˈlaɪtə(r)]—writer[ˈraɪtə(r)]
2. calling [ˈkɔːlɪŋ]— canning [ˈkænɪŋ]
3. meaning[ˈmɪːnɪŋ]—million[ˈmɪljən]
4. bargain[ˈbɑːgɪn]–bugger[ˈbʌgə]
5. prize[praɪz]–press[pres]
6. same [seɪm]— shame [ʃeɪm]
7. lack[læk]— like [laɪk]
8. thought [θɔːt]— sought [sɔːt]
9. worth [wɜːθ]—worse[wɜːs]
10. wise [waɪz]— vice[vaɪs]

二 连读

　　连读就是语速加快时,两个或多个分属不同单词的相邻音连在一起读出的语音现象。连读是英语口语中最普遍、最重要的语音特征之一,也是学生练习听力时面临的较大难题。

　　六级听力中常见的连读现象有以下三种:

1. 第一个单词以辅音结尾,下一个单词以元音开头时,两个词连读。

【例3】 (07-6-18)

M: I could hardly recognize Sam after he got that new job. He's always <u>in a</u> suit <u>and a</u> tie now.

W: Yeah, he was never like that at college. Back then he would've run in an old T-shirt and jeans.

Q: What do the speakers say about Sam?

2.第一个单词以辅音结尾,下一个单词以清辅音[h]开头,前一辅音将击穿清辅音[h],直接与[h]后的元音发生连读。

【例4】　　　　　　　　　　　　　　　　　　　　　　　　　　　(05-1-12)

W: I don't agree with Mr. Johnson on his views about social welfare. He seems to suggest that the poor are robbing the rich.

M: He might have used better words to express his ideas, but I find what he said makes a lot of sense.

Q: What does the man mean?

3.第一个单词以字母 r 结尾,下一个单词以元音开头,原本不发音的字母 r 发辅音[r],与后面的元音发生连读。

【例5】　　　　　　　　　　　　　　　　　　　　　　(06-6-Passage One)

So I stilled myself, began to work seriously for another year and reapplied. Happily I received notice of my admission.

连读问题对策

1. 反复聆听、跟读,熟悉连读现象。

对于听不清的连读音,首先反复聆听几遍,尽量将其听懂;如无论如何无法听懂,则应对照原文,再次反复聆听、跟读、模仿,直到完全熟悉该连读现象。

2. 把握习语和词组内部单词之间的连读现象。

平时记忆听力习语和词组时,应注意将其内部单词之间固定的连读现象当成习语或词组的组成部分一块进行记忆。

Exercise 2　　　　**Read after me**

朗读下列短语和句子,注意连读现象。

1. brush up
2. make it up
3. punish him
4. turn off
5. make a lot of sense
6. Will you fetch it for me?
7. I came out well in that photograph.
8. I feel like a fish out of water doing that job.
9. You can set your watch by the time he starts his class.
10. I feel as if I were twenty years younger when I stay with young men.

三 同化

同化是指语速加快时,某些语音连读从而导致的语音变化。这种音变现象既发生在词与词之间，也发生在词的内部，如：last year［lɑːstjɪə］→［lɑːstʃɪə］，education［'edjukeɪʃən］→［'edʒukeɪʃən］等。

常见的四个同化音变是：

［t］＋［j］读作［tʃ］	如：not yet［'nɔtjet］→［'nɔtʃet］；don't you［'dəʊntjuː］→［'dəʊntʃuː］
［d］＋［j］读作［dʒ］	如：send you［'sendjuː］→［'sendʒuː］；would you［'wudjuː］→［'wudʒuː］
［z］＋［j］读作［ʒ］	如：because you［bɪ'kɔzjuː］→［bɪ'kɔʒuː］；seize you［'siːzjuː］→［'siːʒuː］
［s］＋［j］读作［ʃ］	如：kiss you［kɪsjuː］→［kɪʃuː］；issue［'ɪsjuː］→［'ɪʃuː］

【例6】 (07-6-16)

M: I heard you took a trip to Mexico last month. How did you like it?

W: Oh, I got sick and tired of hotels and hotel food. So now I understand the saying, "East, west, home's best".

Q: What does the woman mean?

同化问题对策

1. 进行朗读、跟读，以熟悉四种同化音变。

2. 把握习语和单词内部的同化现象。平时记忆单词时，注意其发音中的同化现象。

Exercise 3 Read after me

朗读下列单词，注意同化现象。

1. graduation
2. schedule
3. miss you
4. set your watch
5. How about you?
6. Don't you think the price is a little steep?
7. Raise your head a little bit.
8. What did you think of the movie?

四 弱读

英语中有些非重读词（主要为助动词、系动词、介词、连词、冠词和人称代词等）有两种读音形式：强读式和弱读式。一般来说，强读式出现在该词在话语中需要特别强调时、或是出现在句首或句末、或是单独出现时，而弱读式出现在该词在句中不需要重读强调时、或是语速加快时。

在日常口语中，是否弱读具有不确定性，它完全取决于说话人当时的语气、情绪、习惯等因素。弱读使实际读音有别于标准音，有的实际读音可能已经面目全非，考生在听音时需特别留意。

常见的词的弱读形式有:

长元音弱化成短元音	如:he[hiː]弱读成[hɪ];been[biːn]弱读成[bɪn]
元音前的辅音省略	如:his[hɪz]弱读成[ɪz];have[hæv]弱读成[æv]
辅音前的元音省略	如:am[æm]弱读成[m];and[ənd]弱读成[nd]
元音弱化成[ə]	如:us[ʌs]弱读成[əs];for[fɔː]弱读成[fə]

有的单词可以有几种弱读式,如:from 的弱读式有[frəm],[frm];them 的弱读式有[ðəm],[əm],[ðm],[m]。

【例7】　　　　　　　　　　　　　　　　　　　　　　　　　(07-6-17)

W: I **am** worried **about** Anna. She **is** really been depressed lately. All **she** does is staying in **her** room all day.

M: That sounds serious. She **had** better see a psychiatrist **at the** consoling center.

Q: What does **the** man suggest Anna do?

弱读问题对策

1. 反复聆听,熟悉弱读。

单词的弱读会导致考生实际听到的发音与自己熟悉的发音出现偏差,因此在平时复习时,考生应留意单词在句中的弱读,并对其进行反复聆听,直至完全熟悉该弱读现象。

2. 熟记常见习语中的弱读。

平时记忆听力短文、对话中的常见习语时,应注意其中是否含有单词的弱读,并将其与这些习语一并牢记。

Exercise 4　　　**Read after me**

朗读下列句子,注意黑体词的弱读。

1. I bought a dog **for** a lot of money.
2. I'll give **him** a present.
3. My brother is taller **than** you.
4. This is **his** coat.
5. I love **them** all.
6. Give me **some** water, please.
7. I never saw **such** a person.
8. How **many** children?
9. I am **from** UK?
10. They **have** been to that country.

（五）失爆和不完全爆破

失爆是指爆破音只保留发音动作,不发出爆破声的语音现象;而不完全爆破是指爆破音只作轻微爆破的语音现象。

常见的失爆和不完全爆破现象有:

失爆	两个爆破音相邻时,第一个爆破音不发出爆破声,稍微停顿后即过渡到后一个爆破音。	爆破音包括:[b],[p],[t],[d],[k],[g]。	如:went_to ['wen(t) tu],sit_down [si(t) 'daun], that_time ['ðæ(t)'taɪm]。
不完全爆破	爆破音后跟摩擦音或破擦音时只作轻微爆破。	摩擦音包括:[f],[v],[s],[z],[r],[h],[θ],[ð],[ʃ],[ʒ] 破擦音包括:[ts],[dz],[tr],[dr],[tʃ],[dʒ]	如:best_friend ['bes(t)'frend], good_job ['gu(d) 'dʒɔb], a_bit_thirsty ['bɪ(t)'θɜːstɪ]
	爆破音后跟鼻辅音或边辅音时只作轻微爆破。	鼻辅音包括:[m],[n],[ŋ] 边辅音包括:[l]	如:good_morning [gu(d) 'mɔːnɪŋ], take_me ['teɪ(k) mɪ], would_like ['wu(d)'laɪk]

其实失爆现象不仅发生在单词之间,也发生在单词内部,如:blackboard['blæ(k)bɔːd],kindness['kaɪn(d)nɪs]等。

【例8】   (05-1-5)

M: Hi, Janet. I hear you've just_returned from a tour of Australia. Did you get a chance to visit_the Sydney Opera House?

W: Of course, I did. It will be a shame for anyone visiting Australia not_to see this unique creation in architecture. Its magnificent_beauty is simply beyond description.

Q: What_do we learn from this conversation?

失爆问题对策

1. 反复聆听,把握失爆现象在听觉上的反映。

平时做听力训练时,遇到没有听出来的失爆现象,应反复聆听并进行跟读,培养自己对失爆现象的辨听能力。

2. 把握听力常见词汇和习语中的失爆现象。

平时在记忆单词或习语时,要注意其发音中是否含有失爆现象,在记住其拼写的同时,还要把握其反映在听觉上的特点。

Exercise 5 　　　　Read after me 　🎧

朗读下列单词、短语和句子,注意失爆现象。

1. topmost   2. advance

3. get_back   4. good_luck

5. I'm not feeling well.　　　　6. I stopped to let the black car pass.

7. Have you got that?　　　　8. But don't expect me to stick to the job.

9. Better luck next time.　　　10. How long will it take me to get there?

六 英美音的差别

　　对中国学生进行英语语音启蒙教育的老师们,由于各种原因,发音多倾向于英音或者英美混杂音,而听力考试中既有英音又有美音,这就造成了很多考生对听力考试中的发音不习惯与不适应,因此熟悉英音和美音在发音上的主要区别对于六级考生来说是相当必要的。

1. 辅音上的差异

1)[r]音

　　在一个单词里,当[r]音位于一个元音的后面时,英式英语中一般不将其发出,而美式英语中则一般将其发出。

【例9】

发音\单词	英音	美音
ladder	[ˈlædə]	[ˈlædər]
apartment	[əˈpɑːtmənt]	[əˈpɑːrtmənt]
conversation	[ˌkɔnvəˈseɪʃən]	[ˌkɔnvərˈseɪʃən]
supervisor	[ˈsuːpəvaɪzə]	[ˈsuːpərvaɪzər]

2)在美音中,当[t]后面跟元音时,[t]发出的并不是清辅音,而是有着明显的浊化味道,使得发出的音更接近[d]的音。

【例10】

发音\单词	英音	美音
letter	[ˈletə]	接近[ˈledər]
matter	[ˈmætə]	接近[ˈmædər]
utter	[ˈʌtə]	接近[ˈʌdər]
contact	[ˈkɔntækt]	接近[ˈkɔndækt]

2. 元音上的差异

1)英音中的[ɑː]音在美音中常发作[æ]音。

【例11】

发音\单词	英音	美音
can't	[kɑːnt]	[kænt]
fast	[fɑːst]	[fæst]
half	[hɑːf]	[hæf]
path	[pɑːθ]	[pæθ]

2）英音中的[ɔ]音在美音中常发作[ɑ:]音。

【例12】

发音　　单词	英音	美音
crop	[krɔp]	[krɑ:p]
ironic	[aɪˈrɔnɪk]	[aɪˈrɑ:nɪk]
polish	[ˈpɔlɪʃ]	[ˈpɑ:lɪʃ]
spot	[spɔt]	[spɑ:t]

3）在美音中，当[ju:]音在[t]、[d]、[n]音后时有的会发成[u:]音。

【例13】

发音　　单词	英音	美音
tune	[tju:n]	[tu:n]
due	[dju:]	[du:]
duplicate	[ˈdju:plɪkeɪt]	[ˈdu:plɪkeɪt]
dual	[ˈdju:əl]	[ˈdu:əl]

3. 某些特殊单词的英美音

　　除了以上几点区别，另外还有一些难于归类的单词在也存在英音和美音上的差别。

【例14】

发音　　单词	英音	美音
neither	[ˈnaɪðə]	[ˈni:ðər]
either	[ˈaɪðə]	[ˈi:ðər]
record (n.)	[ˈrekɔ:d]	[ˈrekərd]
dictionary	[ˈdɪkʃənɪ]	[ˈdɪkʃəneri]
laboratory	[ləˈbɔrətrɪ]	[ˈlæbrətɔ:rɪ]

英美音问题对策

1. 多读、多练，纠正不规范的发音。

　　由于[r]音类似于汉语中的"儿化音"，所以滥发[r]音是造成考生失分的重要原因之一。针对这一问题，建议考生通过多读、多练，纠正错误和不规范的发音，使自己的发音更标准。

2. 利用题型、选项等特点"绕道而行"。

　　在尽力克服发音障碍的同时，要运用相关技巧，如题型、场景、选项特点等"绕道而行"，避免因发音障碍造成失分。

二、语调进阶

　　对语言的理解有两个层面，即字的表面意义和字里行间所暗含的真正意义。

书面语言是通过逐字逐句的阅读去理解,而口语则可通过语调这一手段去理解,这是口语语言更生动、更丰富的一个重要表现。人们将同一组排序相同的词用不同的语调表达,就会具有不同的意义和情感。

一 常用语调

英语中的基本语调有以下两种:

降调	降调的基本含义是"结束"、"肯定"。句子的语调从第一个重读音节开始依次递降,在句末最后一个重读音节上语调滑落下降。
升调	升调的基本含义是"未结束"、"不肯定"。句子的语调从第一个重读音节开始依次递降,在句末最后一个重读音节上语调上升。

【例15】 　　　　　　　　　　　　　　　　　　　　(新06-12-11)

M: I need to find a ↘dentist. You said you ↘know Dr. Smith well. Do you recommend ↗her?

W: Well, I had to see her a few ↘times, but what impressed me most were the magazines in her waiting ↘room.

Q: What does the woman ↘imply?

另外,降调和升调还可以组合成降升调、升降调和升降升调。降升调在英语中也比较常用,它多用于表示"对比"、"态度保留"和"有言外之意";升降调常用于表示"语气强烈"、"惊奇"和"自满得意"等感情;升降升调常用于表示"自信"、"欢快"和"洋洋自得"等感情。

二 常用句式的基本语调

1. 陈述句用降调

陈述句在陈述一件事时用降调。

【例16】 　　　　　　　　　　　　　　　　　　　　(新06-12-12)

W: I'm afraid I can't show you the apartment at the ↘moment, because the tenant is still living in ↘it. It's really a lovely place with a big kitchen and a sunny window for only $200 a ↘month.

M: Sounds good, but we really can't rent an apartment without seeing it ↘first.

Q: What do we learn from the conversation?

2. 一般疑问句用升调

【例17】 　　　　　　　　　　　　　　　　　　　　(新06-12-17)

M: Have the parts we need for the photo copying machine arrived ↗yet?

W: I ordered them last week, but something is holding them up.

Q: What does the woman say about the parts needed for the photo copying machine?

3. 特殊疑问句用降调

【例18】　　　　　　　　　　　　　　　　　　　　　　　　（新06-12-14）

> W: How did you feel when you found out you had high blood ⟍pressure?
>
> M: Shocked! The problem for me was that there were no symptoms; it seemed to have sneaked up on me.
>
> Q: What does the man ⟍mean?

4. 反问句用升调

【例19】　　　　　　　　　　　　　　　　　　　　　　　　（05-12-5）

> M: Jean really lost her temper in Dr. Brown's class this morning.
>
> W: Oh, did ⟋she? But I think her frankness is really something to be appreciated.
>
> Q: What does the woman mean?

5. 反意疑问句的语调

反意疑问句前一部分用降调,后一部分有时用升调,有时用降调。

提问者对所提的问题有很大把握,想让对方证实时,用降调;提问者对所提问题没有把握,希望对方回答时,用升调。

【例20】　　　　　　　　　　　　　　　　　　　　　　　　（06-12-6）

> W: Your chemistry examination is ⟍over, ⟍isn't ⟍it? Why do you still look so worried?
>
> M: I don't know. It wasn't that the questions were too hard or there were too many of them. But I'm still feeling uneasy because the exam didn't seem to have much to do with the course material.
>
> Q: What does the man mean?

【例21】　　　　　　　　　　　　　　　　　　　　　　　　（03-1-9）

> W: I don't imagine you have any interest in attending that lecture on ⟍drawing, ⟋ do ⟋you?
>
> M: Oh, yes, I do. Now that you remind me of it.
>
> Q: What do we learn about the man from the conversation?

6. 祈使句的语调

表示命令、语气强硬的祈使句,句末用降调。

表示鼓励、态度亲切或客气的请求的祈使句,句末用升调。

表示恳求、责备,或表示关心的急切警告时,第一重读音节用降调,句末用升调。

【例22】　　　　　　　　　　　　　　　　　　　　　　　　（05-6-6）

> M: Hurry ⟍up, ⟍Linda! I hear that there are not many tickets left for the football match.

W: I am ready now. ⤴Let's ⤴go. It is the early bird that catches the worm.

Q: Why did the man ask the woman to hurry up?

【例23】　　　　　　　　　　　　　　　　　　　　　　　　　　　(05-6-3)

M: I found that one of my schoolmates uses drugs. How can I help him, Mom?

W: ⤵Stay away from him, ⤴son. Never think that you can talk him out of the habit if he is addicted. But perhaps you can talk to your teacher about the matter.

Q: What's the woman's advice to her son?

7. 感叹句的语调

感叹句表示强烈感叹时用降调;感叹句表示惊奇时用升降调。

【例24】

W: Our school has just built some new apartments near campus, but one bedroom runs for 500 dollars a month.

M: ⤴500 ⤵dollars! That's a bit beyond the reach of most students!

Q: What does the man mean?

【例25】

W: How time ⤵flies! It's almost lunchtime. Thanks for showing us around, Carol.

M: No problem. Any time.

Q: Why does the woman thank Carol?

8. 选择问句的语调

选择问句的语调主要有两种:

一是在说话人所说的几项选择中,前面的选择事项都用升调,最后一个选择事项用降调,中间的连接词(如 or)用平调。

二是在还有其他选择没有说出来的情况下,所有的选择事项均用升调。

【例26】

1. A: Would you like ⤴coffee or ⤵tea?

　　B: Would you like ⤴coffee, or ⤴tea or …?

2. A: Is your car ⤴blue, ⤴green, or ⤵red?

　　B: Is your car ⤴blue, ⤴green, or ⤴red or…?

三　不同语调的不同含义

不同的语调可以用来表达不同的意思与情感。语调与说话人所表达的意思、态度和感情密切相关。一个句子用不同的语调来读,就表达不同的意思。

1. 陈述句表示疑问用升调。

【例27】

1. A: You are interested in this ↘movie. (陈述)

   B: You are interested in this ↗movie? (疑问)

2. A: He has gone to ↘ London. (陈述)

   B: He has gone to ↗ London? (疑问)

2. 陈述句表示安慰、鼓励和友好用升调。

【例28】   (03-6-3)

M: Hey, where did you find the journal? I need it, ↘too.

W: Right here on the shelf. Don't ↗worry, John. I'll take it out on my card for both of us.

Q: What does the woman mean?

3. 陈述句表示观点有所保留、态度有所怀疑或犹豫、有言外之意、或是下文有转折 (如 but …) 时用降升调。

【例29】   (03-1-8)

M: How do you like the way I've arranged the furniture in my living room?

W: ↘↗Fine. But I think the walls could do with a few paintings.

Q: What does the woman suggest the man do?

4. 陈述句用于纠正某人的话或者表示相反意见时用降升调。

【例30】   (06-6-9)

W: I am worried about Jenny going to college. College students are so wild nowadays.

M: Actually, only a few are ↘like ↗that. Most students are too busy studying to have time to cause trouble.

Q: What does the man imply?

5. 长句中句首状语一般为升调。

【例31】   (00-1-1)

W: Have you heard about the plane crash yesterday? It caused a hundred and twenty deaths. I am never at ease when taking a flight.

M: ↗Though we often hear about air crashes and serious casual ↗deeds, flying is one of the safest ways to travel.

Q: What do we learn from this conversation?

6. 并列句的两个部分意思联系紧密, 前一个分句用升调, 后一个分句用降调; 并列句的两个部分意思联系不紧密, 或具有同等重要性时, 两个分句都用降调。

【例32】 (06-6-1)

M: Mary, could you please tell Thomas to contact me? I was hoping he will be able to help me out with the freshmen orientation program next week.

W: I would certainly tell him if I saw ↗him, but I haven't seen him around for quite a few ↘days.

Q: What does the woman mean?

【例33】 (新 06-12-17)

M: It's quite clear for my visit: this is a full-size, comprehensive university. So why is it still called a college?

W: The College of William and Mary is the second oldest institution of higher learning in this country. We have nurtured great minds like Thomas ↘Jefferson and we are proud of our ↘name.

Q: What do we learn from this conversation about the College of William and Mary?

7. 列举并列的几项事物时,前面的事物用升调,后面的事物用降调。

【例34】

1. There is ↗a book, ↗two notebooks and ↘a pen on the desk.
2. Some warm-blooded animals, like ↗the cat, ↗the dog or ↘the wolf, do not need to hibernate.

　　以上,我们分别对六级考试中经常涉及的几种语音和语调现象进行了介绍。然而,在实际的日常交流中,这些语音、语调现象往往都是同时发生的,很难截然分开。因此,考生在对各种现象进行分别了解的基础上,应结合大量的听力实践对语音、语调有一个综合性的把握,这样才会更有实用价值。

分主题词汇

听力与阅读不同,考生在听的过程中没有反复思考的时间,因此,考生必须能够在瞬间把握所听到的词语和句子的含义。

六级听力所涉及的题材十分广泛,包括校园生活、日常生活以及工作、交通、旅游、文化、科普等方方面面。熟练掌握与这些题材相关的常用词语和习惯搭配,对于听音时有效捕捉关键词、迅速把握所听到词语和句子的含义会有非常大的帮助。

一、日常生活类

购物消费

convenience store 便利店

chain store 连锁店

supermarket 超市

department store 百货大楼

mall 购物中心

outlet 廉价商店

grocery 杂货店

salesman 售货员

customer 顾客

complaint 投诉

display 展示

counter 柜台

balance 余额,结余

budget 预算

luxurious items 奢侈品

bargain 便宜货,讨价还价

catalog 商品目录

famous brands 名牌

stationery 文具

cosmetics 化妆品

sports goods 体育用品

electronic products 电子类产品

digital video camera 数码摄像机

Women's wear 女士服装

Men's wear 男士服装

discount 折扣

shopping list 购物单

family size/pack 家庭装(的商品)

receipt 收据

on sale 出售,减价出售

sell out 售完

out of stock 没货,脱销

in stock 有现货,有库存

deliver 送货

opening time 开业时间

closing time 停业时间

in season 正合时令

past the prime 过了最好的时候

居家琐事

trivial affairs 日常琐事

housework 家务活

housekeeper 管家

housemaid 女佣

housewife 家庭主妇
laundry 洗衣店
iron 熨斗
fix the dinner 摆下饭桌
clear up 清理
in a mess 杂乱
hoover 吸尘器
vacuum cleaner 真空吸尘器
cleaning and washing 洗洗刷刷
keep an eye on 照料
household expenses 家务开支
keep down the expenditure 降低开支
budget 预算
economical 经济的,节俭的

open an account 开户
deposit 存款
withdraw 取(钱)
interest rate 利率
exchange rate 汇率
property 财产
debt 债务
pay off 还清
addresser 寄信人
addressee 收信人
parcel 包裹
postage 邮费
registered letter 挂号信
zip/ postal code 邮政编码

日常交往

leisure time 闲暇时间
date 约会
call on sb. 拜访某人
take a message 捎口信
keep contact 保持联系
hospitable 好客的

telephone booth 公用电话亭
pay phone 投币式公用电话
long-distance call 长途电话
hang up 挂断电话
hold on 别挂断电话
operator 接线员

休闲娱乐

hobby 爱好
keep pets 养宠物
tame dogs 驯狗
gardening 园艺
play chess 下象棋
play cards 打牌
computer games 电脑游戏
gossip 闲话;喜欢谈论别人私生活的人
TV channels 电视频道
broadcast 广播,播放
live broadcast 现场直播
programme 电视节目
documentary 纪录片
commercial advertisement 商业广告

TV theatre 电视剧场
tennis court 网球场
football match 足球比赛
the World Cup 世界杯
entertainment industry 娱乐业
performance 表演
violence movie 暴力片
comedy 喜剧
tragedy 悲剧
horror movie 恐怖片
plot 情节
entertaining 有趣的,愉快的
enthusiastic 热情的
clap 拍掌,鼓掌

外出就餐

waiter/ waitress (男/女) 服务员	pork 猪肉
order 点菜	beef steak 牛排
menu 菜单	rare 半熟的
snack 快餐	medium 中等熟的
dessert 甜点	done 老的,煮熟了的
burger 汉堡	join in sb. for dinner 与…共进晚餐
cheese 芝士,奶酪	treat 款待,宴请
appetizer 开胃菜	make a reservation 预定
red wine 红酒	cater 提供饮食及服务
toast 烤面包,吐司	have a picnic 野餐
fried chips 炸薯条	buffet 自助餐
junk food 垃圾食品	Go Dutch 各人付各人的账,AA 制
roast 烤肉	treat 请客,招待
mutton 羊肉	change 零钱,找零

住房搬家

landlord/landlady 房东	settle 定居
tenant 房客	downtown 市中心
apartment/flat 公寓	suburb 郊区
residence 居住,住所	neighborhood 邻近地区
monthly rent 月租	transportation 交通
spare rooms 空房,客房	subway entrance 地铁入口
available 可利用的	put up with the noise 容忍噪音
accommodate 供给住宿或房间	house-warming party 乔迁喜宴

装饰维修

furnished 已装修的	fix 维修
unfurnished 未装修的	install 安装
furniture 家具	maintenance man 维修工
decoration 装饰	plumber 水管工人
painting 画	washing machine 洗衣机
cupboard 衣柜	refrigerator/ fridge 电冰箱
shower 淋浴	light bulb 电灯泡
sink 下水槽	heater 加热器
pipe 管道	furnace 暖气锅炉,熔炉
leak 漏水	air conditioner 空调

二、学校生活类

注册

register 注册,报到,登记	orientation 新生入学导向
enrolment 登记,入学	student ID card 学生证
dean 系主任	recommendation letter 推荐信
department 系,学部	application form 申请表

选课

semester 学期	required/compulsory course 必修课
quit 放弃	optional/elective class 选修课
drop a course 放弃一门课程	curriculum 课程
take a course 选课	linguistics 语言学
pick up 学习,选择	philosophy 哲学
major in 主修	psychology 心理学
outline 大纲,概要	literature class 文学课

听课

professor 教授	take notes 记笔记
supervisor 导师	specialist vocabulary 专业词汇
tutor 家教	build the interest 培养兴趣
teaching assistant 教学助理	absence 缺席
faculty 全体教员	presence 出席
seminar 专门研讨会	active involvement 积极参与
give a lecture 作讲座	punctual 守时,准时
make a speech 发表演讲	skip the class 逃课
make a presentation 作陈述或介绍	make something up 弥补

作业

assignment 作业	have one's hands full with 忙于做…
homework 家庭作业	deadline 最后期限
experiment report 实验报告	an extension of the deadline 延时
figure out 想出	criticism 批评,批判
hand in 上交	feedback 反馈

读书

book review 书评	periodical 期刊
journal 定期刊物	editorial 社论
magazine 杂志	extra copy 额外的副本

volume 册

reference book 参考书

subscribe to 订阅

out of stock 脱销

out of print 已绝版

handover edition 精装本

paperback edition 平装本

publication 出版,出版物

publishing house 出版社

get through the novel 通读小说

read selectively 选择性阅读

buy out the bookstore 买了很多书

学习

swot/ grind 用功的学生

go over/ review 复习

improvement 进步,提高

lack confidence in 缺乏信心

distraction 使人分心的事物

concentration 集中

enthusiasm 热情

diligence 勤奋

come up with 赶上

be strict with 对…严厉

考试论文

quiz 小测验

standardized tests 标准测试

national test 统考

earn a credit 修学分

cancel/call off 取消

postpone/ put off 推迟

reschedule 重新安排时间

passing score 及格分

score/ mark 分数

paper 论文

draft 初稿

school of thought 思想学派

research method 研究方法

stay up 熬夜

cheat 作弊

fall short of one's expectation 出乎意料

disappointing 令人失望的

satisfactory/satisfying 令人满意的

毕业进修

graduation 毕业

graduate 毕业生

postgraduate 研究生

further study 进修

advanced study 进修

study abroad 留学

学费及奖学金

tuition 学费

fee 学杂费

grant 助学金

financial aids 助学金(总称)

fellowship/scholarship 奖学金

a student loan 学生贷款

课余活动

participate in 参加,参与

participant 参加者,参与者

enroll in 登记

take part in 参加,参与

sign up for 参加(俱乐部、课程等)

taste 兴趣,爱好

speech contest 演讲比赛

run for 竞选

vote 选票

election campaign 选举活动

| campaign manager 活动负责人 | candidate 候选人 |
| the student union 学生会 | chairman 主席 |

三、职场工作类

求职面试

job hunting 找工作	inexperienced 没有经验的
want ads 招聘广告	unemployment 失业
position 职位	lose one's job 失业
opening/vacancy 空缺	full-time job 全职工作
opportunity 机会	part-time job 兼职工作
inquiry 询问	do odd jobs 做零工
consult 咨询	fire 解雇
resume 简历	hire 雇佣
application letter 求职信	retire 退休
interview 面试	job-hopping 跳槽
interviewee 面试者	take over 接管,接任
interviewer 面试官	appointment 任命
impression 印象	be no match for sb. 不能与某人相比
confident 自信的	turn down 拒绝

工作往来

appointment 约会	be involved in 参与
clients 客户	in charge of 负责
get along with 与…相处	proposal 建议书
assistance 帮助,协助	transfer 调职
cooperation 合作	be on business 出差

工作态度

attitude 态度	hard-working 工作努力的
personality 品质	perseverance 坚持不懈
active/positive 积极的	hang on 坚持
negative 消极的	struggle 奋斗
optimistic 乐观的	overwork 加班
pessimistic 悲观的	work addict 工作狂
determined 有决心的	overwhelmed 疲倦的
forgetful 健忘的	workload 工作负担
diligent 勤奋的	wear out 疲劳
responsible 有责任感的,负责的	complain 抱怨

work like a horse 辛勤工作 | devote oneself to sth. 致力于…

工作成绩

career 事业 | symbol 象征
achievement 成就 | tribute 赞美
contribution 贡献 | pioneer 先驱,开拓者
deserve 值得,应得 | blaze a trail 开路,开先河
worthy 值得的 | worldwide recognition 举世公认

四、科学技术类

生物

biology 生物学 | respiratory system 呼吸系统
cell 细胞 | hibernation 冬眠
cell nucleus 细胞核 | predator 食肉动物
protein 蛋白质 | capture 捕获
tissue 组织 | survive 生存
genetics 遗传学 | adapt to/adjust to 适应
genetic engineering 遗传工程 | disguise 伪装
tube baby 试管婴儿 | defense 防御
digestive system 消化系统 | warning color 警戒色

天文地理

astronomy 天文学 | geography 地理
observatory 天文台 | South Pole 南极
universe 宇宙 | North Pole 北极
cosmos 宇宙 | equator 赤道
light year 光年 | latitude 纬度
galaxy 银河系 | longitude 经度
solar system 太阳系 | iceberg 冰山
outer atmosphere 大气层 | volcano 火山
satellite 卫星 | erupt 爆发
geology 地质学 | earthquake 地震

现代科技

high-tech 高科技 | cyber 网络
portable computer 手提电脑 | log in/on 登陆
Internet 因特网 | hacker 黑客
website 网址 | computer virus 计算机病毒

bug killer 杀毒软件	surf on the Internet 网上冲浪
virtual community 虚拟社区	distance learning 远程学习
chat room 聊天室	advanced technology 先进技术
on-line shopping 在线购物	telecommute 远程办工

气候

weather forecast 天气预报	windy 有(大)风的,多风的
sunny 阳光充足的	breezy 有微风的
cloudy 多云的	foggy 有雾的
drizzle 毛毛雨	icy 冷的
light rain 小雨	chilly 严寒的
heavy rain 大雨	freezing 寒冷的
shower 阵雨	frigid 严寒的
pour 倾盆大雨	blizzard 大风雪
downpour 倾盆大雨	snowstorm 暴风雪
thunderstorm 雷雨	severe winter 寒冷的冬季
rain cats and dogs 下倾盆大雨	temperature 温度

五、社会问题类

环境问题

environment protection 环境保护	purify 净化
reclaim 开垦,改造	radiation 辐射
deforestation 滥砍滥伐	drought 干旱
over-fishing 过度捕鱼	dust-storm 沙尘暴
dump 倾倒	acid rain 酸雨
ecosystem 生态系统	greenhouse effects 温室效应
vegetation 植物,植被	global warming 全球变暖
oxygen 氧气	sensitive to climate 对气候敏感的
ozone layer 臭氧层	endangered species 濒危物种
deterioration 恶化	rare 稀有的
pollution 污染	wipe out 清除,消亡
recycle 回收再利用	extinction 灭绝
circulation 流通,循环	conservation 保护,保存

移民种族

Industrial Revolution 工业革命	migrate 移居
famine 饥荒	immigration 移民
refugee 难民	settlement 定居

cultural conflict 文化冲突   racial 种族的

multiculturalism 跨文化   discrimination 歧视

diverse 多样的,多元的   segregation 隔离

descendant 后代,后裔   look down upon 看不起,轻视

妇女问题

women's liberation 妇女解放   compensate 补偿

women's movement 妇女运动   abuse 虐待

professional women 职业女性   domestic violence 家庭暴力

sexism 性别歧视   traffic in women 贩卖妇女

discrimination 歧视   divorce 离婚

政治经济

international organizations 国际组织   unstable 不稳定

institution 机构   terrorism 恐怖主义

alliance 联盟   reform 改革

cooperation 合作   crisis 危机

politics 政治   economic recession 经济衰退

rebel 暴乱   economic depression 经济萧条

strike 罢工   break out 爆发

六、文化习俗类

文化艺术

mass media 大众媒体   classical literature 古典文学

animation 动画片的制作   masterpiece 名著,杰作

musical 音乐片   aesthetic 美学的

Academy Award 金像奖   graffiti 涂鸦

fashionable 时尚的   oil painting 油画

outmoded/outdated 过时的   sculpture 雕塑

popular with 流行   dignity 尊严

catch on 流行   individual 个人的

Yuppie/Yuppy 雅皮士   confrontation 冲突

Hippie/Hippy 嬉皮士   offensive 冒犯的,无礼的

art works 艺术作品   cultural shock 文化冲击

社会习俗

exotic 有异域情调的   proper conduct 得体的举止

custom 风俗   good-mannered 文明的,有礼貌的

costume 服饰   ill-mannered 无教养的

blunt 唐突的,不圆通的	tradition 传统
taboo 禁忌	wedding ceremony 结婚典礼
behavior 行为	bride 新娘
interaction 互动	bridegroom 新郎
practice 惯例	engagement 订婚

七、旅游交通类

火车

railway station 火车站	carriage 车厢
express train 快车	sleeping car 卧铺车厢
a non-stop train 直达火车	one-way/single ticket 单程票
transfer 转车	return /round-trip ticket 往返票
platform 站台	booking office 订票处
schedule 时刻表	information booth 问讯台

汽车

commuter 通勤者	jay-walker 乱穿马路的行人
rush hour 高峰时间	make a wrong turn 拐错弯
traffic jam 交通拥挤,塞车	traffic accident 交通事故
hold up 阻塞,抑制	ticket 罚单
handbrake 手刹车	driver's license 驾驶执照
park a car 停车	fast lane 快行车道
break the traffic rule 违反交通规则	one-way street 单行道
run a red light/ jump the light 闯红灯	intersection 十字路口
speeding 超速	give a ride 搭车
zebra 斑马线	shuttle 班车

飞机

airport 机场	board 登机
economy class 经济舱	checking counter 检票处
first class 头等舱	passport 护照
business class 商务舱	visa 签证
see off 送行	air/ plane crash 空难
airline 航线	miss flight 误机
flight 航班	stopover (旅程中的)中途停留
departure time 起飞时间	switch to a different flight 换乘飞机
check in 办理登机手续	behind schedule 晚点
safety inspection 安检	airsick 晕机
declare 申报通关	jet lag 飞行时差反应

参观游览

tourist 游客	scenic resort 旅游胜地
take a vacation 休假	historic spots 历史名胜
sightseeing 观光,游览	landscape 风景
travel agency 旅行社	fantastic scene 奇异的景象
book a room 预订房间	beyond description 难以描述
reception desk 接待处	take a picture 拍照
service counter 服务台	pose 摆姿势
check in 住宿登记	press the shutter 按快门
check out 结账离开	run out of film 胶卷用完
set off to the seaside 去海滨	broaden one's horizon 开阔眼界

八、医疗健康类

疾病和症状

epidemic 流行病	have a temperature 发烧
bird flu 禽流感	sore throat 嗓子疼
SARS 非典型性肺炎	runny nose 流鼻涕
infectious illness 传染病	diarrhea 腹泻
contagion 传染	stomachache 胃痛
symptoms 症状	cavity 牙洞
attack/access/fit 发作	toothache 牙疼
coughing fit 咳嗽发作	dental decay 龋齿
sneeze 打喷嚏	allergy 过敏
fever 发烧	fracture 骨折

看病就医

cure 治愈	fill the prescription 抓药
treat 治疗	pill 药片
fill teeth 补牙	dosage 剂量
take temperature 量体温	take injection 打针
examine 检查	vaccinate 注射疫苗
prescription 处方	surgery 外科手术
physical inspection 体检	operation 手术

医院和医生

infirmary 学校医院	emergency room 急诊室
clinic 诊所	ward 病室
the dentist's 牙科诊所	physician 内科医师

surgeon 外科医生	anesthetist 麻醉师
	减肥锻炼
put on weight 增加体重,变胖	exercise machine 健身器械
overweight 超重	watch your diet 注意饮食
lose weight 减肥	on diet 节食
keep-fit class 健身班	physical exercise 锻炼
fitness center 健身中心	slimming drug 减肥药
	身体状况
be in good shape 身体健康	as fit as a fiddle 身体非常好
be out of shape 身体不好	feel under the weather 身体不舒服
be in poor shape 身体状况不佳	recovery 恢复

Exercise 专项练习   🎧 边听边记

1. Claim the _____ at the _____.

2. I'd like a _____ and fried _____.

3. Are you going to order from the _____, or would you like to try out _____?

4. I got an _____ to a _____ planning _____.

5. I'm a _____ student on an _____ program. I'm doing _____ mainly in the Education Department.

6. I am sure you can't find a better _____ elsewhere.

7. You probably haven't heard that the professor _____ the exam until _____ notice.

8. I guess it's something I haven't _____ _____ _____ for yet.

9. I didn't have enough time to _____ my lessons.

10. Maybe you should _____ yourself in a place that has fewer _____.

11. Hopefully you had no problem going through the _____ _____ with the tightening _____ _____.

12. We all talk about how _____ we are, but in fact women are still not _____ _____.

13. Nowadays you can't _____ on a company for _____ _____ any more.

14. _____ whenever I get into the pool my right leg _____.

15. Could you have your _____ _____ as soon as possible? I really can't _____ in such a _____.

第一篇 基础知识必备 6

16. You know, more and more people are _____ for _____ and 边听边记
    _____ jobs.

17. Do you know which date Ray would like us to hand our _____
    in?

18. We've been working on this _____ for so long that my eyes
    are starting to _____.

19. Here is a great _____ in _____ of foreign travel and learning
    foreign language.

20. It would be more _____ to take the train. But I guess we
    should watch our _____.

21. I'm trying to decide whether or not to take _____ of it. The
    _____ might be too great for me.

22. The _____ already knows that _____ the seminars is a
    _____ for completing the _____.

23. The only way to beat the _____ when you do the _____
    shopping on Saturday is to be here when they open at nine
    o'clock _____.

24. The restaurant doesn't seem to get enough _____. I think they
    should be doing better since there's no _____ along this street.

25. The _____ for the existence of a university is that it _____
    the connection between knowledge and the _____ for life, by
    _____ the young and the old in the _____ consideration of
    learning.

【参考答案】

1. Claim the baggage at the terminal.
2. I'd like a cheeseburger and fried chips.
3. Are you going to order from the menu, or would you like to try out buffet?
4. I got an invitation to a financial planning seminar.
5. I'm a graduate student on an exchange program. I'm doing courses mainly in the
   Education Department.
6. I am sure you can't find a better bargain elsewhere.
7. You probably haven't heard that the professor postponed the exam until further
   notice.
8. I guess it's something I haven't acquired a taste for yet.
9. I didn't have enough time to preview my lessons.
10. Maybe you should seat yourself in a place that has fewer distractions.

27

11. Hopefully you had no problem going through the <u>checking</u> <u>procedure</u> with the tightening <u>security</u> <u>measures</u>.

12. We all talk about how <u>liberated</u> we are, but in fact women are still not <u>equally</u> <u>treated</u>.

13. Nowadays you can't <u>depend</u> on a company for <u>lifetime</u> <u>employment</u> any more.

14. <u>Recently</u> whenever I get into the pool my right leg <u>aches</u>.

15. Could you have your <u>refrigerator</u> <u>fixed</u> as soon as possible? I really can't <u>concentrate</u> in such a <u>noise</u>.

16. You know, more and more people are <u>competing</u> for <u>fewer</u> and <u>fewer</u> jobs.

17. Do you know which date Ray would like us to hand our <u>assignments</u> in?

18. We've been working on this <u>proposal</u> for so long that my eyes are starting to <u>blur</u>.

19. Here is a great <u>argument</u> in <u>favor</u> of foreign travel and learning foreign language.

20. It would be more <u>relaxing</u> to take the train. But I guess we should watch our <u>expenses</u>.

21. I'm trying to decide whether or not to take <u>advantage</u> of it. The <u>responsibility</u> might be too great for me.

22. The <u>faculty</u> already knows that <u>attending</u> the seminars is a <u>requirement</u> for completing the <u>program</u>.

23. The only way to beat the <u>crowds</u> when you do the <u>grocery</u> shopping on Saturday is to be here when they open at nine o'clock <u>sharp</u>.

24. The restaurant doesn't seem to get enough <u>customers</u>. I think they should be doing better since there's no <u>competition</u> along this street.

25. The <u>justification</u> for the existence of a university is that it <u>preserves</u> the connection between knowledge and the <u>enthusiasm</u> for life, by <u>uniting</u> the young and the old in the <u>imaginative</u> consideration of learning.

常考语法

　　听力中涉及的主要是一些比较基本的语法现象,如虚拟语气、比较级和最高级、情态动词等。即便如此,由于听力考试的时间紧,思考时间有限,所以,考生只有熟练掌握这些语法现象,才能在听音时迅速反应出所听话语的含义,在听力考试中做到游刃有余。

一、虚拟语气

　　虚拟语气是英文中的重要语法现象之一,同时也是六级听力考试中涉及的重要考点之一。

一　if引导的虚拟条件句

　　虚拟条件句,又称非真实条件句,它所表示的假设是根本不可能或不太可能发生或实现的情况。

　　主、从句谓语的基本形式如下:

时间 ＼ 形式	if 从句	主句
与现在事实相反	were/did	would/should/might/could + do
与过去事实相反	had been/had done	would/should/might/could + have done
与将来事实相反	should/ were to + do	would/should/might/could + do

【例1】 (03-9-2)

[A] The woman has a very tight budget.	W: I certainly would like to buy the fur coat I saw on the department store, but I don't have enough money.
[B] He does not think the fur coat is worth buying.	
[C] He's willing to lend the woman money for the fur coat.	M: Well, if you had budgeted your money better, you'll be able to buy it now.
[D] The woman is not careful enough in planning her spending.	Q: What does the man imply?

【解析】男士用虚拟条件句"if you had budgeted your money better"表示对过去事实的一种假设,暗含事实上"The woman hasn't budgeted her money better."之意,故答案为[D]。

二　含蓄虚拟条件句

　　含蓄虚拟条件句是指假设的情况并不以条件从句的形式表示出来,而是通过

without，but for，but that，otherwise，or 等词或短语引出。

【例2】 (03-6-4)

[A] She suggested a way out of the difficulty for the man.	M: Thank you for your helpful assistance. Otherwise, I'd surely have missed it. The place is so out of the way.
[B] She took the man to where he wanted to go.	W: It was a pleasure meeting you. Goodbye!
[C] She came a long way to meet the man.	Q: Why did the man thank the woman?
[D] She promised to help the man.	

【解析】男士话中的"I'd surely have missed it"明显使用了虚拟语气(谓语为 would have done 的形式)，由此可知 otherwise 在这里相当于虚拟条件句"if there weren't your helpful assistance"，实际情况是由于女士的帮助，男士没有错过"it"，由后一句可知 it 指代 the place，故答案为[B]。

三　wish 后的虚拟语气

　　动词 wish 后的宾语从句一般用虚拟语气，表示不太可能或没有把握实现的愿望。其谓语动词有三种形式：表示对现在的愿望，用 were 或动词的过去式；表示对过去的愿望，用 had + 过去分词或 would/could have + 过去分词；表示对将来的愿望，用 would/should/could/might + 动词原形。

【例3】 (05-12-7)

[A] He shows great enthusiasm for his studies.	M: Your son certainly shows a lot of enthusiasm on the tennis court.
[B] He is a very versatile person.	W: I only wish he'd show as much for his studies.
[C] He has no talent for tennis.	Q: What does the woman imply about her son?
[D] He does not study hard enough.	

【解析】wish 后的从句，谓语动词为 could + 动词原形，由此可知此句使用虚拟语气，表达不太可能实现的愿望。女士通过虚拟语气 I only wish he'd show …表达了希望儿子对学习可以表现出与网球同样的热情(enthusiasm)的愿望，这表明事实上女士的儿子对学习的热情不高(does not study hard enough)，故答案为[D]。

四　if only 后的虚拟语气

　　"if only"后面的句子常用虚拟语气，表达对无法实现的愿望的一种感叹或惋惜，意为"要是…就好了！"。其谓语动词有三种形式：表示对现在的愿望，用 were 或动词的过去式；表示对过去的愿望，用 had + 过去分词或 could have + 过去分词；表示对将来的愿望，用 would + 动词原形。

【例4】　　　　　　　　　　　　　　　　　　　（04-6-5）

[A] The man is not suitable for the position.	M: I wonder if you find my experience relevant to the job.
[B] The job has been given to someone else.	
[C] She had received only one application letter.	W: Yes, certainly. But if only you had sent in your application letter a week earlier.
[D] The application arrived a week earlier than expected.	Q: What does the woman imply?

【解析】if only 后面句子的谓语动词为 had + 过去分词，由此可知此句使用了虚拟语气，表达一种不可能实现的愿望。女士的意思是说"要是你早一个星期发简历就好了"，实际是在暗示男士简历投晚了，工作已经给别人了，故答案为[B]。

二、反意疑问句

反意疑问句可以表示真实的疑问，也可以表示说话者的某种倾向、强调或反问。

一　基本构成

标准的反意疑问句包括主句和尾句两个部分。前一部分主句为陈述句，后一部分尾句由助动词或情态动词加主语（主语一般与前面的陈述句相同，且须使用指代陈述句主语的代词）构成。若主句为肯定式，尾句一般用否定式；若主句为否定式，尾句一般用肯定式。

如：It's very stuffy here, isn't it?

　　It's not easy to choose, is it?

二　答语

回答反意疑问句，一般须用 yes 或 no。

1. 主句为肯定，尾句为否定

如：– We were late, weren't we?　我们晚了，是不是？

　　– Yes, we were.　是的，我们晚了。（肯定回答）

　　– No, we weren't.　不，我们没晚。（否定回答）

2. 主句为否定，尾句为肯定

如：– You won't go to the party, will you?　你不去参加晚会，是吧？

　　– No, I won't.　是的，我不去。（肯定回答）

　　– Yes, I will.　不，我会去。（否定回答）

三　特殊反意疑问句

1. 同向反意疑问句

前面讲到标准的反意疑问句是"主句肯定则尾句否定，主句否定则尾句肯定"，如果一个反意疑问句的主句和尾句同时都肯定或同时都否定，则称其为同向反意疑问句。不同于一般情况的反意疑问句，同向反意疑问句一般用来表示"关心,惊讶,怀疑,愤怒,讥讽"等感情。这类反意疑问句的主句常会省略,因而增加了理解的难度。

如:You look pale. You are not feeling well, aren't you? (表示关心)

So that's your little trick, is it? (表示讥讽)

2. 非严格语法意义上的反意疑问句

英语中有少量非严格语法意义上的反意疑问句,形式固定,不随其前面的陈述句的变化而变化,这种反意疑问句是希望听话人作出反应。常用的有:eh? right? don't you think? am I right? isn't that so? 等。

如:It's really a nice day, right?

He won't accept the offer, don't you think?

（四）反意疑问句的题型特点

1. 有答语的反意疑问句

1) 反意疑问句出现在第一个说话人的话中,第二个说话人给出回答。

2) 问题主要是考查第二个说话人对第一个说话人所提出问题的回答是肯定还是否定。

3) 第二个说话人的回答是出题的重点,也是答案的关键所在。

【例5】　　　　　　　　　　　　　　　　　(03-1-9)

| [A] He'll give a lecture on drawing.
 [B] He doesn't mind if the woman goes to the lecture.
 [C] He would rather not go to the lecture.
 [D] He's going to attend the lecture. | W: I don't imagine you have any interest in attending that lecture on drawing, do you?
 M: Oh, yes, I do, now that you remind me of it.
 Q: What do we learn about the man from the conversation? |

【解析】女士的话中出现反意疑问句,男士对其做出回答 yes, I do(不,我有兴趣去听讲座),表明了态度,并且后面补充说明了原因 now that you remind me of it(既然你提醒了我),故答案为[D]。

2. 没有答语的反意疑问句

1) 反意疑问句出现在第二个说话人的话中,后面没有对其作出回答。

2) 问题一般是考查反意疑问句隐含的陈述语气,即说话人想要表达的观点或陈述的事实。

3) 抓住了反意疑问句的主句,也就抓住了答案。

【例6】　　　　　　　　　　　　　　　　　(02-1-2)

| [A] Its results were just as expected.
 [B] It wasn't very well designed.
 [C] It fully reflected the students' ab- | M: How many students passed the final physics exam in your class?
 W: Forty, but still as many as 20 percent of |

	the class failed. Quite disappointing, isn't
[D] Its results fell short of her expectation.	it?
	Q: What does the woman think of the exam?

【解析】女士话中的的反意疑问句其实是陈述考试结果令人失望这一事实,而不是针对这一事实提出问题,故答案为[D]。fall short of … expectation ≈ quite disappointing。

三、比较结构

形容词、副词的比较级和最高级,以及 as … as, compared with 等引出的比较结构经常是六级听力理解的设题点。出现比较结构的句子往往提供重要的信息或者就是答案的出处。

一 同级比较

as … as … 表示"和…一样";not so/as … as … 表示"不像…一样"。

【例7】 (04-6-11)

[A] He set up the first university in America.	Few people can stand for the spirit of early America as much as Benjamin Franklin. He lived through almost the whole of the 18th century.
[B] He was one of the earliest settlers in America.	
[C] He can best represent the spirit of early America.	
[D] He was the most distinguished diplomat in American history.	11. What does the speaker say about Benjamin Franklin?

【解析】文章在比较处提到 Few … as much as Benjamin Franklin,意思是"几乎没有人像 Benjamin Franklin 那么…",由此可知 Benjamin Franklin 是最(best)…的,故答案为[C]。

二 形容词、副词的比较级

1.单纯表示两者之间的比较

常与 than 连用,前面经常会有 much, even, still, further 等副词修饰,用来加强语气。

【例8】 (06-6-7)

[A] He has learned a lot from his own mistakes.	W: Your dog certainly seems to know you are his master. Did you have to punish him very often when you trained him?
[B] He is quite experienced in taming wild dogs.	
[C] He finds reward more effective than punishment.	M: I found it's much better to praise him when he obeys and not to be so fussy when he makes mistakes.

| [D] He thinks it important to master basic training skills. | Q: What does the man say about training dogs? |

【解析】男士话中的比较结构 it's much better to praise him …表明他认为 reward（奖励）比 punishment（惩罚）更 effective（有效），故答案为[C]。

2. more … than 表示"与其…不如…"

【例9】 (05-12-9)

| [A] Its rapid growth is beneficial to the world.

[B] It can be seen as a model by the rest of the world.

[C] Its success can't be explained by elementary economics.

[D] It will continue to surge forward. | M: Professor Stevenson, as an economist, how do you look upon the surging Chinese economy? Does it constitute a threat to the rest of the world?

W: I believe China's economic success should be seen more as an opportunity than a threat. Those who looked upon it as a threat overlooked the benefits of China's growth to the world's economy. They also lack understanding of elementary economics.

Q: What does Professor Stevenson think of China's economy? |

【解析】女士话中的比较结构 more as an opportunity than a threat 表明女士即 Professor Stevenson 认为中国的经济增长"与其说是威胁不如说是机遇"。听音时如抓住男士话中 benefits 一词就可基本确定答案为[A]。

3. more and more 表示"越来越…"

【例10】 (04-1-2)

| [A] The air pollution is caused by the development of industry.

[B] The city was poor because there wasn't much industry then.

[C] The woman's exaggerating the seriousness of the pollution.

[D] He might move to another city very soon. | W: I can't bear the air pollution in this city any more. It's getting worse and worse.

M: You said it! We've never had so many factories before.

Q: What does the man mean? |

【解析】女士话中的比较结构 worse and worse 表达了女士的想法:城市空气污染变得越来越严重了,男士话中的 You said it!（你说的太对了!）表明男士赞同女士的想法,他还说以前可没有 so many factories,由此可推断男士认为空气污染是由工业发展引起的,故答案为[A]。

4. the more …, the more … 表示"越…,就越…"

如:The more you learn, the more you earn.

The purer the diamond, the more valuable it is.

三 形容词、副词的最高级

1. 单纯表示三者或三者以上之最

【例11】 (04-6-1)

[A] Dick's trousers don't match his jacket.	W: Oh, Dick. You're wearing a black jacket but yellow trousers. It's the strangest combination I've ever seen.
[B] Dick looks funny in that yellow jacket.	
[C] The color of Dick's jacket is too dark.	M: I know. I got up late and dressed in a hurry. I didn't realize my mistake until I entered the office.
[D] Dick has bad taste in clothes.	Q: What does the woman think of the way Dick dressed?

【解析】女士用最高级"the strangest"表达她对男士穿着的不赞同,说明女士认为男士穿的衣服搭配地不协调,故答案为[A]。

2. one of the + 形容词最高级

常用于表示某事物"非常…"。

【例12】 (01-1-1)

[A] The man thinks traveling by air is quite safe.	W: Have you heard about the plane crash yesterday? It caused a hundred and twenty deaths. I am never at ease when taking a flight.
[B] The woman never travels by plane.	
[C] Both speakers feel nervous when flying.	M: Though we often hear about air crashes and serious casual deeds, flying is one of the safest ways to travel.
[D] The speakers feel sad about the serious loss of life.	Q: What do we learn from this conversation?

【解析】由男士话中的 flying is one of the safest ways to travel 可知他认为飞机是一种相当安全的旅行方式。one of the safest ways ≈ quite safe,故答案为[A]。

四、强调

一 强调句型

强调句型的基本结构是"It + 系动词 be + 被强调成份 + 关系代词 who/that + 句子的其他成份"。

如:原句:Jim bought a book yesterday.

强调主语:**It was Jim** who bought a book yesterday.

强调宾语:**It was a book** that Jim bought yesterday.

强调时间状语:**It was yesterday** that Jim bought a book

需要注意的是,有三类句子成份不可以用这个强调句型进行强调,即表语、谓语动词和 though,although,whereas 等引导的让步状语从句或对比状语从句。

二 谓语动词的强调

强调谓语动词时,通常在该谓语动词前面加助动词 do 或 does(过去时用 did),来加强语气,一般译为"务必,一定,确实"等。

【例13】 (02-6-19)

[A] One of Etna's recent eruptions made many people move away. [B] Etna's frequent eruptions have ruined most of the local farmland. [C] Etna's eruptions are frequent but usually mild. [D] There are signs that Etna will erupt again in the near future.	Let's take Mount Etna for example. It does erupt frequently, but those eruptions are usually minor. 19. What will people living near Mount Etna do in the face of its eruptions?

【解析】句中谓语动词 erupt 前出现的助动词 does 起强调作用,其所在句子为本题答案的出处,故答案为[C]。

五、情态动词

情态动词只有情态意义,即它所表示的是说话人对动作的观点,如需要、可能、意愿或怀疑等。

英语的情态动词主要有 can(could),may(might),must,have to,shall,should,will(would),need,ought to 等。

一 情态动词表推测

1. must do/ must have done(一定…)

前者表示对现在或将来事实的肯定推测,后者表示对过去事实的肯定推测。

【例14】 (02-6-7)

[A] Neither of their watches keeps good time. [B] The woman's watch stopped 3 hours ago. [C] The man's watch goes too fast. [D] It's too dark for the woman to read her watch.	W: It's awfully dark for 4 o'clock. Do you think it's going to rain? M: You'd better do something about that watch of yours. It must have stopped hours ago. Mine says 7. Q: What conclusion can we draw from this conversation?

【解析】男士话中的 must have stooped 表示对过去的一种肯定的推测,表明女士的表很可能几小时前就停了,故答案为[B]。

2. can't do/can't have done(不可能…)

前者对现在或将来事实的否定推测,后者表示对过去事实的否定推测。

【例15】 (06-6-10)

[A] It was applaudable.	W: You didn't seem terribly enthusiastic about the performance.
[B] It was just terrible.	
[C] The actors were enthusiastic.	M: You must be kidding. I couldn't have clapped any harder. My hands are still hurting.
[D] The plot was funny enough.	Q: What does the man think of the performance?

【解析】男士说他 couldn't have clapped any harder(不可能鼓掌得更卖力了),是对过去事情的可能猜测,表明电影 was applaudable(很受欢迎),故答案为[A]。

二 情态动词 + have done 表虚拟

1. should/shouldn't have done

表示"本应该做某事而实际上没有做"或"本不应该做某事但实际上却做了"的含义。

如:You shouldn't have come. 你本不应该来。

You should have finished it. 你本应该做完的。

2. might have done

表示"本来可以做某事而实际上却没有做"的含义。

如:He might have come earlier. 他本可以来得更早一些的。

3. needn't have done

表示"本来没有必要做某事而实际上却已经做了"的含义。

如:She needn't have bought it. 她本不需要买它。

【例16】 (05-1-2)

[A] Mr. Johnson's ideas are nonsense.	W: I don't agree with Mr. Johnson on his views about social welfare. He seems to suggest that the poor are robbing the rich.
[B] He quite agrees with Mr. Johnson's views.	
[C] Mr. Johnson is good at expressing his ideas.	M: He might have used better words to express his ideas, but I find what he said makes a lot of sense.
[D] He shares the woman's views on social welfare.	Q: What does the man mean?

【解析】男士话中的 might have used 表示他认为 Mr. Johnson 原本可以使用(但实际上却没有使用)better words,说明男士对 Mr. Johnson 的措辞不认同,之后男士通过 but 转折表达其真实意图,即他认为 Mr. Johnson 的观点很有道理,故答案为[B]。若不能正确理解 might have used 的含义,就可能误选[C]。

Exercise　　　　专项练习　　　🎧 边听边记

1. [A] They will accept the translation work even if they had taken the night class.

   [B] They will not accept the translation work even if they hadn't taken the night class.

   [C] They will accept the translation work because they do not have enough money.

   [D] They will not accept the translation work because they do not have enough time.

2. [A] Not getting what he wants.

   [B] A custom that is new to him.

   [C] Calling up customers.

   [D] Some of his good friends.

3. [A] It doesn't matter which color the man chooses.

   [B] It's a difficult decision.

   [C] She doesn't like either color.

   [D] The man should choose a different room.

4. [A] Going to see the new kid is the best thing they can do.

   [B] They should go to see the man's father.

   [C] A guy named Tom will go to a new place.

   [D] The woman might go with the man to see his mother.

5. [A] The woman likes the modern art in a higher degree.

   [B] The woman likes the classical art better.

   [C] The woman likes neither the modern art nor the classical art.

   [D] The woman likes the modern art just as he likes the classical art.

6. [A] She went to the party without knowing it.

   [B] She was invited to the party.

   [C] She didn't want to be present for the party.

   [D] She was absent from the party.

7. [A] The weatherman is often wrong.

   [B] The weatherman is usually good at making forecasts.

   [C] It is going to be sunny tomorrow.

   [D] It is going to rain tomorrow.

8. [A] It's more fashionable.　　　[B] It's larger inside.

   [C] It's more functional.　　　[D] It's nicer-looking inside.

9. [A] They spent three hundred dollars on their vacation.

[B] They had only three hundred dollars in the bank.

[C] They lost their bankbook.

[D] They drew more money than they should have from the bank.

10. [A] He suggests that she visit Belgium.

[B] He suggests that she work harder.

[C] He suggests that she listen more.

[D] He suggests that she get a tutor.

边听边记

【答案与解析】

1.

[A] They will accept the translation work even if they had taken the night class. [B] They will not accept the translation work even if they hadn't taken the night class. [C] They will accept the translation work because they do not have enough money. [D] They will not accept the translation work because they do not have enough time.	W: I suppose we should accept the translation work, but I don't see how we can afford it in the future. M: If only we hadn't taken a night class this week. Q: What can we learn about the man and the woman from the conversation?

【解析】男士通过含有虚拟语气的句子 If only we hadn't taken a night class this week(要是不用上夜校课就好了)表明,他们这周要上夜校的课,所以没有足够的时间做翻译工作。

2.

[A] Not getting what he wants. [B] A custom that is new to him. [C] Calling up customers. [D] Some of his good friends.	M: I wish I could get used to this American custom of using first names. W: I usually call just my good friends by their first names. Q: What is the man complaining about?

【解析】男士用含有虚拟语气的句子 I wish I could …表示他希望自己能够习惯美国使用名字的习俗,由此可知男士是在抱怨一种新的习俗。

3.

[A] It doesn't matter which color the man chooses. [B] It's a difficult decision. [C] She doesn't like either color. [D] The man should choose a different room.	M: I haven't decided which color to paint my room, white or yellow? W: It isn't easy to choose, is it? Q: What does the woman mean?

【解析】男士不知道把墙刷成白色好还是黄色好,女士通过反意疑问句 It isn't easy to choose,is it? 表示这确实是 a difficult decision(不太容易做的决定)。

4.

[A] Going to see the new kid is the best thing they can do.	M: My father wants me to go to see a new kid——a guy named Tom. How about going with me?
[B] They should go to see the man's father.	
[C] A guy named Tom will go to a new place.	W: Okay. I might go as well. Nothing better to do.
[D] The woman might go with the man to see his mother.	Q: What can we learn from the conversation?

【解析】男士邀请女士一起去看一个叫 Tom 的孩子,女士说反正自己也觉得 Nothing better to do(没什么其他更好的事可做),就答应和男士一起去,也就是说女士认为去看 Tom 是 the best thing they can do。

5.

[A] The woman likes the modern art in a higher degree.	M: I went to a modern art exhibition yesterday. It is really abstract. Do you like the modern art?
[B] The woman likes the classical art better.	
[C] The woman likes neither the modern art nor the classical art.	W: I certainly do, yet not so much as the classical art.
[D] The woman likes the modern art just as he likes the classical art.	Q: What can we learn from the conversation?

【解析】男士询问女士是否喜欢 the modern art,女士回答说喜欢,但接着女士又在转折词 yet 之后用否定同级比较结构 not so much as the classical art 表示她更喜欢古典艺术。

6.

[A] She went to the party without knowing it.	M: There was a party on our school campus last Saturday evening. Did you go?
[B] She was invited to the party.	W: Had I known about the party, I would have been present for it.
[C] She didn's want to be present for the party.	
[D] She was absent from the party.	Q: What do we learn about the woman?

【解析】女士通过含有虚拟语气的句子 Had I known … , I would have been … 表示如果她知道关于聚会的消息,她就参加了,言外之意就是实际上她并不知道这个消息,所以没有参加聚会。

7.

[A] The weatherman is often wrong.	W: The weatherman says the storm is getting worse.
[B] The weatherman is usually good at making forecasts.	M: If he's as good as he usually is at·making forecasts, we will probably have blue skies tomorrow.
[C] It is going to be sunny tomorrow.	
[D] It is going to rain tomorrow.	Q: What does the man mean?

【解析】女士说天气预报员说将有更猛烈的暴风雨,男士通过条件句 If he's as good as he usually is at making forecasts, we will probably ... 表示,如果他的预报像往常一样"准"的话,那明天应该是晴天,言外之意是天气预报员常常出错。

8.

[A] It's more fashionable.	W: Which of the two cars we saw today do you prefer?
[B] It's larger inside.	M: I think the red one looks very nice, but the black one has more room inside, so I like it better.
[C] It's more functional.	
[D] It's nicer-looking inside.	Q: Why does the man like the black car better?

【解析】男士话中的比较结构 the black one has more room 表明黑色车的车内空间更大,所以他更喜欢黑色的车。

9.

[A] They spent three hundred dollars on their vacation.	W: I just got a statement from the bank. It says I've drawn $300 more than I have in my account.
[B] They had only three hundred dollars in the bank.	M: Well, we did spend a lot on our vacation. In fact, we didn't know exactly how much was in our account.
[C] They lost their bankbook.	
[D] They drew more money than they should have from the bank.	Q: What can we learn about the speakers from the conversation?

【解析】女士说银行通知说她的账户 drawn $300 more than ...（透支了300美元）,由此可知他从银行账户中支取的数额超出了应该支取的范围。

10.

[A] He suggests that she visit Belgium.	W: I spend hours going over the French lessons in my spare time. But I don't seem to be able to carry on a decent conversation in French.
[B] He suggests that she work harder.	

[C] He suggests that she listen more. [D] He suggests that she get a tutor.	M: You should take some private lessons from the new Belgium student. You'd surely make progress then. Q: What advice does the man give the woman?

【解析】男士通过情态动词 should 建议女士去 take some private lessons from the new Belgium student(让那个新来的比利时学生给她讲一下课),即建议她找一个辅导老师教她。

听音素质培养

一、保持良好的心态

很多考生由于在中学时未能接受充分的听力训练,加之受方言等因素的影响,英语发音不太标准,所以听力基础十分薄弱,一遇到听力考试就心慌,心理负担比较重。

由于心里太紧张,考生往往一开始会有几个单词或句子听不进去,从而严重影响整体的听音效果。可见,控制自己的紧张情绪,全神贯注地投入到考试中去,是十分重要的。

实际上,听力理解过程不是被动的接受,而是在积极参与的过程中运用自己已有的知识(包括语法、词汇、常识等)对所听到的内容进行解码,然后进行筛选、过滤、整理、分类,这是一个重新组合的过程。人们在接收信息的过程中,都会自觉地将自己所掌握的知识(包括背景知识)同其听到的内容联系起来,这种背景知识和输入信息的结合就是预测、挑选、吸收和综合的过程。

在听力理解的过程中,注意力必须高度集中,沉着应变,心里万万不可紧张。若偶尔遇到一个或几个生词,不要慌张,可置之不理,因为个别单词往往不会影响对整个句子或段落的理解。如果一遇到生词就停下来,会引起连锁反应,结果什么也听不懂。遇到实在不会做的题,不要反复琢磨,应赶快放弃,专心听后面的内容。听完后必须对所听到的内容进行分析、综合、推理、判断,挑选出和问题有关的信息,放弃无关紧要的信息。

二、学会用英语思维

听的时候尽量避免将每个单词和句子翻译成汉语,这样做一是浪费时间,二是影响理解,因为两种语言的结构和思维不尽相同,不是所有的英语都有相对等的汉语。在短暂的15秒钟内,既要听,又要理解、记忆、翻译,还要进行综合判断,这是不可能的,而且会影响听力理解的效果。最好的办法是逐渐培养英语思维,不但可以节约时间,还可以提高理解能力。

【例】   (05-12-8)

[A] John has lost something at the railway station.	M: We're supposed to meet John here at the railway station.
[B] There are several railway stations in the city.	W: That's like looking for a needle in a hay stack.
[C] It will be very difficult for them to find John.	Q: What does the man imply?
[D] The train that John is taking will arrive soon.	

【解析】女士说他们要去火车站接 John,男士说那就像是 a needle in a hay stack
（大海捞针）一样难,与 very difficult for them to find John 同义,只要知道这一点
很快就可以得出答案。

三、听力训练方法

多听是提高听力的最主要途径。考生在听力训练时可以采取以下步骤:

1. 先按试题要求听录音并做题。
2. 查对答案。分清哪些是真正听懂的,哪些是碰对的,哪些是根本没有听懂的。
3. 打开原文,把没有听懂的部分找出来,弄明白。
4. 合上书,再听一遍。看看刚才没听懂的部分再听时是否能够听懂。如果仍旧
   不懂,要明白是什么原因,比如是发音问题(连音、省音、弱读等)、生词太多,
   还是句子结构复杂,或者是语句中隐含的意思比较模糊。可以再回到原文书
   面材料中去理解,但要特别注意的是,对照原文边看边听是没有效果的。

四、练好基本功,功到自然成

毫无疑问,应试技巧是有效的,也是十分重要的,但不应指望技巧解决所有的
问题。技巧也必须在一定语言能力的基础上才能发挥作用,考生不能只依赖技巧
而忽视了听力实力的提高。了解基本的语音知识,熟记(不只是认识)一定数量的
核心词汇,熟练掌握英文的常用句型结构,熟悉英文的常用人名、地名及数字表达
法等,对于听力的提高都是十分必要的。

应试技巧是用在考场上的,考生在平时的听力训练中一定要脚踏实地,不懂
的问题要彻底搞懂,下次再出现同样的问题就不会有障碍。问题一个个消灭了,
能力自然就上来了,应对考试也就不成问题了。

短对话高分必备

Part 2

本篇首先对短对话题中的常考场景及常考句式进行了归纳和总结，之后对短对话各类题型的解题方法和解题技巧进行了详尽的讲解，并配备专项练习加以巩固，最后设置了短对话综合训练题，供考生进行自测训练。

常考场景

短对话题是各类考试中最常见、最固定的一种听力试题类型。六级考试改革以后,短对话的数量由每套 10 道题变为 8 道题,但考查内容和难度未有变化。

短对话涉及的场景比较广泛,但以贴近学生学习和日常生活的场景为主。主要有以下几类:

一、校园生活类

这类场景主要围绕学生的学习和生活展开,涉及入学、办手续(注册)、选课、听课、作业、论文、借书、买书、学习、考试、课余活动、住宿问题等一系列话题。

场景规律

高中毕业规划:上大学还是工作? 选择什么专业以及选择的理由是什么? 家长的意见如何?

入学:入学注册手续。刚入校不熟悉环境,可能需要问路或打听一些情况,学校或学生会也可能会组织介绍或参观校园的活动。另外有些学生还需要申请助学贷款。

选课:新学期开始或期末要选修课程,选什么课程? 选几门课程? 课程负担太重是否该放弃某一门?

听课或听讲座:对课程、讲座和教师的评价。课程是否有趣? 老师讲的能不能理解? 讲座是否吸引人?

买书、卖书:书店的书可能会有脱销的时候。高年级的学生,尤其是毕业生,会将用过的书卖掉,低年级的学生则会购买。

借书、还书:用学生证或者借阅证到图书馆借书。书要按时归还,但有时会因疏忽而忘记归还或将书弄丢,因而不得不交罚款。学校或学生个人会订阅期刊杂志。

作业或论文:老师布置的作业或论文一般都较难或较多,为了完成作业或赶交论文,有时还得熬夜或同其他同学合作来加快速度。作业或论文上交以后,老师会给评语或建议,往往是需要改进。

学习:家长谈论孩子的学习大多是担心孩子不用功。学习需要一个安静的环境,但却常常受到干扰。努力学习却收效甚微或成绩不理想。不要过分看重成绩,重要的是学到知识,另外应该找出原因或解决办法。

考试:临近考试,才知道抓紧时间复习,有人甚至会选择逃课。考试之后会担心结果,并会相互打听。

课余活动：	学校常常举办一些比赛或开展一些义务性活动，报名前会做一些准备活动。对于参加比赛，往往由于缺乏信心而比较犹豫；而对于那些义务性活动，一般都会积极报名参加。
同学交往：	联系方式有写信、发电子邮件或打电话等。面对别人的缺点或者错误应该怎么做，一般是保持距离或尽量帮助。

【例1】 (07-6-12)

[A] He enjoys finding fault with exams.	W: I've never seen you have such confidence before an exam.
[B] He is sure of his success in the exam.	M: It's more than confidence. Right now I feel that if I get less than an A, it'll be the fault of the exam itself.
[C] He doesn't know if he can do well in the exam.	Q: What does the man mean?
[D] He used to get straight A's in the exams he took.	

【解析】本对话的话题是关于考试。男士说如果他这次考试拿不到 A，那一定是 the fault of the exam itself（考试本身的问题），可见他 sure of his success in the exam，由此可知答案为 [B]。

【例2】 (03-1-8)

[A] She lacks confidence in herself.	M: The university is going to hold an interesting competition on computer programming. Many of my friends have signed up for it. How about you?
[B] She is not interested in computer programming.	
[C] She has never signed up for any competition before.	W: Do you think I could ever win anything if I took part in it?
[D] She is sure to win the programming contest.	Q: What do we learn from the conversation about the woman?

【解析】本对话的话题是关于校园竞赛。女士话中的反问句 Do you think I could …？表明她对自己在竞赛中获奖 lack confidence（缺乏自信），由此可知答案为 [A]。

二、日常生活类

这类场景主要涉及与日常家庭生活相关的话题，包括购物、洗衣、收拾屋子、家庭理财以及其他一些居家琐事等。

场景规律

购物价格:	顾客往往会觉得价格太高,跟售货员或店主讨价还价,但售货员或店主很少会让步。
顾客投诉:	顾客可能会对产品的某一方面瑕疵、服务员的态度等问题进行投诉,圆满解决的情况较多。
营业时间:	要熟悉周围市场、商店或购物中心的营业时间,如果去的时间不对很可能会赶上关门。
家庭关系:	夫妻关系、父母和子女关系以及家族成员之间的关系等。常涉及到夫妻不合、离婚、父母和子女之间的代沟等话题。
家庭财务:	家庭财务由谁负责。管理好家庭财务很重要,一般对话中涉及到入不敷出的情况占多数。到银行办理开户、存钱、取钱等业务。
家庭分工:	男士是否应该分担家务活;女性是否应该出去工作;如何处理工作和家庭的矛盾。
家务劳动:	家务劳动包括洗衣、做饭、收拾屋子等,有的是自己来做,有的是雇人来做。
干洗衣服:	在干洗店洗衣服的情况较多,常会涉及到什么时候送去洗,什么时候洗好,什么时候取回来,以及由谁来取等事宜。
交流心得:	在解决理财、教育孩子或养宠物等问题上哪一种方法更好。
邮局业务:	到邮局办理寄信、拍电报、买邮票、寄包裹等业务。经常是发生在邮局里的一段对话,要求能够根据关键词判断出对话发生的场景。

【例3】 (06-6-2)

[A] Set the dinner table. [B] Change the light bulb. [C] Clean the dining room. [D] Hold the ladder for him.	M: Susan, I am going to change the light bulb above the dining room table. Will you hold the ladder for me? W: No problem. But be careful while you're up there. Q: What does the man want the woman to do?

【解析】本对话的话题是关于居家琐事。男士请女士帮忙 hold the ladder(扶梯子),女士说 no problem,由此可知答案为[D]。

【例4】 (03-9-4)

[A] The lens. [B] The price. [C] The flash. [D] The leather case.	M: I saw your advertisement in the morning paper concerning the X-20 model. The lens seem to be excellent, and the flash is not bad. But don't you think the price is a little steep? W: I think it's a good buy. The price includes the leather case, you know. Q: What does the man dislike about the camera?

【解析】本对话的话题是关于购物。男士通过反问句 don't you ...？表示他觉得照相机的价格 a little steep（有点高），即他 dislike（不满意）照相机的 price，由此可知答案为[B]。

三、职场工作类

这类场景主要涉及学生假期兼职、毕业生找工作、招聘面试、工作安排、工作状态、同事相处等话题。

场景规律

假期兼职：有的学生假期会放弃回家，而选择做一些兼职，比如在学校图书馆、餐馆或加油站等地。

寻找工作：通过报纸上的广告或招聘会找工作，并投递简历与求职信。可能会出现简历投晚了以致没有空缺的情况。

工作招聘：对工作候选人作出评价，认为谁比较合适并陈述理由。

工作面试：面试迟到往往说明对面试不够重视，会严重影响到面试的结果；初次面试难免会紧张，周围人往往会提一些建议；面试完了会跟别人谈论一下自己的表现以及预测面试结果。

工作情况：有一大堆事情要做以至于不能做别的事情。因为工作忙,经常会有一些员工抱怨。

工作安排：经常会因为某种原因推迟或取消原来安排,这时需向对方说明原因。

职位任免：表现不佳就可能会遭解雇；相反,杰出的表现则会得到上司的青睐而得以升迁。

【例5】 (07-6-15)

[A] More money.	W: I hear your boss has a real good impression of you
[B] Fair treatment.	and he is thinking about giving you two more days
[C] A college education.	off each month.
[D] Shorter work hours.	M: I hope not. I'd rather get more work hours so I can
	get enough bucks to help out my two kids at college.
	Q: What does the man truly want?

【解析】本对话的话题是关于工作目标。男士说他不希望老板给他放假,因为他想 get enough bucks to ...（赚更多的钱来供孩子上大学）,由此可知答案为[A]。more money ≈ enough bucks。

【例6】 (04-6-5)

| [A] The man is not suitable for the position. | M: I wonder if you find my |
| [B] The job has been given to someone else. | experience relevant to the job. |

| [C] She had received only one application letter.
[D] The application arrived a week earlier than expected. | W: Yes, certainly. But if only you had sent in your application letter a week earlier.
Q: What does the woman imply? |

【解析】本对话的话题是关于求职应聘。女士使用虚拟语气 if only you had sent …（要是你早点递上求职信就好了），暗示男士简历投晚了，这份工作已经 given to someone else，由此可知答案为[B]。

四、健康医疗类

这类场景主要涉及到看病就医、健康状况、锻炼身体、健身减肥等话题。

场景规律

生病就医：生病了应及时吃药就医。应主动向医生询问病情或寻求建议。

医院诊所：经常是一段发生在医生和病人之间的对话，需通过关键词判断出谈话场景。

减肥方式：节食减肥，结果往往不尽如人意；健身减肥，效果往往比较显著。

锻炼目的：有人是为了强身，有人是为了减肥。

健康习惯：要养成良好的健康习惯，要听从医生的建议放弃吸烟、喝酒等不良习惯。

【例7】　　　　　　　　　　　　　　　　　　　　　　　　　　(07-6-17)

| [A] Cheer herself up a bit.
[B] Find a more suitable job.
[C] Seek professional advice.
[D] Take a psychology course. | W: I'm worried about Anna. She's really been depressed lately. All she does is staying in her room all day.
M: That sounds serious. She'd better see a psychiatrist at the consoling center.
Q: What does the man suggest Anna do? |

【解析】本对话的话题是关于心理健康。男士通过典型的建议句式 She'd better … 建议 Anna 去 see a psychiatrist at the consoling center（去慰藉中心看精神病医师），由此可知答案为[C]。

【例8】　　　　　　　　　　　　　　　　　　　　　　　　　　(06-6-8)

| [A] At a bookstore.
[B] At the dentist's.
[C] In a restaurant.
[D] In the library. | M: I am afraid there won't be time to do another tooth today. Make sure you don't eat anything like steaks for the next few hours, and we'll fill the other cavity tomorrow.
W: All right. Actually, I must hurry to the library to return some books.
Q: Where does the conversation most probably take place? |

【解析】本对话的话题是关于看牙医。由信息词 tooth，cavity（齿洞）等关键词可推知谈话地点为 the dentist's（牙科诊所），由此可知答案为[B]。

五、旅游交通类

这类场景主要涉及旅行前准备、旅行选择的交通手段、旅行时的情形、旅行的感受、接人送人、交通状况、交通违章、交通事故等话题。

场景规律

旅行准备：准备旅行必备品，确定交通方式，预定旅馆，请人照看房子或宠物。

旅行情况：去哪里旅行，那里的风景如何，旅行者的感觉如何。

接人送人：可能是机场或车站。对话中常涉及时间、航班或车次，有时会因为人多、航班晚点、工作忙等原因接不到要接的人或无法为别人送行。

交通方式：经常会涉及到各类交通工具的优缺点，哪个更安全、更快、更舒适、更经济实惠？

交通时刻：汽车、火车或飞机等因某种原因延误或者取消。

交通状况：高峰期交通堵塞经常导致上班上学迟到。

交通违章：有时会因为超速行驶或闯红灯等违章行为而被罚款。

交通事故：事故原因（多为人为原因），事故伤亡情况，事故后果。

【例9】 (07-6-16)

[A] She was exhausted from her trip.	M: I heard you took a trip to Mexico last month. How did you like it?
[B] She missed the comforts of home.	W: Oh, I got sick and tired of hotels and hotel food. So now I understand the saying, "East, west, home's best".
[C] She was impressed by Mexican food.	
[D] She will not go to Mexico again.	Q: What does the woman mean?

【解析】本对话的话题是关于旅行感受。女士说她 got sick and tired of hotels and hotel food（生病了并且很厌烦旅馆和旅馆的食物），还说自己现在才明白那句谚语"East，west，home's best"（金窝，银窝，不如自己的草窝）的含义，由此可知她 missed the comforts of home（想念家里的舒适），由此可知答案为[B]。

【例10】 (03-6-5)

[A] The company has trouble printing a schedule.	W: We are informed that the 11:30 train is late again.
[B] The speakers arrived at the station late.	M: Why did the railway company even bother to print the schedule?
[C] The train seldom arrives on time.	Q: What do we learn from the conversation?
[D] The schedule has been misprinted.	

【解析】本对话的话题是关于交通时刻。女士话中的火车 late again 以及男士话中的反问句 Why did the railway company …？（铁路公司干吗还要费事印时刻表呢）表明，火车 seldom arrives on time（很少能准点到达），由此可知答案为[C]。

六、饮食娱乐类

这类场景主要涉及吃饭地点、点菜、对饭菜及用餐环境的评价，以及观看电影、观看演出、购票、评论电影或演出等话题。

场景规律

外出就餐：多是朋友、同事之间请客，或是因为朋友或亲属到来、累了不想做饭而选择出去吃。

邀请就餐：一般拒绝的情况居多，拒绝的原因经常会通过 but 转折引出。

就餐地点：讨论去哪家餐馆吃，如西餐厅还是中餐厅、日本菜还是意大利菜？

点菜：　服务生会递上菜谱，有时会推荐一些特色菜或特价菜。点菜时可能会互相征求意见，有时会因身体情况而不能吃某些食物。

评菜：　讨论对某家餐馆的印象，如就餐环境、饭菜味道等，一般不满意的情况居多。

娱乐项目：常涉及到的有音乐会、演唱会、电影、体育比赛等。

观点演出：邀请别人观看演出得看对方的时间安排，如对方拒绝一般会补充说明理由，如接受会表示非常高兴接到邀请。

票的话题：演出的票很早就会卖光，得趁早购买。

评论演出：演出有的很精彩，有的很糟糕，对话中常会涉及一些表达观点的特殊句式。

【例 11】　　　　　　　　　　　　　　　　　　　（新 06-12-18）

[A] The food served in the cafeteria usually lacks variety. [B] The cafeteria sometimes provides rare food for the students. [C] The students find the service in the cafeteria satisfactory. [D] The cafeteria tries hard to cater to the students' needs.	W: The cafeteria provided many kinds of dishes for us today. Did you notice that? M: Yes, kind of rare, isn't it? Q: What does the man imply?

【解析】本对话的话题是关于外出就餐。女士提到今天 the cafeteria（自助餐馆）的菜式很丰富，男士说这种情况 kind of rare（很少有），由此推知通常情况下 the cafeteria 的食物种类很少，由此可知答案为[A]。cater to one's needs 意为"迎合某人的需求"。

【例12】 (06-12-2)

[A] Go to an art exhibition.	M: Hi, Donna, are you interested in going to an
[B] Dine out with an old friend.	art exhibition on Sunday? A friend of mine is showing some of her paintings there. It's
[C] Attend the opening night of a play.	the Opening Night. Free drinks and food.
[D] See his paintings on display.	W: Well, actually, I don't have anything planned. It sounds kind of fun.
	W: What did the man invite the woman to do on Sunday?

【解析】本对话的话题是关于参观展览。男士邀请女士参加周日的 art exhibition，女士接受了邀请，由此可知答案为[A]。

七、住家搬房类

这类场景主要涉及旅馆住宿、租房买房、居住环境、装饰装修、房屋维修等话题。

场景规律

旅馆住宿：住宿条件如何？价格如何？是否客房已满？询问旅馆的路线。

租房信息：租房者向房东或者同事、朋友打听房子出租的消息，包括房子的内部结构、房租等。多数情况下，房子不能满足租房者的要求，需要做这样那样的调整。

居住环境：包括住所离工作、学习的地点的远近，交通情况等。郊区房租便宜但离上班、上学的地方较远，交通也不方便；市区生活方便但房租贵，那就要看租房者自己的意愿和条件了。

装饰装修：房子都有哪些设备和装饰品。家具是否齐全，是否需要添置。

房屋维修：房子出现水管漏水或洗衣机坏了等问题时请人维修。

【例13】 (新 06-12-12)

[A] The man will rent the apartment when it is available.	W: I'm afraid I can't show you the apartment at the moment, because the
[B] The man made a bargain with the landlady over the rent.	tenant is still living in it. It's really a lovely place with a big kitchen and a
[C] The man insists on having a look at the apartment first.	sunny window for only $200 a month.
[D] The man is not fully satisfied with the apartment.	M: Sounds good, but we really can't rent an apartment without seeing it first.
	Q: What do we learn from the conversation?

【解析】本对话的话题是关于租房。男士通过 but 转折提出要 seeing it first（先看看公寓的情况），然后再决定是否租住，由此可知答案为[C]。

【例14】 (05-6-9)

[A] The man should phone the hotel for directions.	M: Excuse me, but could you tell me how to get to the Friendship Hotel? I thought it was on this corner, but I seem to have made a mistake.
[B] The man can ask the department store for help.	
[C] She doesn't have the hotel's phone number.	W: I am sorry, but I am a stranger here myself. Maybe you can try calling them. There is a phone over there outside the department store.
[D] The hotel is just around the corner.	Q: What does the woman mean?

【解析】本对话的话题是关于寻找旅馆。男士向女士询问如何到达 Friendship Hotel，女士建议他 try calling them（往宾馆打电话）问问，由此可知答案为[A]。

八、气候环境类

这类场景主要涉及气候、温度、环境污染以及其对人们生活的影响等方面的话题。

场景规律

天气变化：天气变化无常，不发生变化的天气是不可能存在的，有人因此感冒，有人因此不得不改变行程。

天气影响：天气经常会影响到人们的出行或活动安排。经常因为天气变化而造成某次出行或某项活动的延误或耽搁。

环境污染：环境污染现在十分严重，需要全社会的关注，要从个人做起。影响环境的因素有很多，其中有很多是人为因素。

【例15】 (04-6-3)

[A] The temperature is not as high as the man claims.	M: Excuse me, Madam. Is the air-conditioning on? This room is getting as hot as a furnace.
[B] The room will get cool if the man opens the windows.	
[C] She is following instructions not to use the air-conditioning.	W: Sorry, sir. A new epidemic called SARS is threatening us right now. As a preventative measure, we are told to let in fresh air by opening the windows and not to use air conditioners.
[D] She is afraid the new epidemic SARS will spread all over town.	Q: What does the woman mean?

【解析】本对话的话题是关于室内空气。女士说为了预防 SARS,她被告之不要 use air conditioners（使用空调）,要让空气流通,由此可知答案为 [C]。preventative measure 意为"预防措施"。epidemic 意为"流行性的"。

【例16】   (04-1-2)

[A] The air pollution is caused by the development of industry.	W: I can't bear the air pollution in this city any more. It's getting worse and worse.
[B] The city was poor because there wasn't much industry then.	M: You said it! We've never had so many factories before.
[C] The woman's exaggerating the seriousness of the pollution.	Q: What does the man mean?
[D] He might move to another city very soon.	

【解析】本对话的话题是关于环境污染。男士说过去没有 so many factories（这么多的工厂）,言外之意是说 air pollution（空气污染）是由 factories（即 the development of industry）造成的。You said it!（你说得太对了!）是表示赞同对方看法的一种常用句式。

Exercise   专项练习   🎧 边听边记

1. [A] They won't miss any of the movie.
   [B] The previews began 15 minutes ago.
   [C] The beginning of the movie is not important.
   [D] He doesn't want to miss the previews.
2. [A] She suggests that the man try the restaurant across the road.
   [B] She suggests that the man go to a party.
   [C] She suggests that the man reserve a table again.
   [D] She suggests that the man visit someone's house.
3. [A] Borrow her book.
   [B] Check the classroom again.
   [C] Buy a new book.
   [D] Ask about the book at the information desk.
4. [A] She has to take three more courses this spring.
   [B] She'll be able to finish them in the summer term.
   [C] She'll wait until fall to take them.
   [D] She has already completed them.
5. [A] At the doctor's office.
   [B] At the reception desk of a health service.

[C] At the hotel.　　　　　　　[D] In a shop.

6. [A] Visit his friends.　　　　　[B] Go to a concert.

[C] Buy something in a shop.　[D] Take a trip on the canals.

7. [A] He can't find the new building.

[B] He had a bigger apartment before.

[C] He's not accustomed to the new building.

[D] He's having a hard time finding an apartment.

8. [A] Eat before seeing the movie.

[B] See the movie immediately.

[C] Get the first theater seat.

[D] Stay in town for a while.

9. [A] His classmate.　　　　　　[B] His teacher.

[C] His partner.　　　　　　　[D] His boss.

10. [A] The winter has just begun.

[B] Once it starts to snow, it'll snow a lot.

[C] They're ready for the snow.

[D] It has been snowing for some time.

【答案与解析】

1.

[A] They won't miss any of the movie.	W: If we don't leave soon, we'll miss the beginning of the movie.
[B] The previews began 15 minutes ago.	
[C] The beginning of the movie is not important.	M: We've still got some time. They always show fifteen minutes of previews before it starts.
[D] He doesn't want to miss the previews.	Q: What does the man mean?

【解析】本对话的话题是关于观看电影。女士说要是再不快点就会错过电影的开头部分，而男士却说 fifteen minutes of previews before it starts（在电影开始前有 15 分钟的预告时间），暗示了他们不会 miss any of the movie（错过电影的任何部分）。

2.

[A] She suggests that the man try the restaurant across the road.	M: I booked a table! I asked the receptionist to reserve a table.
[B] She suggests that the man go to a party.	W: I'm sorry, sir. No one told me about it. Why don't you try the restaurant across the road?
[C] She suggests that the man reserve a table again.	
[D] She suggests that the man visit someone's house.	Q: What does the woman suggest?

【解析】本对话的话题是关于外出就餐。女士用反问句 why don't ...？建议男士 try the restaurant across the road(试一下马路对面的那家餐馆),由此可知答案为[A]。

3.

[A] Borrow her book. [B] Check the classroom again. [C] Buy a new book. [D] Ask about the book at the information desk.	M: Can I borrow your algebra textbook? I left mine in the classroom, and it was gone when I went back. W: That happened to me once. I'd almost given up on finding it until I checked it at the lost-and-found at the information desk downstairs in the lobby. Q: What does the woman imply the man should do?

【解析】本对话的话题是关于遗失物品。男士说他的书丢了,女士说她也曾遇到过这样的事情,后来在 the lost-and-found at the information desk(失物招领处)找到了,其言外之意是建议男士去失物招领处问一下。

4.

[A] She has to take three more courses this spring. [B] She'll be able to finish them in the summer term. [C] She'll wait until fall to take them. [D] She has already completed them.	M: Are you going to graduate this spring? W: I still have two more required courses, luckily, they are both being given this summer, so I don't have to wait until fall. Q: What does the woman say about her required courses?

【解析】本对话的话题是关于必修课。女士说她仍有 two more required courses (两门必修课),并且说它们 being given this summer(都设在今年夏天),所以她 don't have to wait until fall,由此可知答案为[B]。

5.

[A] At the doctor's office. [B] At the reception desk of a health service. [C] At the hotel. [D] In a shop.	M: I feel like I'm burning up. W: Let's take your temperature and have a look at your throat. Open your mouth wide and say "Ah" … Now unbutton your shirt and let me listen to your heart and lungs. Take a deep breath please. And another. That'll do. Q: Where does this conversation most probably take place?

【解析】本对话的话题是关于看病就医。对话中出现的 take one's temperature（量体温），look at your throat, listen to your heart and lungs 等都是医生给病人做检查时的常用语,故对话最有可能发生在 doctor's office。

6.

[A] Visit his friends.	M: I'm only here for two days. What
[B] Go to a concert.	can I see in two days?
[C] Buy something in a shop.	W: Two days isn't very much of course,
[D] Take a trip on the canals.	but you should certainly take a trip on
	the canals.
	Q: What can the man do in two days?

【解析】本对话的话题是关于旅行。男士说他只在这呆两天,女士建议他 take a trip on the canals（到运河上游览观光）。

7.

[A] He can't find the new building.	W: How do you like your new
[B] His new apartment is not big enough.	apartment?
[C] He's not accustomed to the new bui-	M: Well, it's quite nice really, although
lding.	I'm having a hard time getting used
[D] He's having a hard time finding an	to such a big building.
apartment.	Q: What is the man's problem?

【解析】本对话的话题是关于搬入新公寓。男士说虽然新房子很漂亮,他却得花一段时间 getting used to such a big building（适应这样的大房子）,由此可知答案为[C]。

8.

[A] Eat before seeing the movie.	W: We really must go to the new movie in
[B] See the movie immediately.	town.
[C] Get the first theater seat.	M: That's a good idea! But let's eat first.
[D] Stay in town for a while.	Q: What does the man want to do?

【解析】本对话的话题是关于饮食娱乐。女士想去看新上映的电影,男士则说 let's eat first,由此可知,男士是想先吃完饭再去看电影。

9.

[A] His classmate.	W: This is the third time you have been late this week,
[B] His teacher.	Robert. You'll have to do better than that, or I might
[C] His partner.	find it necessary to let you go.
[D] His boss.	M: It won't happen again, I assure you.
	Q: Who is speaking to Robert?

【解析】本对话的话题是关于上班迟到。女士说男士是本周第三次迟到了,要是他下次不表现得好点儿,她就会 let you go(把他解雇了)。由说话者的口气可推知这是老板跟雇员之间的对话。

10.

[A] The winter has just begun.	M: I think it's starting to snow.
[B] Once it starts to snow, it'll snow a lot.	W: Starting to snow? The ground's already covered.
[C] They're ready for the snow.	Q: What does the woman mean?
[D] It has been snowing for some time.	

【解析】本对话的话题是关于天气。男士说外面好像开始下雪了,女士通过反问句 Starting to snow? 否定男士的说法,还说 The ground's already covered(地面早已经被雪覆盖了),由此可知,雪已经下了一段时间了。

第二章 常 考 句 式

英语听力考试中,尤其是短对话题中,经常会涉及到一些表示转折、比较、建议或请求等的特殊句式,而对这些句式的正确理解往往就是答对该题的关键。因此熟悉和掌握六级考试中常考的特殊句式,将有助于考生在考试中更加准确、快速地抓取关键点,直抵答案所在。

一、转折句式

转折句式指的是先说明原本的意图或情势,然后经 but 等词进行转折来说明后来的实际想法或事实结果的句式。设题点往往在转折词之后。

 常见转折

1. but 转折

如:I'd like, **but** we have visitors from Finland.

Neither do I. **But** I think we should get it over with.

2. however, though, yet 等转折

如:He once told me that he had bought a big house, **yet** he is still sharing an apartment with Mark.

Though we often hear about air crashes and serious casual deeds, flying is one of the safest ways to travel.

二 解题技巧

1. 转折词之后为听音重点。

如果听到 but, however 等表示转折的词语,应该重点留意后面的内容,答案往往就在其中。

2. 抓住说话人的语气。

说话人往往是"先肯定某件事,然后通过转折表达出真实的意图",听音时应根据说话人的语气进行判断。

【例1】 (98-1-2)

[A] She is going to Finland. [B] She has visitors next week. [C] She has guests at her home. [D] She has just visited him this week.	M: Why don't you come to our house for dinner some time next week? W: I'd like to, but we have visitors from Finland, perhaps next week. Q: Why can't the woman accept the man's invitation?

【解析】男士邀请女士去他家吃晚饭，女士通过"先肯定后转折"的句式 I'd like to, but … 表示自己不能接受邀请，but 后陈述了理由（have visitors next week），由此可知答案为[B]。

三 误区警示

1. 不要被转折词前面的内容误导。

　　如果出现 but 等转折词，重点往往在后面，因此要注意不要受前面内容的影响而误选。

2. 切勿听到什么选什么。

　　这类题目的干扰项往往针对 but 等转折词前面的内容而设，而且经常是细节再现，因此要注意不要听到什么就选什么。

【例2】 (06-6-1)

[A] She met with Thomas just a few days ago. [B] She can help with the orientation program. [C] She is not sure she can pass on the message. [D] She will certainly try to contact Thomas.	M: Mary, could you please tell Thomas to contact me? I was hoping he will be able to help me out with the freshmen orientation program next week. W: I would certainly tell him if I saw him, but I haven't seen him around for quite a few days. Q: What does the woman mean?

【解析】根据女士话中的"先肯定后转折"（certainly … , but … ）的语气可以判断出女士没有把握一定能把口信传到，由此可知答案为[C]。注意不要被 but 前的内容误导而选[D]。orientation 意为"入学导向"。

二、条件句式

　　听力对话题中经常会涉及到一些表示条件的句式，其往往是表达说话人观点、态度的重点句型。

一 两种条件句

1. 真实条件句

　　真实条件句常用于表示事情发生的条件，实现的可能性较大。

如：**If it rains**, we won't go to the park.

　　Please tell him the truth **if he comes**.

2. 非真实条件句

　　非真实条件句，即虚拟条件句，常表示与现实相反的情况，实现的可能性较小。

如：**If I were** you, I would not do that.

　　We would have bought that desk **if we had** enough money that day.

二 解题技巧

1. 熟悉引出条件的常见词语。

    主要包括: unless, as long as, if only, lest(以防), with/without, otherwise, but for(要不是因为)等。

2. 区分真实条件句和虚拟条件句。

    判断是真实条件句还是虚拟条件句主要根据谓语动词的形式,关于虚拟条件句谓语动词的形式,在第一篇介绍常考语法时已经详细列出。

3. 搞清虚拟条件所指时间。

    如果是虚拟条件句,一定要搞清楚它所表示的时间究竟是与现在、过去还是将来相反。

4. 反着选答案。

    解答虚拟语气题型有一条重要的思路就是"反着选答案",因为虚拟语气是表达与事实相反的情况,答案往往就是虚拟条件句中所隐含的真实情况。

5. 注意隐含的虚拟条件句。

    but for, otherwise, without 所引出的短语,经常表示一种隐含的虚拟条件,听音时要留意。

【例3】 (03-9-2)

[A] The woman has a very tight budget.	W: I certainly would like to buy the fur coat I saw on the department store, but I don't have enough money.
[B] He does not think the fur coat is worth buying.	
[C] He's willing to lend the woman money for the fur coat.	M: Well, if you had budgeted your money better, you'll be able to buy it now.
[D] The woman is not careful enough in planning her spending.	Q: What does the man imply?

【解析】男士话中的虚拟语气 if you had budgeted … better(如果你能够更好地预算自己的钱的话)隐含的事实是女士 has a very tight budget(目前的预算很紧张),由此可知答案为[D]。

三 误区警示

1. 时态问题常出错。

    虚拟语气中的时态所表示的时间比事情实际发生的时间要提前,比如虚拟条件句中的一般过去时是表示现在或将来的情况,而虚拟条件句中的过去完成时表示的则是过去的情况。

2. 切勿听到什么选什么。

    虚拟语气是表示与事实相反的情况,如选项都是表示事实情况的,那么一定要注意不要听到什么选什么,要根据录音内容综合判断。

【例4】

(06-6-4)

[A] He has managed to sell a number of cars.	W: How come Jim lost his job?
[B] He is contented with his current position.	M: I didn't say he had lost it. All I said was if he didn't get out and start selling a few cars instead of idling around all day, he might find himself looking for a new job.
[C] He might get fired.	Q: What does the man say about Jim?
[D] He has lost his job.	

【解析】对话中男士通过虚拟语气（might find ... a new job）表达了对 Jim 可能失去工作的担忧。might find himself looking for a new job ≈ might get fired（可能被解雇）。这是一个与现在或将来事实相反的虚拟语气，而不是与事实过去相反，因此选项[D]是错误的。所以，考生除了掌握"反着选"的技巧，还要留心时态问题。

三、请求和建议句式

谈话的一方向另一方提出请求或建议是六级听力考试中常出现的一类场景,因此掌握一些表达请求或建议的常用句式,将对理解对话和解答问题有很大帮助。

一 常见句式

1. had better do sth. （最好⋯）

如: **You'd better go** someplace where there are fewer distractions.

  Next time **you'd better choose** a comedy.

2. How about/What about doing sth.? （⋯怎么样?）

如: **How about using** our dining-room for the meeting?

  What about seeing a film tonight?

3. Why not/Why don't ... ?

如: **Why don't** you try the one near the railway station?

  Why not read it in the library and save the money?

4. should/ shouldn't do ...

如: You **should** try the place where I go.

  You've been working like a horse. You **should** take a vacation.

5. might as well do sth. （最好还是⋯）

如: You **might as well** simply skip the class and apologize to the professor later.

  You **might as well** go to the east wing first to take a look at the Chinese booth.

6. Can't /Don't/ shouldn't/ ... ? （反问句表达建议）

如: **Can't you** drop one course and pick it up next semester?

  Shouldn't we get a telephone installed in the hall?

7. Let's/Let me do ... （祈使句表达建议）

如: **Let me** make some coffee to warm us up.

　　Let's go shopping.

8. maybe …

如: **Maybe** you can try calling them.

　　Maybe instead of studying in your dorm, you'd better go …

9. Can/Will/Could/Would you (please) do … ?

如: **Will you hold** the ladder for me?

　　Could you tell me how to get to the Friendship Hotel?

10. Would you mind doing sth. ?

如: **Would you mind** saving the stamps for me?

　　Would you mind closing the door?

解题技巧

1. 熟悉表达请求或建议的句式。

　　　只有熟练掌握表达请求或建议的常用句式,才能在听音时快速准确的抓住关键信息点。

2. 留意对话中的动词。

　　　这类句式表达的内容一般都是建议或请求某人做某事,因此句式中的动词往往是答案所在或能够揭示出关键的信息。

【例 5】　　　　　　　　　　　　　　　　　　　　　　　　　　(05-1-8)

[A] Ask Joe to apologize to the professor for her. [B] Skip the class to prepare for the exam. [C] Tell the professor she's lost her voice. [D] Attend the lecture with the man.	W: Hi, Joe. I wonder if you could do me a favor and tell the professor I've lost my voice. so I can't attend this morning's class. I need the time to study for tomorrow's exam. M: I don't think it's wise to say so, since you are not going to give the lecture. You might as well simply skip the class and apologize to the professor later. Q: What will the woman probably do?

【解析】男士通过典型的建议句式 you might as well … 建议女士 skip the class (逃课),由此可推知女士接下来很可能会 skip the class to prepare for the exam (逃课准备考试)。

误区警示

1. 注意区分建议与反问句式。

　　　反问句除了表达建议以外,还可以表达很多含义,因此听音时要注意区分。

2. 注意说话人的语气。

　　　有时说话人在提出建议或请求的同时,还会在语气中带有否定、责备等感情色彩,听音时应特别注意。

【例6】 (03-6-6)

[A] Not to subscribe to the journal.	M: Maybe I ought to subscribe to the Engineering Quarterly. It contains a lot of useful information.
[B] To buy the latest issue of the magazine.	
[C] To find a better science journal in the library.	W: Why not read it in the library and save the money?
[D] Not to miss any chance to collect useful information.	Q: What is the woman's advice to the man?

【解析】女士通过典型的建议句式 Why not ...? 建议男士 read it in the library,即暗示男士 not to subscribe to the journal(不要订阅期刊),由此可知答案为[A]。

四、否定句式

六级听力考试中的很多题目都与英语的否定表达有关。说话人的话语中含有明显的否定标志是考生最熟悉的一种否定表达,也比较容易理解,关键是要掌握一些常见的否定词。但有时说话人的话语中没有否定标志,而在含义上却是否定的,即暗示否定。这类句式往往是表达说话人持肯定/否定、赞成/反对意见的重点句式,要求考生对其含义是肯定还是否定给予准确判断。

常见否定表达

1. 含有否定标志的表达

常见否定词或短语有:no,not,none,nobody,never,nothing,neither,nor,hardly,rarely,little,few,without,not ... at all,not ... until,nothing but,no sooner ... than,hardly ... when 等。

2. 不含有否定标志的表达

常见的暗含否定意义的词或短语有:deny,fail,refuse,ignore,dislike,overlook,miss,doubt,lack,against,beyond,unless,instead of,far from,short of,other than(除了),rather than(而不是),too ... to(太…而不能…),anything but(一点也不,根本不),The last thing + 定语从句等。

3. 双重否定

同一个句子里出现两个否定词,即否定之否定,这种结构叫做双重否定结构。

如:**Unless** you have visited that place, you probably **never** known of it.

Without your help, we **couldn't** have succeeded in the experiment.

4. 否定转移

在含有表示"相信"或"臆测"等含义的动词的复合句中,在形式上是否定主句谓语,实则是否定从句谓语。常见的这类动词有: believe, think, imagine, feel, expect, suppose 等。

如: I **don't think** your choice is right.

  They **didn't believe** it was wise for me to give up my present job.

二 解题技巧

1. 听力时留意对话中的否定词。

    注意对话中出现的是一个否定词还是两个否定词(即双重否定表示肯定)、是明示否定词还是暗含否定意义的词,尤其注意与选项中否定词相关的信息。

2. 正确选项一般不是原文的细节再现。

    考查否定句式的试题答案一般都不能够从原文中直撷,而大多是对话内容的同义转述或由对话内容推断出来的。

【例7】   (新 06-12-12)

[A] The man will rent the apartment when it is available.	W: I'm afraid I can't show you the apartment at the moment, because the tenant is still living in it. It's really a lovely place with a big kitchen and a sunny window for only $200 a month.
[B] The man made a bargain with the landlady over the rent.	
[C] The man insists on having a look at the apartment first.	
[D] The man is not fully satisfied with the apartment.	M: Sounds good, but we really can't rent an apartment without seeing it first.
	Q: What do we learn from the conversation?

【解析】男士话中的双重否定结构 but we really can't ... without ... 表明他坚持要先看看公寓再考虑是否要租,由此可知答案为[C]。

三 误区警示

1. 否定对象易出错。

    否定转移中,否定词修饰限制的不是紧随其后的谓语动词,而是后面从句的谓语动词,或是整个句子,听音时一定要特别注意。

2. 切忌听到否定选否定。

    在听力考试中,考完全否定的形式并不多见,也就是说考生在对话中听到了否定句,而答案也为否定句的比率较低。

【例8】   (05-12-1)

[A] The dean should have consulted her on the appointment.	M: The dean just announced that Dr. Holden's going to take over as chairman of the history department.
[B] Dr. Holden should have taken over the position earlier.	
[C] She doesn't think Dr. Holden has made a wise choice.	W: I knew it all along! He's the obvious choice. All the other candidates are no match for him!

[D] Dr. Holden is the best person for the chairmanship.	Q: What does the woman mean?

【解析】女士话中的否定结构 All … no match for him（所有的…都不能与他相比）转换成了选项[D]中的肯定结构 Dr Holden is the best person（他是最好的人选），由此可知答案为[D]。

五、反问句式

反问句式是英语中常见的句式之一,也是六级听力考试中的一个重要考查点。反问句是为了达到某种修饰效果,不需要回答,含义相当于陈述句。一般来说,反问句的肯定结构表示否定意义,否定结构表示肯定意义。一般疑问句及由 what、how 等引导的疑问句均可成为反问句。

一　反问句所表达的含义

反问句常用来表示建议、责怪、批评、惊讶等含义,掌握其常见的含义及表达方式往往是正确理解说话人意图的关键。

1. 表示异议

如: Do you think is it necessary?

　Does it matter?

2. 表示责怪或批评

如: Shouldn't you be studying in the room now?

　How could you keeping going on line so long?

3. 表示拒绝

如: Don't you think it is a little far?

　Do you think I will go to his home again?

4. 表示建议

如: Why not go to the zoo together with us?

　Why don't you choose that green one?

二　解题技巧

1. 听音辨意。

　反问句一般要采取重读、放慢语速、突出语调等措施对反问的部分进行强调,在听觉上极易被考生捕获。

2. 听到的反意即是解。

　反问句直接表达出作者的真实意图,其肯定结构表达否定含义,否定结构表达肯定含义,因此答案往往就是听到内容的反向含义。

【例9】　　　　　　　　　　　　　　　　　　　　　　　　　(03-9-7)

[A] Everyone enjoyed himself at John's parties.	M: Shall we go to John's house-warming party this weekend? Everyone is invited.

[B] The woman didn't enjoy John's parties at all. [C] It will be the first time for the man to attend John's party. [D] The woman is glad to be invited to John's house-warming party.	W: Well, you know what John's parties are like. Do you think I will go again? Q: What can be inferred from the conversation?

【解析】对话中女士用反问句 do you think I will go again? 表示她不会再参加 John 的派对,由此可知答案为[B]。

三 误区警示

1. 莫把反问当疑问。

   反问句多采用一般疑问句的形式,考生不要一听到助动词或系动词开头的句子就以为是一般疑问句而失去"戒心",从而错选答案。

2. 切勿会错意。

   Why not do sth.? 表示提出建议,虽形式上是否定的(带有否定词 not),但其实际意义却是肯定的,是在建议某人做某事;而 Why do sth.? 形式上是肯定的,但实际意义却是否定的,是在希望某人不要做某事。

【例10】   (05-12-4)

[A] They join the physics club. [B] They ask for an extension of the deadline. [C] They work on the assignment together. [D] They choose an easier assignment.	M: The assignment on physics is a real challenge. I don't think I can finish it on time all by myself. W: Why don't we join our efforts together? It may be easier then. Q: What does the woman suggest?

【解析】对话中女士采用反问句 why don't ...? 建议由他们 join ... efforts(共同来完成作业),由此可知答案为[C]。

六、推测句式

情态动词 must,can't 等经常用于表示对过去或现在的肯定或否定推测,这也是听力考试中的重要设题点之一。

一 常见句式

1. 肯定推测

   must do/must have done 意为"一定⋯",前者表示对现在或将来事实的肯定推测,后者表示对过去事实的肯定推测。

2. 否定推测

   can't do/can't have done 意为"不可能⋯",前者表示对现在或将来事实的否定推测,后者表示对过去事实的否定推测。

3. 不确定推测

　　may do/might do 和 may have done/might have done 意为"可能、可以…",前者表示对现在或将来事实的可能性推测,后者表示对过去事实的可能性推测。

二 解题技巧

1. 抓住情态动词。

　　不同的情态动词表达的推测含义不同,听音时应注意抓取关键情态动词。

2. 答案往往是经过推断得出。

　　说话者表达的是对过去或现在事实的一种推测,而问题往往需要考生从说话人的推测中推断出其中隐含的事实细节。

【例11】　　　　　　　　　　　　　　　(98-6-1)

| [A] He thinks that there won't be enough seats for everybody.
[B] He thinks that the speaker won't show up.
[C] He thinks the seminar won't be open to the public.
[D] He thinks that there might not be any more tickets available. | W: Friday's speaker is supposed to be wonderful. Are you going to attend the seminar on that day?
M: Yes. But I haven't been able to get the ticket yet. Since the lecture is open to the public, I imagine that the tickets may have already been sold out.
Q: Why is the man afraid he won't be able to attend the seminar? |

【解析】男士话中的可能性推测 the tickets may have already been sold out 表示他觉得票可能早就卖光了,由此可知答案为 [D]。

三 误区警示

1. 注意区分是单纯表示情态,还是表示推测。

　　要根据情态动词后面动词的形式,以及说话人的语气和所表达的意思,区分情态动词的不同含义。比如 must 作为情态动词可意为"必须",而表示推测时,则意为"一定"。

2. 注意不要与情态动词在虚拟语气中的用法混淆。

　　情态动词 + have done 经常用于表达一种虚拟概念,如 couldn't have done 可表示"本不能做某事实际却做了",要注意将其与情态动词表示对过去事实的推测的用法区分开。

【例12】　　　　　　　　　　　　　　　(04-1-1)

| [A] She knows where Martha has gone.
[B] Martha will go to the concert by herself. | M: Did you see Martha just now? I want to ask her to go with us to the concert tonight. |

[C] It is quite possible for the man to find Martha.	W: She must be around somewhere. You may still be able to catch her.
[D] The man is going to meet Martha at	Q: What does the woman mean?

【解析】由女士话中的推测语气（must be，may）可推出答案为 [C]（quite possible）。must do sth. 表示对现在事实的肯定推测；may do sth. 表示对现在事实的一种可能性推测。

Exercise　专项练习　　🎧 边听边记

1. [A] At home.　　　　　　[B] At the beach.
   [C] In the mountains.　　[D] In a foreign country.
2. [A] She is really an unlucky person.
   [B] She is a good story teller.
   [C] She is an unbelievable person.
   [D] What she said is not always true.
3. [A] The man just makes a joke.
   [B] The man does not like sunbath.
   [C] The woman is going to learn swimming.
   [D] The woman has no idea how to swim.
4. [A] Continue to read.　　　[B] Meet the woman for coffee.
   [C] Make some coffee.　　[D] Go out with some friends.
5. [A] They should take the elderly relative for a drive in the country.
   [B] The elderly relative should stay at home.
   [C] They should take the elderly relative to the downtown.
   [D] They should take the elderly relative for a drive in the town.
6. [A] The shops are not crowded in December.
   [B] Many people go shopping in winter.
   [C] Many people don't like shopping in December.
   [D] People stay at home because of the cold weather.
7. [A] John has been forgetful lately.
   [B] John is a wise leader.
   [C] Running for election has taken too much of John's time.
   [D] John now acts less friendly.
8. [A] He needs help finding a place to live.
   [B] There aren't enough rooms available in the dormitories.

[C] He can't afford to live on campus.

[D] He doesn't want to live in university housing.

9. [A] Put posters up at different schools.

[B] Advertise the concert on the radio.

[C] Make the concert free to the public.

[D] Ask the school radio station to play more music.

10. [A] John refused to offer help to others.

[B] John was in need of help.

[C] John refused Henry's assistance.

[D] John didn't want assistance from others.

边听边记

【答案与解析】

1.

[A] At home.	W: I wonder if we'll ever get the sand off our suitcases.
[B] At the beach.	M: We wouldn't have the sand at all if we hadn't spent our vacation at the beach. Next year, let's go to the mountains or just have a nice and quiet vacation at home.
[C] In the mountains.	
[D] In a foreign country.	
	Q: Where did they spend their vacation?

【解析】男士用虚拟语气 if we hadn't … 说要是他们没有 spent … vacation at the beach（在海边度假），他们的手提箱上就不会弄的都是沙子，由此可知他们去海边度假了。if + 过去完成时表示对过去事实的一种假设。

2.

[A] She is really an unlucky person.	W: Have you known anyone as unlucky as Mary Green? The most terrible things keep happening to her.
[B] She is a good story teller.	
[C] She is an unbelievable person.	M: Yes, if you can trust what she says, but most of her stories are pretty unbelievable in my opinion.
[D] What she said is not always true.	
	Q: What's the man's opinion of Mary Green?

【解析】男士对女士说如果她相信 Mary 的话，她可以那么认为，但是在他看来 most of her stories are pretty unbelievable（大多数话都不可信）。

3.

[A] The man just makes a joke.	M: Aren't you going to swim? We drove
[B] The man does not like sunbath.	fifty miles to come here not just for a

[C] The woman is going to learn swimming.	sunbath.
[D] The woman has no idea how to swim.	W: Are you kidding? Don't you know I can't swim?
	Q: What can we learn from the conversation?

【解析】男士建议女士游泳,女士用反问句 Don't you know I can't swim? 回答男士,言下之意就是她不会游泳。

4.

[A] Continue to read.	W: Hey, Larry. Wanna meet a few of us for coffee in a little while?
[B] Meet the woman for coffee.	M: Hmm. I would if I weren't so far behind in this reading I'm doing for history.
[C] Make some coffee.	
[D] Go out with some friends.	Q: What will the man probably do?

【解析】女士邀请男士一块去喝咖啡,男士用虚拟条件句 I would if I... 表示要是他没有 far behind in this reading 他就会去,由此可推知,男士要继续阅读。

5.

[A] They should take the elderly relative for a drive in the country.	W: It's always a bit difficult with elderly relative. She hates noise, so perhaps we should take her out of town.
[B] The elderly relative should stay at home.	
[C] They should take the elderly relative to the downtown.	M: Why not take her for a drive in the country?
[D] They should take the elderly relative for a drive in the town.	Q: What does the man suggest?

【解析】女士说不知道该带她 elderly relative(年迈的亲戚)去哪玩,男士通过反问句 Why not take ... 建议女士开车带她的亲戚去乡下,由此可知答案为[A]。

6.

[A] The shops are not crowded in December.	M: There are too many people here. Let's go to some other place.
[B] Many people go shopping in winter.	W: All right. But cold weather in December can not keep people away from the busy shops.
[C] Many people don't like shopping in December.	
[D] People stay at home because of the cold weather.	Q: What does the woman mean?

【解析】女士先答应男士的建议,之后用 but 转折句说,12 月的寒冷天气不能 keep people away from the busy shops,也就是说在寒冷的天气仍然有许多人购物。

7.

[A] John has been forgetful lately.	M: Have you noticed how John's changed since he became student government president?
[B] John is a wise leader.	
[C] Running for election has taken too much of John's time.	W: I think the whole thing has gone to his head, and he used to be so sociable and open.
[D] John now acts less friendly.	Q: What does the woman mean?

【解析】女士说 John 曾经是多么的 sociable and open(友善和坦率),言外之意是说他现在 less friendly(不那么友善了)。used to do 表示"过去常常…",常暗含对现在的否定。

8.

[A] He needs help finding a place to live.	W: Will you be living in the dormitory this year?
[B] There aren't enough rooms available in the dormitories.	
[C] He can't afford to live on campus.	M: Yes, if I can't help it. I've been thinking of renting an apartment off campus with some friends of mine.
[D] He doesn't want to live in university housing.	Q: What does the man imply?

【解析】女士问男士今年是否还住在宿舍里,男士回答说 if I can't help it(如果没有办法了)还是会住的,并且还考虑要租房,由此推断他不想住在学校宿舍里。

9.

[A] Put posters up at different schools.	W: We need to let everyone know about the benefit concert, but we don't have much money for advertising.
[B] Advertise the concert on the radio.	
[C] Make the concert free to the public.	M: How about using the school radio station? They broadcast three public service announcements.
[D] Ask the school radio station to play more music.	Q: What does the man suggest that they do?

【解析】女士想为音乐会做广告,男士则建议她利用 school radio station(学校的广播站),由此可知答案为[B]。How about … 是常用来表达建议的句型。

10.

| [A] John refused to offer help to others. | W: Hello, Henry, I'm surprised to see you here, so you haven't gone to help John. |
| [B] John was in need of help. | |

[C] John refused Henry's assistance.

[D] John didn't want assistance from others.

M: I'd like to, but he turned down all offers of assistance.

Q: What does Henry mean?

【解析】女士对男士（Henry）没有去帮助 John 感到很吃惊，男士说他本来想去的，但是 John turned down all offers of assistance（拒绝让所有人帮忙）。

解 题 攻 略

　　根据选项的内容,六级听力短对话可分为事实状况题、行为活动题、观点态度题、地点场景题、谈论话题题、身份关系题和数字信息题七大类。

一、事实状况题

一　背景知识

　　问题是关于陈述谈话的一方或双方说了什么,所处状态,做某事的原因何在,结果如何。

　　提问方式通常为:

　　What do we learn from this conversation?

　　What does the man mean?

　　What can be inferred from the conversation?

　　这类试题要求考生在听懂对话内容的基础上,捕捉到或推断出谈话一方或双方所陈述的事实,如发生了什么事,某事的原因何在或结果如何等。在对话中说话人可能不直接表达出事实,而是采用一种间接的方式,如采用虚拟、反问等特殊表达,考生要进行综合判断。

　　考生在复习时应注意积累与这些场景相关的词汇和其他背景知识,可参照第一篇第二章中的分主题词汇和本篇第一章中的场景规律介绍。

二　解题技巧

1. 捕捉关键词。

　　要注意抓取事情的原因、结果等细节信息。

2. 理解同义转述。

　　正确选项一般是对话内容中关键词的同义转述,因此要注意同义词语的替换或句式上的变换。

3. 抓住选项关键点。

　　要对各选项涉及的关键信息进行标记,根据问题对号入座。

【例1】　　　　　　　　　　　　　　　　　　　　　　　　　　(新06-12-17)

[A] They can't fit into the machine.	M: Have the parts we need for the photo copying machine arrived yet?
[B] They have not been delivered yet.	
[C] They were sent to the wrong address.	W: I ordered them last week, but something is holding them up.

| [D] They were found to be of the wrong type. | Q: What does the woman say about the parts needed for the photo copying machine? |

【解析】事实状况题。女士话中的 something is holding them up 表明她订购的影印机部件还没有寄到，由此可知答案为[B]。hold sth. up 意为"耽误,使不能进行"。

三 误区警示

1. 注意多义词。

在不同的语境中,同一个词的含义会发生变化,不懂得应变就会误听。如"ticket"既有"票"的意思,又有"罚单"的意思,如果只知其一,就有可能选错答案。

2. 切忌违背常理。

这类题型多与日常生活联系紧密,听到线索词语时要大胆按照常理或者常识去判断,而不要过多设想一些有违常理的情况。

【例2】　　　　　　　　　　　　　　　　　　　　　　　　(06-6-6)

| [A] He was fined for running a red light.
[B] He was caught speeding on a fast lane.
[C] He had to run quickly to get the ticket.
[D] He made a wrong turn at the intersection. | W: Oh! Boy! I don't understand how you got a ticket today. I always thought you were slow even driving on the less crowded fast lane.
M: I'm usually careful. But this time I thought I could get through the intersection before the light turned.
Q: What do we learn about the man? |

【解析】事实状况题。由女士话中的 got a ticket(被开罚单)和男士话中的虚拟语气 I thought I could … before the light turned(我以为我能在红灯前过去的)可推知,男士因为闯红灯而被 fined(罚款),答案为[A]。注意 ticket 在此处不是表示"票",而是表示"罚单"。fast lane 意为"快行车道"。

二、行为活动题

一 背景知识

问题是关于谈话的一方或双方做过、正在做、准备去做什么或一方建议另一方去做什么。

提问方式通常为:

What will the man/woman most probably do?

What are the speakers probably going/trying to do?

What does the woman suggest doing?

这类试题的情景往往是谈话的一方向另一方提出请求或者建议其做某事,因此掌握一些表达请求或建议的常用句式,将对这类题目的解答有很大帮助。本篇第二章中已经对常见的请求或建议句式有过比较详尽的介绍,复习时可参照。

这类试题答案的摄取可能是直接引用原文,或是原文的同义转述,或者需要经过推理分析,前两种情况居多。

二 解题技巧

1. 根据选项特点判断题型。

   一般来说这类试题的选项都是动词短语形式,且动词一般为动词原形或动词的现在分词形式。

2. 听音时留意对话中的动词,尤其注意与选项中动词相关的信息。

   在留意动词的同时,要记录一些与该动词相关的重要信息,尤其是不单是一个选项中的动词在对话中出现的时候,只有留意与动词相关的信息,才能根据问题对号入座。

3. 注意表示请求、建议或提议的短语或句式。

   行为活动类试题的对话中经常会包含提出请求或建议的句式或短语,这些句式后面的内容有可能就是建议去做或准备去做的行为活动,很可能与答案直接相关,因此听音时需重点留意。

【例3】   (07-6-11)

[A] Surfing the net. [B] Watching a talk show. [C] Packing a birthday gift. [D] Shopping at a jewelry store.	W: Jim, you are on the net again? When are you going to get off? It's the time for the talk show. M: Just a minute, dear. I'm looking at a new jewelry site. I want to make sure I get the right gift for Mum's birthday. Q: What is the man doing right now?

【解析】行为活动题。根据女士话中的 are you on the net again? When are you going to get off?(你又在上网吗?你什么时候出发?)可知,男士正 on the net(在上网);而男士话中的 I'm looking at a new jewelry site(我正在看一个新的珠宝网站)也说明男士正在上网。surf the net ≈ on the net,由此可知答案为[A]。

三 误区警示

1. 注意区分建议与实际发生的动作。

   有些建议是在事情发生后才提出的,实际上动作并没有进行。

2. 不要听到什么选什么。

   有时对话中会出现多个动词,选项中经常会有据此而设的干扰项,因此切忌捕捉到一个信息就妄下推断。

【例4】 (07-6-14)

[A] Study for some profession. [B] Attend a medical school. [C] Stay in business. [D] Sell his shop.	M: Tom must be joking when he said he plans to sell his shop and go to medical school. W: You are quite right. He is just kidding. He's also told me time and time again he wished he'd studied for some profession instead of going into business. Q: What will Tom probably do according to the conversation?

【解析】行为活动题。男士说 Tom 打算 sell his shop(卖掉店铺)去医学院一定是 joking,女士表示赞同,由此可知 Tom 实际上并没打算 sell his shop,即他会 stay in business(继续经营他的店铺),故答案为[C]。注意不要抓住对话中的某个动词短语(sell his shop,go to medical school 或 studied for some profession 等)就妄下结论。

三、观点态度题

一 相关背景

问题是关于谈话一方对另一方或第三方的行为、品德、观点等的态度或评价。提问方式通常为:

What does the woman feel about?

What does the woman/man mean /imply?

How does the woman /man feel about … ?

What does the woman/man think of … ?

这类试题主要考察考生对谈话者所表达的态度或感觉的理解。这类试题有的能直接听到答案,但更多的需要一定的分析与思考。

六级听力短对话中,说话人的观点态度,往往可以通过对话中某个(些)带有感情色彩的词语或表达方式判断出来,这就需要我们熟悉并掌握这类词语或表达方式的含义及用法。

表示观点态度的常见词语有:

赞成	approve;agree;share;prefer;wise;reasonable;favorable
反对	disapprove;disagree;unwise;ridiculous;foolish;childish
赞赏	admire;appreciate;think much of;be proud of
批评	critical;criticize;ironic;find fault with
喜欢	love;enjoy;favorite;favor;wonderful;fascinating;funny

怨恨或生气	boring/bored；a shame；hate；hatred；regret；angry；anger；irritated
自信或自负	confident；arrogant；proud
积极或消极	active；positive；negative
失望或灰心	disappointed；discouraged
乐观或悲观	optimistic；pessimistic
自私或无私	selfish；unselfish
漠然或热情	indifferent；careless；enthusiastic

表达观点态度的常用短语与句式有：

| 短语 | as for somebody；in one's opinion；according to me；as for me |
| 句式 | I think/believe/find/guess/imagine/consider that …；as far as I know；as far as something is concerned |

解题技巧

1. 根据选项特点判断问题类型。

　　观点态度类试题的选项中一般都含有一些引出观点态度的动词或短语,常见的有：think, believe, find, guess, imagine, consider, as far as I know 等。根据这类线索词判断出试题类型以后,可以更有针对性地去留意对话中说话人对自己观点态度的陈述,尤其注意带有褒贬色彩的词语。

2. 抓住对话中的一些标识性词语。

　　听音时应注意抓住一些表明上下文间的因果、转折、比较与对照或举例等逻辑关系的标识性词语(如：but, instead 表转折；if, as long as 表条件；because, due to 表原因；there fore,consequently 表结果),尤其是转折后的内容,往往表达作者的真实观点或态度,常为考查重点。

3. 听话听音。

　　在口语中,重读是用来表达说话人的情感、态度的最有效手段之一,因此,考生要留意重读语气的形容词、副词和动词,善于以此来推断讲话者的真正意思。

【例5】 (00-1-9)

[A] The man should stick to what he's doing.	M: I think I'm going to give up playing tennis. I lost again today.
[B] The man should take up a new hobby.	
[C] The man should stop playing tennis.	W: Just because you lost? Is that a reason to quit?
[D] The man should find the cause for his failure.	Q: What does the woman imply?

【解析】观点态度题。由女士话中的反问语气可知,她不赞成男士 quit(放弃),即她认为男士应该 stick to what he's doing(坚持下去),由此可知答案为[A]。如果没有体会到这里的反问语气,则很容易误选[C]。

三　误区警示

1. 注意区分人物之间不同的观点。

　　对话中两人的观点和态度有可能不同,因此分清问题所指非常重要。

2. 通常对话中不会直接出现答案。

　　说话人的观点态度往往需要通过说话人的语气或根据其说话内容进行推断才能得出,因此对话中一般不会直接出现答案。

【例6】　　　　　　　　　　　　　　　　　　　　　(07-6-13)

[A] The man is generous with his good comments on people.	W: Just look at this newspaper, nothing but murder, death and war! Do you still believe people are basically good?
[B] The woman is unsure if there will be peace in the world.	M: Of course I do. But newspapers hardly ever report stories about peace and generosity. They are not news.
[C] The woman is doubtful about newspaper stories.	Q: What do we learn from the conversation?
[D] The man is quite optimistic about human nature.	

【解析】观点态度题。女士问男士是否还相信 people are basically good(人是善良的),男士给予了肯定回答(Of course I do),由此可推知男士对人的善良天性持 optimistic(乐观的)态度,由此可知答案为[D]。对话中并没有直接表明男士的态度,需要通过双方的对话内容进行推测。

四、地点场景题

一　背景知识

问题是关于对话发生的场合、地点或者涉及到的人或事物所处的位置。

提问方式通常为:

Where is the conversation most probably taking place?

Where are the two people?

这类试题要求考生根据对话所提供的环境或情节来判断事件发生的地点、准备去的地点或谈话发生的地点等。主要分为两种:

一是对话中含有多个地点场所,问题要求从中辨别出符合要求的地点。

二是对话中并未提到具体地点,问题要求根据对话内容推断出该地点场所。

此类题目相对简单,只要掌握考试中常见的场景和一定的相关词汇,即可根据对话中出现的关键词语判断出对话涉及的地点场景。

常见的地点场景包括:

诊所或医院(clinic or hospital)	餐馆(restaurant)
学校或校园(school or campus)	书店(bookstore)
火车站(railway station)	机场(airport)
邮局(post office)	图书馆(library)
银行(bank)	旅馆(hotel)

各场景相关词汇在第一篇第二章中已有介绍,可参照记忆。

二 解题技巧

1. 多个地点:依赖笔记,把握提问中的关键词。

   对话中提到几个地点,就其中某一个进行提问,解题关键在于区分细节,并注意抓住提问中的关键词。

2. 单个地点:抓住与特定地点相关的常用词或短语。

   对话中并未提到具体场所,问题要求根据对话内容推测出谈话场所或某人的去向。该类题要求考生能抓住标志信息,即与特定地点相关的最常用词或短语。

【例7】   (06-6-8)

[A] At a bookstore.	M: I am afraid there won't be time to do another tooth tod-ay. Make sure you don't eat anything like steaks for the next few hours, and we'll fill the other cavity tomorro-w.
[B] At the dentist's.	
[C] In a restaurant.	
[D] In the library.	W: All right. Actually, I must hurry to the library to return some books.
	Q: Where does the conversation most probably take place?

【解析】地点场景题。只要抓住对话中"tooth"和"cavity"这两个线索词就可以推出两人的谈话发生在"牙科诊所"。

三 误区警示

1. 切忌听到什么选什么。

   对话中如果出现明确的地点,往往会不止一个,考生需记录与所听到地点相关的细节信息,然后根据问题确定答案。切不可听到某个地点就匆匆作答。

2. 切忌违背常规逻辑。

   听到线索词语时要大胆按照常规逻辑去判断,而不要设想一些特例。

【例8】   (04-6-7)

[A] At a shopping cent-er.	M: Er… Hi, could you tell me where electronic products are displayed? I want to see some TVs, digital video

| [B] At an electronics company.
[C] At an international trade fair.
[D] At a DVD counter in a music store. | cameras, DVD players, that sort of thing.
W: Well. Several countries are displaying electronic products. China's selection is very large this year. You might as well go to the east wing first to take a look at the Chinese booth.
Q: Where is the conversation most probably taking place? |

【解析】地点场景题。由对话中的 displayed(展示),several countries 和 Chinese booth(中国展区)等关键信息词可推断,对话最有可能发生在一次 international trade fair(国际展览会)上。注意不要抓住 electronic(电子的)一词而误选[B]。

五、谈论话题题

一 背景知识

问题是关于对话中所谈论的话题或对象。

提问方式通常为:

What are they talking about?

What are the speakers talking about?

这类试题往往需要考生根据一些关键信息推断出对话所谈论的主题。

考生在平时训练中,应留意与某类场景相关的话题和词语,并加以记忆。在第一篇第二章中已经对常考场景相关的词语进行了归纳和总结,以供大家巩固记忆。

二 解题技巧

1. 根据选项特点判断问题类型。

一般来说,谈论话题题的选项概括性都较强,且常为短语;另外,各选项所陈述的内容往往差别较大。

2. 捕捉与话题相关的关键词。

一般来说,该类题型比较简单,只要能捕捉到对话中与该话题相关的关键词,即可判断出对话谈论的内容。

【例9】 (02-6-1)

| [A] Registering for courses.
[B] Getting directions.
[C] Buying a new computer.
[D] Studying sociology. | W: The deadline for the sociology and computer courses is the day after tomorrow.
M: But I haven't decided which courses to take yet?
Q: What are the man and woman talking about? |

【解析】谈论话题题。选项均为动词-ing 短语,且内容差别较大,故本题很可能属于考查"谈论话题"类型。由女士话中的关键词 sociology and computer courses 和

男士话中的关键词 courses 和 take 可推知对话谈论的主题是 registering for courses(选修课程)。动词 take 可以表示"选(课)"。

三 误区警示

1. 集中抓"面",而不是"点"。

　　只要能够通过某些属于某一话题的关键词语判断出对话所谈论的主题内容即可,而不需要将对话中的具体词语或内容都搞清楚。

2. 不要只从对话一方的话语中寻找答案。

　　由于是考查谈话主题,因此双方的话语都应含有与主题相关的线索词。

【例10】　　　　　　　　　　　　　　　　　　　　　　　　　（99-6-5）

[A] How to use a camera.	W: Can you show me how to use this, John?
[B] How to use a washer.	M: It is fully automatic. All you have to do is
[C] How to use a keyboard.	focus on the scene and press the button here.
[D] How to use a tape recorder.	Q: What are they talking about?

【解析】谈论话题题。由对话中 how to use this、focus on the scene(将镜头对准要拍摄的画面)、press the button(按钮)等关键词语可推知对话双方正在谈论如何使用照相机。

六、身份关系题

一 背景知识

　　问题是关于对话双方的关系或对话中某个人物的身份职业等。

　　提问方式通常为:

What is the probable relationship between the (two) speakers?

What is the most probable relationship between Jim and Bob?

What's the woman's job?

What most probably is Mary?

　　这类试题的对话中,一般不会直接交代出说话人的身份或说话人之间的关系,需要考生根据对话中的关键词语以及说话人的语气来进行推断。

　　这类试题相对比较简单,考生只要抓住那些体现人物身份或关系的关键词即可。如果考生熟悉六级听力短对话中常涉及到的人物身份或人物关系,将更加有能够在考试时有的放矢。

　　常考人物关系或职业身份:

人物关系主要包括:	服务人员与顾客（waiter/waitress—customer）
夫妻（husband—wife）	主人与客人（host/hostess—guest）
父子（father—son）	警察与司机（policeman—driver）
母子（mother—son）	图书管理员与借阅者（librarian—reader）
师生（teacher—student）	

同学 (schoolmates)	医生 (doctor)
同事 (colleagues)	秘书 (secretary)
雇主与雇员 (boss—secretary/employee)	老板 (boss)
医生与病人 (doctor—patient)	服务员 (waiter/waitress)
房东与租房者 (landlord/landlady—tenant)	家庭角色 (husband，wife，son，daughter，girlfriend…)
职业身份主要包括：	修理工 (repairman，electrician，plumber，technician)
教授 (professor)	

二 解题技巧　　　　　　　　　　　　　　　　　　　　　　　　⌄⌄

1. 注意称呼语。

    对话中的称呼语往往会直接暴露出说话人的身份或说话双方的关系,比如 Mr. 一词就表明对方很可能是自己的上级或老师,因此在听音时要注意捕捉这类词语。

2. 注意人物语气。

    由于说话人的身份、说话人之间的关系不同,说话的语气和态度也有所区别,师生之间、夫妻之间、家长与孩子之间以及老板与员工之间的说话方式和语气均有自己的特点,这是听音时要抓住的关键点之一。

3. 捕捉关键词语。

    解答这类试题,要熟悉体现某种人物关系或某种职业的相关词汇,捕捉有关信息,然后判断、推测人物之间的关系或人物身份。

【例11】　　　　　　　　　　　　　　　　　　　　　　　　　　　（01-1-7）

[A] An auto mechanic.	W: This is Mrs. Starched. My heater is not getting any power and the weatherman says the temperature is to fall below zero tonight. Could you get someone to come over and fix it?
[B] An electrician.	
[C] A carpenter.	
[D] A telephone repairman.	M: This is the busiest time of the year, but I'll speak to one of our men about going over some time today.
	Q: Who did Mrs. Starched want to come over?

【解析】身份关系题。通过关键词 heater（加热器）,getting power（通电）,以及 fix it 可推知 Mrs. Starched 想要请的人应该是一名 electrician（电工）。

三 误区警示　　　　　　　　　　　　　　　　　　　　　　　　⌄⌄

i. 不要只在一方的谈话中寻找关键词。

    对人物关系或人物身份的判断往往不是只根据一方话中的关键词,而要结合对话双方的说话语气及关键词才能作出准确判断,因此要注意不能只关注一方的话语。

2. 不要听到什么选什么。

对话中明确出现的人名或某个人物身份往往作为干扰项在选项中出现,其为答案的可能性较小,在选择时要慎重。

【例12】 (06-6-5)

[A] Tony's secretary. [B] Paul's girlfriend. [C] Paul's colleague. [D] Tony's wife.	M: Hello, Mary. This is paul at the bank. Is Tony home? W: Not yet. Paul. I don't think you can reach him at the office now, either. He phoned me five minutes ago to say he was stopping for a hair-cut on his way home. Q: Who do you think the woman probably is?

【解析】身份关系题。选项表明本题为考查"身份角色"类型,根据选项中 girlfriend, wife 可知,本题应该是问对话中女士的身份。男士询问女士 Tony 是否在家,由此可初步确定答案为[D],即女士最可能是 Tony's wife,再根据女士所说的 He phoned me…on his way home 即可进一步确定答案为[D]。听音时一定要注意辨别选项中出现的人名,搞清人物关系。

七、数字信息题

背景知识

问题涉及到时间、年龄、数量、速度、价格等信息。

提问方式通常为:

What time did Suzy leave home?

How much does one ticket cost?

When is the train leaving?

这类试题对话中一般不会只出现一个数字,答案往往需要进行简单的运算才能得出。

解题技巧

1. 速记信息。

这类对话题中一般都不会只出现一个数字,因此一定要速记对话中出现的数字及相关要点信息。

2. 听清问题。

注意做这类题目时,必须清楚地抓住问题是针对什么提问,然后才能根据记录的信息将答案对号入座。

【例13】　　　　　　　　　　　　　　　　　　　　　　　(97-6-1)

[A] On Thursday night. [B] On Monday night. [C] On Friday morning. [D] At Thursday morning.	M: Good morning. I'm here to see Mr. Adison. W: Mr. Adison went to Washington last Monday for a conference and he will be back on Thursday night. If you like, you may come again on Friday morning. Q: When will Mr. Adison return?

【解析】数字信息题。对话中一共出现了三个时间:Last Monday, Thursday night, Friday morning,听音时要注意记录三个时间分别对应的事件: Adison went to Washington, Adison back, may come again,然后根据问题对号入座。

三　误区警示 ≫

1. 不要直摄答案。

如果是纯粹的数字题的话,答案往往不是原文中数字信息的再现,一般都需要经过简单的运算。

2. 切忌只抓数字。

这类对话题中一般不会只出现一个数字,而且往往需要结合与数字相关的信息才能得出答案,因此听音时在抓住数字的同时,一定要注意记录与其相对应的关键信息。

【例14】　　　　　　　　　　　　　　　　　　　　　　(04-6-3)

[A] At 10:30. [B] At 10:25. [C] At 10:40. [D] At 10:45.	M: So when are the other guys going to get here? The train is leaving in 10 minutes. We can't wait here forever. W: It's 10:30 already. They're supposed to be here by now. I told everybody to meet here by 10:15. Q: When is the train leaving?

【解析】数字信息题。男士说火车将在 10 minutes 后发车,女士说现在已经 10:30 了,经过简单的运算即可知火车发车的时间应该是 10:40。

Exercise 专项练习 　　　🎧 边听边记

1. [A] Getting another ticket at the door.
   [B] Canceling the concert.
   [C] Exchanging the ticket for a better one.
   [D] Trying to sell the ticket.

2. [A] He'll probably quit school to play tennis.
   [B] He's teaching a tennis class now.
   [C] He's trying to relax this semester.

[D] He's busy with sports and schoolwork.

3. [A] Doctor and patient.　　　[B] Passenger and conductor.

　　[C] Daughter and father.　　[D] Customer and salesman.

4. [A] It is difficult for the old people to learn mathematics well.

　　[B] The old people find mathematics easier than they thought.

　　[C] The old people take longer to learn mathematics as well as the young people.

　　[D] The old people haven't spent much time in studying mathematics.

5. [A] Get some coins at the cafe.

　　[B] Buy her a cup of coffee at the cafe.

　　[C] Get some coffee from the machine.

　　[D] Try to fix the machine.

6. [A] At the library.　　　　[B] In the classroom.

　　[C] In the office.　　　　[D] At the bookstore.

7. [A] The cause of the flood.

　　[B] The effects of the flood.

　　[C] The heroic fight against a flood.

　　[D] Floods of the past twenty years.

8. [A] Uncle and niece.　　　[B] Father and daughter.

　　[C] Aunt and nephew.　　[D] Mother and son.

9. [A] $6.25.　　　　　[B] $13.5.

　　[C] $6.75.　　　　　[D] $27.

10. [A] He'll see if they have the best quality paper.

　　[B] The best quality paper she wants is out of stock.

　　[C] She's bound to find the best quality paper somewhere else.

　　[D] He can't find the best quality paper for her.

【答案与解析】

1.

[A] Getting another ticket at the door.	M: I have an extra ticket to the concert tonight. Would you like to come along?
[B] Canceling the concert.	W: Thanks, but I already have my own ticket. Perhaps you can sell the other one at the door.
[C] Exchanging the ticket for a better one.	
[D] Trying to sell the ticket.	Q: What does the woman suggest?

【解析】行为活动题。男士说他有 an extra ticket to the concert（一张多余的音乐会门票），希望女士能和他一起去，女士说她已经有票了，并建议男士 sell the other one（卖掉那张多余的票）。

2.

[A] He'll probably quit school to play tennis. [B] He's teaching a tennis class now. [C] He's trying to relax this semester. [D] He's busy with sports and school work.	M: Have you seen Tom at all this semester? I used to see him everywhere! ... But now, he's never around. W: Well, he's got a really heavy course load and he is on the tennis team now! Q: What does the woman say about Tom?

【解析】事实状况题。女士说 Tom 有很重的 course load（课业负担），并且他现在 on the tennis team（在网球队），由此可知，Tom 现在忙于 sports and schoolwork。

3.

[A] Doctor and patient. [B] Passenger and conductor. [C] Daughter and father. [D] Customer and salesman.	W: Excuse me. Could you tell me at which stop I should get off for the city council? And how much is the fare? M: Of course. You can get off at Linden Street. I'll let you know when we get there. The fare is fifty cents. Q: What is the probably relationship between the two speakers?

【解析】身份关系题。由对话中的关键词 stop, get off, the fare（费用）可以判断出，对话最有可能发生在乘客与售票员之间。

4.

[A] It is difficult for the old people to learn mathematics well. [B] The old people find mathematics easier than they thought. [C] The old people take longer to learn mathematics as well as the young people. [D] The old people haven't spent	W: What about the group who studies mathematics? M: We have carried out some very interesting experiments. Although the old people take longer to learn, eventually they perform as well as the young people. But as to mathematics, that's a different story.

| much time in studying mathematics. | Q: As to mathematics, what does the man mean? |

【解析】观点态度题。男士说老人学习某种事物时，虽然花的时间比较长，但最终的学习效果跟年轻人的一样好，but 之后又说，至于学习数学，that's a different story（那是另一回事），言外之意是说学习数学对于老人有点困难。

5.

[A] Get some coins at the cafe.	W: I'm out of coins for the slot machine. Do you have any?
[B] Buy her a cup of coffee at the cafe.	
[C] Get some coffee from the machine.	M: I don't have any either. But I'll get some from the cafe.
[D] Try to fix the machine.	Q: What does the man offer to do?

【解析】行为活动题。女士问男士有没有硬币，男士回答说他也没有，但他会 get some from the café（去咖啡馆换一些）。slot machine 意为"自动售货机"。

6.

[A] At the library.	W: Can I help you?
[B] In the classroom.	M: Yes. I am a bit confused. My sociology class is supposed to read a chapter in a book called *Sociology and the Modern Age*. According to the syllabus, the book is in the library, but I haven't been able to find it.
[C] In the office.	
[D] At the bookstore.	Q: Where does the conversation most probably take place?

【解析】地点场景题。男士说他修的社会学课程要求他读一本书，Syllabus（教学大纲）上说这本书 in the library，但是他 haven't been able to find it，说明对话发生在图书馆里。

7.

[A] The cause of the flood.	M: This is the worst flood for the past twenty years. It has caused much damage and destruction.
[B] The effects of the flood.	
[C] The heroic fight against a flood.	W: Look at the prices of fruits and vegetables. No wonder they are so expensive.
[D] Floods of the past twenty years.	Q: What are they talking about?

【解析】谈论话题题。男士说这是二十年来 the worst flood（最严重的一次洪灾），导致了 much damage and destruction（很大的损失）；女士补充说现在水果与蔬菜价格也因此被抬得很高，可见两人讨论的是洪灾的带来的影响。

8.

[A] Uncle and niece.	M: Yes, Mary, how are you? Is there anything wrong?
[B] Father and daughter.	W: Oh, no, no. I'm just calling to see if everything is O-K with you and Mom. It's been quite a while since I saw you last time.
[C] Aunt and nephew.	
[D] Mother and son.	Q: What might be the relationship of the speakers?

【解析】身份关系题。由女士话中的 you and Mom 以及对话双方说话的语气可推知,这可能是父女间的谈话。

9.

[A] $6.25.	W: This morning we went to that new shoe store and bought t-wo pairs of leather shoes for the price of one.
[B] $13.5.	
[C] $6.75.	M: Mary told me that you each got a nice pair for $13.5.
[D] $27.	Q: What's the regular price for one pair of leather shoes?

【解析】数字信息题。女士说她用买一双皮鞋的钱买了两双,而每双皮鞋只用了13.5 美元,由此可知,按照正常的价格,一双鞋应该是 27 美元。

10.

[A] He'll see if they have the best quality paper.	W: I'm looking for the best quality paper to have my thesis typed on. I don't see any on the shelf.
[B] The best quality paper she wants is out of stock.	
[C] She's bound to find the best quality paper somewhere else.	M: I think I saw some in the stockroom this morning. I'll check.
[D] He can't find the best quality paper for her.	Q: What did the man tell the woman?

【解析】事实状况题。女士想找一些质量好的纸打印论文,男士说他早上在stockroom(储藏室)看到一些,并且说他会去 check(查看一下),由此可知答案为[A]。

综合训练

Exercise 1

🎧 边听边记

11. [A] The woman doesn't want to go to any more barbecues.
    [B] The guests are late because of the weather.
    [C] Everybody should help with the cooking.
    [D] The weather wasn't good at the last barbecue.

12. [A] By enjoying themselves.
    [B] By doing a kind of important work.
    [C] By enough leisure activities.
    [D] By doing some form of work positively.

13. [A] Doctor.   [B] Clerk.   [C] Professor.   [D] Waitress.

14. [A] It's new.   [B] It's dull.
    [C] It's not clean.   [D] It has a broken handle.

15. [A] The man must be a very slow driver.
    [B] She did a lot of walking in Florida.
    [C] Most people make the trip in about a week.
    [D] She got to Florida long before the man did.

16. [A] Answer only the difficult questions.
    [B] Answer as many questions as he finds helpful.
    [C] Answer the questions that aren't in the textbook.
    [D] Get help with his homework.

17. [A] Women have got as much freedom as they could want.
    [B] Women are struggling for their rights.
    [C] The man understands what this Women's Lib business is all about.
    [D] She doesn't think that British women have got as much freedom as wanted.

18. [A] She forgot to write down the message.
    [B] She had to try several times to get her call through.
    [C] She didn't understand the caller's message.
    [D] She didn't get to the phone on time.

Exercise 2

♫ 边听边记

11. [A] She wants to work again tomorrow.

[B] She's willing to stop working.

[C] She wants to consider half a day's work as a full day.

[D] She's unhappy to work so long without pay.

12. [A] He puts the information on top of his desk.

[B] The top of his head hurts.

[C] He doesn't know the answer right now.

[D] He's afraid that very few people are registered.

13. [A] She doesn't want to ask Mr. Jones herself.

[B] She doesn't want to work for Mr. Jones.

[C] Mr. Jones may have broken the radio.

[D] Mr. Jones might fix the radio.

14. [A] They don't have to go to the concert.

[B] His brother should let them use the car.

[C] The subway was fine with her.

[D] A car wouldn't be any faster.

15. [A] Peter is visiting his mother.

[B] Peter will be unable to come.

[C] Peter's mother is coming for dinner.

[D] Peter can't hear them.

16. [A] A carpenter built it for students.

[B] The drama students designed and made it.

[C] The drama students built most of it.

[D] A special designer made it.

17. [A] He began working on his degree more than five years ago.

[B] He finished his degree a long time ago.

[C] It took him the least time of anyone to finish his degree.

[D] He will be working on his degree for at least five more years.

18. [A] In a department store.　　　[B] In a bank.

[C] At a tourist bureau.　　　[D] At a hotel.

Exercise 3

11. [A] Traveling a lot.　　　[B] Getting a lot of exercise.

[C] Working hard.　　　[D] Waiting for the train.

12. [A] They will find the trouble.

   [B] They should carry the parts outside.

   [C] They should practice working together.

   [D] They should follow the directions.

13. [A] He fixes the bicycles.　[B] He raises sheep.

   [C] He sells chairs.　　　[D] He's a gardener.

14. [A] The woman doesn't like orange juice.

   [B] The woman is as clumsy as ever.

   [C] The man was in a car crash this morning.

   [D] The man broke the container of juice.

15. [A] Steve looks good in anything.

   [B] He knew someone who looked like Steve.

   [C] He wishes he had a jacket like Steve's.

   [D] Steve should get a new jacket.

16. [A] At the information desk.[B] On the platform.

   [C] On the train.　　　　[D] Near the stairs.

17. [A] In a school.　　　[B] At the post office.

   [C] In a courtroom.　　[D] In a packing plant.

18. [A] She hasn't gone camping for several weeks.

   [B] She likes to take long camping.

   [C] She prefers not to go camping on weekends.

   [D] She takes a long time to plan her trips.

🎧 边听边记

答案与解析

Exericise 1

11.

[A] The woman doesn't want to go to any more barbecues.	W: This barbecue sure beats the last one we went to, huh?
[B] The guests are late because of the weather.	M: That's right. Everyone had to spend the whole time inside. Good thing the weather decided to cooperate this time around.
[C] Everybody should help with the cooking.	
[D] The weather wasn't good at the last barbecue.	Q: What can be inferred from this conversation?

【解析】事实状况题。女士说这次的烧烤一定会胜过上一次，男士表示赞同，并且说 good thing the weather decided to cooperate this time around（这次如果天气愿意合作就好了），言外之意是说上次天气不好，由此可知答案为 [D]。

12.

[A] By enjoying themselves. [B] By doing a kind of impo- rtant work. [C] By enough leisure activit- ies. [D] By doing some form of w- ork positively.	M: Kathy, do you think that in order to lead a ba- lanced life, people need some form of work? W: Yes, I do. But I think it's equally important th- at their attitude to work should be positive. If one is going to look on work as slavery, something that one does, so that one will enjoy one's leisure or whatever after it, then I don't think there can be very much satisfaction in it. Q: According to the woman, how can people lead a balanced life?

【解析】观点态度题。男士问为了平衡的生活,人是否需要工作,女士给予肯定回答,紧接着说她认为 attitude to work should be positive(对工作持积极的态度)同样很重要,由此可知答案为[D]。

13.

[A] Doctor. [B] Clerk. [C] Professor. [D] Waitress.	W: Now, would you please fill out these customs forms for each package? Please state clearly the contents a- nd value of each, and the name and address of the returnee. Better in block letters. M: There, I think I've filled out everything correctly. Q: What is the woman's occupation?

【解析】身份关系题。女士话中的 fill out...forms for... package(填写包裹单子),contents and value(内容及价值),the name and address of the returnee 等都为填表时邮局工作人员的常用语,由此可知女士为邮局职员。

14.

[A] It's new. [B] It's dull. [C] It's not clean. [D] It has a broken handle.	W: I'm having trouble in slicing the bread with this knife. M: Oh. Sorry about that. I haven't gotten round to sharpening it yet. Q: What can be inferred about the knife?

【解析】事实状况题。女士说这把刀切不开面包,男士表示抱歉,并说他还没腾出时间 sharpen(磨快)它,可见这把刀比较 dull(钝)。get round to do...意为"腾出时间来做…"。

15.

[A] The man must be a very slow driver.	M: It took me five days to drive down to Florida,
[B] She did a lot of walking in Florida.	
[C] Most people make the trip in about a week.	W: Five days? I could have walked there in less time.
[D] She got to Florida long before the man did.	
	Q: What does the woman mean?

【解析】观点态度题。男士说他开车去 Florida 花了 five days,女士表示惊讶,说她走路去都花不了那么多时间,言外之意就是说男士开车太慢。

16.

[A] Answer only the difficult questions.	M: Do we have to do all the practice questions in the back of the textbook? Couldn't we just do a few?
[B] Answer as many questions as he finds helpful.	
[C] Answer the questions that aren't in the textbook.	W: Well, it's entirely for our own benefit. No one ever said we had to do any.
[D] Get help with his homework.	Q: What does the woman imply the man should do?

【解析】行为活动题。男士问是不是非要做书后的 all the practice questions,女士回答说这完全是 for our own benefit(为我们自己好),没有人要求我们必须全部做完,言外之意是说男士应该尽可能地多做题,由此可知答案为[B]。

17.

[A] Women have got as much freedom as they could want.	M: I've never understood what this Woman's Lib business is all about. I can understand women in some countries struggling for their rights. But it strikes me that here in Britain women have already got as much freedom as they could possibly want.
[B] Women are struggling for their rights.	
[C] The man understands what this Women's Lib business is all about.	
[D] She doesn't think that British women have got as much freedom as wanted.	
	W: You are fooling.
	Q: What does the woman mean?

【解析】观点态度题。男士说他认为英国的妇女已经 got as much freedom as they could possibly want(获得的她们想要的自由),女士则说男士 fooling.(太傻了),这说明她不认同男士的看法。

18.

| [A] She forgot to write down the message. | M: Any message for me? |
| [B] She had to try several times to get her | W: Someone did call. But there was |

call through.

[C] She didn't understand the caller's message.

[D] She didn't get to the phone on time.

so much static I couldn't make out what he was saying.

Q: What does the woman mean?

【解析】事实状况题。男士问有没有他的电话留言,女士回答确实有人打过电话,但因为有太多 static(静电干扰),所以分辨不出对方在说什么,由此可知女士没有 understand the caller's message。

Exericise 2

11.

[A] She wants to work again tomorrow.

[B] She's willing to stop working.

[C] She wants to consider half a day's work as a full day.

[D] She's unhappy to work so long without pay.

M: We've looked long enough for a Saturday afternoon.

W: OK. Let's call it a day.

Q : What did the woman mean?

【解析】事实状况题。男士说他们盼望周六下午的到来,并到已经盼了很长时间了,女士说 Let's call it a day(今天的工作就到这吧),由此可知答案为[B]。

12.

[A] He puts the information on top of his desk.

[B] The top of his head hurts.

[C] He doesn't know the answer right now.

[D] He's afraid that very few people are registered.

W: Bob, can you tell me what percentage of the United State population is registered to vote?

M: Off the top of my head, I'm afraid I don't know.

Q: What does Bob mean?

【解析】事实状况题。女士问男士美国人口当中有多少人登记投票,男士回答说 Off the top of my head(他也不知道),由此可知答案为[C]。

13.

[A] She doesn't want to ask Mr. Jones herself.

[B] She doesn't want to work for Mr. Jones.

[C] Mr. Jones may have broken the radio.

[D] Mr. Jones might fix the radio.

M: My radio doesn't work. What do you think I should do?

W: I don't know what to do with it. But Mr. Jones may help you.

Q: What does the woman mean?

【解析】事实状况题。男士说他的收音机坏了,女士也不知道该怎么办,她说 Mr. Jones may help …(Mr. Jones 可能能帮男士),由此可知答案为[D]。

14.

[A] They don't have to go to the concert.	M: I'd like to drive to the concert, but my brother has the car tonight.
[B] His brother should let them use the car.	W: Who needs a car? We can take the subway if we go a little earlier.
[C] The subway was fine with her.	Q: What does the woman mean?
[D] A car wouldn't be any faster.	

【解析】事实状况题。男士说他想开车去音乐会,女士说不用开车,她觉得 take the subway(乘坐地铁)就可以了,由此可知答案为[C]。

15.

[A] Peter is visiting his mother.	W: Do you think we should invite Peter for dinner?
[B] Peter will be unable to come.	M: His mother's here for a visit.
[C] Peter's mother is coming for dinner.	Q: What does the man mean?
[D] Peter can't hear them.	

【解析】事实状况题。女士打算请 Peter 一起吃晚饭,男士说 Peter 的妈妈来看望 Peter 了,言外之意是说 Peter 不会来的。

16.

[A] A carpenter built it for students.	M: Did the drama students build all the scenery for the program?
[B] The drama students designed and made it.	W: No, they had a carpenter make it according to their design.
[C] The drama students built most of it.	Q: Where did the scenery come from?
[D] A special designer made it.	

【解析】事实状况题。男士问是不是这些学生布置了节目需要的场景,女士说他们 had a carpenter make it(找工匠做的),由此可知答案为[A]。

17.

[A] He began working on his degree more than five years ago.	M: How long has Alex been working on his degree, five years?
[B] He finished his degree a long time ago.	W: At least that long.
[C] It took him the least time of anyone to finish his degree.	Q: What is the woman saying about Alex?
[D] He will be working on his degree for at least five more years.	

【解析】事实状况题。男士问女士 Alex 学习了多长时间,有五年吗? 女士回答说 At least that long(至少有那么长时间了),由此可知答案为[A]。

18.

[A] In a department store.	M: May I help you?
[B] In a bank.	W: Yes. I'd like to cash these travelers' checks first,
[C] At a tourist bureau.	and then open a savings account.
[D] At a hotel.	Q: Where does this conversation probably take place?

【解析】地点场景题。由对话中的 cash checks(兑支票)和 open a savings account (开储蓄账户)可以推断出,对话很可能发生在银行。

Exericise 3

11.

[A] Traveling a lot.	W: John seems to have lost a lot of weight
[B] Getting a lot of exercise.	recently.
[C] Working hard.	M: Yes, he's been training hard with the soccer
[D] Waiting for the train.	team.
	Q: What has John been doing?

【解析】行为活动题。女士说 John 最近看起来瘦了,男士说因为 John 最近 training hard with the soccer team(正在足球队努力训练),由此可知答案为[B]。

12.

[A] They will find the trouble.	M: Have you ever put one of these together
[B] They should carry the parts o-utside.	before?
[C] They should practice working together.	W: No, never. But I think if we carry out th-ese instructions exactly, we won't have any trouble.
[D] They should follow the direct-ions.	Q: What does the woman mean?

【解析】行为活动题。女士说要是我们严格地 carry out these instructions(按说明书上的指示做),我们就不会遇到麻烦了,由此可知,女士认为他们应该 follow the directions。

13.

[A] He fixes the bicycles.	M: The front tire is flat, and the seat needs to be r-aised.
[B] He raises sheep.	
[C] He sells chairs.	W: Why not take it to Mr. Smith?
[D] He's a gardener.	Q: What kind of work does Mr. Smith probably do?

【解析】事实状况题。男士说车前胎瘪了,车座也需要提高,女士建议他去找 Mr. Smith 帮忙,由此可知 Mr. Smith 很可能是修自行车的。

14.

[A] The woman doesn't like orange juice. [B] The woman is as clumsy as ever. [C] The man was in a car crash this morning. [D] The man broke the container of juice.	W: I just made up a quart of orange juice this morning, and now I can't find it anywhere. Do you know what happened to it? M: Did you hear a crash earlier? That was it. I'm just as clumsy as ever. Q: What is the problem?

【解析】事实状况题。女士说她早上做的桔子汁不见了,问男士看到没有,男士回答说 Did you hear a crash earlier?（没听到摔碎声吗?),是他太笨了,把它摔了,由此可知答案为[D]。

15.

[A] Steve looks good in anything. [B] He knew someone who looked like Steve. [C] He wishes he had a jacket like Steve's. [D] Steve should get a new jacket.	W: Steve looks good in that old jacket, doesn't he? M: I still wish he'd get a new one. Q: What is the man's opinion?

【解析】观点态度题。女士说 Steve 穿那件旧夹克看起来不错,男士用虚拟语气说他还是希望 Steve 能 get a new one,由此可知答案为[D]。

16.

[A] At the information desk. [B] On the platform. [C] On the train. [D] Near the stairs.	M: Where have you been all this time? The train is about to leave. W: I'm sorry, Jim, I'm late, but I was waiting for you at the information desk upstairs. It's lucky I thought to look for you here on the platform. Q: Where did the woman think they were supposed to meet?

【解析】事实状况题。男士问女士刚才跑哪去了,女士说她刚才一直在楼上的 information desk(服务台)等男士,由此可知女士本来认为他们是在 information desk 碰面。

17.

[A] In a school. [B] At the post office. [C] In a courtroom.	M: Your honor! I would like to bring the jury's attention to some points that I feel are relevant to the case at this time.

[D] In a packing plant.	W: Counselor, you may address the jury this afternoon. The court will now recess for one hour for lunch. Q: Where is this conversation taking place?

【解析】地点场景题。由对话中的关键词 jury(陪审团),case(案件),counselor(律师), recess(休庭)等可以推断出,对话发生在 courtroom(法庭)。

18.

[A] She hasn't gone camping for several weeks. [B] She likes to take long camping [C] She prefers not to go camping on weekends. [D] She takes a long time to plan her trips.	M: Janet's quite enthusiastic about camping, isn't she? W: Yes, she often goes for weeks at a time. Q: What does the woman say about Janet?

【解析】事实状况题。男士问女士 Janet 是不是非常喜欢 camping(野营),女士给予肯定回答,而且说 Janet 每次都是 goes for weeks,由此可知答案为[B]。

第三篇

长对话高分必备

Part 3

本篇首先介绍了长对话的常考场景和出题重点，之后详细讲解了解答长对话题应掌握的一些听前预测技巧和边听边记技巧，并配有专项练习和综合训练题，以供考生对知识进行巩固提高。

常考场景

六级听力长对话一共两组,平均长度在 270 词左右,每组长对话由一男一女两个人的对话组成,每组对话约包含 7—10 轮对话,后设 3—4 题,共 7 题。题目的顺序一般是按照对话的顺序分布。

与听力短文类似,长对话都有一个主题,双方围绕该主题展开对话,一般一篇长对话的场景构成包括如下要点:

1. 谈话的时间、地点以及人物。
2. 谈话双方的关系,如朋友、同学、师生、同事等。
3. 谈论的话题,如学习、工作、购物、娱乐、旅行等。
4. 双方的态度或观点。
5. 谈话的结果,如作出决定或约定、提出建议等。

一、职场工作类

这类题材主要涉及招聘面试、工作经历、工作内容、工作交流或工作中遇到的问题等。

情景设计	谈论话题
工作招聘	招聘职位,招聘手段,招聘要求
工作面试	应聘职位,工作内容,工作时间,工作经验,工作资历,工作待遇,工作福利,最终决定
工作安排	具体负责的内容,负责人,完成时间
工作交流	对工作的感受,对待遇、工作时间、同事的看法,工作的前途
暑期兼职	兼职工作的内容,待遇如何,工作与学习的冲突

二、旅游交通类

这类题材主要涉及旅行计划、旅行安排、旅行感受、交通状况、交通方式、交通事故等。

情景设计	谈论话题
旅行计划	确定旅行地点,了解旅行地点的情况,准备旅行必备品,确定交通方式,预定旅馆,请人照看房子或宠物
旅行情况	旅行地点的风光景色如何,旅行者的感受如何
交通状况	交通拥挤,上下班高峰,车辆拥堵,尾气排放污染空气

交通方式	各类交通工具的优缺点,哪个更安全、更快、更舒适、更经济实惠
事故违章	事故原因(多为人为原因),事故伤亡情况,事故后果,违章现象,违章惩罚,交通法规

三、新闻采访类

这类题材包括电台报道和电视报道,内容涉及广泛,以社会问题、政治事件或人物报道为主。

情景设计	谈论话题
时事报道	事件的起因,目前的情况,影响事件的因素,将来的趋势
人物采访	人物简介,人物成就或地位,对某个问题的看法,对某项成就或研究的介绍

四、日常生活类

这类题材主要涉及购物休闲、邻里相处、家庭事务等。

情景设计	谈论话题
日常购物	购物需求,商品情况,讨价还价,服务态度,商品质量,顾客投诉
休闲娱乐	休闲方式,休闲时间,休闲必备品,休闲与工作的冲突
家庭事务	家庭分工,家庭财务,家庭关系,孩子学习,装饰装修,住房搬家
邻里相处	邻里往来,邻里纠纷,纠纷原因,解决办法,结果如何

五、文化教育类

这类题材主要涉及到文化习俗、艺术时尚、教育制度、学校介绍、学生学习和生活等。

情景设计	谈论话题
文化习俗	不同的风俗习惯,文化冲突,文化交流
艺术时尚	音乐影视,艺术展览,电影电视,流行趋势,时尚观念,时尚变化
教育制度	当前的问题,改革,措施,影响
学校介绍	学校历史,学校设施,学校地位,学校成就,学校政策
学生学习	专业选择,选课上课,借书买书,作业论文,考试,毕业
学生生活	课余活动,公益活动,朋友相聚,学生干部竞选
学生住宿	校内住宿,校外住宿,住宿条件,室友相处
假期安排	打工经历,结伴旅游,假期培训

六、社会问题类

这类题材主要涉及环境污染、动物保护、能源问题、妇女问题、暴力犯罪等社会现象或社会问题。

情景设计	谈论话题
环境污染	污染严重性,污染原因,环保措施
动物保护	濒危动物,灭绝原因,保护区建立,动物保护意识
能源问题	能源枯竭,解决能源问题的紧迫性,解决措施,节约能源,开发能源
妇女问题	妇女地位,妇女运动,妇女角色,职业妇女,家庭妇女,离婚
暴力犯罪	社会治安,青少年犯罪,媒体中的暴力宣传,解决办法

七、科普知识类

这类题材主要涉及到自然现象、生物生态、科技发展等。

情景设计	谈论话题
自然现象	气候变化,地理变迁,自然灾害,温室效应,全球变暖
生物生态	动植物介绍,生物进化,濒危物种,生态环境,生态平衡
科技发展	太空探索,计算机技术,医学、科技上的新发明或新发现,对人类的影响

Exercise 专项练习 ∩ 边听边记

Conversation One

1. [A] In 1959.　　　　　　　[B] In 1960.
　 [C] In 1961.　　　　　　　[D] In 1916.

2. [A] In 1941.　　　　　　　[B] In 1942.
　 [C] In 1943.　　　　　　　[D] In 1944.

3. [A] It was his experience in India that inspired his film *Eastern Moon*.
　 [B] He stayed in Indonesia for 18 years, and he met his wife there in 1965.
　 [C] His second novel named *The Cold Earth* was a best seller.
　 [D] He has never been to Indonesia.

Conversation Two

4. [A] A student.　　　　　　[B] A doctor.
　 [C] An academic adviser.　　[D] An assistant professor.

5. [A] About 12.　　　　　　　[B] 12 at most.

[C] More than 36.　　　　　[D] No less than 12.

6. [A] She's been in the United States before.

[B] She'd like to go fast in her studies.

[C] She must take exams on audited courses.

[D] She would rather take fewer classes than fail any.

【答案与解析】

Conversation One

【听力原文】	【答案解析】
W: Now let's go back to your first novel, *Rag Doll*. When did you write that?	1. When did the writer leave school?
M: *Rag Doll*, yes. [1] I wrote that in 1960, a year after I left school.	【解析】选[A]。推断题。男士即 the writer 说他写第一本小说是在 1960 年，那时他离校一年了，由此可知他是 1959 年毕业的。
W: [2①] How old were you then?	
M: [2②] Um, eighteen? Yes, eighteen, because a year later I went to Indonesia.	
W: Mm. And of course it was your experience in Indonesia that inspired your film *Eastern Moon*.	2. When was the writer born?
M: Yes, that's right, although I didn't actually make *Eastern Moon* until 1978.	【解析】选[B]。推断题。男士说他写书那年是 1960 年，女士问他那时多大，男士回答说应该是 eitheen（18 岁），由此可知男士生于 1942 年。
W: And you worked in television for a time too.	
M: Yes, I started making documentaries for television in 1973, when I was thirty. That was after I gave up farming.	
W: Farming?	
M: Yes, that's right. You see, I stayed in Indonesia for eight years. I met my wife there in 1965, and after we came back we bought a farm in the West of England in 1970. A kind of experiment, really.	3. Which statement below is true according to the conversation?
W: But you gave it up three years later.	【解析】选[C]。细节题。男士提到他的第二本小说名叫 *The Cold Earth*，并且说它是 a best seller（畅销书）。
M: Well, yes. You see it was very hard work, and I was also very busy working on [3①] my second novel, *The Cold Earth*, which came out in 1975.	
W: Yes, [3②] that was a best-seller, wasn't it?	
M: [3③] Yes, it was, and that's why only two years after that I was able to give up television work and concentrate on films and that sort of thing. And after that...	

Conversation Two

【听力原文】	【答案解析】

M: How do you do? Miss Wu. Please have a seat.

W: Thank you.

M: Now then, let's look at your transcript. You got your Bachelor of Arts in English and now you want to get your Master's in Education, right?

W: Right.

M: You'll need 36 credit hours, of which 15 must be from the English Department and 15 from the Education Department. For the remaining six credit hours, you can either write a thesis or take two selected courses.

W: Right now, this is very confusing to me, but I'm sure it will straighten out in my mind as I learn more about it.

M: [4①]Let's program your courses. Since you have had English Literature, you should take American Literature and American Prose and Fiction. Your transcript indicates that your English background is strong, so I don't think you will have any problem with it.

W: How many credits for each course?

M: Three. You should also take two three-credit courses in the Education Department. [4②] I suggest Educational Psychology and Audiovisual Methods and Aids. That will give you [5]12 hours altogether, which is the minimum for a full-time student.

W: Excuse me, sir. Actually I am a part-time student so I would like to audit one course. Since this is my first time in the United States, [6] I don't want to fail any classes and would therefore prefer a somewhat lighter program.

M: That's correct. In fact, you must maintain a "B" average to earn your Master's. In other words, if you get a "C", you will need an "A" to balance it. If you get a "D"…

W: I surely don't want to get any "D" or "F". Therefore, like the tortoise in the fable, I'd better go slowly but surely.

M: That's a good idea.

4. Who is the man?

【解析】选[C]。推断题。由 Let's … , I suggest… 等内容可知男士给女士解答了很多有关修学分的问题并提出了许多建议，由此可推断男士是一个 academic adviser（学院指导老师）。

5. How many hours must a full-time student have in one semester?

【解析】选[D]。细节题。男士提到 12 hours 是 the minimum for a full-time student，即一个 full-time student 一个学期中至少要修 12 小时课时。

6. What conclusion may be drawn about Miss Wu from the conversation?

【解析】选[D]。细节题。女士提到她不想 fail any classes and would therefore prefer a somewhat lighter program，即她宁愿少选几门课程，也不想有不及格的科目。would rather … than… 意为"宁愿…，而不愿…"。

出 题 重 点

第二章 **Chapter 2**

　　长对话不同于短对话,信息量较大,而且问题是在整组对话之后提出,这使得考生很难抓住关键信息,记住要点内容。因此,熟悉和掌握长对话的出题重点,将有助于考生在听音时更加快速准确地抓住关键信息。

一、对话的开头处

　　对话的开头部分一般都会引出谈话的主题,比较容易设主旨题,主要考查对谈话主题或所涉及场景的把握。

【例1】 (710分样卷-Conversation One-19)

[A] To interview a few job applicants.	M: Morning, Brenda.
	W: Good morning, Mr. Browning.
[B] To fill a vacancy in the company.	M: Er, did you, did you put that ad in yesterday?
	W: Yes, yesterday afternoon.
[C] To advertise for a junior sales manager.	M: The ad for a junior sales manager, I mean.
	…
[D] To apply for a job in a major newspaper.	19. What did Mr. Browning ask Brenda to do?

【解析】本题的设题点在开头处。根据原文中 did you put that ad in yesterday? 和 The ad for a junior sales manager 可知,Mr. Browning 是要求 Brenda 在报纸上刊登一则招聘广告。本题只需抓住 ad 一词(advertisement 的缩写)即可确定答案为[C]。

二、对话的结尾处

　　对话结尾往往会涉及对话双方的态度、建议或决定等总结性的内容,而且经常能够进一步体现对话的主题及场景,也是出题者设题时考虑的重点。

【例2】 (710分样卷-Conversation One-21)

[A] Not clearly specified.	…
[B] Not likely to be met.	W: Well sir, I wish you the best of luck and hope…
[C] Reasonable enough.	M: Well, yes?
[D] Apparently sexist.	W: …I think you're asking an awful lot.
	21. What does Brenda think of the qualifications Mr. Browning insists on?

【解析】本题的设题点在结尾处。根据女士在结尾处所说的 you're asking an awful lot 可推知,她认为 Mr. Browning 的要求太多,不大可能会得到满足,故答案为[B]。

三、对话中问答处

长对话由于仍然是以对话形式出现,双方会就对话主题进行讨论,故其中经常会包含一些对话双方的一问一答,这些地方往往是长对话设题的重点。

【例3】 (710分样卷-Conversation One-20)

[A] A hard working ambitious young man.	W: What kind of person have you got in mind for this job?
[B] A young man good at managing his time.	M: Oh, well, somebody fairly young, you know, twenty something, like 21, or 25. A man, I think. …
[C] A college graduate with practical working experience.	W: Erm, what sort of a young man have you …?
[D] A young man with his own idea of what is important.	M: …, someone with plenty of ambition, plenty of drive. …
	20. What kind of person will meet the job requirements?

【解析】本题的设题点在问答处。根据对话中 fairly young, plenty of ambition, plenty of drive 等关键词可知,招聘者想要寻找的是一个工作努力、有抱负的年轻小伙子,故答案为[A]。

四、对话中逻辑关系处

长对话中经常会涉及到表示转折、因果等逻辑关系的短语或句式,这些地方也很受出题人的青睐。

【例4】 (新06-12-Conversation Two-23)

[A] Bad weather.	W: What were the circumstances? Were there bad weather, a fire, or engine failure?
[B] Human error.	M: Apparently, there were some low clouds in the area, but mostly it was just miscommunication between the pilots and the air traffic controllers.
[C] Breakdown of the engines.	23. What was the cause of the tragedy?
[D] Failure of the communications system.	

【解析】本题的设题点在问答处和转折处。女士问男士事故发生时情形如何,男士通过 but 转折引出悲剧发生的主要原因 miscommunication between the pilots and the air traffic controllers(飞行员和控制人员的沟通失误),这明显属 human error(人为失误),故答案为[B]。

五、对话中列举或举例处

对话中出现列举或举例的地方往往也是出题的重点,因此,当听到 such as,

for example，for instance，the first，the second 等一类词语时，应加以留意。

【例5】   (07-6-Conversation One-21)

［A］Took balanced meals with champagne. ［B］Ate vegetables and fruit only. ［C］Refrained from fish or meat. ［D］Avoided eating rich food.	W: Well，I didn't drink any alcohol or coffee and I didn't eat any meat or rich food. I drink a lot of water and fruit juice and I eat the meals on the well-being menu. They are lighter. They have fish，vegetables and noodles，for example. And I did some of the exercises in the program. 21. What did the woman do to follow the well-being menu?

【解析】本题的设题点在举例处。女士说她不吃 meat or rich food（肉或高脂肪的食物），但是会 drink a lot of water and fruit juice（喝很多水和果汁），并且会 eat the meals on the well-being menu（健康菜单上的食物），包括 fish，vegetables 和 noodles，故答案为［D］。本题答案虽并未直接来自于所举例子，但该例子内容可作为排除干扰项的主要依据。

六、对话中比较或对比处

含有形容词、副词的比较级或最高级，以及 as...as，compared with，in contrast 等引出比较结构的句子往往提供重要信息或者就是答案的出处，这些地方也是长对话设题的重点之一。

【例6】   (新 06-12-Conversation One-20)

［A］Trim the apple trees in her yard. ［B］Pick up the apples that fell in her yard. ［C］Take the garbage to the curb for her. ［D］Remove the branches from her yard.	W: Well，I don't think you're quite finished yet—some of the larger branches fell over into my yard，and I think you should come and get them. 20. What did the woman ask the man to do?

【解析】本题的设题点在比较处。女士说 some of the larger branches 掉进了她的院子里，要求男士 come and get them，由此可知她是想让男士把掉到她院子里的苹果枝清走，故答案为［D］。

七、对话中数字信息处

对话中出现年代、价格、时间等相关信息的地方，也经常被作为长对话设题的一个重点，但要注意，除了单纯地考查数字或时间以外，还经常会考查与数字或时间相关的其他细节信息。

【例7】   (新 06-12-Conversation Two-24)

[A] Two thousand feet. [B] Twelve thousand feet. [C] Twenty thousand feet. [D] Twenty-two thousand feet.	M: The pilots were told to descend to "two-two thousand" feet. …Unfortunately, the terrain of the mountains in Norweija extends up 20,000 feet. 24. How high are the mountains in Norweija?

【解析】本题的设题点在数字信息处。抓住男士话中的 the terrain of the mountains in Norweija extends up 20,000 feet,即可确定 Norweija 地区的山有两万英尺高,故答案为[C]。terrain 意为"地带,地势"。

Exercise   专项练习   🎧 边听边记

Conversation One

1. [A] She won the money on a lottery.
   [B] She won the money on the premium bonds.
   [C] She earned the money by her hard work.
   [D] She inherited the money from her uncle.

2. [A] A cheque book.   [B] A cheque card.
   [C] An instruction book.   [D] Nothing.

3. [A] In a bank.   [B] In a shop.
   [C] In a bookstore.   [D] In a restaurant.

Conversation Two

4. [A] She wants to buy things at a discount using the card.
   [B] She wants to go to Hawaii over the school break.
   [C] She hopes to establish a good credit rating.
   [D] She doesn't want to borrow from her parents.

5. [A] People generally have a difficult time getting out of debt.
   [B] Students often apply for more credit cards than they need.
   [C] The interest rates on student cards are very high.
   [D] Credit cards often have a credit limit.

6. [A] She hopes that someone will give her the money.
   [B] She plans on getting rid of her student credit cards.
   [C] She is going to return the items she purchased on the card.
   [D] She is going to make a budge that will help her get out of this mess.

【答案与解析】

Conversation One

【听力原文】	【答案解析】
M: Now, Miss Andrews, how much do you actually want to deposit with us in your new account? W: Well, [1] it's just around two thousand pounds that I won on the premium bonds. M: Right, er … now do you want a deposit or a current account? W: Well, I want to be able to take my money out at any time. M: I see. So you probably want a current account. W: Well, if you say so. I've only had a post office savings account until now. M: Well, [2] with a current account you can have a cheque book, or you can come into the bank and take the money out as you like. Of course, there's no interest on a current account. W: Not at all? M: No. If you put it into a seven day's deposit account, of course, you get interest, but in a current account, none. W: Well, most people have current accounts, don't they? M: Well, they do if they've not got an awful lot of money and they need to use it regularly. Eh… so that's probably the best thing for you. W: Well, you'll give me a cheque book, won't you? M: I'll give you a cheque book immediately, yes, er… W: Do you need my signature? M: Ah yes, we'll need er … two or three specimen signatures… W: OK. And I will get a cheque card… I mean one of those cards which I'm allowed to use for up to fifty pounds a day. M: Eh, eh, now we don't actually give a cheque card until you've had an account with us for six months. W: Six months? M: Yes, we have to see how the accounts going, you see.	1. Where did the woman get the money? 【解析】选 [B]。细节题。本题的设题点在数字信息处。女士明确提到这2,000多英镑是她通过 the premium bonds(有奖债券)获得的。 2. What will the woman be given after opening the account? 【解析】选 [A]。细节题。本题的设题点在条件处。男士说如果女士开一个 current account(活期账户),就可以获得 a cheque book(支票簿)。 3. Where did the woman work in the past? 【解析】选 [B]。细节题。本题的设题点在转折处。女士说她过去 work in a shop,如果没有支票卡他们

W: But that's crazy. [3]I mean I used to work in a shop and we'd never accept cheques without a cheque card. I mean no one will accept my money. M: Well, this is how we work. W: Well, I'll think about it.	就不能接受支票，由此可知女士以前在一家商店工作。used to do 意为"过去…"。

Conversation Two

【听力原文】	【答案解析】
M: Hi, Sis. I just came over to drop off the DVDs you wanted, and…Hey, wow! Where did you get all of this stuff? W: I bought it. What do you think of my new entertainment center? And the wide screen TV… M: Bought it? W:…and my new DVD player. Here, let me show you my stereo. You can really rock the house with this one. M: But where did you get the money to buy all this? You didn't borrow money from mom and dad again, did you? W: Of course not. I got it with this! M: Let me see that…Have you been using dad's credit card again? W: No. It's mine. It's a student credit card. M: A student credit card? How did you get one of these? W: I got an application in the mail. M: Well. Why did you get one in the first place? W: Listen. [4]Times are changing, and having a credit card helps you build a credit rating, control spending, and even buy things that you can't pay with cash… M: I don't want to hear it. How does having a student credit card control spending? It sounds you've spent yourself into a hole. Anyway, student credit cards just lead to impulse spending…as I can see here. [5]And the interest rates of student credit cards are	4. What is one reason to explain why the woman obtained a student credit card? 【解析】选[C]。细节题。本题的设题点在问答处和因果处。男士问女士为什么要申请学生信用卡，女士回答拥有信用卡有助于 build a credit rating（树立信用度），由此可知女士申请信用卡的一个原因就是想要 establish a good credit rating。 5. According to the man, what is one reason for not having a credit card? 【解析】选[C]。推断题。本题的设题点在并列处。男士提到 the interest rates of student credit cards are usually sky high，由此可知男士不想用信用卡的一个原因是他认为学生信用卡的利息太高。 6. What does the woman imply about how she plans on resolving her credit card problems?

usually sky high, and if you miss a payment, the rates, well, just jump!

W: Ah. The credit card has a credit limit…

M: …of $20,000?

W: No, not quite that high. Anyway…

M: I've heard enough. How in the world are you going to pay your credit card bill?

W: [6]Um, with my birthday money? It's coming up in a week.

M: Hey, let's sit down and talk about how you're going to pay things back, and maybe we can come up with a budget that will help you get out of this mess.

【解析】选[A]。推断题。本题的设题点在反问处。男士问女士打算如何还信用卡的账单，女士话中的反问句 with my birthday money? 表明，她希望过生日时会有人给她钱，那样她就可以还账单了。

听前预测技巧

长对话的篇幅较长,涉及的信息较多,想要抓住所有的信息几乎是不可能的,因此,在听音前阅读选项、利用选项信息了解听力的弦外之音、从选项中寻找突破点,就变得尤其重要。

听力题中很多选项都有比较明显的特点,或者使用某种专门的表达形式,如均为动词原形或均为人物角色等;或者含有一些标志性的词语,通过这些选项特点我们便可以推测问题可能考查的核心内容。另外,我们经常可以通过对选项的分析,排除一些比较明显的干扰性,缩小听音范围,从而在听音时更有针对性。

技巧一:各题主题揭示对话主题

将各题所考查的主题内容结合在一起,往往可得出整篇对话的主题。如果某一题目是考查对话主题,其中的一个选项明显能够概括其他各题选项的内容,那么该选项很可能为答案。

【例1】 (710 分样卷-Conversation One)

【预览选项】	【听前预测】
19. [A] To interview a few job applicants. [B] To fill a vacancy in the company. [C] To advertise for a junior sales manager. [D] To apply for a job in a major newspaper. 20. [A] A hard – working ambitious young man. [B] A young man good at managing his time. [C] A college graduate with practical working experience. [D] A young man with his own idea of what is important. 21. [A] Not clearly specified. [B] Not likely to be met. [C] Reasonable enough. [D] Apparently sexist.	预览三道题各选项,由 19 题中的 interview, applicants, vacancy, advertise for a manager, apply for a job 等词语可以推测对话与刊登招聘广告或应聘工作有关。而 20 题中 hard – working, ambitious, good at managing his time, with practical working experience, with his own idea 等词语则表明对话中还涉及到对所招聘人员的要求。

【听音验证】

M: Morning, Brenda.

W: Good morning, Mr. Browning.

M: Er, did you, did you put that ad in yesterday?

W: Yes, yesterday afternoon.

M: The ad for a junior sales manager, I mean.

W: Yes, it went into the Standard and the Evening News.

M: That's good. Erm, well …

W: What kind of person have you got in mind for this job?

M: Oh, well, somebody fairly young, you know, twenty something, like 21, or 25. A man, I think.

W: A man?

M: We really need a man for the position. Yes, I mean, its really too demanding. The sort of situations they get into are much too difficult for a young woman to deal with, erm …

W: Erm, what sort of a young man have you got in mind?

M: Oh, you know, a good education, polite, responsible, and easy to get along with. What I don't want is one of those young men just out of university, with exaggerated ideas of his own importance.

W: Yes, erm, what sort of education are you actually looking for?

M: Well, you know, a couple of A levels. Must have English, of course.

W: Yes, I think you're asking quite a lot. I mean you're not really prepared to pay all …

M: No, I'm not prepared to give him a big salary to start with. Nevertheless, I want someone with plenty of ambition, plenty of drive. You know, not looking at the clock all the time.

W: Well sir, I wish you the best of luck and hope you have some very successful interviews.

M: Well, yes?

W: Because personally I think you're asking an awful lot.

技巧二：选项均以动词的某种形式开头

含有这类选项的问题为考查"行为活动"类型。根据动词的不同形式，问题考查的重点也可能不同。

选项均以动词原形开头，问题大多是关于建议某人做某事，有时也表示为了某种目的要做某事。

选项均为动名词，问题大多是关于正在进行的动作或者计划打算。

选项为不定式，问题很可能是关于做某事的目的，或是计划、承诺或要求做某事。

【例2】 　　　　　　　　　　　　　　（新 06-12-Conversation One-21）

【预览选项】	【听前预测】
[A] File a lawsuit against the man. [B] Ask the man for compensation. [C] Have the man's apple tree cut down. [D] Throw garbage into the man's yard.	选项均为动词原形,故本题应该是考查某人的行为活动。四个选项均是针对男士的行为,故本题很可能是关于某人与男士发生争吵或冲突时所采取的应对措施。

【听音验证】

…

W: Get the branches off my property or I'll have to sue you.

M: Yeah? For what?! You're taking those law classes too seriously! I've gotta go, I have to pick up my son.

…

21. What did the woman threaten to do?

【例3】 　　　　　　　　　　　　　（710 分样卷-Conversation One-19）

【预览选项】	【听前预测】
[A] To interview a few job applicants. [B] To fill a vacancy in the company. [C] To advertise for a junior sales manager. [D] To apply for a job in a major newspaper.	选项均为不定式短语,故本题应该是考查某人将要采取的行动。[A]、[C] 是关于招聘工作(interview, advertise),[B]、[D] 则是关于申请工作(fill, apply for),故听音时应留意该行为是关于招聘还是应聘。

【听音验证】

M: Morning, Brenda.

W: Good morning, Mr. Browning.

M: Er, did you, did you put that ad in yesterday?

W: Yes, yesterday afternoon.

M: The ad for a junior sales manager, I mean.

…

19. What did Mr. Browning ask Brenda to do?

技巧三:选项中含有表示意愿或建议的词

　　如果选项中含有 should, had better, would like 等一类的词语,问题很可能是考查"观点或建议"。

【例4】　　　　　　　　　　　　　　　　　　(新 06-12-Conversation Two-25)

【预览选项】	【听前预测】
[A] Accurate communication is of utmost importance. [B] Pilots should be able to speak several foreign languages. [C] Air controllers should keep a close watch on the weather. [D] Cooperation between pilots and air controllers is essential.	由选项中的 should 可推知,本题应该是考查某人的观点或建议。选项内容表明问题应该与确保安全飞行的因素有关。
【听音验证】	

...

M: Sadly enough, yes they did. It was a really bad mistake. Many people died as a result of the simple misunderstanding.

W: Wow, that's a powerful lesson on how important it can be to accurately commu-unicate to each other.

...

25. What lesson could be drawn from the accident?

技巧四:选项中含有表示评论或感受的动词

如果选项中含有 think, like, dislike, enjoy, agree, disagree, mind 等一类的词语,听力材料或问题很可能与对某人或某事物的评价或感受有关。

四个选项中如均含有表示评论或感受的词,则表示问题是关于对人或事物的评价或感受;如其中只有个别选项含有表示评论或感受的词,则表示听力材料中很可能涉及到对人或事物的评价或感受,问题则不一定会涉及。

【例5】　　　　　　　　　　　　　　　　(710 分样卷-Conversation One-21)

【预览选项】	【听前预测】
[A] Not clearly specified. [B] Not likely to be met. [C] Reasonable enough. [D] Apparently sexist.	四个选项中均含有表示评论的词语(specified, reasonable 等),故问题很可能是关于某人对某事物的看法。
【听音验证】	

...

W: Yes, erm, what sort of education are you actually looking for?

M: Well, you know, a couple of A levels. Must have English, of course.

W: Yes, I think you're asking quite a lot. I mean you're not really prepared to pay all

...

M: No, I'm not prepared to give him a big salary to start with. Nevertheless, I want someone with plenty of ambition, plenty of drive. You know, not looking at the clock all the time.

W: Well sir, I wish you the best of luck and hope you have some very successful interviews.

M: Well, yes?

W: Because personally I think you're asking an awful lot.

21. What does Brenda think of the qualifications Mr. Browning insists on?

技巧五:选项中含有比较结构

如果选项中含有形容词或副词的比较级或最高级,或是其他表示比较的词语,则听力材料或问题很可能涉及人或事物之间的异同点或优劣的比较。

四个选项中如均含有比较级或表示比较的词,则表示问题是关于人或事物之间的比较;如其中只有个别选项中含有比较级,则表示听力材料中很可能涉及到人或事物之间的比较,问题内容则不一定会涉及。

【例6】   (710 样卷-Conversation One-22)

【预览选项】	【听前预测】
[A] Their competitors have long been advertising on TV. [B] TV commercials are less expensive. [C] Advertising in newspapers alone is not sufficient. [D] TV commercials attract more investments.	由选项中的 advertising on TV, advertising in newspapers 以及比较级 less expensive, attract more 可知本题很可能涉及到电视广告和报纸广告之间优劣的比较。故听音时应留意比较级或其他陈述二者优劣特点的词句。
【听音验证】	
… W: Marketing has some interesting ideas for television commercials. M: TV? Isn't that a bit too expensive for us? What's wrong with advertising in the papers, as usual? W: Quite frankly, it's just not enough anymore. … 22. Why does the woman suggest advertising on TV?	

技巧六:选项均为名词短语

如选项均为概括性较强的名词或是名词性的短语,且各项内容差异较大,问题则很可能是关于对话所谈论的主题或对话中出现的某一事件或问题的主题。

【例7】　　　　　　　　　　　　　　　　(710 分样卷-Conversation Two-22)

【预览选项】	【听前预测】
[A] The latest developments of an armed rebellion in Karnak. [B] The fall of Karnak's capital city into the hands of the rebel forces. [C] The epidemic that has just broken out in the country of Karnak. [D] The peace talks between the rebels and the government in Karnak.	选项均为名词短语,且概括性均较强,故本题很可能考查对话的主旨。由 armed rebellion, the rebel forces, peace talks between the rebels and the government 等词以及多次出现的 Karnak 可推知本对话很可能与 Karnak 国反政府武装叛乱有关。

【听音验证】
W: We now interrupt our regular scheduled news program to bring you live up-to-date coverage on the civil unrest in the newly formed country of Karnak, where our man Stan Fielding is stationed. Stan …   M: This is Stan Fielding reporting live from the suburbs of the capital city. Just 20 minutes ago, rebel forces launched the biggest offensive against the ruling government in the 18- month conflict here in this country.   …   22. What is the news coverage mainly about?

技巧七:与其余选项内容不同的选项往往不是答案

　　如果某一选项明显与对话主题不相关,那么该选项往往不是答案。

　　如果某一选项明显与其他三个选项内容不同,即与该题主题明显不相关,那么该选项往往不是答案。

【例8】　　　　　　　　　　　　　　　　(新 06-12-Conversation One-19)

【预览选项】	【听前预测】
19. [A] He picked up some apples in his yard. [B] He cut some branches off the apple tree. [C] He quarreled with his neighbor over the fence. [D] He cleaned up all the garbage in the woman's yard. 20. [A] Trim the apple trees in her yard. [B] Pick up the apples that fell in her yard. [C] Take the garbage to the curb for her. [D] Remove the branches from her yard.	由各选项中的 apple, tree, yard, branches, trim(修剪)等词可推知对话主题应该与苹果树枝条和院子有关,再根据选项中出现的 quarreled, lawsuit(诉讼), compensation(赔偿), concession(让步), court(法庭)等词可推知对话还可能涉及到对话双方的争吵。

21. [A] File a <u>lawsuit</u> against the man.

[B] Ask the man for <u>compensation</u>.

[C] Have the man's <u>apple tree</u> cut down.

[D] Throw garbage into the man's <u>yard</u>.

22. [A] He was ready to make a <u>concession</u>.

[B] He was not prepared to go to <u>court</u>.

[C] He was not intimidated.

[D] He was a bit concerned.

19 题各选项中谓语动词的过去式形式表明本题应该是考查男士过去的活动。[A]、[B]、[C]均与苹果树和院子有关，只有[C]是关于 fence(栅栏)，与其他三项内容差别较大，且与其他各题选项内容均不相关，故[C]为答案的可能性较小。

【听音验证】	【答案解析】
W: Hello, Patrick, is that you? M: Yeah, Jane, what can I do for you? W: I was calling about the apple tree that you were trimming yesterday. M: That was hard work! …	19. What did the man do yesterday? 【解析】选[B]。由女士话中的 the apple tree that you were trimming yesterday 可知男士昨天给苹果树剪枝了。trim 意为"修剪，修整"。

技巧八:包含其他选项内容的选项往往不是答案

有的选项明显包含其他选项的含义,那么该选项往往不是答案。

【例9】 (托福)

【预览选项】	【听前预测】
[A] She was <u>impressed</u> by it. [B] It was <u>a waste of money</u>. [C] She was <u>amazed</u> it had opened so soon. [D] She didn't <u>like</u> it as much as the other wings.	由选项中的 impressed, a waste of money, amazed, like 等可推知本题是针对对某事物的看法设题的。选项[A]说"it"给她留下了深刻印象,选项[C]说她对"it"这么快就开张(或开放)感到吃惊,其含义包含[A]的含义在内,故[C]很可能不是答案。

【听音验证】	【答案解析】
M: Hey, how was your trip? W: Wonderful. I spent most of my time at the art museum. I especially liked the new wing. I was amazed to hear the guide explain all the problems they had building it. …	34. What did the woman think of the new wing of the museum? 【解析】选[A]。由对话中出现的 amazed, unusual, impressive 等可知女士对美术馆新侧厅的修建费用以及修建过程中的种种问题大感吃惊,并且对里面的设计印象非常深刻,故答案为[A]。

技巧九：明显不符常理的选项往往不是答案

有的选项明显不符合该对话情景下的常识或常理，那么该选项往往不是答案。

【例10】 （新 06-12-Conversation Two-25）

【预览选项】	【听前预测】
[A] Accurate communication is of utmost importance. [B] Pilots should be able to speak several foreign languages. [C] Air controllers should keep a close watch on the weather. [D] Cooperation between pilots and air controllers is essential.	由选项中的 should 可推知，本题应该是考查某人的观点或建议。选项内容表明问题应该与确保安全飞行的因素有关。[B]是说飞行员应该会说几门外语，这不大合乎常理，因为飞国内行线的飞行员并不一定要会好几门外语，故[B]为答案的可能性较小。
【听音验证】 ... M: Sadly enough, yes they did. It was a really bad mistake. Many people died as a result of the simple misunderstanding. W: Wow, that's a powerful lesson on how important it can be to accurately communicate to each other.	【答案解析】 25. What lesson could be drawn from the accident? 【解析】选[A]。对话的最后女士总结了这次事故的教训：how important it can be to accurately communicate to each other，答案是对此的同义转述。utmost 意为"极大的"。

技巧十：意思相近的选项往往都不是答案

【例11】 （新 06-12-Conversation One-22）

【预览选项】	【听前预测】
[A] He was ready to make a concession. [B] He was not prepared to go to court. [C] He was not intimidated. [D] He was a bit concerned.	由选项中的 concession（让步）, go to court, intimidate（威胁）, concerned（担心）等词可推测问题应该与男士对某事的反应有关。[A]是说他准备让步，[B]是说他不准备上法庭，二者都表示男士要"妥协退让"的含义，故很可能都不是答案。
【听音验证】 ... M: Get the branches off my property or I'll have to sue you.	【答案解析】 22. What was the man's reaction to the woman's threat? 【解析】选[C]。女士对男士说让他等着收

M: Yeah? For what?! ... W: You'll be hearing from me. M: Yeah, yeah. See you in court, Jane.	法庭的传票（hear from me），男士的回答 "Yeah, yeah. See you in court（法庭见）" 表明他根本 not intimidated（不怕威胁）。

Exercise　　　专项练习　　　🎧 边听边记

Conversation One

1. [A] It is very hot.　　　　　　[B] It is very cold.
   [C] It is very uncomfortable indoors. [D] It is too dark inside.

2. [A] To see an outdoor movie.
   [B] To go for a walk.
   [C] To see an indoor movie.
   [D] To go out to have a meal.

3. [A] No good films are shown in the summer.
   [B] They cannot hear properly at outdoor movie.
   [C] They cannot eat their meals comfortably.
   [D] It will be very crowded.

Conversation Two

4. [A] Ruthless.　　　　　　　　[B] Intelligent.
   [C] Motherly.　　　　　　　　[D] Warm-hearted.

5. [A] Because of being shot.
   [B] Because of the shock of a car.
   [C] Because of the shock of the cold water.
   [D] Because of the fire.

6. [A] To find a vet for the rabbit.
   [B] To build a fire for the rabbit.
   [C] To have a rest.
   [D] To have something to eat.

Conversation Three

7. [A] Changing work schedules.
   [B] Looking for work.
   [C] Who can replace the man.
   [D] Work on their assignments.

8. [A] She needs a new job.
   [B] Her professor doesn't want her to work.
   [C] She wants to have time to do her assignment.
   [D] She doesn't think she can do the assignment herself.

9. [A] He is strict.
   [B] He doesn't give breaks to students who are late.
   [C] He marks hard.
   [D] He gives a lot of assignments.

10. [A] Because another person who needs part-time work can fill in.
    [B] Because another person will switch shifts.
    [C] Because the professor may give an extension.
    [D] Because Greg will get her another job.

边听边记

【答案与解析】

Conversation One

【听力原文】	【答案解析】
M: I want to do something tonight for a change, let's go to the movies. W: [1] In this heat? Are you joking? M: We can go to an outdoor movie. Do you think I'd suggest an indoor one in the middle of the summer in San Diego? W: [2] I'd rather go out for a meal. M: Yes, that sounds a better idea. The outdoor movies are so uncomfortable. W: Why don't we do both at the same time? We could pick up some take-away food and eat it in the movie. M: That sounds like fun. W: But they never show any good films in the summer. At least not any of the new ones. All you get is the old classics. M: And what's wrong with them? W: Oh nothing, it's just that we've seen them all half a dozen times. M: But that's why they're classics. [3]My main objection to outdoor movies is that you can never hear properly. You hear all the traffic from outside. Well, but we can find a foreign film with subtitles, then you don't need to hear the sound. W: Supposing it's a musical. M: Oh, trust you to say that! I think it would be fun to sit	1. Why does the woman not want to go to an indoor movie? 【解析】选[A]。推断题。男士建议女士晚上去看电影,女士反问道 In this heat?(那多热啊) Are you joking?(没开玩笑吧),由此可知女士觉得看室内电影太热了,所以不想去。 2. What does the woman like to do? 【解析】选[D]。细节题。女士说她更愿意 go out for a meal(出去吃饭)。would rather do 意为"宁愿,更愿意"。 3. Why does the man object to going to the outdoor movie?

watching an old film and eating a meal at the same time.

W: Last time I went to an outdoor movie, I bought a bar of chocolate to eat as I went in. It was a horror film and I was so shocked I just sat there holding my bar of chocolate until the interval when I found out it had melted in my hand and run all down my dress. That was an expensive evening one.

M: Well, we won't go and see a horror film, darling, and take-away meals don't melt.

【解析】选[B]。细节题。男士说他反对看 outdoor movies（室外电影）的主要原因是他们 can never hear properly（听不清楚电影的声音），因为室外汽车噪音太大。

Conversation Two

【听力原文】

W: So in your book why do you focus more on Bonnie than you have on Clyde?

M: Bonnie had something which Clyde completely lacked. Clyde, not intelligent. He was just a rather stupid hoodlum. Bonnie was a much warmer, more generous person.

W: [4] But she could be very ruthless, couldn't she? I mean what about that policeman she shot in Grapevine, Texas? Didn't she laugh about it?

M: Well, first of all, we don't know if that's what actually happened. A farmer says he saw her shoot the second policeman and then laugh. That's the only evidence we have that she actually did that. But even if the story is true, the whole incident illustrates this warmer, almost motherly side to her character.

W: Motherly? How does the incident of shooting a policeman illustrate that she was motherly?

M: You see, the day before the shooting, Bonnie and Clyde were driving about with Bonnie's pet rabbit in the car. Clyde started complaining because the rabbit stank. So they stopped and washed the rabbit in a stream. [5] The rabbit almost died because of the shock of the very cold water. Bonnie got very worried, and wrapped the rabbit in a blanket and held it close to her as they drove on.

W: Well, Bonnie seemed to love that rabbit very much.

【答案解析】

4. What was Bonnie thought by the interviewer?

【解析】选[A]。细节题。男士认为 Bonnie 非常 warmer（热情）和 generous（大方），女士即 interviewer 则认为 Bonnie 非常 ruthless（残忍），因为 Bonnie 曾经杀了一位警察还能笑得出来。

5. Why did Bonnie's pet rabbit almost die?

【解析】选[C]。细节题。男士提到 Clyde 和 Bonnie 在小溪里给 Bonnie 的宠物兔洗了澡，因为 the shock of the very cold water，宠物兔差点死去。

6. Why did Bonnie make Clyde stop the

M: Yeah. [6] The next morning, when the rabbit still wasn't any better, she made Clyde stop and build a fire. She was sitting in front of that fire, trying to get the rabbit warm when the two policemen drove up and got out. Probably the policemen had no idea who was there. They just wanted to see who was burning a fire and why. A moment later, as we know, they were both dead.

W: You mean all because of that pet rabbit which Bonnie wanted to mother?

M: Right. Clyde was something like a pet rabbit, too. She was attracted to him because he was weaker than she was and needed someone to mother him. It's strange but strong, intelligent women are often attracted to such men ... , weaker than they are ... , men who are like children, or pet rabbits.

car the next morning? 【解析】选［B］。细节题。男士提到第二天 Bonnie 看到兔子的情况仍然没有好转，于是就让 Clyde 把车停下，build a fire（生一堆火），想让她的兔子暖和过来。

Conversation Three

【听力原文】	【答案解析】

W: Hi, Mark, I was about to go look for you. You're a hard man to find these days. Where've you been all week?

M: Here, there and everywhere but getting nowhere. So, what's up with you?

W: [7][8] Well, I have a paper due this coming Monday and I'm wondering if it's possible to switch shifts so I can have the weekend free to finish my paper. I know you've got exams a couple of weeks from now, so I thought I could free up a weekend for you at that time.

M: That's a tough one, Jane. I promised my folks to visit them this weekend and they're really looking forward to seeing me. Have you check with Martin? Perhaps he can help you out.

W: Yes, I did. He can't do it either since he has an exam next week. He said he's behind on his reading and wants to spend time to do some catching up.

7. What are the speakers discussing?
【解析】选［A］。主旨题。对话一开始，女士提到她赶着完成一篇论文，想和男士商量能不能和他 switch shifts（换班），接下来整段对话都是围绕这一话题展开，由此可知两人正在讨论换班事宜。

8. Why does the woman need to solve the problem?
【解析】选［C］。细节题。女士想换班的原因是下周一 have a paper due（要交论文），所以她想 have the weekend free（利用周末）来完成论文。

9. What can be inferred about the professor?

M: That's too bad. I wish I could help you. Wait a minute, I have an idea. [10①] I know Greg is looking for some part-time job. Maybe you can look him up for help.

W: Yeah, that's right. I almost forgot about him. He mentioned once he could do replacement work anytime, since he's only taking one course this semester. I am praying that he will help me [9] because this professor is really sticky about late assignment. You know how much he knocked down Theresa on her last assignment.

M: Not to worry. [10②] I know Greg has a lot of free time on his hands.

W: Great. Thanks for reminding me about Greg. I'll let you know what happens.

M: No problem, I hope you can get your work done on time.

【解析】选[A]。推断题。女士说教授 sticky about late assignment(不同意迟交作业)，而且还举了一位女同学的例子来说明这一点，由此推断教授对学生十分严厉。

10. Why may this problem be solved for the woman?

【解析】选[A]。细节题。男士说 Greg 有空余的时间，因为他正在寻找 part time job(兼职工作)，由此可知男士建议女士可以找 Greg 帮忙来解决她的问题。

边听边记技巧

第四章 Chapter 4

长对话的篇幅较长,想要听过之后就能将主要的内容都清楚地记在脑子里,几乎是不可能的。考生只有听一遍的机会,只能边听、边记、边答。

边听边记是听力中一项非常重要的技能,但是作笔记并不是要把听到的每一个单词都记下来,笔记无非是帮助记忆的手段,只要能把重要的信息用可识别的符号记录下来,就算达到了目的。因此为了提高听与记的效率,应注意把握一定的技巧和原则。

技巧一:抓住首尾句

主题句常常是在对话的开头,它对整个对话的内容起一个概括和提示的作用,实际上是说话人所谈论的中心话题。长对话中的第一题很可能是针对对话的开头提问,考查考生对整篇对话的主题或所谈话题的把握。

结尾处往往涉及到某种建议、决定或下一步要做的事情,它对整个对话起到一个总结的作用。长对话的最后一题经常是针对对话的结尾设题,故留意结尾处的关键动词对解题至关重要。

【例1】 (07-6-Conversation Two-19)

【预览选项】	【边听边记】
[A] To go sightseeing.	M: Hi, Ann, welcome back. How's your trip to
[B] To have meetings.	the states?
[C] To promote a new champagne.	W: Very busy, [19]I had a lot of meetings. ...
[D] To join in a training program.	19. Why did the woman go to New York?

【解析】选[B]。细节题。对话一开始,男士就问女士去美国的旅行怎么样,女士回答说很忙,她 had a lot of meetings(要参加很多会议),由此可知女士去纽约是去参加会议。

技巧二:留意对话中的一问一答

长对话中,对话双方往往出现多个一问一答,而这恰恰是长对话的一个出题重点,对话后面问题往往就是对话原文中问题的照搬或同义转述,因此其答案就是对话中紧接问题之后的答语,而且一般不会有同音或近音词的干扰,因此对于这类题目答案的基本原则就是"听到什么选什么"。

【例2】 (07-6-Conversation Two-25)

【预览选项】	【边听边记】
[A] Data collection.	W: What's your line of business, Mr. Johnson?
[B] Training consultancy.	M: We are a training consultancy.

［C］Corporate management.

［D］Information processing.

25. What is the man's line of business?

【解析】选［B］。细节题。女士的提问即为本题的提问,答案就在男士接下来的回答中。女士问男士 What's your line of business(做哪一行),男士回答说他们是 a training consultancy(一家培训咨询公司),由此可知答案为［B］。

技巧三:留意重复率较高的词或短语

对话的主要内容理所当然会得到说话人的强调,而一个非常重要、也是非常明显的强调方式就是重复,而且重复的词语往往能够揭示对话的主题。因此,对那些对话双方多次提到的词语或内容应进行重点记忆。

【例3】   (710 分样卷-Conversation Two-22)

【预览选项】	【边听边记】
［A］The latest developments of an armed rebellion in Karnak. ［B］The fall of Karnak's capital city into the hands of the rebel forces. ［C］The epidemic that has just broken out in the country of Karnak. ［D］The peace talks between the rebels and the government in Karnak.	W: … bring you live up-to-date coverage on the civil unrest in the newly formed country of Karnak … M: … , rebel forces launched the biggest offensive against the ruling government in the 18-month conflict here in this country. … … M: … , rebel forces are also using heavy artillery to pound the positions of government forces around the city center. Rebel forces are closing in, … … M: … this war-torn country … , but that is always a concern if this war lingers on. … 22. What is the news coverage mainly about?

【解析】选［A］。主旨题。主旨题的答案往往在开头或结尾,而本题的答案就出自开头的第一句。选项中的 latest(最新的)对应该句中的 live up-to-date(最新直播),armed rebellion(武装叛乱)对应 unrest(动乱)。另外,对话的主题往往会得到多次重复,因此根据后面多次出现的 rebel forces,conflict,war 等与"叛乱"相关的词语,也可判断本题答案为［A］。

技巧四:留意选项中的要点内容

正确选项往往与原文相似,或是原文的同义表达,而错误选项也往往是根据原文而设,因此应注意提取选项中的关键点,在听音时留意其是否在文中出现并对其相关信息加以记录。

【例4】 *(710分样卷-Conversation Two-25)*

【预览选项】	【边听边记】
[A] Inadequate medical care. [B] Continuing social unrest. [C] Lack of food, water and shelter. [D] Rapid spreading of the epidemic.	W: ... what other pressing concerns are there for the citizens of the city? M: Well, since the beginning of the conflict, starvation, and lack of clean water and adequate shelter have been the biggest daily obstacles facing the citizens of this war-torn country. 25. What is the pressing concern of the citizens of Karnack?

【解析】选[C]。细节题。四个选项中只有[C]项内容在对话中出现,其他三项均未涉及到,故只要抓住对话中 starvation, and lack of clean water and adequate shelter 或其部分内容,即可判断答案为[C]。starvation 意为"饥饿"。

技巧五:留意数字、人名、地名、时间、年代等相关信息

遇到数字、人名、地名、时间、年代时要对相关信息作简要记录,尤其是选项中出现相互类似的概念时,在听音时更应重点留意。

【例5】 *(710分样卷-Conversation Two-24)*

【预览选项】	【边听边记】
[A] Late in the morning. [B] Early in the afternoon. [C] Sometime before dawn. [D] Shortly after sunrise.	M: ... Rebel forces are closing in, and it's feared that they will be able to take the capital building before daybreak where, it is believed, many government officials are holding out. 24. At what time of day do you think this news report is being made?

【解析】选[C]。细节题。根据原文中 ... it's feared that they will ... before daybreak 可知,当时报道的时间应该是在 before daybreak(黎明破晓前)。dawn 相当于 daybreak。

技巧六:注意使用缩略语

作笔记一定要迅速,要想在有限的时间内尽可能比较全面的记录重点信息,使用一定的缩略语和熟悉的符号是十分必要的。

一 利用数学符号

如 equal 写成"=";"≠"表示"unequal";"↑"表示 increase/up;"←"表示 result from/because/since/for/as;"→"表示 lead to/result in/has become/turn into;"↓"表示 decrease/drop/dip/fall;"≈"表示 about/almost;">"表示 more than;"<"表示 less than;"+"表示 include/cover;"–"表示 exclude 等。

二　利用数字和其他固定符号

能用阿拉伯数字或其他固定符号代表的词全部用符号代替，这样既能节约时间，又能避免拼写错误，如：twenty 记作 20；nineteen eighty four 记作 1984；dollar 记作 $；pound 记作£；11 in the morning 记作 11 a. m.；11 in the evening 记作 11 p. m. 等。

三　创造自己的速写符号

在平时的训练中也可以使用和创造一些符合自己习惯的缩略语和符号，如 u 可代表 understand(ing)；m 可代表 minute；s 可代表 second；h 可代表 hour；imp. 可代表 important/importance；nec. 可代表 necessary 等。

Exercise　　　专项练习　　　🎧 边听边记

Conversation One

1. [A] Granny.　　　　　　[B] Grandfather.
   [C] Old people in general.　[D] The younger generation.
2. [A] A widowed mother should live with one of her married children.
   [B] A widowed mother should live with her son instead of her daughter.
   [C] A widowed mother should live alone or go to the nursing home.
   [D] A widowed mother should live with one of her brothers.
3. [A] Because the number of such homes is strictly limited.
   [B] Because the cost is too high for the average family to afford.
   [C] Because old people are strongly opposed to the idea of being sent to nursing homes.
   [D] Because old people prefer living with their children.

Conversation Two

4. [A] Eighty-one years old.
   [B] Eighty-three years, eleven months and fifteen days old.
   [C] Eighty-three years, ten months and fifteen days old.
   [D] Eighty-three years, nine months and fifteen days old.
5. [A] Having lived the longest life in Bristol.
   [B] Having failed the driving test the most times in Britain.
   [C] Having been driving the longest time in Britain.
   [D] Having lived the longest life in Britain.
6. [A] Because she often quarrels with examiners.
   [B] Because she does not allow the examiners sitting by her to

speak.

〔C〕Because she is always late for the exams.

〔D〕Because she cannot drive round corners.

Conversation Three

7. 〔A〕A half day.　　　〔B〕A full day.

〔C〕A day and evening.　　〔D〕A half day and a full day.

8. 〔A〕In the theatre.

〔B〕At the restaurant.

〔C〕In the hotel room.

〔D〕At home.

9. 〔A〕A tour lasting a whole week.

〔B〕A tour lasting a whole day.

〔C〕A tour lasting a day and an evening.

〔D〕A tour lasting two days.

10. 〔A〕70 pounds.　　　〔B〕140 pounds.

〔C〕30 pounds.　　　〔D〕170 pounds.

【答案与解析】

Conversation One

【听力原文】	【答案解析】
W: Now Professor Taylor, in your latest book *Granny Doesn't Live Here Any More*, you suggest that Granny is a problem, and she is going to become even more of a problem in the future. M: Yes, [1] in fact it's not only Granny who is a problem, it's Grandfather, too, and old people in general. W: It seems very sad that parents should give so much of their lives to bringing up their children and then, when they become old, be regarded as a problem. M: Our research was mainly carried out in Britain. [2] In many countries it is still regarded as quite natural that a widowed mother should go to live with one of her married children, but in Britain, certainly during the last thirty or forty years, there has been considerable resistance to this idea. W: And when Granny gets very old, then the situation becomes even worse, doesn't it?	1. What problem are they talking about? 【解析】选〔C〕。细节题。女士认为男士即Taylor教授的书中预示Granny将成为a problem，男士说并不只是Granny，而是old people in general(所有的老年人)都将成为以后的问题。 2. According to the conversation, what is regarded quite natural in many countries? 【解析】选〔A〕。细节题。男士说在许多国家里

M: Yes, as long as old people are able to look after themselves, the system works quite well. Once they can't, everything changes.

W: Well, [3①] presumably a point comes when old people have to go into a nursing home or something similar.

M: [3②] But the number of places in old people's homes provided by the State is strictly limited. There are private nursing homes, but the cost is away out of reach of the average family.

W: And how do you see the situation developing in the future?

M: Well, obviously a lot of money is going to have to be spent. But it's difficult persuading people to do this. There aren't many votes for politicians in providing nursing homes for the elderly.

W: You don't see a reversal of this trend, with Granny going back to live with the family.

M: I think this is most unlikely.

a widowed mother should go to live with one of her married children(守寡的母亲与结了婚的子女居住)是很常见的事。

3. Why can't all the old people be sent to nursing homes run by the state?
【解析】选［A］。细节题。女士说到时候很多老人就不得不去 nursing home(养老院)或类似的地方养老，男士说但这种 old people's homes provided by the state(国立养老院)的数量是 strictly limited(非常有限的)，因此不是所有的老人都能进国立养老院。

Conversation Two

【听力原文】

M: Good evening and welcome to "Interesting Personalities". Tonight we've got a real treat in store for you. We have here in the studio Mrs. Annie Jarman of Bristol. Say hello to the listeners, Mrs. Jarman.

W: Hello.

M: Now Mrs. Jarman is eighty-four years old.

W: [4] Eighty-three years, ten months and fifteen days.

M: Good, well, now that we've got that out of the way. [5] Mrs. Jarman holds the English record for having failed her driving test the most times.

W: I'm still trying.

M: Now precisely how many times have you failed your driving test, Mrs. Jarman?

W: Well, the last attempt last Wednesday brought it up to fifty-seven times.

【答案解析】

4. How old is Mrs. Jarman?
【解析】选［C］。细节题。男士在介绍女士即 Mrs. Jarman 时说，她今年 eighty-four years old，但接下来 Mr. Jarman 纠正说自己是 Eighty-three years, ten months and fifteen days。

5. What kind of record does Mrs. Jarman hold?
【解析】选［B］。细节题。男士说 Mrs.

M: What is the cause of this record number of failures?

W: Bad driving.

M: Yes, but in what way do you drive badly?

W: I hit things. That's the really big problem, but I'm working on that. Also [6]I can't drive round corners. Each time I come to a corner I just drive straight on.

M: And how many examiners have you had in all this time?

W: Fifty-seven.

M: But why do you drive so badly?

W: I blame the examiners. It's all their faults. They don't do their job properly.

M: But they have to tell you where to go, Mrs. Jarman. How long do your tests usually last, Mrs. Jarman?

W: Two or three minutes. They've usually jumped out by then. Except the last one.

M: And how long did that last?

W: Four hours and twenty-five minutes, exactly, from beginning to end. I got on the motorway and as I told you I can't turn right or left, so we didn't stop until I hit a post box just outside London.

Jarman 创下了英国 failed her driving test the most times 的纪录，由此可知 Mrs. Jarman 是英国驾驶执照考试中不过关次数最多的人。

6. Why has she failed all the tests?

【解析】选[D]。细节题。女士说她考试屡次失败是因为她开车技术很烂，她不会 drive round corners(开车拐弯)，每次遇到拐弯处她都是直直开过去了。

Conversation Three

【听力原文】

W: So you have a half day, a full day and a day and evening tour of London?

M: Yes.

W: Well, [7①][9①] perhaps we should take the full day and evening tour. Give my children the opportunity to see everything.

M: Won't that be a bit tiring for them?

W: [7②] Yes. It's better if we don't include them on the evening part.

M: Not the theatre and the dinner entertainment?

W: Yes. Now, can you tell me what the cost will be?

M: [9②][10①] For the full tour? Seventy pounds per head.

【答案解析】

7. How long does the woman want to take tour of London for her children?

【解析】选[B]。推断题。女士开始说要选择 the full day and evening tour，但是怕孩子们太累，于是最后决定不让孩子们参加 evening part，为他们选择了 a full day tour。

W: [10②] So that would be 140 pounds for myself and my husband. What about the children?

M: We have half price for children and if they're not going to the theatre or the dinner, we could let them have the full day tour for thirty pounds each.

W: That's fine. I mean, what will we be actually seeing?

M: Well, here's a brochure for you to read, but I can quickly run through the main items of the tour with you.

W: Yes...

M: Then you're taken to see the Changing of the Guard and you'll see Buckingham Palace ...

W: Oh, that sounds perfect.

M: Now in the afternoon, you'll be taken to London Zoo.

W: Oh.

M: And from there we just go round the corner to Madame Tussaud's to see the waxworks and after that right next door to the London Planetarium, where you'll see the stars simulated by laser beams.

W: What a full day!

M: Yes, we do let you have a couple of hours' rest before taking you on to the theatre and dinner in the evening.

W: [8]Oh, that's good. I'll be able to get the children off to bed or settled down watching television or something. Well, that sounds marvellous.

8. In the evening, where will the children be?

【解析】选 [D]。细节题。女士说她晚上会先 get the children off to bed (哄孩子睡觉), 或让他们看会儿电视什么的, 由此可知孩子们晚上会呆在酒店房间里。

9. What does the full tour mean?

【解析】选 [C]。细节题。女士说她想选 the full day and evening tour, 之后询问价格是多少, 男士回答说 for the full tour, 价格是每人 70 英镑, 由此可推知, the full tour 应该指的就是 the full day and evening tour, 即 a tour lasting a day and an evening。

10. How much will the full tour cost for each of the adults?

【解析】选 [A]。细节题。男士说 for the full tour, 价格是 seventy pounds per head, 女士说那她和她丈夫共交 140 pounds, 由此可知每个成年人应交 70 pounds。

综 合 训 练

Exercise 1

边听边记

Conversation One

19. [A] Agent and customer.   [B] Husband and wife.
    [C] Boss and secretary.   [D] Interviewer and interviewee.
20. [A] A clerk in the personnel department.
    [B] Manager and Head Waiter.
    [C] Waiter.
    [D] Assistant manager.
21. [A] At home.   [B] In Hotel Scandinavia.
    [C] In this restaurant.   [D] At her friend's home.

Conversation Two

22. [A] Because she wanted a job as a waitress.
    [B] Because King Hotel dining room was closing down.
    [C] Because she wanted more time to study.
    [D] Because her pay was too low.
23. [A] At weekends.   [B] On weekdays.
    [C] Late in the week.   [D] On Thursday,Friday and Sunday.
24. [A] The manager would contact Linda Brown before May 1st.
    [B] Linda Brown got the job.
    [C] The manager promised Linda Brown a pay rise.
    [D] The manager was not very satisfied with Linda Brown.
25. [A] $1.80 an hour.   [B] $18 an hour.
    [C] $18 a day.   [D] $80 a day.

Exercise 2

Conversation One

19. [A] English.   [B] Biology.
    [C] Math.   [D] Spanish.
20. [A] She likes it very much. [B] She doesn't think it is useful.
    [C] She likes only biology. [D] She doesn't like it.

21. ［A］Driving a cab.　　　［B］Driving a bus.
　　［C］Working at the gas station.［D］Working at restaurant.

边听边记

Conversation Two

22. ［A］They are designed to measure children's intelligence.
　　［B］They are intended to test linguistic and numerical skills.
　　［C］They are designed to test why some children perform better at school.
　　［D］They are intended to find out why some children are not appreciated.

23. ［A］Because they are not brighter than others.
　　［B］Because they don't have good education.
　　［C］Because they are not doing the things they are best at.
　　［D］Because they are not duly encouraged in life.

24. ［A］They don't have proper education.
　　［B］They don't get enough encouragement.
　　［C］Their parents are not responsible.
　　［D］They are not good with words and numbers.

25. ［A］A child with a high IQ will be successful when he grows up.
　　［B］Some children's abilities can not be easily measured.
　　［C］A child should be judged on his IQ level.
　　［D］Being happy in life is being good at everything.

Exercise 3

Conversation One

19. ［A］To get the government to restore the funding to the organization.
　　［B］To raise awareness of the importance of recycling.
　　［C］To force the government to change its mind over a decision.
　　［D］To increase funding to the organization.

20. ［A］Sign a petition.
　　［B］Dump garbage on the city lawn.
　　［C］Put their garbage in the street.
　　［D］Hold a demonstration.

21. ［A］The station will play music.
　　［B］The host will take in caller.
　　［C］The station will have another guest.

[D] The host will continue asking questions.

Conversation Two

22. [A] Italy.　　　　　　[B] Portugal.
    [C] Costa Rica.　　　　[D] Spain.

23. [A] She has difficulty in finding a suitable hotel.
    [B] She has never been abroad.
    [C] She can't book tickets for her family now.
    [D] She has to take her children with her.

24. [A] It should be on the beach.
    [B] It should have a swimming pool.
    [C] It should be quiet.
    [D] It should be in the downtown.

25. [A] Joan has decided not to stay in that hotel.
    [B] Joan has decided to use the tent.
    [C] The ad turned out to be a lie.
    [D] Charles advises Joan to have a try.

答案与解析

Exericise 1

Conversation One

【听力原文】	【答案解析】
M: Good evening, Miss Malinen. Won't you sit down?	19. What's the relation-
W: Good evening. Thank you.	ship between the two
M: Now, I notice you left the Hotel Scandinavia in 1980. What are you now?	speakers? 【解析】选[D]。推断
W: I'm spending a few months going over my English and getting to know the country better.	题。对话结尾处,男士 问女士还想了解这份工 作其他方面的什么问
M: And you want to work in England too. Why?	题,女士回答说她想知
W: I like getting some experience abroad, and I like England and English people.	道 what sort of salary were you thinking of paying?
M: Good. Now I see from the information you sent me that you've worked in your last employment for nearly four years. Was that a large restaurant?	(工作薪水多少),由此可 知他们应当是 interviewer 和 interviewee 的关系。
W: Medium-size for Finland, about forty tables.	20. Who is the man?
M: I see. Well, you'd find it rather different here. Ours is much smaller restaurant, we have only ten tables.	【解析】选[B]。细节题。

【听力原文】	【答案解析】
W: That must be cosy. M: [20]I'm the Restaurant Manager and Head Waiter, so you'd be working directly under me. You'd be responsible for looking after five tables normally, bringing in the dishes from the kitchen, serving the drinks, and if necessary looking after the bills. So you'd be kept pretty busy. W: I'm used to that. In my last position we were busy most of the time. M: Good. [19①]Now, is there anything you'd like to ask about the job? W: [19②] Well, the usual question—what sort of salary were you thinking of paying? M: We pay our waiters forty pounds a week, and [21] you would get your evening meal free.	对话中男士明确说他是 the Restaurant Manager and Head Waiter(饭店经理兼领班)。 21. Where is the woman going to have her dinners? 【解析】选[C]。推断题。对话中女士问起自己的薪水时，男士说每周付给她40英镑，另加 evening meal free(免费晚餐)，由此可知女士将在她应聘成功的这家饭店吃晚饭。

Conversation Two

【听力原文】	【答案解析】
M: Miss Linda Brown, right? W: Yes, that's right. M: Please take a seat. W: Thank you. M: So you're interested in a job as a waitress. W: That's right. I saw your sign in the window asking for a part-time waitress. M: Mm, have you worked as a waitress before? W: Yes. I've worked as a waitress for three years at several different restaurants. M: I see. Are you working now? W: Yes, at the King Hotel dining room on Park Avenue. M: They have a very nice dining room there. Why do you want to leave? W: [22] Because I can't work full time at the moment. I'm taking some courses at university and need more time to study. M: I see. What days are you available?	22. Why did Linda Brown want to change her job? 【解析】选[C]。细节题。女士即 Linda Brown 说她离开那家公司的原因是自己目前无法 work full time(做全职工作)，因为她在大学选修了几门课，need more time to study(需要更多的时间学习)。 23. On what days did the interviewer say that they needed help? 【解析】选[C]。细节题。男士即 interviewer 说他们要找的人要能在 late in the week(一周的

【听力原文】	
W: I'm free all day Thursday and Friday, Saturday and Sunday. M: That suits us very well actually. [23] We're looking for someone who can help us late in the week when we get very busy. That's Thursday afternoon, Friday afternoon and evening as well as Saturday. The restaurant is closed on Sunday. W: That's fine with me. M: [24①] When can you start? W: Is the first of next month all right with you? M: That's fine. The first of May. Yes, that's good. [24②] [25] By the way, you'll get ＄1.80 an hour, with tips, of course. W: [24③] Good. Thank you very much.	后几天时间)工作,因为餐馆那个时候会很忙。 24. What was the result of the interview? 【解析】选[B]。推断题。对话最后,男士问女士 When can you start?(什么时候能开始工作),并且他们还谈了薪水的问题,女士最后表示感谢,显然女士即 Linda Brown 是被这家公司录用了。 25. How much money will the manager pay Linda Brown? 【解析】选[A]。细节题。对话最后,男士告诉女士她的薪水是＄1.80 an hour(每小时1.80美元)。

Exericise 2

Conversation One

【听力原文】	【答案解析】
M: Nancy, what classes are you taking this semester? W: I'm not sure yet. I want to take two English courses and maybe Spanish. And I'll probably have to take math. M: [19①] Aren't you going to take biology? That's a required class you know. W: [19②] I already took it. No more science classes for me. [20] Science just isn't something I like. What are you taking? M: Only biology and English. W: How come you're only taking two classes? M: I have to work this year. I couldn't get a student loan so I don't have enough money to study full-time. W: What kind of job are you going to get? M: That's the problem. I've tried all the gas stations and the restaurants, but nothing. [21] I'm going to try a few cab companies tomorrow. I like to drive.	19. What class won't Nancy take this semester? 【解析】选[B]。细节题。男士问女士是否准备 take biology(选修生物课程),女士即 Nancy 回答说她 already took it(已经修过了),由此可知她不会修的课程就是生物课。 20. How does Nancy feel about science? 【解析】选[D]。细节题。对话中女士明确说 Science just isn't something I like(她不喜欢自然科学课程)。 21. What kind of job will the man try to get?

W: My brother's a bus driver. He likes it.

M: Well, I'll see what happens tomorrow. By the way, have you seen Dave yet? He just got back yesterday.

W: Oh? Where did he go? I hadn't heard that he was going anywhere.

M: He went to Europe. He was there for three weeks.

W: Well, how did he like it?

M: He said Germany was nice but he didn't care for the rest of it. He said he didn't like France or Spain at all.

W: I went to Spain once and I really liked it. But the place I like most was Switzerland. I spent two weeks visiting my uncle there. It's great.

M: I hope that I can get to Europe someday.

【解析】选[A]。细节题。男士说他第二天会去 cab companies（出租汽车公司），试试看能不能找到工作，因为他喜欢驾车，由此可知他将会去试试看能不能找到一份开出租车的工作。

Conversation Two

【听力原文】	【答案解析】
W: Why is it that some children perform much better than others at school?	22. What is the basic purpose of IQ tests?
M: Obviously, certain children are brighter than others, but it's not as simple as that. A lot of emphasis is placed on intelligence measured by tests.	【解析】选[B]。细节题。男士明确提到 IQ tests 的目的是测试 linguistics and numerical skills（语言和数字运算能力）。
W: [22①] The so-called IQ tests?	
M: Yes. [22②] Basically they are intended to test linguistics and numerical skills, so some children are bound to suffer. This is very unfortunate. A child with an average IQ may turn out to be successful when he grows up.	23. According to the man, why are there so many unhappy adults in the world?
W: What you're saying is that [25] some children have abilities that are not easy to measure, that aren't appreciated.	【解析】选[C]。细节题。男士认为很多成年人不快乐的原因是他们没有 doing the things they are best at。
M: Precisely. And if these skills are not spotted sufficiently early, they cannot be developed. [23] That's why, in my view, there are so many unhappy adults in this world. They are not doing the things they are best at.	24. Why can't some children do well in school examinations?
W: I see.	【解析】选[D]。推断题。男士说在学校里，只有那些擅长语言和数字的孩子才可能取得好成绩，由此可知那
M: But at school, [24] only those children who are	

【听力原文】	【答案解析】
good with words and numbers, they probably do well in school examinations. W: Right. Is there anything a parent can do to help in this case? M: Yes. In my opinion, a child should be judged by his individual talents. After all, being happy in life is putting your skills to good use, no matter what they are.	些不擅长语言和数字的孩子成绩不好。 25. What can we learn from this interview? 【解析】选[B]。细节题。女士说有些孩子的能力 are not easy to measure（很难测量），男士非常同意这个观点。

Exericise 3

Conversation One

【听力原文】	【答案解析】
M: Today, our guest on Student Radio West Mark is student organizer and well-known Biology major and activist, Marcy Reynolds. Marcy, welcome to the show. First, can you give us some ideas about your work? W: Well, [19] we've been trying to pressure the local government to resume funding of its recycling center. As you may know, they cut off funding to the main plan Our group called Restoring Recycling Radars (or RRR) for funding. We hope to succeed in not only getting the funding restored, but also increased. M: Since you have repeatedly said in the previous interview in the newspaper that the city government doesn't care about this. So my question is: why would they listen to your group? W: Well, we've been advocating these issues for a long time and now the council is pretty split on this issue. So a push in the right direction couldn't hurt. M: Any light, so far, at the end of the tunnel? W: Plenty. [20] The council wasn't happy about the garbage we dumped on the City Hall lawn, but they got the message. Now, they're reviewing their actions and voting tomorrow in a special council meeting. M: Well, thanks for that briefing and it was a pleasure once	19. What is the goal of the organization? 【解析】选[C]。细节题。女士说政府削减了对 recycling center（循环中心）的投资，她所在的组织试图对政府施加压力以促使政府 resume（继续）对这一项目投资。 20. What form of protest did the RRR use? 【解析】选[B]。细节题。女士说政府对她所在组织在 the City Hall lawn 上 dumped garbage（倾倒垃圾）的行为非常不满，由此可知她们采取的抗议形式就是在市政厅草坪上倒垃圾。 21. What will happen after the show? 【解析】选[A]。推断题。对话结尾处，男士说不要走

once again to talk with you. [21] Stay tuned now for some fine tunes from our DJ …	开，接下来是由 DJ 带来的 fine tunes(美妙金曲)，由此可知电台接下来将要播放歌曲。

Conversation Two

【听力原文】	【答案解析】
W: Charles, I want to ask if you know anything about hotels on Costa Brava. M: What? No, I'm afraid I can't be much help to you there. W: Well, it's just that [22] we've been thinking of taking the family to Spain this summer and [23] at this rather late stage we're trying to organize ourselves a suitable hotel. But I thought that you'd been to the Costa Brava. M: It's certainly a bit late. Have you looked at the ads? W: Well, yes. As a matter of fact, I was reading one ad only this morning in the Sunday paper, which sounded marvelous. M: For a hotel? W: Yes. Just outside Barcelona. [24] It said that this hotel was right on the beach, and that's essential as far as we're concerned. M: I know just how it is. W: And all the rooms have balconies facing the sea and overlooking the beach. M: Expensive? W: No. That was the remarkable thing about it. You know, even allowing for a bit of exaggeration in the ad, it seemed to have a lot to offer. M: Which is unlikely with yours, from the sound of it. W: Well, yes, but you can never tell, can you? And the food's good. M: Of course. [25] The only way to find out for certain is to go and try it. And that's taking rather a risk. W: Yes, I agree with you.	22. Where is Joan's family going to spend summer? 【解析】选 [D]。细节题。女士即 Joan 说这个夏天她准备 taking the family to Spain。 23. What is the problem that Joan has? 【解析】选 [A]。细节题。女士即 Joan 说她想订 a suitable hotel(一个舒适的酒店)，由此可知 Joan 面临的问题是要找一间舒适的酒店。 24. What is essential to Joan about a hotel? 【解析】选 [A]。细节题。女士即 Joan 说她中意的酒店一定要 right on the beach(在海滩边)，这是她最关心的。 25. Which of the following statements is true? 【解析】选 [D]。细节题。对话最后，男士(Charles)对女士(Joan)说验明真相的唯一办法就是 try(去尝试)，也就是说男士建议女士去 have a try。

短文理解高分必备

Part 4

本篇主要涉及短文理解的题型特征和出题重点，以及解答短文理解题时应采用的解题步骤和解题技巧，并配有专项练习和综合训练题，从而使考生对短文理解实现全面的掌握。

题型特征

短文理解部分一般由3篇短文构成,长度大约在240—260词之间,每篇短文后有3—4道题,共10道题。

短文理解内容、题材比较丰富,考生需要了解记忆的信息相对较多,考生往往抓不住中心,记不住要点,不知全文的关键所在,因此难度相对而言较大。考生要想取得比较好的成绩,一是要强化听、记的能力,二是要扩大自己的知识面,熟悉短文理解常考的题材,这对提高短文听力理解能力非常有用。

一、常考题材

一 人物故事类

这类题材主要涉及人物的生平事迹、工作和生活经历、奇闻趣事等。这类题材还可以分为大人物类和小人物类。大人物类的文章主要介绍大人物的生卒年月、性格特点、主要事迹、经历或贡献等;小人物类的文章主要介绍小人物的性格特点、生活和工作经历以及人生感悟等。

例如:07年6月的Passage Two(一个由车祸中舍已救人行为引发的故事),06年12月老题型的Passage One(最早的美国装饰艺术品收藏家之一)和06年6月的Passage One(一名想成为理疗师的女孩)等。

二 社会问题类

这类题材主要涉及妇女问题、移民问题、残疾人问题、环境污染、动物保护、能源短缺、社会安全和暴力犯罪等。

例如:06年12月老题型的Passage Three(残疾人问题),03年9月的Passage Three(移民问题)和03年6月的Passage One(一次防洪演习)等。

三 社会习俗类

这类题材主要涉及饮食习惯、礼仪差异、婚丧嫁娶的风俗、文化冲击、文化交流以及各地风土人情等。

例如:07年6月Passage One(美国人如何看待新年),05年1月Passage Two(亚洲文化与美国文化的不同)和04年6月Passage Two(Yuppies的另类饮食习惯——食用昆虫)等。

四 科学技术类

这类题材主要涉及自然现象、自然灾害、生态平衡、生物科学、技术发展、医学进步、人体保健、太空探索以及海洋资源等。

例如：06 年 6 月 Passage Three（动物如何自我保护），05 年 1 月的 Passage Three（药物的副作用）和 04 年 1 月的 Passage Two（如何保护牙齿）等。

五　工作生活类

这类题材主要涉及日常工作、日常生活、交通出行、朋友往来、休闲旅行、购物消费和社会服务等。

例如：07 年 6 月 Passage Three（美国人的工作状态），04 年 6 月的 Passage Three（银行开设上网服务）和 04 年 1 月的 Passage One（金门大桥的渡船）等。

六　文化教育类

这类题材主要涉及学校教育、法律法规等，内容主要是关于美国社会的文化教育现象。

例如：06 年 12 月新题型的 Passage Two（帮助文盲学会读写），06 年 12 月老题型的 Passage Two（语言的发展趋势）和 05 年 12 月的 Passage Three（学校处理逃学问题的对策）等。

除了以上六种常考题材外，短文理解偶尔还会涉及到美国的政府政策、法规惯例等方面的题材，如 05 年 12 月的 Passage Two（美国的国旗法）。

考生在平时复习时除了注意扩充各类题材的相关知识以外，还要注意积累与各题材相关的词汇和短语，这样才能在考试时更加迅速、准确地理解短文内容。

二、考查方式

短文理解主要考查考生对文章大意、中心思想、重要细节的理解与领会；对短文中的某一事实或人物相关的细节内容的辨认能力；以及根据所获取的相关信息对文中的某些细节进行联想、判断和推理的能力。

一　主旨题

主旨题在一套考题中所占比例很小，一般只有一道，有时甚至没有。但这并不意味着理解短文的主旨大意不重要，事实上，只有把握了原文的大意才能更加深入透彻地理解细节。

常见的提问方式如：

What is the speaker mainly talking about?

What message does the speaker wish to convey?

What does the story try to tell us?

二　细节题

细节题主要考查对短文的细节内容的辨认或对其确切含义的理解，主要是针对短文中的人名、地名、时间、原因、数据、目的、年代等细节内容进行提问。细节题是六级考试中出现频率最高的一种题型，10 道题中通常占 5 道以上，有时多至8、9 道。

常见的提问方式如：

Why did many countries think highly of Gabriela Mistral?

What protects the sea dragon from the meat eater's attack?

Which reason for student's absences is discussed in great detail?

三　推断题

推断题主要考查考生对文章重要细节引申含义的理解及考生的推理判断能力，这类题难度相对较大，因为它不仅要求考生在听音过程中捕捉到相关的细节信息，还要求考生对这些细节进行深层次的理解和把握。在实际考试中，推断题所占比例时多时少，有时一道都没有，但有时多达5道，而且最近几年有上升的趋势。

常见的提问方式如：

What can be inferred from the passage?

Why did the taxi driver ask the speaker how long he has been in the US?

According to the passage, what type of food or drink is most likely to cause dental decay?

【例1】　　　　　　　　　　　　　　　　　　（06-6-Passage Three）

18. [A] How animals survive harsh conditions in the wild.

　　[B] How animals alter colors to match their surroundings.

　　[C] How animals protect themselves against predators.

　　[D] How animals learn to disguise themselves effectively.

19. [A] Its enormous size.

　　[B] Its plant-like appearance.

　　[C] Its instantaneous response.

　　[D] Its offensive smell.

20. [A] It helps improve their safety.

　　[B] It allows them to swim faster.

　　[C] It helps them fight their predators.

　　[D] It allows them to avoid twists and turns.

【听力原文】	【答案解析】
[18①]Over time animals have developed many ways to stay away from predators. A [18②] predator is an animal that hunts and eats other animals. Hiding is one of the best ways to stay alive. Some animals hide by looking like the places where they live. To see how this works, let's look at the sea dragon. It's a master of disguise.	18. What is the speaker mainly talking about? 【解析】选[C]。主旨题。主旨题的答案往往在短文的开头或结尾,而本题的答案出处就是短文开头的第一句。由该句可知本文主要是讨论many ways to stay

The sea dragon is covered with skin that looks like leaves. [19] The skin helps the dragon look like a piece of seaweed. A hungry meat eater would stay away from anything that looks like seaweed. Other animals stay safe by showing their colors. They want other animals to see them. Scientists call these bright colors warning colors. You have probably seen animals that have warning colors. Some grasshoppers show off their own bright colors. Those colors don't just look attractive; they tell their enemies to stay away. Of course, hungry [18③] predators sometimes ignore the warning. They still go off the grasshopper. If that happens, the grasshopper has a backup of defense. It makes lots of foams. The foams taste so bad that the [18④] predator won't do it again. Color doesn't offer enough protection for some other animals. They have different defenses that help them survive in the wild. Many fish live in groups or schools. [20]That's because of the safety in numbers. At the first sign of trouble, schooling fish swim as close together as they can get. Then the school of fish makes lots of twists and turns. All that movement makes it hard for [18⑤]predators to see individuals in a large group.

stay away from predators, 即 how animals protect themselves against predators(动物如何保护自己免受食肉动物的侵食), 由此可知答案为[C]。另外, 短文中多次出现了 predator 一词, 抓住该词也有助于本题答案的选择。

19. What protects the sea dragon from the meat eater's attack?
【解析】选[B]。推断题。本题的答案不是对话中某个细节的再现, 而是在细节基础上的推理。由文中的 The skin helps the dragon look like a piece of seaweed. 一句可推知, 是 plant-like appearances(像海草的外表)保护了 sea dragon 免遭食肉动物的攻击。

20. According to the passage, why do many fishes stay in group?
【解析】选[A]。细节题。本题的答案是对话中的细节再现。由文中的 That's because of the safety in numbers. 一句可知, 许多鱼 stay in group 是为了 safety(安全)。只要抓住 safety 一词即可确定答案为[A]。

Exercise 专项练习   🎧 边听边记

Passage One

1. [A] We eat more food than primitive people do.
   [B] We eat a great variety of food.
   [C] We eat a lot of food that is very expensive.
   [D] Most food we eat is produced in other countries.
2. [A] It is needed to adjust the temperature of our bodies.
   [B] It is our second need.

∩ 边听边记

[C] We need it to cover our bodies.

[D] Weather is changing all the time.

3. [A] It remains the same for many years.

[B] It can only keep us from the weather.

[C] It depends on a number of conditions.

[D] It is not very important compared with food and clothing.

4. [A] Food and Clothing.

[B] Food—Human Basic Need.

[C] Material Comforts.

[D] Human Basic Needs.

Passage Two

5. [A] Stars usually stick to their own acting styles.

[B] Stars may not be able to speak the local dialect.

[C] Stars may share the audience's attention with the story.

[D] It was not easy for him, a fresh hand, to invite stars to join him.

6. [A] He was born in the early 1970s.

[B] He grew up in Henan province.

[C] He was popular in Henan province.

[D] The story had to do with his own experience.

7. [A] It entered the 2005's Oscar Contest.

[B] It has been welcomed only in China.

[C] It started its production in spring, 2005.

[D] It has been publicly shown in spring, 2005.

Passage Three

8. [A] Because he led his teams to many championships.

[B] Because he set as many as 65 different records.

[C] Because he still played the game after he retired.

[D] Because he didn't stop playing even when he was seriously injured.

9. [A] He lost the final chance to win a championship.

[B] He was knocked out.

[C] He broke a bone in the wrist.

[D] He was awarded with a $1.5 million house.

10. [A] To break the previous records.

[B] To buy a luxury house.

[C] To win one more championship for his team.

[D] To play against the New York team once again.

【答案与解析】

Passage One

【听力原文】	【答案解析】
We can agree with primitive man that[4①] food is a basic need, [1] but we differ from him in our food wants because of the wide variety of food we have available compared with him; we have a wider choice. Take fruit, for example, not only can we enjoy the fruits grown in our country, but because of modern methods of transport and food preservation, we can also enjoy more fruits from foreign countries thousands of miles away, whereas primitive man is limited in his choice to the kinds of fruit which actually grow where he lives. However they differ in satisfying their hunger, primitive and civilized men both experience the basic need for food. The same is true of [4②] the second of our human need. [2] Clothing is necessary to regulate the heat of our bodies. Since we live in a temperate climate we need more clothes than people living in tropic conditions. Likewise, our clothing needs to change with seasons. [3][4③] Shelter, the third of our needs, depends upon the climate, the skill of the builder, one's social position, and the materials available. The simple shelter of primitive man would not do for us, and yet it satisfies his needs. The three-bedroom suburban house of the average family would not be grand enough for a rich family, and yet the modern house contains many of the material comforts which were denied to the Kings and Queens of old.	1. With regard to food, how are we different from the primitive people? 【解析】选[B]。细节题。文章开头提到我们与古代人在食物摄取上有差别是因为我们现在有 wide variety of food（更加丰富的食物品种）可供选择，也就是说，在食品方面，我们不同于古代人的就是 we eat a great wariety of food。 2. Why does clothing need to change with seasons? 【解析】选[A]。细节题。文中明确提到，衣服是用来 regulate（调节）身体的温度的，因此我们需要随季节的变化增减衣物。 3. What can we learn about shelter—our third need? 【解析】选[C]。推断题。文中提到，shelter（住所）会因天气、建造者的技艺、材料等而有所不同，由此可知 shelter 要根据很多情况而定。 4. What is the best title for this passage? 【解析】选[D]。主旨题。文章从始至终分别讲了三个人类最基本的需要：food，clothing，shelter。因此，文章的最佳题目应当是 Human Basic Needs。

Passage Two

【听力原文】	【答案解析】

【听力原文】

Gu Changwei was the first Chinese cinematographer to be nominated for an Oscar, and he is regarded by Zhang Yimou as the best cinematographer in China. Gu was behind the camera for many of Zhang Yimou's famous films including the one that rocketed Zhang to fame: "*Red Sorghum*". And now this master of the visual has taken on his first directing role with the film "*Peacock*". So Gu Changwei has come out from behind the camera into the spotlight.

Gu Changwei is very serious about his directing "*Peacock*". To get the authentic atmosphere, Gu took his film crew to the city of Anyang in central China's Henan province where the story takes place, to shoot the film. [5] He chose all new actors because he didn't want "star" appeal to weaken the power of the story, and he also had his actors trained in the local dialect. For this film Gu has been able to get out from behind the camera to manage every aspect of the film, and to realize his own ideals in movie-making.

"*Peacock*" is about the life of an average family in a small town in Henan province in the late 70s and early 80s. [6] Gu chose this story for his first movie because he grew up during this same period and it struck a chord with him.

"*Peacock*" wrapped up production in June, 2004. At the end of October, 2004, Gu took "*Peacock*" to his Alma Mater, the Beijing Film Academy, one of the most famous film colleges in China, to hold a preview. The film was warmly received by both teachers and students. [7] It's released in China in February, 2005, and entered in Berlin Film Festival at the same time. It has been welcomed greatly abroad.

【答案解析】

5. Why didn't Gu employ "stars" in his film?
【解析】选[C]。细节题。文中提到,顾长卫之所以不使用明星是怕"star"appeal(明星魅力)削减the power of the story(故事本身的吸引力)。

6. Why did Gu choose such a story for his first movie?
【解析】选[D]。细节题。文中提到,顾长卫选择这样的故事作为他的第一部电影是因为他grew up during the same period(成长于同一时代),故事struck a chord with him(引起他内心的共鸣)。

7. What can we learn about the film "*Peacock*" from the passage?
【解析】选[D]。细节题。文章结尾处提到,这部影片is released in China in February,2005(是在2005年2月在国内上映的)。in February ≈ in spring。同时,该影片参加了Berlin Film Festival(柏林电影节),并且welcomed greatly abroad(在国外也受到了极大的好评)。

Passage Three

【听力原文】

Wilt Chamberlain is retired now, but he used to be a famous basketball player. [8] He has set sixty-five different records, and still holds many of them. During the final years of his career, he drew a large salary and became very wealthy. He, even built himself a $1.5 million house. Yet, despite his personal success, he led his teams to only one championship. His teams often won enough games to qualify for the final rounds, but they almost always lost in the finals. As a result, [10] Wilt became determined to win one more championship before he retired.

In 1972, while Wilt was playing against a New York team, he fell down and hit his wrist on the floor. He felt pain immediately and knew that he had hurt himself badly. When a doctor examined Wilt, the doctor confirmed Wilt's fears. [9] The doctor told Wilt that he had broken a bone in the wrist and that he could not play any more.

Wilt ignored his doctor's advice. The next night, with his many fans watching in amazement, he not only played the entire game, but also he was outstanding. His team won the game and the championship. Wilt had his wish—to be a winner one last time.

【答案解析】

8. Why was Wilt Chamberlain considered a famous basketball player?

【解析】选[B]。细节题。文章开头处提到,Wilt Chamberlain(威尔特·张伯伦)创下了65项不同的记录,直到现在还有许多记录未曾被他人打破。选项[B]是原文的细节再现。

9. What happened to Wilt Chamberlain during a match in 1972?

【解析】选[C]。细节题。文中提到,Wilt Chamberlain 在1972年的一场比赛中摔倒在地,医生诊断他 had broken a bone in the wrist(伤到了腕关节的骨头)。

10. What was Wilt Chamberlain determined to do before he retired?

【解析】选[C]。细节题。文中提到,Wilt Chamberlain 所在的篮球队总是能打进决赛,但没能再次夺冠,所以他决定在退役之前要 win one more championship(再赢得一次冠军)。

第二章 出题重点

短文理解的信息量较大,而且问题是在整篇文章之后提出来的,使得考生很难抓住关键信息,记住要点内容。因此,只有熟悉和掌握短文理解的常见出题点,才能在听音时更有针对性,从而更加快速、准确地抓住关键信息。

一、短文首尾处

短文的开头与结尾,尤其是开头,是设题的重点,一般是考查对短文主旨或所讨论话题的把握。短文的主题句一般都出现在开头,而且往往是第一道题的答案出处。而短文的结尾也往往对整篇文章的内容起一个概括和提示的作用,因此同样不可忽视。

【例1】 (05-12-Passage Two-14)

[A] By making laws.	
[B] By enforcing discipline.	Laws have been written to govern the use
[C] By educating the public.	of the American National Flag and to ensure
[D] By holding ceremonies.	proper respect for the flag. …
	14. How do Americans ensure proper respect

【解析】主旨题。本题的设题题眼在短文的开头。

【例2】 (05-1-Passage Two-17)

[A] Getting rich quickly.	… A major difference between American
[B] Distinguishing oneself.	culture and most East Asian cultures is that in
[C] Respecting individual rights.	East Asia, the community is more important than
[D] Doing credit to one's community.	the individual. Most Americans are considered a success when they make a name for themselves.
	17. What is encouraged in American culture according to the passage?

【解析】细节题。本题的设题题眼在短文的结尾。

二、短文中列举或举例处

短文中为说明一个问题,常常会使用列举或进行举例,这些地方往往是考查的重点。因此当听到 such as, for example, for instance, the first, the second 等一类的词语时,应加以留意。

【例3】　　　　　　　　　　　　　　　　　　　　　　　　　　　（03-9-Passage One-11）

| [A] Rally support for their movement.
[B] Liberate women from tedious housework.
[C] Claim their rights to equal job opportunities.
[D] Express their anger against sex discrimination. | ... Women's liberation groups in Britain, for example, have used graffiti to show their anger at the sex discrimination of many advertisements where women's bodies are used to sell goods. ...
11. What do women's liberation groups in Britain do with graffiti? |

【解析】细节题。本题的设题题眼在列举处。

三、短文中逻辑关系处

　　转折处，尤其是 but 之后，不仅是对话题的考查重点，在短文理解中也常常备受关注。另外表示并列、因果、条件等其他逻辑关系的地方往往也是短文理解的出题重点。因此，当短文中出现 as well as, not only ... but also ... , but, however, because, since, so, if, even if/even though 等表示逻辑关系的连接词的时候，需重点关注。

【例4】　　　　　　　　　　　　　　　　　　　　　　　　　　　（04-6-Passage Two-17）

| [A] It will be consumed by more and more young people.
[B] It will become the first course at dinner parties.
[C] It will have to be changed to suit local tastes.
[D] It is unlikely to be enjoyed by most people. | ... But until our attitudes to food change fundamentally, it seems that insect-eaters will remain a select few.
17. What does the speaker say about the future of this type of unusual food? |

【解析】细节题。本题的设题题眼在 but 转折处。

四、短文中强调处

　　强调的地方肯定是短文的重点所在，因此短文中的强调句型以及 especially, particularly 等强调处也是考查的重点之一。

【例5】　　　　　　　　　　　　　　　　　　　　　　　　　　　（02-6-Passage Three-19）

| [A] One of Etna's recent eruptions made many people move away.
[B] Etna's frequent eruptions have ruined most of the local farmland. | ... Let's take Mount Etna for example. It does erupt frequently, but those eruptions are usually minor. ... |

[C] Etna's eruptions are frequent but usually mild. [D] There are signs that Etna will erupt again in the near future.	20. What will people living near Mount Etna do in the face of its eruptions?

【解析】细节题。本题的设题题眼在强调处。

五、短文中比较或对比处

短文中的形容词或副词的比较级和最高级、as … as 同级比较,以及 while,whereas, in contrast, compared with 等引出的对比结构也经常是短文理解的设题题眼之一。

【例6】　　　　　　　　　　　　　　　　　　　　(03-1-Passage One-14)

[A] There were fewer fish in the river. [B] Over-fishing was prohibited. [C] The local Chamber of Commerce tried to preserve fishes. [D] The local fishing cooperative decided to reduce its catch.	… However, my studies indicate that they took fewer fish because there were fewer fish to catch, not because they were trying to preserve fishes … 14. Why was the annual catch of fish in the Biramichi River reduced according to the speaker?

【解析】细节题。本题的设题题眼在比较处。

六、短文中数字信息处

短文中经常会涉及到时间、价格、数量等与数字相关的信息,这些数字以及与这些数字相关的重点信息,常常是短文理解的重要设题题眼之一。

【例7】　　　　　　　　　　　　　　　　　　　　(06-6-Passage Two-17)

[A] She won the 1945 Nobel Prize in Literature. [B] She was the first woman to win a Nobel Prize. [C] She translated her books into many languages. [D] She advised many statesmen on international affairs.	… In 1945, she gained worldwide recognition by winning the Nobel Prize in literature, the first South American to win the prize. 17. How did Gabriela Mistral become famous all over the world?

【解析】细节题。本题的设题题眼在年代处。

七、短文中目的处

短文中涉及目的、目标的地方也经常受出题人的青睐,这类题目的选项多为动词原形或不定式短语。

【例8】 (03-9-Passage One-11)

[A] Rally support for their movement. [B] Liberate women from tedious housework. [C] Claim their rights to equal job opportunities. [D] Express their anger against sex discrimination.	Writing on walls is a way to comment on the world we live in. Women's liberation groups in Britain, for example, have used graffiti to show their anger at the sex discrimination of many advertisements where women's bodies are used to sell goods. 11. What do women's liberation groups in Britain do with graffiti?

【解析】细节题。本题的设题题眼在目的处。

八、短文中定语从句处

短文中的定语从句,尤其是非限制定语从句经常是短文理解的设题题眼之一,定语从句的内容往往就是答案所在或为解题提供重要的信息提示。

【例9】 (新06-12-Passage Three-35)

[A] In areas with few weeds and unwanted plants. [B] In areas with a severe shortage of water. [C] In areas lacking in chemical fertilizer. [D] In areas dependent on imported food.	Scientists say Low Till Farming is becoming popular in South Asia, which is facing a severe water shortage. 35. Where is Low Till Farming becoming popular?

【解析】细节题。本题的设题题眼在定语从句处。

九、短文中 it 形式主语或宾语处

it 常用来代替不定式、动名词短语或从句充当形式主语或形式宾语,这也是短文理解的重要设题题眼之一,题目的答案往往出自 it 所代替的真正主语。

【例10】 (新06-12-Passage One-29)

[A] He grieved to death over the loss of his wife. [B] He committed suicide for unknown reasons. [C] He was shot dead at the age of 40. [D] He died of heavy drinking.	It is said that he was found dead after days of heavy drinking. 29. How did Edgar Allen Poe's life come to an end?

【解析】细节题。本题的设题题眼在形式主语处。

Exercise 专项练习 🎧 边听边记

Passage One

1. [A] They have found cures and prevention for some diseases and learned about others.

   [B] They have founded many health programs for people.

   [C] They have cured people of serious diseases.

   [D] They have learned about other people's diseases.

2. [A] Their companies have a fund for each employee.

   [B] The insurance companies pay for them.

   [C] The government pays some amount of money for them.

   [D] They pay by health plans of the companies and health insurance.

3. [A] People who are in need of help.

   [B] Medical scientists.

   [C] Older people, poor people and people with long-term illness.

   [D] People with diseases like cancer.

Passage Two

4. [A] Residential area and gardens.

   [B] Shopping centers and gardens.

   [C] Parking lots and residential area.

   [D] Shopping centers or parking lots near stadiums or gymnasiums.

5. [A] They have to break into the car.

   [B] Five percent of the cars are left unlocked.

   [C] They sometimes simply get in the car with the keys in the ignition.

   [D] They often knock out the driver and get the car away.

6. [A] Young people who want to ride a car for joy.

   [B] Professionals who need vehicles.

   [C] People who lack money to buy a car.

   [D] People who like excitement.

Passage Three

7. [A] Because flowers are commonly recognized romantic gifts.

   [B] Because flowers are easy to get.

   [C] Because there are too many kinds of flowers.

[D] Because flowers are easy to wither and fall.

8. [A] He will pick one rare kind of flower.

　[B] He will choose the customary red roses.

　[C] He will choose the person's favorite flower.

　[D] He will present the flower in person.

9. [A] Whether the gifts are standard romantic ones or not.

　[B] The present-receiver's taste and the length of the relationship.

　[C] Whether the gifts are expensive or not.

　[D] Whether the gifts are thoughtful or not.

Passage Four

10. [A] About 70%.　　　　[B] Nearly 60%.

　　[C] Almost 50%.　　　[D] About 12%.

11. [A] After research showed health benefits of sports.

　　[B] After people learned sports from magazine covers and postage stamps.

　　[C] After scientific evidence of health benefits of sports was shown on TV ads.

　　[D] After an increasing number of races were held in American cities.

12. [A] Different Forms of Exercise.

　　[B] Exercise—The Road to Health.

　　[C] Scientific Evidence of Health Benefits.

　　[D] Running—A Popular Form of Sport.

【答案与解析】

Passage One

【听力原文】	【答案解析】
Americans are proud of the medical achievements made in their country. [1]Medical scientists have found cures and prevention for such diseases as polio and tuberculosis. They have learned a great deal about cancer and heart disease. American hospitals are the most modern and best-equipped medical facilities in the world. But this degree of excellence has been expensive. Medical costs in the United States are very high. There is no national health	1. What have American medical scientists done? 【解析】选[A]。细节题。本题的设题点在短文开头处。短文开头提到,美国人为他们的医学成就感到自豪,医学科学家已经能够治疗和预防 polio(小儿麻痹症)以及 tuberculosis(肺结核)这样的疾病,同时对癌症和心脏病也有很多的了解。

plan for Americans, yet there are many programs available for this purpose. [2①] Many people have health plans at the companies where they work. Under these plans, the company pays a fixed sum of money regularly into a fund. Then when the employee needs medical help, he can use money from the fund to pay for it. [2②] Other people have health insurance. They pay insurance premiums each month to insurance companies, which then pay for medical expenses when they are needed. [3] The government has health insurance programs for older people, poor people and those with long-term illness. These programs make medical care available to those without their own health insurance.

2. How do Americans pay for health costs?

【解析】选[D]。细节题。本题的设题点在列举处。文中提到,他们通过公司的 health plans(健康计划)和 health insurance(健康保险)来支付医疗费用。

3. Who are helped by government health insurance programs?

【解析】选[C]。细节题。本题的设题点在短文结尾处。短文最后提到政府有健康保险计划来帮助 older people, poor people and those with long-term illness(老年人、穷人和有慢性疾病的人)。

Passage Two

| 【听力原文】 | 【答案解析】 |

Good evening. I know many of you students are the proud owners of your first motor vehicle and this evening I want to talk to you about some of the things you can do to make sure your car or motorbike isn't stolen. I will start with a few facts and figures to put you in the picture. Car theft is a wide spread problem. In this country alone one car is stolen every 32 seconds. That's almost a million cars each year. And of those, 40% are never recovered. And don't think that just because your car might be a bit old and beaten-up looking no one will steal it. Any car can be stolen. Anywhere.

Most thefts occur in residential areas, often the front of the house or even from inside the garage. [4] Some areas that are especially dangerous are shopping centers and parking lots, particularly at sports events.

Most car thieves don't need to break into the car. [5] They usually gain entry through unlocked doors and many times they find the key in the ignition. In fact,

4. What is the place where car theft is most likely to occur?

【解析】选[D]。细节题。本题的设题点在强调处。文中提到,失窃事件大多数发生在 residential areas(住宅区),但是最危险的地方是在 shopping centers(购物中心)、parking lots(停车场),尤其是在举行运动赛事附近的地方。

5. What can we learn on how car thieves commit the crime?

【解析】选[C]。细节题。本题的设题点在并列处。文中提到盗车贼经常能够进入未锁的汽车,并且很多时

one in five stolen cars had the keys left in the car. Isn't that amazing? Twenty percent of drivers left the keys in the ignition of an unlocked car!

[6] Who steals cars? Well, there are basically two kinds of car or bike thieves: joy riders aged about 15 to 21, and professionals. This last group usually needs less than one minute to break into a locked car and they often steal cars to use in other crimes such as robberies. You are much less likely to get your car back if it's stolen by a professional, and if it's stolen by a joy rider chances are it'll be a wreck when you do get it back. Joy riders have a very high accident rate.

候会发现 the key in the ignition(汽车钥匙就在发动机上)。

6. Who usually steal cars?
【解析】选[A]。细节题。本题的设题点在列举处。文中提到盗车贼有两大类，一类是 joy riders aged about 15 to 21(喜欢驾车的年轻人)，另一类是 professionals(专业盗车贼)。

Passage Three

【听力原文】	【答案解析】

Romantic gifts are often very hard to pick out. These gifts can highly range in price and thought. Some people would prefer a thoughtful gift that is inexpensive while others value expensive gifts. For Americans, standard romantic gifts include flowers, jewelry, and candy. [7]These gifts don't take much thought because they are commonly recognized romantic gifts. However, some people would rather have a present that is personalized than one picked from a list of commonly given presents. For instance, when giving someone flowers, red roses usually signify love and passion. [8] If someone wanted to personalize this gift more, they would choose the person's favorite flower instead of the customary red roses. A thoughtful gift that is sentimental can be just as valuable as the most expensive necklace.

[9] Not only must one take into account a person's taste, the length of the relationship also usually determines the kind of gift one gives. For example, people who have not been dating for very long should stay away from very expensive

7. Why do flowers don't take much thought in American's eyes?
【解析】选[A]。细节题。本题的设题点在因果处。文中提到对于美国人来说，flowers、jewelry(珠宝)和 candy(糖果)本身并不会传递太多的想法，因为人们普遍认为它们是 romantic gifts。

8. What will a person do if he wants to personalize a gift more?
【解析】选[C]。细节题。本题的设题点在条件处。文中提到如果有人想送更加个性化的礼物，他就会送对方 favorite flower 而不是常规的 red roses。

9. What should be taken into account when presenting a gift?
【解析】选[B]。细节题。本题的设题点在并列处。文中提到在挑选礼物时，对方的 taste(品

gifts. Expensive gifts tend to suggest a very serious relationship. Unless this is the intention of the giver, costly presents should be avoided to prevent any misunderstandings about the depth of the relationship.

位）和 the length of the relationship(友谊时间的长短)决定了该送什么样的礼物。

Passage Four

【听力原文】

America is a country on the move. In unheard numbers, people of all ages are [12①] exercising their ways to better health. According to the latest figures, [10]59 percent of American adults exercise regularly—up 12 percent from just two years ago and more than double the figure of 25 years ago. Even non-exercisers believe they would be more attractive and confident if they were more active.

It is hard not to get the message. The virtues of physical fitness are shown on magazine covers, postage stamps, and television ads for everything from beauty soaps to travel books. [11]Exercise as a part of daily life did not catch on until the late 1960s when research by military doctors began to show the health benefits of doing regular physical exercises. Growing publicity for races held in American cities helped fuel a strong interest in the ancient sport of running. Although running has leveled off in recent years as Americans have discovered equally rewarding—and sometimes safer—forms of exercise, such as walking and swimming, running remains the most popular form of exercise.

As the popularity of [12②]exercise continues to mount, so does scientific evidence of its [12③] health benefits. The key to fitness is exercising the major muscle groups vigorously enough to approximately double the heart rate and keep it

【答案解析】

10. According to the passage, what was the percentage of American adults doing regular physical exercises two years ago? 【解析】选[C]。推断题。本题的设题点在数字处和比较处。文中提到,最新数字表明,定期锻炼的 American adults 的比率是59%,比前两年 up 12 percent (增长了12%),由此可知两年前定期锻炼的 American adults 的比率是47%,不到50%。

11. When did a growing interest in sports develop? 【解析】选[A]。细节题。本题的设题点在时间状语处。文中提到,作为 daily life 的一部分,exercise 直到20世纪60年代才 catch on (流行)起来,那时 military doctors 所做的 research 表明经常锻炼身体 show the health benefits(有益健康)。

12. Which of the following would be the best title for the passage? 【解析】选[B]。主旨题。文章开头提到,各年龄段的人都通过 exercising 来 better health (改善身体状况),接着又反复提到 exercise,还提到 exercise 有 health

doubled for 20 to 30 minutes at a time. Doing such [12④] physical exercises three times or more a week will produce considerable [12⑤] improvements in physical health in about three months.

benefits, 改善了人们的 physical health, 由此可知全文都是围绕锻炼对人身体健康的益处展开的。

解 题 步 骤

听力短文理解相对来说信息量较大,听的过程中不仅要求考生要捕捉到具体的语言细节,还要结合自己的知识去分析和归纳,从语篇上对短文进行整体性把握和理解。因此,掌握科学有效的解题步骤是十分必要的。

第一步:浏览选项,推测主题。

根据各题选项中出现的相同或相关词语,推测出短文的大致主题,这样可以更容易、更准确地理解短文内容。

第二步:推测问题,确定听音重点。

很多选项都有比较明显的特点,或者使用某种专门的表达形式,如均为动词原形或均为人物角色等;或者含有一些标志性的词语,如均含有 should(很可能是针对建议提问)或均含有描述某人性格或某事特点的词语。通过这些选项特点及选项内容,我们便可以推测问题可能考查的核心内容,从而在听音时更有针对性。

第三步:听音时迅速记录关键信息。

听音时,要重点关注短文的开头和结尾部分,另外要留意与选项相关的信息,结合选项要点对关键信息加以记录或注释。

第四步:结合问题和笔记得出答案。

结合第二步分析,搞清问题是针对什么进行提问的,再根据前面抓往的信息,对号入座,得出答案。

【例】   (06-6-Passage One)

11. [A] Social work.   [B] Medical care.
    [C] Applied physics.   [D] Special education.

12. [A] The timely advice from her friends and relatives.
    [B] The two-year professional training she received.
    [C] Her determination to fulfill her dream.
    [D] Her parents' consistent moral support.

13. [A] To get the funding for the hospitals.
    [B] To help the disabled children there.
    [C] To train therapists for the children there.
    [D] To set up an institution for the handicapped.

第一步:浏览选项,推测主题。

预览三道题各选项,由 medical care(医疗护理),hospitals,以及 therapists(治

疗专家)可推测本文可能与医疗工作有关;而由 special education
(特殊教育),disabled(残疾的)和 handicapped(残疾的)可推测本文还可能与残疾
人特殊教育有关,但12、13 题各选项并没有涉及到任何有关教育的问题。因此综
合来看,本文主题很可能是与残疾人医疗工作有关。

第二步 推测问题,确定听音重点。

11 题四个选项均为某一学科领域,由第一步的主题分析可初步判断本题答案
可能为[B],听音时再确认具体是哪个领域。

12 题选项特点表明本题很可能是关于影响她做某种决定的因素(friends and
relatives, parents, training, determination)。[A]、[C]、[D]都是来自"人"的主观
因素,只有[B]是客观因素,故可初步排除。听音时主要判断是来自"谁"的因素。

13 题选项均为不定式形式表明本题是考查做某事的目的或原因。[A]是有
关资金问题,偏离主题,可初步排除。听音时需留意以下要点:help disabled
children;train therapists;set institution for handicapped。

第三步 听音时迅速记录关键信息。

听力原文如下:

> Born and raised in central Ohio, I'm a country girl through and through. [11]
> I'm currently studying to become a physical therapist, a career path that marks a
> greater achievement for me. At Ohio State University, admission into the physical
> therapy program is intensely competitive. I made it pass the first cuts the first year
> I applied, but was turned down for admission. I was crushed, because for years I
> have been determined to become a physical therapist. I received advice from
> friends and relatives about changing my major and finding another course for my
> life. I just couldn't do it. I knew I could not be as happy in another profession.
> [12] So I stilled myself, began to work seriously for another year and reapplied.
> Happily I received notice of my admission. Later, I found out that less than 15%
> of the applicant had been offered positions that year. Now in the first two years of
> professional training, I couldn't be happier with my decision not to give up on my
> dream. My father told me that if I wanted it badly enough, I would get in. Well,
> Daddy, I wanted it. So there.
>
> After graduation, I would like to travel to another country, possibly a Latin
> American country and [13] work in a children's hospital for a year or two. So many
> of the children there are physically handicapped but most hospitals don't have the
> funding to hire trained staff to care for them properly. I would like to change
> that somehow.

第四步 结合问题和笔记得出答案。

11. What is the speaker's field of study?

【解析】本题是问说话者研究的领域是什么。根据短文中" studying to become a

physical therapist"可知说话人目前在学习成为一名理疗师,而
physical therapist 明显属于 medical care 的范畴,故答案为[B]。

12. According to the speaker, what contributed to her admission to Ohio State University?

【解析】本题是问说话者被俄亥俄州立大学录取的原因是什么。根据短文中"So I stilled myself, began to work seriously for another year and reapplied"可以知道说话人继续努力,矢志不渝地为实现自己的梦想而奋斗,故答案为[C]

13. Why does the speaker want to go to a Latin American country?

【解析】本题是问说话者想去拉美国家的原因是什么。根据短文中"work in a children's hospital for a year or two. So many of the children there are physically handicapped but most hospitals don't have the funding to hire trained staff to care for them properly. I would like to change that somehow."可知这是说话人帮助拉美贫困国家和地区的残疾儿童的意愿,故答案为[B]。

Exercise　　　　　专项练习　　　🎧 边听边记

Passage One

1. [A] People with light colored skin, hair or eyes.
   [B] People with dark colored skin, hair or eyes.
   [C] People with a history of sunburns early in life.
   [D] People with a family history of skin cancer.

2. [A] Colthes the weave of whose material is dense, and color is light.
   [B] Clothes the weave of whose material is loose, and color is dark.
   [C] Clothes which is wet, and whose material is bleached cotton.
   [D] Clothes which is dry, and whose material is natural cotton.

3. [A] Wear wet swimsuit and sunglasses.
   [B] Put on a swimsuit which can prevent sunrays.
   [C] Put on a thick amount sunscreen on all areas of skin that will get sun.
   [D] Don't put on sunscreen.

Passage Two

4. [A] Once a week.　　　　[B] Twice a week.
   [C] Once a month.　　　[D] Twice a month.

5. [A] No one.　　　　　　[B] One young man.
   [C] His son.　　　　　　[D] Mathew.

6. [A] Because that was how he liked it.
   [B] Because he wanted to show the hairdresser his dissatisfaction.
   [C] Because he was used to the new hairstyle.
   [D] Because he liked to be different from others.

Passage Three

🎧 边听边记

7. [A] Club members.　　[B] College freshmen.

[C] Photographers.　　[D] Film fans.

8. [A] Go and see films on video.

[B] See documentaries on sporting events.

[C] Watch news about campus life.

[D] Attend a video-making lesson.

9. [A] Paying less money to use all the equipment.

[B] Taking video films back to home.

[C] Paying no membership fee.

[D] Paying less for video tapes.

Passage Four

10. [A] Bring a bouquet of flowers when you go to the party.

[B] Send a bouquet of flowers afterwards with a thank-you note.

[C] Bring a bottle of wine instead of a bouquet of flowers.

[D] Bring a bouquet of flowers and a bottle of wine.

11. [A] If someone is dead, send carnations.

[B] If someone is ill in hospital, send carnations.

[C] If you are invited to a dinner party, send red roses to the hostess.

[D] If you are in love with someone, send red roses.

12. [A] How to hold a dinner party.

[B] How to send flowers.

[C] Good manners at a French dinner party.

[D] Different countries have different manners.

【答案与解析】

Passage One

【听力原文】	【答案解析】
Skin cancer is one of the most common forms of cancer. The risk increases in summer because ultraviolet rays from the sun are the main cause of skin cancer. Tanning beds can also be high in UV radiation. Anyone can get skin cancer, [1] but people with light colored skin, hair or eyes are at greatest risk. A history of sunburns early in life also increases the risk. So does a family history of	1. Who doesn't easily get skin cancer? 【解析】选[B]。推断题。文中提到,有 light colored skin, hair or eyes 的人 at greatest risk(危险最大),由此可推断,不容易得 skin cancer 的人应该有 dark colored skin, hair or

skin cancer. The sooner skin cancer is found the easier it is to treat. The two most common forms of skin cancer are called basal cell and squamous cell cancers. They can develop as flat, discolored areas or as raised growths, often with a rough surface. Melanoma is far more dangerous. Melanomas can appear even in areas of the body that do not get a lot of sun. Without early treatment, deadly melanomas can quickly spread within the body. Hats, sunglasses and clothing offer protection from harmful sunrays, but that can depend. [2]Experts say the denser the weave of the material, the less ultraviolet radiation reaches the skin. Also, darker colors may offer more protection, and natural cotton can block more than bleached cotton. When clothing is wet or stretched, however, it lets more UV radiation pass through. Choose sunscreen products and sunglasses designed to protect against both UV-A and UV-B rays. Experts at the Centers for Disease Control and Prevention remind people to put on sunscreen before they go outdoors. UV levels can be high even on cloudy days. [3] Put a thick amount on all areas of skin that will get sun. Put on more sunscreen if you stay in the sun for more than two hours, and after you swim or sweat a lot from activities.

eyes。

2. What kind of clothes is good in preventing sunrays?

【解析】选[D]。细节题。文中提到，the weave of the material（衣料）越denser（密），皮肤受到的 ultraviolet radiation（紫外线辐射）越少；dark colors 能提供更多的保护，而且 natural cotton（天然棉）比 bleached cotton（漂白棉）阻挡的紫外线要多；衣服 wet or stretched（潮湿或被拉平）的时候，皮肤受到的紫外线辐射越多，由此可推知天然棉制衣服和干衣服可以很好地阻挡紫外线。

3. If you go out to swim, what should you do before you go?

【解析】选[C]。细节题。文章结尾处提到外出时要在所有能晒到的地方 put a thick amount 的防晒霜，如果在太阳底下超过 2 个小时和刚 swim 回来或由于运动出汗过多，就应该 put on more sunscreen。

Passage Two

| 【听力原文】 | 【答案解析】 |

Mathew lived in a big city, and [4] his hair was always cut by the same hairdresser. Mathew went to him once a month.

The hairdresser had a very small shop near Mathew's office, and [5] he worked alone, but he always cut Mathew's hair exactly as Mathew liked it, and while he was doing it, the two men talked about football or cricket.

4. How often did Mathew go to the old hairdresser?

【解析】选[C]。细节题。文章开头处明确提到，Mathew 每次都找 the same hairdresser（理发师）理发，去的频率是 once a month（一个月一次）。

But the hairdresser was an old man, and one day, when Matthew was sitting in his chair, and his hair was being cut as usual, the old man said to him, "Mathew, I'm going to be 65 years old next month, so I'm going to retire. I'm going to sell my shop to a young man who wants to be a hairdresser. The shop's being paid for by the young man's father."

Mathew was very sad to hear this, because he enjoyed talking to the old man, and he was also worried that his hair would not be cut as well by the new young man as it had been for so many years by his old friend. He went to the shop again the next month, and the new man was there. He cut Mathew's hair, but he did it very badly.

The next month, Mathew went into the shop again. The young man asked him how he would like his hair cut, and Mathew answered, "Please cut it very short on the right, but leave it as it is on the left. It must cover my ear. On the top, cut all the hair away in the middle, but leave a piece at the front which can hang down to my chin." The young man was very surprised when he heard this. "But sir," he said, [6①]"I can't cut your hair like that!"

[6②]"Why not?" Mathew asked. "That's how you cut it last time."

5. Whom did the old hairdresser work with?
【解析】选[A]。细节题。文中明确提到，这位老理发师 worked alone（单独一个人工作），所以 No one 和他一起工作。

6. Why did Mathew ask the new hairdresser to cut his hair very badly the second time?
【解析】选[B]。推断题。文章结尾处提到，Mathew 第一次去 new hairdresser 的店时，new hairdresser 给 Mathew 理了一个很怪的头型，当 Mathew 第二次去并要求再理一次这样的头发时，new hairdresser 说自己不会 cut your hair like that（不会剪那样的头型），而 Mathew 说 that's how … last time（new hairdresser 上次就是这么剪的），这句话表现出了 Mathew 对 new hairdresser 的 dissatisfaction（不满）。

Passage Three

【听力原文】

Well, [7①]I'd like to tell you something about the video club. It's one of the most popular clubs in the college. We have about 80 members at the moment. The club is one of the oldest in the college. In fact it began in 1981. I've been a member for two years and I've been the President since January. Um, we do three things really. Our main job is to rent films on video and show these in the Student Common Room, [8①]that's on Tuesday and Friday evenings

【答案解析】

7. Who are the listeners of the talk?
【解析】选[B]。推断题。文章一开头就为大家介绍 in the college 影音俱乐部的详细情况并且在短文结尾处欢迎听众入会，由此可推断听众应该是大学里新入学的学生。

8. What can you do at 7:50

at eight o'clock. Then we also make our own video films. We've got two portable cameras, two studio cameras, an editing suite and a TV studio, so we can achieve quite professional results. [8②] And, in addition, we make a short magazine-type program each week. It's about ten minutes long and we show it just before the films on Tuesday and Friday evenings. Just very simple things: College sports results, um, [8③] any college news, things like that. Of course, [9] membership of the club is completely free, and our members can use all the equipment as often as they like to make their own films. But you do have to pay for the video tape! So lastly, [7②] if anyone is interested in joining, please come and see me in the studio any time this week.

every Tuesday and Friday evening?
【解析】选[C]。推断题。文中提到,俱乐部制作的十分钟校园短片将会在每周二和每周五电影放映之前播放,短片内容是关于 any college news(校园内所有新闻)的,而电影是 8 点钟开始,由此可知每二和每周五的 7：50 可以看校园生活新闻。

9. What is one of the privileges members of the video club can enjoy?
【解析】选[C]。细节题。文中提到加入俱乐部是 completely free(完全免会费的)。而且可以免费 use all the equipment,但是使用者 have to pay for the video tape。

Passage Four

【听力原文】	【答案解析】
[12①] If you are ever lucky to be invited to a formal dinner ｐ...in Paris, remember that the French have their own way of doing things, and that [12②] even your finest manners may not be "correct" by French custom. Here I, the marketing director of the Ritz Hotel in Paris, Will explain how it works. [12③] The first duty of the guest is to respond to the invitation within 48 hours. And, the guest may not ask to bring a guest because the hostess has chosen her own. [10] Flowers sent in advance are the preferred gift. They may also be sent afterwards with a thank-you note. The type of flowers sent has a code of its own, too. [11] One must never send chrysa-	10. If you are too busy to send flowers in advance, what should you do? 【解析】选[B]。细节题。文中提到 flowers sent in advance(提前送花)是一种 preferred gift(较好的礼物),但是你也可以在事后送花,并附上 thank-you note(感谢之语)。 11. What can we learn about sending flowers? 【解析】选[D]。细节题。文中提到每种花都有自己的花语,人们认为,chrysanthemums(菊花)是 too humble a flower for

nthemums because they are considered too humble a flower for occasion. Carnations are considered bad luck, and calla lilies are too reminiscent of funerals. A bouquet of red roses is a declaration of romantic intent. Don't send those unless you mean it,—and never to a married hostess. And though the French love wine, [12④] you must never bring a bottle to a dinner party. Why, it's as if you feared your hosts would not have enough wine on hand, and that's an insult. You may, however, offer a box of chocolates, which the hostess will pass after dinner with coffee.

If an invitation is for eight o'clock, the considerate guest arrives at 8:15. Guests who arrive exactly on time or early are mere thoughtless ones who are not giving the hostess those last few minutes she needs to deal with details and crisis. [12⑤] The "correct" guest arrives between 15 to 20 minutes after the hour because dinner will be served exactly 30 minutes past the time on the invitation.

occasion（上不了台面）的花；carnations（康乃馨）代表 bad luck；calla lilies（马蹄莲）让人想到 funerals（葬礼）；red roses 有浪漫之意但不宜送给 a married hostess，所以 sending flowers 时应注意各种花语。

12. What is the passage mainly about?

【解析】选[C]。主旨题。文章开头提到，当你被邀请参加一个正式的 dinner party in Paris 时，要注意你的 manners，接着身为法国专业人士的说话者对 manners 给出了一系列建议：the first duty … you must never … the "correct" guest arrives … ，由此可知短文的主要内容是关于 Good manners at a French dinner party（法式晚宴上的得体举止）。

第四章 解题攻略

短文理解是相对较难的一种听力题型，平时训练时必须采取合理的解题步骤，并掌握一些有针对性的解题技巧，这样才能在考试时做到游刃有余，轻松拿下短文理解。

攻略一：听音前预测内容与问题

预测的成败主要取决于考生对文章题目的理解、掌握的背景知识、所捕捉到的关键词以及对语言环境的熟悉程度。听前快速浏览选项，可以对全文内容有个大概了解，通过纵向、横向比较能够发现一些解题的重要信息。对于听音前的预测技巧，可参照第三篇长对话高分必备中第三章的内容。

攻略二：抓住文章的首尾句

主题句常是文章的第一句话或最后一句（个别情况主题句也出现在段落的中间），它们对整篇文章的内容起一个概括和提示的作用，实际上是文章的中心论点或者是说话人对所谈内容的观点和态度。

在听短文时应尽快抓住能概括短文中心思想的主题句和关键词，这样就能比较容易地听懂短文的内容，更有助于主旨题的解答。

1. 主题句在段首

听清开场白，对于了解文章的主题、理解后面的内容非常重要。而且第一道题经常是根据短文的开头而设。

2. 主题句在结尾处

主题句出现在段落结尾时，是先摆出一些事实或情节，然后归纳总结本段的主题。

攻略三：注意关联词，把握短文发展的脉络

短文中常使用一些连接手段使文章成为一个有机的整体，这些连接手段经常是一些表示并列、转折和因果等关系的连词或副词，它们把短文串在一起，表明上下文的逻辑关系。熟悉这些关联词，就能有效地顺着短文的思路，比较完整地理解短文的内容。而且这些关联词出现的地方往往是短文理解设题的重点。

常见的关联词有：

表举例	such as, namely, that is, for example, for instance
表并列	and, also, besides, furthermore, in addition, what's more

表因果	because, because of, therefore, since, as a result
表顺序	first, last, before, after, next, then, follow, originally
表转折或让步	although, but, however, in spite of, otherwise
表对比或比较	compared with, while, whereas, as … as, than

攻略四：记录关键信息，作简要笔记

对关键信息作适当的笔记不仅有利于进一步明确短文的中心思想，而且有利于抓住所考察细节内容。但是一定要注意，笔记记录的应该是一些关键的信息点，为了提高笔记的效率，应注意把握一定的原则，第三篇第四章已经对此进行了比较详细的阐述，考生在复习时直接参考即可。

攻略五：注意与主题相关的细节

短文理解所考查的细节一般都与主题密切相关，故明显与主题无关的选项往往可以首先排除，而听音时应重点留意那些与主题关系密切的选项。

攻略六：唯一听到的常为解

如果听到的某个细节正好在某个选项中出现，而其他选项均没有涉及短文内容，那么该选项往往为答案。

【例1】 (06-6-Passage One)

【预览选项】	【听前预测】
11. [A] Social work. [B] Medical care. [C] Applied physics. [D] Special education.	预览三道题各选项，由 medical care（医疗护理），hospitals，以及 therapists（治疗专家）可推测本文可能与医疗工作有关；而由 special education（特殊教育），disabled（残疾的）和 handicapped（残疾的）可推测本文还可能与残疾人的特殊教育有关，但 12、13 题各选项并没有涉及到任何有关教育的问题。因此综合来看，本文主题很可能是关于残疾人的医疗工作。
12. [A] The timely advice from her friends and relatives. [B] The two-year professional training she received. [C] Her determination to fulfill her dream. [D] Her parents' consistent moral support.	11. 四个选项均是某一学科领域，由前面对主题的分析可推断本题答案为 [B] Medical care 的可能性较大，听音时再确认具体是哪个领域。
13. [A] To get the funding for the hospitals. [B] To help the disabled children	12. 选项特点表明本题很可能是关于影

there.
[C] To train therapists for the children there.
[D] To set up an institution for the handicapped.

响"她"做某种决定的因素(friends and relatives, parents, training, determination)。听音时主要判断是来自"谁"的因素。

13.选项均为不定式形式,表明本题很可能是考查做某事的目的或原因。[A]是有关资金问题,偏离主题,不大可能为答案。听音时需留意以下要点: help disabled children; train therapists; set institution for handicapped。

【听音验证】

Born and raised in central Ohio, I'm a country girl through and through. [11] I'm currently studying to become a physical therapist, a career path that marks a greater achievement for me. At Ohio State University, admission into the physical therapy program is intensely competitive. I made it pass the first cuts the first year I applied, but was turned down for admission. I was crushed, because for years I have been determined to become a physical therapist. I received advice from friends and relatives about changing my major and finding another course for my life. I just couldn't do it. I knew I could not be as happy in another profession. [12] So I stilled myself, began to work seriously for another year and reapplied. Happily I received notice of my admission. Later, I found out that less than 15% of the applicant had been offered positions that year. Now in the first two years of professional training, I couldn't be happier with my decision not to give up on my dream. My father told me that if I wanted it badly enough, I would get in. Well, Daddy, I wanted it. So there.

After graduation, I would like to tr-

【答案解析】

11. What is the speaker's field of study?
【解析】选[B]。推断题。本题是问说话者研究的领域是什么。根据文中的 studying to become a physical therapist 可知说话人目前在学习成为一名理疗师,而 physical therapist 明显属于 medical care 的范畴,由此可推断说话人的学习领域属于 medical care(医疗)范畴,故答案为[B]。解答此题时切忌将 physical therapist(理疗师)中的 physical 与 physics(物理学)联系起来而误选[C]。

12. According to the speaker, what contributed to her admission to Ohio State University?
【解析】选[C]。推断题。本题是问说话者被俄亥俄州立大学录取的原因是什么。根据文中 So I stilled myself, began to work seriously for another year and reapplied. 一句可知说话人坚持自己的梦想,并努力为实现梦想而奋斗,由此可推断她最终被录取是因为她 determination to fulfill her dream(实现梦想的决心),故答案为[C]。解答本题要注意不能根据只言片语妄下结论,如听到 received advice from friends and relatives 就误选[A]。

13. Why does the speaker want to go to a Latin American country?
【解析】选[B]。细节题。本题是问说话

avel to another country, possibly a Latin American country and [13] work in a children's hospital for a year or two. So many of the children there are physically handicapped but most hospitals don't have the funding to hire trained staff to care for them properly. I would like to change that somehow.

者想去拉美国家的原因是什么。根据据文中 work in a children's hospital for a year or two. So many of the children there are physically handicapped but most hospitals don't have … 可知说话人想去拉美国家是为了 help the disabled children there(帮助那里的残疾儿童),故答案为[B]。

【例2】 (04-1-Passage Two)

【预览选项】	【听前预测】
14. [A] Coca Cola.　　[B] Sausage. 　　[C] Milk.　　　　[D] Fried chicken. 15. [A] He has had thirteen decayed teeth. 　　[B] He doesn't have a single decayed tooth. 　　[C] He has fewer decayed teeth than other people of his age. 　　[D] He never had a single tooth pulled out before he was fifty. 16. [A] Brush your teeth right before you go to bed in the evening. 　　[B] Have as few of your teeth pulled out as possible. 　　[C] Have your teeth X-rayed at regular intervals. 　　[D] Clean your teeth shortly after eating.	14. 由 15、16 题各选项内容可推测本文主题应该是关于牙齿保健。而本题选项都是食物或饮料,结合对文章主题的分析,本题很可 问哪种东西对牙齿有 。根据常识,四种食物或饮料中 Coca Cola 最容易伤害牙齿,因为其含糖量较高。 15. 选项表明本题考查的是某人的牙齿状况(是否有蛀牙)。[A]、[B]、[C] 都是关于蛀牙的问题,[D] 则是关于拔牙的问题,故可初步排除。 16. 选项表明本题考查的是保护牙齿的正确方法。根据对前两题的分析可推知,本题很可能是关于预防蛀牙的方法,并且很可能与饮食有关。因此[B]、[C] 为答案的可能性较小;而[A]、[D] 为答案的可能性较大。
【听音验证】	【答案解析】
How many teeth have you had filled in the past 2 years? If you follow the advice of Dr. Forstic, you may be able to reduce the number of your visit to a dentist. Dr. Forstic conducted a two-year survey to find out how to prevent or reduce dental decay. 946 students	14. According to the passage, what type of food or drink is most likely to cause dental decay? 【解析】选[A]。细节题。根据原文中 sugar is a major agent in dental decay, particularly the sugar in sweets,

took part in the experiment. 523 students cleaned their teeth within 10 minutes of eating. When possible, they used tooth-brush. When this was impossible, they washed their mouth thoroughly with water. The remaining 423 students merely cleaned their teeth when they went to bed and when they got up in the morning. All the students had their teeth X-rayed at the end of the first and second years. At the end of the first year, the night-and-morning group had three times as many decayed teeth as the clean-after-each-meal group. At the end of the second year, the latter group had 53% fewer decayed teeth than the former group. [15] Dr. Forstic has cleaned his teeth after every meal for 1 3 years, and has not had a single decayed tooth. [14]He pointed out that sugar is a major agent in dental decay, particularly the sugar in sweets, cakes and soft drinks. Ideally, [16] you should keep a toothbrush in your pocket and use it immediately after you have finished eating. When this is impractical, you can at least make sure that you have a drink of water and let the water through your teeth, to force out any particles of food. Seven out of ten people lose at least half their teeth by the time they are fifty. Many have a complete set of false teeth by that time. In any case, neither toothache nor a visit to a dentist is very pleasant. So, it is worthwhile making an effort to keep your own teeth as long as possible. The main preventive agent is simply water.

cakes and soft drinks(糖是导致龋齿的主要成份,特别是糖果,蛋糕和软饮料中的糖)可知含糖量较高的sweets,cakes 和 soft drinks 最有可能引起蛀牙,而 Coca Cola 是 soft drinks 中的一种,故答案为[A]。

15. What does the passage tell us about the condition of Doctor Forstic's teeth?
【解析】选[B]。细节题。根据原文中的 Dr. Forstic has cleaned his teeth after every meal for 13 years, and has not had a single decayed tooth 可知,Dr. Forstic 坚持13年来每顿饭后都清洁牙齿,所以至今没有一颗蛀牙,故答案为[B]。

16. What does Doctor Forstic suggest to prevent dental decay?
【解析】选[D]。细节题。根据原文中的 you should keep a toothbrush in your pocket and use it immediately after you have finished eating 可知,饭后保持牙齿的清洁是防止蛀牙的有效方法,故答案为[D]。

Exercise 专项练习

边听边记

Passage One

1. [A] On the second Sunday in April.
   [B] On the second Sunday in May.
   [C] On the third Sunday in May.
   [D] On the third Saturday in May.

2. [A] A good dinner.   [B] A day of rest.
   [C] An expensive bed.   [D] A lot of greeting cards.

3. [A] For more than 90 years. [B] For about 190 years.
   [C] For about 50 years.   [D] For over a century.

4. [A] On the third Sunday in May.
   [B] On the third Sunday in June.
   [C] On the second Sunday in May.
   [D] On the second Sunday in June.

Passage Two

5. [A] When they had a party. [B] When they took leave.
   [C] When someone died.   [D] When they met in public.

6. [A] She was too absorbed in her imagination.
   [B] She was so tall that she could not see the ground clearly.
   [C] She was heavy loaded that she could not look down on the ground.
   [D] She was too careful about the milk pail on her head.

7. [A] It is too much to expect for a poor person to become rich.
   [B] We must make careful plans before doing anything.
   [C] We shouldn't expect anything with certainty.
   [D] Best wishes alone is not enough for dreams to come into being.

Passage Three

8. [A] A person who was not afraid of police.
   [B] A person who wanted a profitable job.
   [C] A person who wished to earn $500 with two opportunities.
   [D] A person who was fond of adventure.

9. [A] He did not want the police to suspect him.
   [B] He did not fully believe the advertiser.
   [C] The offer of the advertiser was only $250.
   [D] The advertiser did not want to discuss the job fully on the phone.

10. [A] The advertiser was arrested red-handed.
　　[B] The reader was paid ＄250 as arranged.
　　[C] The life of the advertiser's wife was spared.
　　[D] The reader was bit by the dog.

Passage Four

11. [A] He didn't live very long with them.
　　[B] The family was extremely large.
　　[C] He was too young when he lived with them.
　　[D] He was fully occupied with observing nature.

12. [A] A scientist as well as a naturalist.
　　[B] Not a naturalist but a scientist.
　　[C] No more than a born naturalist.
　　[D] Neither a naturalrst nor a scientist.

13. [A] Full of ambition.　　[B] Knowledgeable.
　　[C] Full of enthusiasm.　　[D] Self-disciplined.

边听边记

【答案与解析】

Passage One

【听力原文】

[1]Mother's Day is celebrated on the second Sunday in May. On this occasion, Mother usually receives greeting cards and gifts from her husband and children. [2]For most mothers, the rarest and best gift is a day of rest. Often, families honor Mother by taking her out for dinner. In some households the husband and children take over meal preparations so that Mom can spend a whole day away from the kitchen. Serving her breakfast in bed is another family ritual. Later in the day, parents may take their children to visit their grandparents.

Flowers are an important part of the holiday. Mothers are often given corsages for the occasion, particularly if they are elderly.

The idea of setting aside a special day to honor mothers did not originate in the United States. In England, Mothering Sunday, celebrated

【答案解析】

1. When is Mother's Day celebrated?

【解析】选[B]。细节题。文章开头明确提到人们在 the second Sunday in May(五月第二个星期天)庆祝 Mother's Day(母亲节)。

2. What is the rarest and best gift for most mothers?

【解析】选[B]。细节题。文章开头明确提到,对于母亲来说,the rarest and best gift 就是 a day of rest(休息一天)。

3. How long has Mother's Day been a national tradition in the United States?

【解析】选[A]。细节题。文中明确提到,从1915年开始,Mother's Day 成为美国一个

during Lent, was once traditional. The Yugoslavs and many other peoples have long observed a holiday for mothers. [3] In the United States, Mother's Day has been a national tradition since 1915.

[4] Father's Day is celebrated throughout the United States and Canada on the third Sunday in June. The holiday customs are similar to Mother's Day. Dad also receives greeting cards and gifts from his family and enjoys a day of leisure.

national tradition(全国性的传统节日),那么到现在应该是 90 多年了。

4. When is Father's Day celebrated?
【解析】选[B]。细节题。文中明确提到,在美国和加拿大, the third Sunday in June(六月第三个星期日)是 Father's Day(父亲节)。

Passage Two

【听力原文】	【答案解析】
One of the most interesting of all studies is the study of words and word origins. Consider again the everyday English expression "Goodbye". [5①] Many years ago, people would say to each other on parting: "God be with you". As this expression was repeated over and over millions of times. It gradually became shortened to "good-bye". From the fables of Aesop, a Greek writer who lived in 550 BC has been translating many common expressions—not only into English, but into many other languages of the world as well. There is a fable of Aesop, which is pop in many languages, is the story of a young farm girl who was going to market carrying a pail of milk on her head. As she walked along, she began to plan what she was going to do with the money she was to get when she sold the milk. She would [6①] buy some chickens. The chickens were going to lay eggs. She would sell the eggs and buy a new dress and hat. The young men of the town would fall in love with	5. When did people say "God be with you" to each other long ago? 【解析】选[B]。细节题。文中提到,很久以前,人们 on parting(离别)的时候说 God be with you。选项[B]是原文的同义转述。 6. Why did the young farm girl carrying a pail of milk on her head strike her foot against a stone? 【解析】选[A]。推断题。文中提到,女孩一直幻想着卖掉牛奶后的种种美丽场景:buy some chickens … chickens lay eggs … sell the eggs … buy a new dress …,所以这个女孩才被一块石头绊倒。 7. What lesson can we draw from the fable of the young girl who was to sell milk in market? 【解析】选[D]。推断题。文章结尾处提到,女孩尽管怀着美好

her. She would marry the richest one, and so forth. Suddenly, with her head high up in the air, [6②]she struck her foot against a stone and fell. All the milk was spilled and she had to return home with nothing at all. [7]The moral of this fable is : don't count your chickens before they are hatched.	的原望,但因不慎,结果什么都没有得到,这个 fable(寓言)的寓意就是 : 不要在鸡 hatched(孵出来)之前 count your chickens,也就是说要想 dreams come into being(实现梦想),光在那里幻想是不够的。

Passage Three

【听力原文】	【答案解析】
The writers of murder stories go to a great deal of trouble to keep the readers guessing right up to the end. In fact, people often behave more strangely in real life than they do in stories. The following advertisement once appeared in a local newspaper: "An opportunity to earn ＄250 in a few minutes. [8]A man willing to take chances, wanted for an out-of-the-ordinary job which can be performed only once. " A reader found this offer very nice and wrote to the advertiser. [9]But being a bit suspicious, he gave a false name. Soon afterwards, he received a reply. Enclosed in the envelope was a typed note instructing him to ring a certain number if he was still interested. He did so and learned on the telephone that the advertiser wanted him "to get rid of somebody" and would discuss it more fully with him the next day. But [10①]the man told the police and from then on acted under their instructions. The police saw the two men meet and watched them as they drove away together. The advertiser told the man he wanted him to shoot his wife. Giving the man some money, the advertiser told him to buy a gun and warned him to be careful of the dog, though it would not bite, it might attract attention. Afterwards, the advertiser suggested that the man should "do the job" the next morning. At the same time	8. What kind of person is asked for in the advertisement in the newspaper? 【解析】选[D]。细节题。文中提到,广告对所招聘的人的要求是 A man willing to take chances(愿意冒险)。 9. Why did the reader give a false name when he answered the advertisement? 【解析】选[B]。细节题。文中明确提到 the reader 看见广告,觉得很有意思就给登广告的人写了一封信,但是他有一点 suspicious(怀疑)这个广告,于是他 give a false name。 10. What was the result after the man told the police of the murder plan? 【解析】选[C]。推断题。文中提到 the reader 把事情告诉了 police,最

he should prepare his wife by telling her that a young man was going to call. After the murder they would meet again outside a railway station and the money would be paid as arranged. The second meeting never took place, for [10②] the advertiser was arrested shortly afterwards and charged with attempting to persuade someone to murder his wife.

后登广告的人 charged with attempting to persuade someone to murder his wife（因蓄意雇凶谋杀自己的妻子）的罪名而 arrested（被捕），由此可推断登广告者的 wife 还活着。

Passage Four

【听力原文】

Looking back on my childhood, [11①][13①] I am convinced that naturalists are born and not made. Although we were all brought up in the same way, my brothers and sisters soon abandoned their pressed flowers and insects. Unlike them, I had no ear for music and languages. I was not an early reader and I could not do mental arithmetic.

I have only a dim memory of the house we lived in, of my room and my toys. Nor do I recall clearly the large family of grandparents, aunts, uncles and cousins who gathered next door. [11②] But I do have a crystal-clear memory of the dogs, the farm animals, the local birds, and above all, the insects.

[12] I am a naturalist, not a scientist. I have a strong love of the natural world and [13②] my enthusiasm has led me into varied investigations. I love discussing my favorite topics and enjoy burning the midnight oil while reading about other people's observations and discoveries. Then something happens that brings these observations together in my conscious mind. Suddenly you fancy you see the answer to the riddle, because it all seems to fit together. This has resulted in my publishing 300 papers and books, which some might honor with the title of scientific research.

【答案解析】

11. Why can't the speaker remember his relatives clearly?
【解析】选 [D]。推断题。文中提到，作者说他认为自然主义者是天生的，又说他记忆很模糊，记不清亲戚们，接着提到他却 have a crystal-clear memory … the insects（对动物昆虫印象深刻），由此可推断，the speaker 之所以记不住亲戚是因为他把心思都花在观察动植物，也就是 nature 上了。

12. According to the passage, what does the author do?
【解析】选 [C]。细节题。文中明确提到，作者是一个 naturalist（自然主义者），而不是 a scientist，即他只是 a naturalist。

13. According to the author, what should a born naturalist be like first of all?
【解析】选 [C]。推断题。文中提到，作者认为 naturalists

But curiosity, a keen eye, a good memory and enjoyment of the animal and plant world do not make a scientist: one of the outstanding and essential qualities required is self-discipline, a quality I lack. A scientist requires not only self-discipline but hard training, determination and a goal. A scientist, up to a point, can be made. A naturalist is born. If you can combine the two, you get the best of both worlds.

are born and not made (自然主义者是天生的不是后天培养的), 也就是说 a born naturalist 本身就很喜欢 nature, 完全出自本人的 enthusiasm, 由此可推断, 天生的自然学家最重要的一点就是 full of enthusiasm。

综 合 训 练

Exercise 1　　　🎧 边听边记

Passage One

26. [A] To show their sense of significance and happiness.
    [B] To show their sense of comfort and leisure.
    [C] To show their sense of leisure and happiness.
    [D] To show their sense of comfort and significance.

27. [A] To shake hands with others.
    [B] To look at the card you receive carefully.
    [C] To put the card you receive into your bag immediately.
    [D] To offer and receive the cards with one hand.

28. [A] They're warm and open.
    [B] They are not very warm but open.
    [C] They're shy but warm.
    [D] They're shy and cool.

Passage Two

29. [A] Abnormal lung.　　　[B] Death.
    [C] Low birth weight.　　[D] Severe breathing problems.

30. [A] About 500,000.　　　[B] About 5,000.
    [C] About 50,000.　　　[D] About 5000,000.

31. [A] It reduces the ability of the heart to correct abnormal heartbeats.
    [B] It will easily cause heart attacks.
    [C] It will increase heartbeats.
    [D] It can damage blood passages around hearts.

Passage Three

32. [A] Why people hold back their tears.
    [B] Why people cry.
    [C] How to restrain one's tears.
    [D] How tears are produced.

33. [A] Only humans respond to emotions by shedding tears.
    [B] Only humans shed tears to get rid of irritating stuff in their

eyes.

〔C〕 Only human tears can resist the invading bacteria.

〔D〕 Only human tears can discharge certain chemicals.

34. 〔A〕 What chemicals tears are composed of.

〔B〕 Whether crying really helps us feel better.

〔C〕 Why some people tend to cry more often than others.

〔D〕 How tears help people cope with emotional problems.

35. 〔A〕 Only one out of four girls cries less often than boys.

〔B〕 Of four boys, only one cries very often.

〔C〕 Girls cry four times as often as boys.

〔D〕 Only one out of four babies doesn't cry often.

Exercise 2

Passage One

26. 〔A〕 A medical magazine.

〔B〕 A police report.

〔C〕 A legal document.

〔D〕 A government information booklet.

27. 〔A〕 To make the front seat passenger wear a seat belt.

〔B〕 To make the front seat children under 14 wear a seat belt.

〔C〕 To stop children riding in the front seat.

〔D〕 To wear a seat belt each time he drives.

28. 〔A〕 You will be taken to court or be fined.

〔B〕 You will go to prison.

〔C〕 You will not be influenced.

〔D〕 You will be taken into custody.

Passage Two

29. 〔A〕 In 1971.   〔B〕 In 1976.

〔C〕 In 1966.   〔D〕 In 1990.

30. 〔A〕 Main Street.   〔B〕 The Sleeping Beauty Castle.

〔C〕 Cinderella's Castle.   〔D〕 The Magic Kingdom.

31. 〔A〕 It is relatively cheap.   〔B〕 It is very expensive.

〔C〕 It just wastes time.   〔D〕 It is vulgar.

Passage Three

32. 〔A〕 Eighty years.   〔B〕 Forty years.

〔C〕 Thirty-five years.   〔D〕 Fifty-three years.

33. 〔A〕 She lost her record.

边听边记

[B] She didn't stop at a red light.

[C] She didn't see a red light.

[D] She stopped at a red light.

34. [A] Because she was too old to make a right judgement.

[B] Because she didn't look at the traffic light.

[C] Because she wanted to break her record.

[D] Because her eyes had become too weak with old age to see the red light.

35. [A] She asked the judge a lot of questions.

[B] She tried hard to thread a needle with a small eye.

[C] She showed the judge her clean record.

[D] She threaded a needle with a small eye very easily.

Exercise 3

Passage One

26. [A] To give lectures.

[B] To organize discussions.

[C] To grade students' papers.

[D] To be a coordinator.

27. [A] From the office.

[B] From the coordinator.

[C] From the university bookstore.

[D] From the lecture room.

28. [A] The study guide.

[B] The course reader.

[C] The textbook by Osborne.

[D] The readings by Bender.

Passage Two

29. [A] Its oil refinery. 　　　[B] Its linen textiles.

[C] Its food products. 　　　[D] Its deepwater port.

30. [A] Soap. 　　　[B] Grain.

[C] Steel. 　　　[D] Tobacco.

31. [A] French refugees arrived.

[B] The harbor was destroyed.

[C] Shipbuilding began to flourish.

[D] The city was taken by the English.

Passage Three

32. [A] Poet.   [B] Journalist.
    [C] Playwright.   [D] Novelist.

33. [A] To visit his brother.
    [B] To attend the New York Film Festival.
    [C] To help with the production of his play.
    [D] To advertise his new film.

34. [A] 12∶10.   [B] 5∶45.
    [C] 6∶30.   [D] 8∶50.

35. [A] He was nervous because he missed the plan.
    [B] The air crash was the most terrible accident he had ever heard.
    [C] He would have been dead if he hadn't overslept.
    [D] He hurt himself while pouring the boiling water.

答案与解析

Exericise 1

Passage One

【听力原文】

We live in a global village, but how well do we know and understand each other?

[26]American executives sometimes signal their feelings of ease and importance in their offices by putting their feet on the desk while on the telephone. In Japan, people would be shocked. Showing the soles of your feet is the height of bad manners. It is a social insult only exceeded by blowing your nose in public.

The Japanese have perhaps the strictest rules of social and business behavior. The Japanese business card almost needs a rulebook of its own. You must exchange business cards immediately on meeting because it is essential to establish everyone's status and position. [27]When it is handed to a person in a superior position, it must be given and received with both hands, and you must take time to read it carefully,

【答案解析】

26. Why do some high-level American managers place their feet on the desk?

【解析】选[D]。细节题。文章开头提到，美国的主管们打电话的时候经常把脚放在桌子上是为了显示出他们在办公室的 feeling of ease and importance（安闲感和重要感）。ease ≈ comfort，importance ≈ significance。

27. What should you do as a junior in Japan while exchanging business cards?

【解析】选[B]。细节题。文中提到，当 a person in a superior position 递给你名片

and not just put it in your pocket! Also the bow is a very important part of greeting someone. You should not expect the Japanese to shake hands. Bowing the head is a mark of respect and the first bow of the day should be lower than when you meet thereafter.

The Americans sometimes find it difficult to accept the more formal Japanese manners. They prefer to be casual and more informal, as illustrated by the universal "Have a nice day!" American waiters have a one-word imperative "Enjoy!" [28] The British, of course, are cool and reserved. The great topic of conversation between strangers in Britain is the weather—unemotional and impersonal. In America, the main topic between strangers is the search to find a geographical link.

时，要用 both hands，而且拿到名片后要 take time to read it carefully，不要直接放在 your pocket 里。

28. How does the passage describe Englishmen?

【解析】选 [D]。细节题。文章结尾处提到，英国人是 cool and reserved（冷漠而且矜持）的。reserved ≈ shy。

Passage Two

【听力原文】

Scientific evidence has been collected to show the danger of second-hand smoke. Now the top doctor in the United States says the evidence cannot be argued: second-hand tobacco smoke is a serious public health risk. Recently Surgeon General Richard Carmona released the government's largest report ever on second-hand smoke. For example, it says nonsmokers increase their risk of lung cancer by up to thirty percent if they live with a smoker. Children who have to breathe second-hand smoke are facing added dangers. These children are at increased risk for sudden infant death syndrome, severe breathing problems and ear infections. The report says smoking by parents also slows lung growth in their children. Children are especially at risk from the poisonous chemicals in tobacco smoke because their bodies are still developing. [29] Smoking during pregnancy can lead to babies with low birth weight. And low birth weight can lead to many health problems. The

【答案解析】

29. What do babies suffer if pregnancy smoking happens?

【解析】选 [C]。细节题。文中提到女性在 pregnancy（怀孕）期间吸烟会使孩子 low birth weight（出生时体重过轻），由此可知答案为 [C]。

30. According to the estimation, how many adults die of second-hand smoke every year?

【解析】选 [C]。细节题。文中明确提到，科学家估计，second-hand smoke（二手烟）每年能夺走大约 fifty thousand

surgeon general says there is no safe level of second-hand smoke. Effects in the blood can be seen after even a short time in a smoky room. [30]Scientists have estimated that second-hand smoke kills about fifty thousand adults in the United States each year. Most of these nonsmokers die from heart disease, but others from lung cancer. Also, an estimated four hundred thirty newborn babies die from sudden infant death syndrome as a result of second-hand smoke. Scientists have identified more than fifty cancer-causing substances in second-hand smoke. Tobacco smoke also damages blood passages. [31] And it reduces the ability of the heart to correct abnormal heartbeats.

（50000）成年人的生命，由此可知答案为[C]。

31. What damage does tobacco smoke take to heart?

【解析】选[A]。细节题。文章结尾处提到，tobacco smoke 会损坏 blood passages（血管），并且会降低心脏 correct abnormal heartbeats（纠正异常心跳）的能力，由此可知答案为[A]。

Passage Three

【听力原文】	【答案解析】
[32]Why do we cry? Can you imagine life without tears? Not only do tears keep your eyes lubricated, they also contain a substance that kills certain bacteria so they can't infect your eyes. Give up your tears, and you'll lose this on-the-spot defense. Nobody wants to give up the flood of extra tears you produce when you get something physical or chemical in your eyes. Tears are very good at washing this irritating stuff out. Another thing you couldn't do without your tears is cry from joy, anger or sadness. [33] Humans are the only animals that produce tears in response to emotions, and most people say a good cry makes them feel better. Many scientists, therefore, believe that [34①] crying somehow helps us cope with emotional situations. Tear researcher, Whitney Fred, is trying to [34②] figure out how it happens. One possibility, he says, is that tears discharge	32. What's the topic discussed in this passage? 【解析】选[B]。主旨题。文章的第一句话 Why do we cry?（人们为什么哭？）明确点明了文章的主题，而且全文都在围绕这个主题展开。 33. What's the difference between human beings and other animals when shedding tears? 【解析】选[A]。推断题。文中明确提到 Humans are … in response to emotions（人类是唯一一种用眼泪来反应感情的动物），由此可推断出，人类与其他动物的区别就是，只有人类 respond to emotions by shedding tears。in response to 相当于 respond to。 34. What is Whitney Fred trying to find out? 【解析】选[D]。细节题。文中提到

certain chemicals from your body, chemicals that build up during stress. When people talk about crying it out, "I think that might actually be what they are doing," he says. If Fred is right, what do you think will happen to people who restrain their tears? [35]Boys, for example, cry only about a quarter as often as girls once they reach teenage years, and we all cry a lot less now than we did as babies. Could it possibly be that we face less stress? Maybe we found another way to deal with it, or maybe we just feel embarrassed.

Whitney Fred 想要 figure out(弄明白) how it happens, 而 it 指的是前一句话的内容, 即 crying somehow helps us cope with emotional situations(痛哭在一定程度上帮助人们解决情感问题)。

35. What does the passage say about teenage boys and girls?

【解析】选[C]。细节题。文章结尾处明确提到 boys … cry only about a quarter as often as girls …(女孩哭的次数是男孩的四倍)。

Exericise 2

Passage One

【听力原文】

More than 30,000 drivers and front seat passengers are killed or seriously injured each year. At a speed of only 30 miles per hour it is the same as falling from a third floor window. Wearing a seat belt saves lives, and it reduces your chance of death or serious injury by more than half.

Therefore drivers or front seat passengers over 14 in most vehicles must wear a seat belt. [26①]If you do not, you could be fined up to $50. It will not be up to the driver to make sure you wear your seat belt. [27]But it will be the driver's responsibility to make sure that children under 14 not to ride in the front unless they are wearing a seat belt of some kind. However, you do not have to wear a seat belt if you are reversing your vehicle or you are making a local delivery or collection using a special vehicle, or [26②]if you have a valid medical certificate which excuses you from wea

【答案解析】

26. Where is this passage probably taken from?

【解析】选[B]。推断题。文章提到, 如果不系安全带, 可能会被 fined up to $50(罚款50美元), 除非有有效的 medical certificate(诊断书)证明不能系安全带, 否则, 一经查处, 可能会被 taken to court(带上法庭)并处以罚款, 由此可推断 the passage 来自于 a police report。

27. What is the driver's responsibility?

【解析】选[B]。细节题。文中提到 the driver's responsibility 是必须确保 children under 14 不能坐在前排, 除非他们系上安全带, 也就是说, 司机的责任就是确保坐在前排的14岁以下的孩子系好安全带。

-ring it. Make sure these circumstances apply to you before you decide not to wear your seat belt. [26③][28]Remember you may be taken to court for not doing so, and you may be fined if you cannot prove to the court that you have been excused from wearing it.

28. According to the passage, what will happen if you have no reason of not wearing your seat belt?

【解析】选[A]。细节题。文章结尾处提到，没有理由不系安全带的人会被 taken to court（带上法庭），并且 be fined（处以罚款）。

Passage Two

【听力原文】

Disney World, Florida, is the biggest amusement place in the world. [29]It opened on October 1, 1971, five years after Walt Disney's death.

There is very little that could be called vulgar in Disney World. [31]It attracts people of most tastes and most income groups, and people of all ages, from toddlers to grandpas. There are two expensive hotels, forests for horseback riding and rivers for boating and some other places. [30]But the main attraction of the place is the Magic Kingdom.

Between the huge parking places and the Magic Kingdom lies a broad man-made lake. In the distance rise the towers of Cinderella's Castle, which, like every other building in the Kingdom, is built of solid materials. Even getting to the Magic Kingdom is quite exciting. You can either cross the lake on a boat, or you can travel around the shore in a steam train.

When you reach the terminal, you walk straight into a little square which faces Main Street. Main Street was built in the late 19th century. There are modern shops inside the buildings and there is no traffic except a horse-drawn streetcar and a double-decker bus. Yet, as you walk through the Magic Kingdom, you are in fact walking on top of a network of underground roads. This is how the shops, restaurants and all the other material needs of the Magic Kingdom are supplied.

【答案解析】

29. When did Walt Disney die?

【解析】选[C]。推断题。文章开头提到，Florida 的 Disney World 是 October 1, 1971 开始营业的，那时 Walt Disney 已去世 five years 了，由此可推断 Walt Disney 是在 1966 年去世的。

30. What is the most favorite place of Disney World?

【解析】选[D]。细节题。文中提到，Florida 的 main attraction 是 the Magic Kingdom（魔幻王国）。

31. What can we learn about Disney world?

【解析】选[A]。推断题。文中提到，Florida 的 Disney World 吸引了 most tastes and most income groups（各种品味、各种收入的人群），游客也有老有少，from toddlers（步履蹒跚的孩子）to grandpas，由此可推断迪斯尼乐园的消费还是 relatively cheap。

Passage Three

【听力原文】	【答案解析】
Mrs. Jones was over eighty, but she still drove her old car like a woman half her age. She loved driving very fast and boasted of the fact that she had never, [32] in her thirty-five years of driving, been punished for a driving offence.	32. How many years has Mrs. Jones been driving? 【解析】选[C]。细节题。文章开头处明确提到 Mrs. Jones 的驾龄是 thirty-five years。
Then one day she nearly lost her record. A police car followed her, and [33] the policemen in it saw her pass a red light without stopping. When Mrs. Jones came before the judge, he looked at her severely and said that she was too old to drive a car, and that [34] the reason why she did not stop at the red light was most probably that her eyes had become weak with old age, so that she simply did not see it.	33. What did Mrs. Jones do one day? 【解析】选[B]。细节题。文中提到，一天，警察看见她 pass a red light without stopping（闯红灯了）。 34. Why did the judge think Mrs. Jones had done so? 【解析】选[D]。细节题。文中提到，法官认为 Mrs. Jones 闯红灯的原因是：her eyes had become weak with old age（年老眼花看不清），所以没看见红灯。
When the judge had finished what he was saying, Mrs. Jones opened the big hand bag she was carrying and took out her sewing. Without saying a word, [35①] she chose a needle with a very small eye, and threaded it at her first attempt.	35. How did Mrs. Jones prove that the judge was wrong? 【解析】选[D]。细节题。文中提到，Mrs. Jones 选了一个有
When she had successfully done this, she took the thread out of the needle again and handed both the needle and the thread to the judge, saying, "Now it is your turn. I suppose you drive a car, and that you have no doubts about your own eyesight."	small eye（小针眼）的针，并且 threaded it at her first attempt（一下子就穿过去了），然后她把针递给法官，让他穿，可是 after
The judge took the needle and tried to thread it. [35②] After half a dozen attempts, he still did not succeed. The case against Mrs. Jones was dismissed and her record remained unbroken.	half a dozen attempts 法官还是 not succeed，这样证明了 Mrs. Jones 的视力很好，法官的判断是错误的。

Exericise 3

Passage One

【听力原文】

Good morning everyone. My name is Paul Stange. [26] I'm the coordinator of this course. It's called South-East Asian Traditions. I'm also the author of the study guide and course reader and you should have those in front of you. As well as these you'll need two textbooks for the course; there is the one by Osborne and there's another by Legge. I'll talk a bit more about the reading materials in a moment. Now if you haven't got these materials, [27] you can buy the textbooks at the university bookshop and you can collect the study guide and the course reader from me on your way out of the lecture.

The purpose of this lecture is simply orientation. What I'm going to do is introduce myself, talk you through the course, and give you some additional advice—apart from what is contained in the study guide—on dealing with the various assignments for the course.

First of all, the materials. You'll find the two textbooks very clear and they give a good, basic coverage of the history of the region. Most of the readings in the reader are fairly easy going, but I have to warn you that two of them are quite difficult. These are the readings by Smail and Bender. And, of these two, [28] the one by Bender is perhaps the more challenging. But don't let that put you off, because understanding these two readings is important to help you develop a clearer understanding of the cultures. In other words they'll help you acquire greater sensitivity to the differences between the various cultures in the region.

Now, the course itself. It's primarily a history course ...

【答案解析】

26. What's the speaker's job for the course?
【解析】选 [D]。细节题。文中说话人明确提到自己是这门课程的 coordinator（协调员）。选项 [D] 是原文的细节再现。

27. Where can students buy the textbooks?
【解析】选 [C]。细节题。文中说话人明确提到，如果学生还没有教科书，他们可以在 the university bookshop（学校的书店）里购买到课本。选项 [C] 是原文的细节再现。

28. Which studying material is more challenging?
【解析】选 [D]。细节题。文中说话人明确提到一共有两本比较难的教科书，一本是由 Bender 编写的，另一本是由 Smail 编写的，而由 Bender 编写的那本 more challenging（更有挑战性）。选项 [D] 是原文的细节再现。

Passage Two

【听力原文】	【答案解析】
[29①]Belfast is the capital of Northern Ireland and a major city in commerce and industry. It is one of the most important ship-building and repairing centers of the United Kingdom, [29②] and has long been known for its linen textiles. Its manufactures include aircraft, guided weapons, and tobacco and food products. A large petroleum refinery here is supplied by imported petroleum which is received at the city's deep-water port. Other imports include grain, coal, chemicals and iron and steel. [30] Among the chief exports are petroleum products, soap, food stuffs and textiles. In Belfast, there are the notable Ulster Museum and the Protestant Cathedral of Saint Anne. As an educational center, the city is home to Queen's University of Belfast and Belfast College of Technology. Although there's evidence that people once settled in this place during the Stone and Bronze Ages, the founding of Belfast dates from 1177 when a Norman castle was erected. Edward Bruce destroyed the settlement in 1315, the year he became the Irish King. The city was taken by the English in the 16th century. In the late 17th century, French refugees arrived here and developed the linen industry. [31] The harbor was improved in the late 18th century and ship-building was begun on a large scale. The city was made the capital of Northern Ireland in 1920. During World War II, Belfast was heavily damaged by German bombing raids. Beginning in 1969, the city was the scene of religious disorder involving civil rights agitation and increased violence.	29. What is Belfast has long been famous for? 【解析】选[B]。细节题。文章开头就提到 Belfast 因它的 linen textiles（亚麻纺织品）而闻名。选项[B]是原文的细节再现。 30. Which of the following does Belfast chiefly export? 【解析】选[A]。细节题。文中明确提到 Belfast 出口的货物里包括 petroleum products（石油产品）、soap（肥皂）、food stuff（食物）和 textiles（纺织品）。选项[A]是原文的细节再现。 31. What happened in Belfast in the late 18th century? 【解析】选[C]。细节题。文中明确提到在 18 世纪晚期 harbor（海港）得到了发展，ship-building was begun on a large scale（造船业发展到很大的规模，十分繁荣）。选项[C]是原文的同义转述。

Passage Three

【听力原文】	【答案解析】
[32]James wrote a play for television, about an immigrant family who came to England from Pakistan, and the problems they had settling down in England. The play was surprisingly successful, and [33] it was bought by an American TV company. James was invited to go to New York to help with the production. He lived in Dulwich, which is an hour's journey away from Heathrow. The flight was due to leave at 8:30 a. m. , so he had to be at the airport about 7:30 in the morning. He ordered a mini-cab for 6:30, set his alarm for 5:45, and went to sleep. Unfortunately he forgot to wind the clock, and it stopped shortly after midnight. Also the driver of the mini-cab had to work very late that night and overslept. James woke with that awful feeling that something was wrong. He looked at his alarm clock. It stood there silently, [34①]with the hands pointing to ten past twelve. He turned on the radio and discovered that it was, [34②] in fact, ten to nine. He swore quietly and switched on the electric kettle. He was just pouring the boiling water in the teapot when the nine o'clock pips sounded on the radio. The announcer began to read the news: "... reports are coming in to a crash near Heathrow Airport. A Boeing 707 bound for New York crashed shortly after taking off this morning. Flight number 2234 ... [35]James turned pale. "My flight," he said out loud. "If I hadn't overslept, I'd have been on that plane."	32. What does James do? 【解析】选[C]。细节题。文章开头明确提到 James wrote a play for television(詹姆斯为电视台写了一个剧本),由此可知 James 是一位 playwright(剧作家)。 33. Why does James go to New York? 【解析】选[C]。细节题。文中提到 James 所写的电视剧被 an American TV company 买走了,这家美国公司还邀请他去美国 help with the production(帮忙生产),所以 James 才去的纽约。选项[C] 是原文的细节再现。 34. When does James' clock stop? 【解析】选[A]。推断题。文中提到,James 醒来时发现钟表的时针 pointing to ten past twelve(12:10),可是实际上当时是 ten to nine(8:50),由此可推断出钟表是在 12:10 停的。 35. Why did James turn pale after hearing the news? 【解析】选[C]。细节题。文章结尾处提到,James 听到飞机失事后,脸色 turned pale,而且还喊着 My flight, if I ... I'd have ... (是他的航班,假如不是睡过头了,他就在那架飞机上了),也就是说如果 James 没有 overslept 的话,他 would have been dead。

短文听写高分必备

Part 5

本篇首先介绍了短文听写的设题重点和基本的解题步骤，之后对短文听写的单词填空和句子填空的解题技巧分别进行了讲解和练习，最后配备了综合训练题，供考生巩固提高。

单词设题点

短文听写是大学英语六级听力考试中唯一的主观题型,包括对听力材料的理解能力(即"听")和一定的书面表达能力(即"写")两方面的测试。六级短文听写的长度一般在 240～260 词之间,包括 8 个单词填空和 3 个句子填空。

单词填空主要集中在名词、动词和形容词三种词性的考查上,偶尔也会涉及到副词。

一、动词的考查重点

动词主要考查其单复数形式、时态和语态以及某些特殊形式的过去式和过去分词以及情态动词、虚拟语气中动词的正确形式。

【例1】   (07-6-36)

> As nurses, we **are** (36) licensed **to** provide nursing care only.(系动词 are 和不定式 to 提示所填词应为动词的过去分词形式)

【例2】   (05-6-S6)

> If the parents **can** (S6) afford **it**, each child will have his or her own bedroom.(情态动词 can 和代词 it 提示所填词应为动词原形)

二、名词的考查重点

名词主要考查单复数问题、表示数量的名词、一些单复数同形的名词,以及常见的一些名词后缀。

要注意根据空格前面的修饰词和后面的谓语动词等线索来判断名词的单复数形式。像 percent, percentage, million, billion 等表示数量的名词与具体数字连用时,一般不用复数形式。

【例3】   (07-6-42)

> ... we have **a legal** (42) responsibility to question that order or refuse to carry it out.(注意名词后缀 -lity)

【例4】   (99-6-S3)

> Mr. Clinton will ask Congress this coming week for nearly **three** (S3) billion **dollars** to fund a five-year program called "America Reads".(数词 three 和表示金钱的名词 dollars 提示所填词应为表示数量的名词)

三、形容词考查重点

形容词主要考查近音易混形容词、分词演化来的形容词、与介词搭配使用的形容词以及带有前缀后缀的形容词。

【例5】 (07-6-41)

... we feel that a physician's order is (41) inappropriate or unsafe, ...（注意否定前缀 -in）

【例6】 (710分样卷-40)

The second charge stemmed from his association with numerous young men who came to Athens from all over the (40) civilized world to study under him.

四、副词的考查重点

副词主要考查用于说明动词发生时的情形或状态的情状副词,以 – ly 结尾的副词居多。

【例7】 (01-1-S2)

You are (S2) constantly harnessing and consuming energy through the intricate (S3) machanism of your body in order to remain in energy balance.（副词 constantly 修饰动词 harnessing）

五、对易混词的考查

英语中存在很多近音异义词或近形异义词,这些词会对听力理解形成很大的障碍,尤其在听写时,更会对考生造成比较大的干扰,影响考生的判断。

【例8】 (07-6-38)

We provide health teaching, (38) assess physical as well as emotional problems, ...（assess 很容易误写成 access）

【例9】 (99-6-S6)

... it would also give (S6) grants to help parents help children read by the third grade, or about age eight.（grants 很容易误写成 grounds）

【常见易混词】

aboard-abroad	accident-incident	adapt-adept-adopt
affect-effect	aspiration-inspiration	altitude-latitude
angel-angle	area-era	assign-a sign
assume-resume	attain-obtain	bald-bold
blush-flush	brake-break	brown-brow

carton-cartoon	casual-causal	cause-course
champion-champagne	collar-color	compliment-complement
contend-content	confirm-conform	contact-contract
council-counsel	commerce-commence	dairy-diary
dessert-desert	decent-descent	delicate-dedicate
drought-draught	dying-dyeing	either-easier
ensure-insure	emigrant-immigrant	eminent-imminent
except-expect	familiar-family-similar	flower-flour
forth-fourth	flew-flu	hanger-hunger
idle-idol	immoral-immortal	literacy-literary
loose-lose	march-match	male-mail
mortal-mental-medal-model	median-medium	overall-overrule
passed-past	pray-prey	police-policy
personnel-personal	phrase-phase	principal-principle
purpose-propose	quite-quiet	recent-resent
road-rowed-rode	sale-sail	site-sight-cite
sweet-sweat	source-sauce	suite-suit
specie-species	scare-scarce	stationery-stationary
story-storey	thought-sought	thin-sin
thing-sing	threw-through	weather-whether
weight-wait	vocation-vacation	vision-version

六、对较难单词拼写的考查

　　六级短文听写经常会涉及对一些拼写较复杂单词的考查,像拼写中含有前缀后缀,或含有重复字母的词汇等,并且这类难词多为名词或形容词。

【例10】　　　　　　　　　　　　　　　　　　　　　　　　　　　(07-6-41)

… we feel that a physician's order is (41) <u>inappropriate</u> or unsafe, … (注意前缀-in)

【例11】　　　　　　　　　　　　　　　　　　　　　　　　　(99-6-S4,S5)

The program would fund the (S4) <u>coordination</u> efforts of 20 thousand reading (S5) <u>specialists</u> and it would … (注意前缀 co-、后缀-tion 和 -ist)

　　常见的前缀有:co-, en(em)-, ex-, over-, un-, in-, (im-, ir-, il-), dis-, non-, re-, de-, mis-等。
　　常见的后缀有:-ism, -al, -able(-ible), -ous, -ness, -ity, -ition(-ion), -ment, -ly, -or 或-er 等。

七、对习惯搭配的考查

　　习惯搭配也是六级短文听写的一个考查点,常见的有形容词与介词,动词与介词,名词与介词,名词与名词的搭配等。

【例12】　　　　　　　　　　　　　　　　　　　　　　　　（07-6-40）

If, *in any* (40) circumstance, we feel that a physician's order is (41) _____ or unsafe. (in any circumstance 是固定短语,意为"在任何情况下")

【例13】　　　　　　　　　　　　　　　　　　　　　　　（710 分样卷-39）

The second charge stemmed from his (39) association *with* numerous young men who came to Athens from all over the civilized world to study under him. (association 后面常接介词 with)

八、对上下文照应或复现的考查

所填词前后句中经常会有与其相照应的词或短语,或是该词的近义或反义复现,这也是短文听写重点考查的内容之一。

【例14】　　　　　　　　　　　　　　　　　　　　　　　　（05-6-S3）

Closely (S2) _____ with the value they *place on* individualism is the importance Americans (S3) assign to privacy. (assign to 是该句前面的 place on 的近义复现)

【例15】　　　　　　　　　　　　　　　　　　　　　　　　（99-6-S6）

The program would *fund* the coordination efforts of 20 thousand reading specialists and it would also give (S6) grants to help parents help children read by the third grade, or about age eight. (give grants to 是前面句中 fund 一词的近义复现)

九、并列、排比或列举处

常见的并列连接词有 and, as well as, or, together with, along with, coupled with, with 等。

【例16】　　　　　　　　　　　　　　　　　　　　　　　　（07-6-38,39）

We *provide* health teaching, (38) assess physical as well as emotional problems, (39) coordinate patient-related services, *and make* all of our nursing decisions based upon what is best or suitable for the patient. (所填词与 provide, make 是并列的谓语动词)

【例17】　　　　　　　　　　　　　　　　　　　　　　　　（07-6-41）

… we feel that a physician's order is (41) inappropriate *or unsafe*, … (所填词与 unsafe 并列充当表语)

十、转折等其他逻辑关系处

常见转折连接词有 but, however, whereas, while, instead 等。

【例18】 (四级 03-1-S5)

Anyone may go there and read anything in the collection. But no one is (S5) permitted to take books out of the building. (but 前说 "anyone 都可以…", 后面应该说 "anyone 都不可以…")

Exercise 专项练习 🎧 边听边记

Air Force One is a Boeing 747-200B aircraft that was extensively modified to meet presidential requirements. The original paint (S1) _____ was designed at the request of President John F. Kennedy, who wanted the airplane to (S2) _____ the spirit of the national character.

In 1990, a modified Boeing 747-200B Air Force One presidential aircraft (S3) _____ the Boeing 707-320 airframe that served the nation's chief executives for nearly 30 years. Today, the chief executive flies aboard a modified 747-200B, the newest and (S4) _____ presidential airplane. The 747 is (S5) _____ suited to support the travel requirements of the president.

The flying "Oval office" has 4,000 square feet of (S6) _____ floor space, which features a conference/dining room, quarters for the president and the first lady, and an office area for senior staff media (S7) _____ and Air Force crews; two galleys "are each (S8) _____ of providing food for 50 people".

About 238 miles of wire wind through the presidential plane. This is more than twice the wiring found in a typical 747. Wiring is shielded to protect it from electromagnetic pulse, which is (S9) _____ by a thermonuclear blast and interferes with electronic signals. The airplane's mission communications system provides worldwide transmission and reception of normal and (S10) _____ communications. The equipment includes 85 telephones, as well as multi-frequency radios for air-to-air, air-to-ground and satellite communications. Air Force One provides longer range for presidential travel and can be (S11) _____ at airports around the world. Modified for aerial refueling, it has virtually unlimited range.

【答案与解析】

【听力原文】	【答案解析】

【听力原文】

Air Force One is a Boeing 747-200B aircraft that was extensively modified to meet presidential requirements. The original paint (S1) <u>scheme</u> was designed at the request of President John F. Kennedy, who wanted the airplane to (S2) <u>reflect</u> the spirit of the national character.

In 1990, a modified Boeing 747-200B Air Force One presidential aircraft (S3) <u>replaced</u> the Boeing 707-320 airframe that served the nation's chief executives for nearly 30 years. Today, the chief executive flies aboard a modified 747-200B, the newest and (S4) <u>largest</u> presidential airplane. The 747 is (S5) <u>ideally</u> suited to support the travel requirements of the president.

The flying "Oval office" has 4,000 square feet of (S6) <u>interior</u> floor space, which features a conference/dining room, quarters for the president and the first lady, and an office area for senior staff media (S7) <u>representatives</u> and Air Force crews; two galleys "are each (S8) <u>capable</u> of providing food for 50 people".

About 238 miles of wire wind through the presidential plane. This is more than twice the wiring found in a typical 747. Wiring is shielded to protect it from electromagnetic pulse, which is (S9) <u>generated</u> by a thermonuclear blast and interferes with electronic signals. The airplane's mission communications system

【答案解析】

S1. 空前的名词 paint 和空后的系动词 was 提示所填词应为名词。scheme 意为"方案"。

S2. 空前的不定式 to 和空后的名词 spirit 提示所填词应为动词原形。reflect 意为"反映"。

S3. 空前的名词 aircraft 和空后的名词 airframe(机身)提示所填词应为动词。根据上下文时态可知所填词应为动词的过去式。replaced 意"取代,代替"。

S4. 空前的并列连词 and 和空后的形容词 presidential 提示所填词应为形容词最高级,与 newest 构成并列结构。largest 意为"最大的"。

S5. 空前的系动词 is 和空后的动词被动式 suited 提示所填词应为副词。ideally 意为"完美地"。

S6. 空前的介词 of 和空后的名词 floor space 提示所填词应为形容词。根据空后的内容 which features a conference … 推测,此处可能是要表示飞机的机内面积,故所填词很可能要表示"内部的"的含义。interior 意为"内部的"。

S7. 空前的名词 media 和空后的并列连词 and 提示所填词应为名词的复数形式,与 crews 构成并列结构,所填词应该也是表示一类人。representatives 意为"代表"。

S8. 空前的系动词 are 和空后的介词 of 提示所填词应为动词的被动式或形容词。由空前的 galleys(厨房)和空后的 providing food for 50 people 推测所填词可能是要表示"能够"的含义。capable 意为"能…的"。

provides worldwide transmission and reception of normal and (S10) <u>secure</u> communications. The equipment includes 85 telephones, as well as multi-frequency radios for air-to-air, air-to-ground and satellite communications. Air Force One provides longer range for presidential travel and can be (S11) <u>self-sufficient</u> at airports around the world. Modified for aerial refueling, it has virtually unlimited range.

S9. 空前的系动词 is 和空后的介词 by 提示所填词应为动词的被动形式。generated 意为"由…产生"。

S10. 空前的并列连词 and 和空后的名词 communications 提示所填词应为形容词,与 normal 构成并列结构。secure 意为"安全的"。

S11. 空前的系动词 be 和空后的介词 at 提示所填词应为动词的被动式或形容词。self-sufficient 意为"自给自足的"。

句子设题点

句子填空要求考生写出所空句子的原文或其要点。根据历年真题,六级短文听写所考查的句子结构一般都比较复杂,通常为并列句或主从复合句,其长度都在 12—30 个单词之间,平均长度约 18 个单词。

一、与主题密切相关的细节内容

段落的主题一般已给出,要求同学们补全支撑细节。

【例1】 (05-6-S10)

> Americans' attitudes about privacy can be hard for foreigners to understand. (S10) American's houses, yards, and even their offices can seem open and inviting. Yet, in the minds of Americans, there are boundaries that other people are simply not supposed to cross. (空格前面一句是该段的主题句,紧接着的一句显然应该用来说明这一主题)

二、段落主题句或结论句

全文的概括性的结论或主题句一般情况下出现在文章开头或末尾,而段落的概括性的结论或主题句多出现在段首或段尾。

【例2】 (05-6-S9)

> Americans assume that (S9) people will have their private thoughts that might never be shared with anyone. Doctors, lawyers, psychologists, and others have rules governing "confidentiality" ... (所填句为该段的主题句,后面的部分是对该句的进一步说明)

三、并列、转折结构处

这类句子中往往含有 and, as well as, but, yet 等标志性的词语。

【例3】 (01-6-S8)

> The term body image refers to the mental image we have of our own physical appearance, **and** (S8) it can be influenced by a variety of factors, including how much we weigh, or how that weight is distributed. (and 提示所填内容的主题与前面一致,应该都是有关 "body image" 的情况)

四、比较或对比处

句子由 whereas，while 等表示对比含义的连词连接，或是句中含有 as ... as，than 等引出的比较结构，或是句中含有形容词或副词的比较级或最高级。

【例4】　　　　　　　　　　　　　　　　　　　　　　　　（710 分样卷-45）

Socrates（45）**had the right to ask for a less severe** penalty，and he probably could have persuaded the jury to change the verdict.（该句中包含比较级 less severe）

五、含有从句的句子

短文听写的句子很少有简单句，因此含有状语从句、同位语从句或定语从句的复合句往往是其命题重点。

【例5】　　　　　　　　　　　　　　　　　　　　　　　　（05-6-S8）

Having one's own bedroom，even as an infant，fixes in a person *the notion that*（S8）she is entitled to a place of her own where she can be by herself，and keep her possessions.（该句为同位语从句）

六、含有非谓语动词短语或独立结构的句子

含有不定式、动名词、分词短语或是分词的独立结构的句子往往也是短文听写重点考查的句式之一。

【例6】　　　　　　　　　　　　　　　　　　　　　　　　（01-1-S8）

The term body image refers to the mental image we have of our own physical appearance，and（S8）**it can be influenced by a variety of factors，including how much you weigh or how that weight is distributed.**（现在分词短语 including ... 在句中充当定语）

七、含有年代等数字的句子

含有数字（年代、增长或降低的数据、百分比、比分等）的句子也是短文听写中的一个考点，听的过程中注意作好笔记。

【例7】　　　　　　　　　　　　　　　　　　　　　　　　（99-6-S10）

The president says many of the Philadelphia summit's corporate sponsors will recruit tutors.（S10）**Dozens of colleges and universities are prepared to send thousands of their students in support of the program.**（dozens of 和 thousands of 均为表示数字的短语）

Exercise 专项练习 🎧 边听边记

Is your family interested in buying a dog? A dog can be a happy addition to your family, but (S1) _____.

Families should sit down and thoroughly discuss the problems involved before buying a dog. Even if the children in your family are the ones who want the dog, (S2) _____. If you don't know much about dogs, it's a good idea to go to the library of the ASPCA for books about various kinds of dogs, as well as books about how to train a puppy. In reading about the different breeds, (S3) _____. When a book describes a dog as an ideal hunting dog, it probably means that the dog won't be happy living in a small apartment. Dog breeds vary in popularity as the years go by.

One of the most popular dogs these days is the German shepherd. (S4) _____. The family should be warned that these dogs grow up to be very big, and may be too powerful for children to handle. (S5) _____. These dogs are very small and easy to train. (S6) _____.

【答案与解析】

【听力原文】

Is your family interested in buying a dog? A dog can be a happy addition to your family, but (S1) <u>if you choose the wrong kind of the dog, the consequences can cause you a lot of trouble</u>.

Families should sit down and thoroughly discuss the problems involved before buying a dog. Even if the children in your family are the ones who want the dog, (S2) <u>the parents are the ones who are really responsible for seeing the animal is properly cared for</u>. If you don't know much about dogs, it's a good idea to go to the library of the ASPCA for books about various kinds of dogs, as well as books about how to train a puppy. In

【答案解析】

S1. 空前的转折连词 but 提示其前后的句子为转折关系,前面说狗可以给家庭增添欢乐,故所填句子可能涉及狗同样会带来麻烦。

【Main Points】if you choose the wrong kind of the dog, the consequences can **bring** you **lots** of trouble

S2. 空前说家庭在决定买狗之前要好好讨论一下,即使是孩子想要一只狗,故所填句子可能涉及家长应该怎么做。

【Main Points】the parents are the **persons** who are really responsible for seeing the animal is properly **taken care of**

S3. 空前说"在阅读关于狗的品种的书时",由此推测所填句子可能涉及想养狗的人读这些书时应当注意些什么。

reading about the different breeds, (S3) you should know that a dog described as very alert may be too jumpy and bouncy. When a book describes a dog as an ideal hunting dog, it probably means that the dog won't be happy living in a small apartment. Dog breeds vary in popularity as the years go by.

One of the most popular dogs these days is the German shepherd. (S4) This is because this kind of dogs provides protection as well as companionship. The family should be warned that these dogs grow up to be very big, and may be too powerful for children to handle. (S5) If space is limited, a toy dog may be a good choice. These dogs are very small and easy to train. (S6) They don't need to be walked daily, since they can exercise in the space available in the home.

【Main Points】you **ought to** know that a dog which is described as very alert may be too **bouncy and jumpy**

S4. 空前说德国牧羊犬是时下最流行的狗之一, 且空前为段首句, 由此推测所填句子是要对上一句进行解释说明。

【Main Points】This is because **the German shepherd** provides protection **and** companionship

S5. 空前说德国牧羊犬会长得很大, 而且孩子可能控制不了, 空后则介绍另外一种体积小而且容易驯养的狗, 由此可知所填句子应该是推荐另外一种不同于德国牧羊犬的狗。

【Main Points】If space is limited, **maybe** a toy dog **is** a good choice

S6. 空前介绍的狗体积小而且容易驯养, 故所填句子可能会对这种狗作进一步说明。

【Main Points】They don't need **walking every day, because** they can exercise in the space available in the home

解题步骤

短文听写比对话和短文理解都更强调对语言的综合运用能力，考生不仅要具有良好的辨音能力，还应具有较强的拼写能力、笔记能力和书面表达能力。

从某种意义上说，短文听写，实际上也是一种完形填空。因为其听力材料的大部分都以书面形式给出，考生可以在听前充分利用上下文进行推测；另外录音共播放三次，为考生提供了更多抓取重要信息的机会。

一般来说，解答短文听写应该采取如下步骤：

第一步：快速浏览卷面材料，了解大意，预测内容

浏览卷面材料时，尤其要关注所给材料的首尾部分以及空格前后的部分，注意要达到以下几个目的：一是掌握篇章大意；二是要确定前 8 个空格要求填写单词的词性、单复数以及时态语态；三是根据上下文推测要填单词的可能含义；四是根据上下文及短文主题推测句子可能陈述的内容。

第二步：听第一遍录音，听为主，记为辅

听第一遍录音时，注意以听为主，记为辅，切忌急于完整地填写每个空格。这一遍的主要任务是理清文章的脉络。

对前面的 8 个空格，要重点搞清空格处单词的含义，千万不要努力去思考单词该如何拼写，以免顾此失彼。不过可以适当作点简单的记录，单词可采用缩写或只记录开头字母。

对于后面的三个句子，注意以听为主，在整体上把握句子含义的前提下，适当记录关键词，一般三、四个单词即可，且不可贪多而影响了对句子含义的理解，甚至影响后面句子的听写。一般说来，名词、动词、形容词、数词这几种词性是关键词；介词、副词、连词、冠词则可以略去不计。

第三步：听第二遍录音，快速记录所缺单词和句子

听第二遍录音时，对于前 8 个单词空格，需尽量将其填写完整；对于后面 3 个句子空格，尽量使用缩略词进行记录，长的词语可以先写开头，对于不重要的冠词、介词等能省则省，争取把重要的信息都抓住。

从历年的考题来看，后面 3 句话一般都比较难，要全部一字不漏地写下来几乎是不可能的。因此考生应该在听懂句子大意之后，用自己的话重新组织出一个句子，并保证不出现语法错误。

考生要切忌两点：一是只将听到的单词写下来，而把没听到的部分空出位置；二是多次涂改句子内容，卷面非常难看。不管捕捉到多少信息，考生都一定要写出一个完整的句子，而且要保持卷面整洁，尽量不要涂改。

第四步：听第三遍录音，补全未填部分，核对已填内容

听第三遍录音时，重点放在空格部分。一方面要对所填内容进行仔细核听；另一方面要重点关注没有听懂或不是很有把握的地方，尽量补全没有写出的内容。尤其是后3个句子，要尽量将句子意思表达得完整、准确。

第五步：通篇阅读，全面检查

三遍录音听完以后，务必进行最后检查。很多同学听完录音以后，往往立刻开始做其他题，而忽视最后的检查工作，其实这种做法是非常不明智的。对短文听写做最后的通篇核查往往可以避免很多低级的错误，减少不必要的失分。

【例】　　　　　　　　　　　　　　　　　　　　　　　　　　　(新 06-12)

> Adults are getting smarter about how smart babies are. Not long ago, researchers learned that 4-day-olds could understand (36) _____ and subtraction. Now, British research (37) _____ Graham Schafer has discovered that infants can learn words for uncommon things long before they can speak. He found that 9-month-old infants could be taught, through repeated show-and-tell, to (38) _____ the names of objects that were foreign to them, a result that (39) _____ in some ways the received (40) _____ that, apart from learning to (41) _____ things common to their daily lives, children don't begin to build vocabulary until well into their second year. "It's no (42) _____ that children learn words, but the words they tend to know are words linked to (43) _____ situations in the home," explains Schafer. "(44) _____ with an unfamiliar voice giving instructions in an unfamiliar setting."
>
> Figuring out how humans acquire language may shed light on why some children learn to read and write later than others, Schafer says, and could lead to better treatments for developmental problems. (45) _____ __. "Language is a test case for human cognitive development," says Schafer. But parents eager to teach their infants should take note: (46) _____ _____. "This is not about advancing development," he says. "It's just about what children can do at an earlier age than what educators have often thought."

36. 空后的并列连词 and 提示所填词应与 subtraction(减法)并列，而"加、减法"在表达中常常并列出现，故所填词很可能表示"加法"的含义。addition 意为"加法"。

37. 空前的限定语 British research 和空后的人名 Graham Schafer 提示所填词很可能是表示 Graham Schafer 的职业或身份。而由后文内容可知，他主要研究婴儿及儿童的认知能力，这属于心理学的范畴，故所填词很可能表示"心理学家"

的含义。psychologist 意为"心理学家"。

38. 空前的 be taught ... to 提示所填词应为动词原形,并能与后面的 the names of objects 构成合理的动宾搭配,而 teach(教)的目的应该是能使婴儿认知或了解某些东西,故所填词很可能是表示"认知、辨识"的含义。recognize 意为"认出"。

39. 空前的 a result that 和空后的名词短语 the received (40) _____ 提示,所填词应该是充当 that 从句的谓语动词,并应该为第三人称单数形式。空前提到,如果不断地给婴儿看一些他们不熟悉的物品并重复告诉他们这是什么,九个月的婴儿也可以记住这些物品的名字,这与后面 children don't begin to build vocabulary until well into their second year 的论断是矛盾的,因此所填动词对后面的宾语 the received (40) _____ 应具有否定或反驳的含义。challenges 意为"挑战"。

40. 所填词应该是后面 that 从句的先行词,应能对从句的内容进行归纳概括,故很有可能是表示一种观点或看法。the received wisdom 意为"被普遍接受的观点或看法"。

41. 分析上下文关系可知,learning to (41) _____ things 与前面的 be taught ... to (38) _____ the names of objects 结构、意义均相近,所以本空所填词应是 38 题所填词的近义复现,即也应表示"认知"或"了解"的含义。identify 意为"识别,了解"。

42. It's no (42) _____ that ... 的句子结构表明,所填词应为一抽象名词。children learn words 是人所共知的常识,所填词应与此语义相符。secret 意为"秘密"。

43. 空前的介词 to 和空后的名词 situations 提示所填词应为形容词。situations 的定语 in the home 说明这里很可能是描述家中"特定的"或"具体的"场景。specific 意为"具体的"。

44. This is the first demonstration that we can choose what words the children will learn and that they can respond to them

〖Main Points〗**This first demonstrates** that we can choose **which** words the children will learn and that they can respond to them

45. What's more, the study of language acquisition offers direct insight into how humans learn

〖Main Points〗**Moreover**, the study **in** language acquisition offers direct insight into **the way** humans learn

46. even without being taught new words a control group caught up with the other infants within a few months

〖Main Points〗even **if they weren't** taught new words a control group caught up with the other infants **in** a few months

Exercise　　　专项练习　　🎧 边听边记

How men first learned to invent words is (S1) _____ ; in other words, the origin of language is a (S2) _____ . All we really know is that men, unlike animals, somehow invented certain sounds to (S3) _____ thoughts and feelings, actions and things, so that they could (S4) _____ with each other, and that later they agreed upon certain signs, called letters, which could be (S5) _____ to represent those sounds, and which could be written down. Those sounds, whether (S6) _____ or written in letters, we call words.

The power of words, then, lies in their (S7) _____ — the things they bring up before our minds. Words become filled with meaning for us by experience; and the longer we live, the more certain words (S8) _____ to us the glad and sad events of our past; and (S9) _____ .

Great writers are those who not only have great thoughts but also express these thoughts in words which appeal powerfully to our minds and emotions. (S10) _____ . Above all, the real poet is a master of words. He can convey his meaning in words which sing like music, and which by their position and association can move men to tears. We should, therefore, (S11) _____ .

【答案与解析】

【听力原文】	【答案解析】
How men first learned to invent words is (S1) <u>unknown</u>; in other words, the origin of language is a (S2) <u>mystery</u>. All we really know is that men, unlike animals, somehow invented certain sounds to (S3) <u>express</u> thoughts and feelings, actions and things, so that they could (S4) <u>communicate</u> with each other, and that later they agreed upon certain signs, called letters, which could be	S1. 空前的系动词 is 提示所填词应为形容词或动词的被动形式。下文没有提到人是如何发明文字的，只提到人们在生活中逐渐为交流创建符号，形成文字,故所填词可能是要表示"不知道的"的含义。unknown 意为"不知道的"。 S2. 空前的不定冠词 a 提示所填词应为单数可数名词。根据 in other words 和前一分句内容推测,所填词可能是要表示"未解之谜"的含义。mystery 意为"谜"。 S3. 空前的不定式 to 和空后的名词 thoughts

（S5）combined to represent those sounds, and which could be written down. Those sounds, whether（S6）spoken or written in letters, we call words.

The power of words, then, lies in their（S7）associations — the things they bring up before our minds. Words become filled with meaning for us by experience; and the longer we live, the more certain words（S8）recall to us the glad and sad events of our past; and（S9）the more we read and learn, the more the number of words that mean something to us.

Great writers are those who not only have great thoughts but also express these thoughts in words which appeal powerfully to our minds and emotions.（S10）This charming and telling use of words is what we call literary style. Above all, the real poet is a master of words. He can convey his meaning in words which sing like music, and which by their position and association can move men to tears. We should, therefore,（S11）learn to choose our words carefully and use them accurately, or they will make our speech silly and tasteless.

提示所填词应为动词原形。由 sounds, thoughts and feelings 推测，此处很可能表示"人发明了一些声音来表达思想和感情"的意思，故所填词很可能表示"表达"的含义。express 意为"表达"。

S4. 空前的情态动词 could 提示所填词应为动词原形，且能与介词 with 搭配。上文提到，人们可以表达自己的情感，那样彼此就可以交流了，故所填词可能要表示"交流"的含义。communicate 意为"交流"。

S5. 空前的系动词 be 和空后的不定式 to 提示所填词应为形容词或动词的被动式。根据句子中的 letters 和 represent those sounds 可以推测所填词可能是要表示"组合"的含义。combined 意为"组合"。

S6. 空后的并列连词 or 提示所填词应为动词的被动形式，与 written 构成并列结构。文字只有书面和口头两种，故所填词很可能表示："口头的，口语的"的含义。spoken 意为"口语的"。

S7. 空前的介词 in 和形容词性物主代词 their 提示所填词应为名词。associations 意为"结合"。

S8. 分析句子结构可知所填词应为谓语动词，并且能与介词 to 搭配。recall 意为"回想"。

S9.〖Main Points〗the more we read and **study**, the more the number of **meaningful words**

S10.〖Main Points〗This charming and **vivid** use of words **we call literary style**

S11.〖Main Points〗learn to choose our words carefully and use them accurately, or **our speech will appear silly and tasteless**

第四章 填词高招

通过空格前后的语法结构、近义词、反义词复现等卷面材料所提供的已知信息来预测空格处的未知信息，可以有效地提高听音的针对性，从而更准确地填出单词。

第一招：利用句子的语法结构

根据句子的主谓搭配、动宾搭配、修饰关系以及虚拟、倒装等语法结构关系，判断所缺单词的成分，从而推测出所填词的词性及形式（名词的单复数或动词的时态、语态等）。

【例1】 (05-6-S7)

> If the parents can afford it, each child will have his or her own bedroom. Having one's own bedroom, even as *an* (S7) _____, fixes in a person the notion that …

【解析】空前的不定冠词 an 提示所填词应为一个以元音音素开头的单数可数名词。本空答案为 infant。

第二招：利用语义连贯

根据上下文中的关键词与空格前后词语在语义上的连贯，判断出所填词可能的含义。

【例2】 (05-6-S6)

> If the parents can (S6) _____ it, each child **will have his or her own bedroom.**

【解析】空前的情态动词 can 和空后的代词 it 提示所填词应为动词原形。if 引导的条件状语从句应是后一句的前提，而要做到每个孩子都有自己的卧室，前提必须是父母能够承担得起费用。本空答案为 afford。

第三招：从逻辑衔接中寻找线索

根据上下文及句际间的逻辑关系，如并列、转折、因果等推测所填词可能的含义（主要通过连接词、介词短语和副词来判断）。

【例3】 (01-1-S7)

However, sometimes the overall energy balance is upset, and your normal body weight will *either fall or* (S7) _____.

【解析】either ... or ... 连接两个语法结构相同的并列成分,用于表示在两个可能性中选择一个。either 后面为动词原形 fall,or 后面也应为动词原形且意思应与 fall 相对。本空答案为 increase。

第四招:注意上下文的照应

根据同一语境中所填词的近义词、反义词、上、下义词推测所填词可能的形式和含义。近义词和反义词的出现常伴有表示并列或转折关系的信号词;上、下义词是指词的总括或分解关系,上义词是总称词,下义词是被包含的个体或种类。

【例4】 (99-6-S6)

The program would *fund* the (S4) coordination efforts of 20 thousand reading (S5) specialists and it would also give(S6) _____ to help parents help children read by the third grade, or about age eight.

【解析】and ... also 提示所填词所表达的含义应与前面的 fund(资助)形成照应,故也应表示"资助"或"补助"等相关含义。本空答案为 grants(补助)。

第五招:注意是否构成固定搭配

根据所填词与其前后词语构成的固定搭配或习惯表达来推测所填词的形式和含义。如动词 + 介词、形容词 + 介词或其他习惯性表达方式等。

【例5】 (05-6-S5)

Americans *have great* (S5) _____ *understanding* foreigners who always want to be with another person, who dislike being alone.

【解析】由空前的 have great 和空后的动名词 understanding,可以比较容易联想到固定搭配 have difficulty (in) doing sth。本题答案为 difficulty。

Exercise　　　　　　　专项练习　　　　　　🎧 边听边记

　　It was an Italian inventor who created the first wireless device for (S1) _____ out radio signals in 1895. But not until the American inventor Leede Forest built the first (S2) _____ vacuum tube in 1906 did we get the first radio as we know it. And the first (S3) _____ radio broadcast was made on Christmas

Eve of 1906. That's when someone working from all (S4) _____ station in Band Rock, Masschusetts, arranged the program of two short musical selections of poem and brief holiday (S5) _____. The broadcast was heard by wireless operators on ships with a radio through several hundred miles. The (S6) _____ year, De Forest began regular radio broadcasts in New York. These programs were (S7) _____ to much of what we hear on the radio today in that De Forest played only music. But because there was still no home radio receivers, De Forest's (S8) _____ consisted of only wireless operators on ships in New York harbor. There is no doubt that radio broadcasting was quite a (S9) _____ in those days. But it took a while to catch on commercially. Why? For the simple fact that only a few people, in fact, only those who tinkered with wireless telegraphs as a (S10) _____ owned receivers. It wasn't until the 1920's that someone envisioned mass appeal for radio. This was radio pioneer, David Sarnoff who (S11) _____ that one day there would be a radio receiver in every home.

〔边听边记〕

〔答案与解析〕

〔听力原文〕	〔答案解析〕
It was an Italian inventor who created the first wireless device for (S1) <u>sending</u> out radio signals in 1895. But not until the American inventor Leede Forest built the first (S2) <u>amplifying</u> vacuum tube in 1906 did we get the first radio as we know it. And the first (S3) <u>actual</u> radio broadcast was made on Christmas Eve of 1906. That's when someone working from all (S4) <u>experimental</u> station in Band Rock, Masschusetts, arranged the program of two short musical selections of poem and brief holiday (S5) <u>greeting</u>. The broadcast was heard by wireless operators	S1. 空前的介词 for 和空后的介词 out 提示所填词应为动词的现在分词形式。由空后的 signals 推测，所填词可能是要表示"发送"的含义。sending 意为"发送"。 S2. 空前的序数词 first 和空后的名词 vacuum tube 提示所填词应为形容词或名词。amplifying 意为"增大的"。 S3. 空前的序数词 first 和空后的名词词组 radio broadcast 提示所填词应为形容词。actual 意为"真正的"。 S4. 空前的泛指形容词 all 和空后的名词 station 提示所填词应为形容词或名词。experimental 意为"实验的"。 S5. 空前的并列连词 and 和名词 holiday 提示所填词应为名词。greeting 意为"祝贺"。 S6. 空前的定冠词 the 和空后的名词 year 提

on ships with a radio through several hundred miles. The (S6) following year, De Forest began regular radio broadcasts in New York. These programs were (S7) similar to much of what we hear on the radio today in that De Forest played only music. But because there was still no home radio receivers, De Forest's (S8) audience consisted of only wireless operators on ships in New York harbor. There is no doubt that radio broadcasting was quite a (S9) novelty in those days. But it took a while to catch on commercially. Why? For the simple fact that only a few people, in fact, only those who tinkered with wireless telegraphs as a (S10) hobby owned receivers. It wasn't until the 1920's that someone envisioned mass appeal for radio. This was radio pioneer, David Sarnoff who (S11) predicted that one day there would be a radio receiver in every home.

示所填词应为形容词。下文提到广播能够有规律地播放了，那么这应该是后来的事，此处是要表示接下来的一年，故所填词可能表示"接下来的，下一个"的含义。following 意为"接下来的"。

S7. 空前的系动词 were 和空后的介词 to 提示所填词应为动词的被动式或形容词。similar 意为"类似的"。

S8. 空前的名词所有格 De Forest's 和空后的动词 consisted 提示所填词应为名词。根据上文的内容和空后的内容 consisted of only wireless operators 推测，所填词是要表示"听众"的含义。audience 意为"听众"。

S9. 空前的不定冠词 a 和空后的介词 in 提示所填词应为单数可数名词。当时 radio broadcast 刚刚建立，在 those days 广播还是一个新奇事物，故所填词是要表示"新事物"的含义。novelty 意为"新事物"。

S10. 空前的不定冠词 a 和空后的动词 owned 提示所填词应为名词。hobby 意为"嗜好"。

S11. 分析句子结构可知所填词在从句中作谓语，且时态与上文一致应为一般过去式。根据空后的 one day，would be 推测，所填词是要表示"预言"的含义。predicted 意为"预言"。

填 句 法 宝

短文听写的句子结构一般都比较复杂,如在不了解其内容的情况下直接听写,很难抓住全部信息。因此,我们应该在听音前根据空格前后的逻辑关系、上下文内容及短文整体脉络和内容对句子可能陈述的主题进行推测,从而在听音时可以更有效地抓取更多的信息。

法宝一:抓住文章和段落的主题句

文章的开头或段首往往会出现主题句,之后的内容进一步展开,说明或论证该主题。抓住这些主题句,把握文章和段落的组织结构,有助于更好地理解文章或段落意义,更容易把握所填单词或句子的含义。

【例1】 (05-6-S8)

Certain phrases one commonly hears among Americans capture their devotion to individualism: "Do your own thing." "I did it my way." "You'll have to decide that for yourself." "You made your bed, now lie in it." "If you don't look out for yourself, no one else will." "Look out for number one." ……

If the parents can (S6) <u>afford</u> it, each child will have his or her own bedroom. Having one's own bedroom, even as an (S7) <u>infant</u>, fixes in a person the notion that (S8) _____. She will have her clothes, her toys, her books, and so on. These things will be hers and no one else's.

【解析】文章的第一句就点出了主题"individualism",接下来就是对这一主题的展开,从各个方面讲述美国人对待隐私的态度。空前的 the notion that 提示所填句应该是 the notion(观念)的同位语,根据本文的主题,该观念很可能与美国人对待隐私的态度有关。本空答案为 she is entitled to a place of her own where she can be by herself, and keep her possessions。

法宝二:根据段落主题推测段落首尾处空格内容

段落的开头或结尾往往起到承上启下的作用,常为主题或总结性的内容,因此应注意根据上下文的细节内容进行总结,推测段首或段尾空格处可能表达的内容。

【例2】 (05-6-S9)

Americans assume that (S9) _____.
Doctors, lawyers, psychologists, and others have rules governing "confidentiality"

that are intended to prevent information about their clients' personal situations from becoming known to others.

【解析】本空考查的是段首句。空后句子谈到医生、律师、精神病专家等职业人士都有规定要为客户保密个人信息,应该是对段首句子的展开,因此所填句很可能是讲美国人认为人们应该有对自己的想法或信息进行保密而不让他人知道的权利。本空答案为 people will have their private thoughts that might never be shared with anyone。

法宝三:理清句子间的逻辑关系

作者在组织篇章和段落时,经常会使用一些表达逻辑关系的词或短语,如顺承关系、因果关系、对比关系、转折关系等。通过分析句子结构,把握这些关键词,理清句子间的逻辑关系,可以推测所填句子所表达的大致含义,从而在听音时更准确地抓取有效信息。

【例3】 (710分样卷-46)

But Socrates, as a firm believer in law, reasoned that it was proper to submit to the death sentence. (46) _____.

【解析】空格前面的句子说苏格拉底是法律的坚定信奉者,他认为服从死刑是应当的,so 表示前后句子是因果关系,因此后面很可能是表达他接受了判决。本空答案为 So he calmly accepted his fate and drank a cup of poison in the presence of his grief-stricken friends and students。

法宝四:根据前后句意推测空格处内容

句与句之间在语义上要保持连贯,因此要利用空格前后句意,对所填句子可能表达的含义进行推测。

【例4】 (01-1-S9)

Research has revealed that about 40 percent of adult men and 55 percent of adult women are dissatisfied with their current body weight. (S9) _____
_____. At the college level, a study found that 85% of both male and female first-year students desired to change their body weight.

【解析】空前描述了对自己体重不满的成年人的比例,空后描述了对自己体重不满的大学新生的比例,由此可推测所填句子很可能是关于某个年龄阶层的人对自己体重的不满情况。

法宝五：明确代词的指代关系

空格后面句子中的代词往往为空格所在句中出现过的词,因此要学会利用后面句子的内容明确代词的指代内容,从而推测所填句要陈述的内容。

【例5】　　　　　　　　　　　　　　　　　　　　　　　　　(01-1-S9)

> The term body image refers to the mental image we have of our own physical appearance , and it (S8) ＿＿＿＿＿＿＿＿＿＿＿＿＿＿＿ .
>
> 【解析】根据上文可知,所填句子的主语 it 指代的是 body image(体形),由此可推知所填句子的陈述对象是"体形"。

法宝六：学会记录关键词

由于句子结构比较复杂,而且时间有限,考生想要在听音时将句子完整地写下来不太现实,因此考生应学会记录关键词,然后调动自己的语法知识、词汇知识、语篇分析能力、语感和思维判断能力,将所记录的关键词整理成完整、准确的句子。可见,足够信息量的笔记是写好要点的重要条件。

首先,要学会使用缩略语。缩略语不一定要求规范,甚至可以用些符号,所记内容不一定要求完整,只要能起到提示的作用,自己能看懂就行了。这里的基本要求是快速、省时,并能表达含义。

其次,要有选择地作笔记。由于短文听写的句子结构都比较复杂,即使使用缩略语也难记下全句,因此考生应有选择地作笔记。英语中的实词具有表意功能,而虚词多具语法功能,所记词应以实词为主。

再次,重点记录句子主干。因为短文听写第二部分只要求写出内容要点,这样考生应重点记录句子的主干中心词,在记下主干的前提下尽可能记全信息。

总之,弄清句子的前后关系并进行适当地分析和推理是准确填写出所填内容的关键。但是,技巧只是提纲挈领的,能帮助提高准确度,但只注重技巧而忽视实践,不多练习也不会取得很好的成绩,因此必须把两者有机地结合起来,才会取得事半功倍的效果。

Exercise　　　专项练习　　　🎧 边听边记

A cab driver taught me a million dollar lesson in customer satisfaction and expectation. (S1) ＿＿＿＿＿＿＿＿＿＿ . It cost me a $ 12 taxi ride.

I had flown into Dallas for the sole purpose of calling on a client. (S2) ＿＿＿＿＿＿＿＿＿＿ . A spotless cab pulled up. The driver (S3) ＿＿＿＿＿＿＿＿＿＿ .
As he got in the driver's seat, he mentioned that the neatly folded

Wall Street Journal next to me was for my use. (S4) _____ 🎧 边听边记

_____. Well! I looked around for a "Candid Camera!" Wouldn't you? I could not believe the service I was receiving! I took the opportunity to say, "Obviously you take great pride in your work. You must have a story to tell."

"You bet," he replied, "I used to be in Corporate America. But I got tired of thinking my best would never be good enough. I decided to find my niche in life where I could feel proud of being the best I could be. I knew I would never be a rocket scientist, (S5) __

_____. I evaluate my personal assets and... Wham! I became a cab driver. (S6) _____

_____. But, to be great in my business. I have to exceed the customer's expectations! I like both the sound and the return of being 'great' better than just getting by on 'average'.

Did I tip him big time? You bet! Corporate America's loss is the traveling folk's friend!

【答案与解析】

【听力原文】	【答案解析】
A cab driver taught me a million dollar lesson in customer satisfaction and expectation. (S1) <u>Motivational speakers charge thousands of dollars to impart this kind of training to corporate executives and staff.</u> It cost me a $ 12 taxi ride. I had flown into Dallas for the sole purpose of calling on a client. (S2) <u>Time was of the essence and my plan included a quick turn around trip from and back to the airport.</u> A spotless cab pulled up. The driver (S3) <u>rushed to open the passenger door for me and made sure I was comfortably seated before he closed the door.</u> As he got in the driver's seat, he mentioned that the neatly folded *Wall Street Journal* next to me was for my use. (S4) <u>He then showed me several ta-</u>	S1. 空前提到一名出租车司机给我上了一堂价值百万的课，空后提到这堂课只花了我 12 美元的车费，由此可推知所填句很可能也与这堂课的费用有关。 【Main Points】Motivational speakers charge thousands of dollars to **give** this **sort** of training to **company** executives and staff S2. 空前提到"我"来到 Dallas 的目的是拜访一个客户，空后说一辆出租车停了下来，由此可推知所填句很可能与"我"的计划或要进行的活动有关。 【Main Points】Time was **essential** and **I planned to have** a quick turn around trip from and back to the airport S3. 由空后的 as he got in the dirver's seat(司机坐回到他的位置时)可推知，司机应该是下了车，结合空前的内容("我

pes and asked me what type of music I would enjoy. Well! I looked around for a "Candid Camera!" Wouldn't you? I could not believe the service I was receiving! I took the opportunity to say, "Obviously you take great pride in your work. You must have a story to tell."

"You bet," he replied, "I used to be in Corporate America. But I got tired of thinking my best would never be good enough. I decided to find my niche in life where I could feel proud of being the best I could be. I knew I would never be a rocket scientist, (S5) but I love driving cars, being of service and feeling like I have done a full day's work and done it well. I evaluate my personal assets and... Wham! I became a cab driver. (S6) One thing I know for sure, to be good in my business I could simply just meet the expectations of my passengers. But, to be great in my business I have to exceed the customer's expectations! I like both the sound and the return of being 'great' better than just getting by on 'average'.

Did I tip him big time? You bet! Corporate America's loss is the traveling folk's friend!

要打车拜访客户)可推知,所填句很可能是关于司机下车为"我"提供服务。

【Main Points】rushed to open **the door for me** and **after he made sure I was comfortably seated, he closed the door**

S4. 空前提到司机提示"我"可以看旁边的 *Wall Street Journal*,空后提到"我"没想到自己会得到这么好的服务,由此可推知所填句很可能是讲述司机为"我"提供的其他服务。

【Main Points】**Then he** showed me **some** tapes and asked me **what music I** would **like**

S5. 空前提到司机说他知道自己不可能成为火箭科学家,空后提到他成了一名出租车司机,由此可推知所填句很可能与他成为出租车司机的原因有关。

【Main Points】but I **like driving**, being of service and feeling like I have done a **whole** day's work and done it well

S6. 由空后 but 转折句可知,司机觉得要想体现出他的工作的伟大,他必须超出顾客的期望,由此可推知所填词很可能与司机满足顾客期望有关。

【Main Points】One thing I know **surely**, to be good in my business I could just **reach my passengers' expectations**

综合训练

Exercise 1

边听边记

The advantages and disadvantages of a large population have long been a subject of discussion among economists. It has been argued that the (36) _____ of good land is limited. To feed a large population, (37) _____ land must be cultivated and the good land worked (38) _____. Thus, each person produces less and this means a lower (39) _____ income than could be obtained with a smaller population. Other economists have argued that a large population gives more (40) _____ for specialization and the development of (41) _____ such as ports, roads and railways, which are not likely to be built unless there is a big (42) _____ to justify them.

One of the difficulties in carrying out a (43) _____ birth control program lies in the fact that official attitudes to population growth vary from country to country depending on the level of industrial development and the availability of food and raw materials. In developing countries where a vastly expanded population is pressing hard upon the limits of food, space and natural resources, (44) _____. In a highly industrialized society the problem may be more complex. (45) _____. When the pressure of population on housing declines, prices also decline and the building industry is weakened. (46) _____ __, rather than one which is stable or in decline.

Exercise 2

Like many other countries, Britain has experienced a great increase in criminal activity of nearly every kind. Nearly five times as many acts of (36) _____ were reported to the police in 1987 as twenty years before. Although most (37) _____ are not caught, those who are caught (38) _____ the courts and

边听边记

prisons. Although the courts try, in (39) _____ at least, to
use probation, community service and other devices to avoid (40)
_____ people to prison, the 50,000 people in prison are more,
in (41) _____ to the population, than in any other Western
European countries. Vast sums are being spent on building new
prisons, but the prisons are still (42) _____. Each prison has
a local Board of Visitors who make reports about (43) _____
and also deal with serious bad behavior. (44) _____
_____. There are several kinds of prisons, (45) _____
_____. Prisoners who want to study for
examination are helped to do so, and there are training courses in
prison. (46) _____.

Exercise 3

The tobacco industry has been large and important to America's
economy ever since colonial farmers grew tobacco for export 300
years ago. Even today tobacco is grown in large (36) _____
along America's Eastern Coast.

Since the 1800's the most (37) _____ form of smoking
tobacco is in cigarettes. Men and women of all (38) _____
smoke cigarettes and there are dozens of (39) _____ sold in
the U. S. Pipe smoking has some (40) _____ and cigars are
usually only smoked by older men. Over the past (41) _____
years, many people have stopped smoking. This (42) _____
away from cigarettes began when lung cancer and other (43)
_____ were linked to smoking. In the 1970's, when taxes on
cigarettes were greatly increased, cigarette smoking became much
more expensive. (44) _____. These three
factors have been the major causes for many people to stop smoking.

Today in the U. S. cigarette smoking is restricted in many
ways. (45) _____. When they are on
public buses, in theaters and in classrooms, they may not smoke at
all. Cigarettes are not advertised on television or radio. Cigarettes
are not advertised on television or radio. (46) _____
_____.

答案与解析

Exericise 1

【听力原文】	【答案解析】
The advantages and disadvantages of a large population have long been a subject of discussion among economists. It has been argued that the (36) <u>supply</u> of good land is limited. To feed a large population, (37) <u>inferior</u> land must be cultivated and the good land worked (38) <u>intensively</u>. Thus, each person produces less and this means a lower (39) <u>average</u> income than could be obtained with a smaller population. Other economists have argued that a large population gives more (40) <u>scope</u> for specialization and the development of (41) <u>facilities</u> such as ports, roads and railways, which are not likely to be built unless there is a big (42) <u>demand</u> to justify them. One of the difficulties in carrying out a (43) <u>world-wide</u> birth control program lies in the fact that official attitudes to population growth vary from country to country depending on the level of industrial development and the availability of food and raw materials. In developing countries where a vastly expanded population is pressing hard upon the limits of food, space and natural resources, (44) <u>the first concern of the government will be to place a limit on the birthrate, whatever the consequences may be</u>. In a highly industrialized society the problem may be more	36. 空前的定冠词 the 和空后的介词 of 提示所填词应为名词。supply 意为"供应"。 37. 空后的名词 land 提示所填词应为形容词。前面提到土壤肥沃的土地有限,那得开垦不好的土地,故填词很可能表达"差的,劣等的"的含义,与后面的 good land 形成对比关系。inferior 意为"劣等的"。 38. 空前的不及物动词 worked 提示所填词应为副词。intensively 意为"集中地"。 39. 空前的形容词比较级 lower 和空后的名词 income 提示所填词应为形容词。前面提到 each person 地里的的产量变少了,那么他们的平均收入也就减少了,故所填词很可能表达"平均的"的含义。average 意为"平均的"。 40. 空前的动词 gives 和形容词比较级 more 与空后的介词 for 提示所填词应为名词。scope 意为"范围"。 41. 空前的介词 of 和空后的介词短语 such as 提示所填词应为名词。由空后 such as... 所举例的内容推测,所填词可能是要表达"公共设施"的含义。facilities 意为"设施"。 42. 空前的形容词 big 和空后的不定式 to 提示所填词应为名词。上文提到,人口多的话就可以建造更多的公路,铁路;可如果人口数量下降,没有了这个需求,这就不可能实现了,故所填词可能是要表示"需求"的含义。demand 意为"需求"。 43. 空前的不定冠词 a 和空后的名词词组

complex. (45) <u>A decreasing birthrate may lead to unemployment because it results in a declining market for manufactured goods</u>. When the pressure of population on housing declines, prices also decline and the building industry is weakened. (46) <u>Faced with considerations such as these, the government of a developed country may well prefer to see a slowly increasing population</u>, rather than one which is stable or in decline.

birth control program 提示所填词应为形容词。world-wide 意为"世界范围的"。

44.【Main Points】the first concern of the government will be to **limit** the birthrate, **whatever consequences there may be**

45.【Main Points】A decreasing birthrate may **bring** unemployment because it results in **the market's declining** for manufactured goods

46.【Main Points】**Facing such considerations**, the government of a developed country may well prefer to see **the population increasing slowly**

Exericise 2

【听力原文】

Like many other countries, Britain has experienced a great increase in criminal activity of nearly every kind. Nearly five times as many acts of (36) <u>violence</u> were reported to the police in 1987 as twenty years before. Although most (37) <u>burglars</u> are not caught, those who are caught (38) <u>overload</u> the courts and prisons. Although the courts try, in (39) <u>theory</u> at least, to use probation, community service and other devices to avoid (40) <u>sentencing</u> people to prison, the 50,000 people in prison are more, in (41) <u>proportion</u> to the population, than in any other Western European countries. Vast sums are being spent on building new prisons, but the prisons are still

【答案解析】

36. 空前的介词 of 和空后的系动词 were 提示所填词应为名词。由上句中的 criminal activity 和所填词所在句子的内容推测,所填词可能是指犯罪行为。violence 意为"暴力"。

37. 空前的形容词 most 和空后的系动词 are 提示所填词应为名词的复数形式。根据句子中的 caught 和 courts and prisons 推测,所填词可能是指犯了某种罪行的人。burglars 意为"盗贼"。

38. 分析句子结构可知,所填词应在定语从句中作谓语,根据上下文的时态判断,所填词应为一般现在时。overload 意为"使…超载"。

39. 空前的介词 in 和空后的短语 at least 提示所填词应为名词。theory 意为"理论"。

40. 空前的动词 avoid 和空后的名词 people 提示所填词应为动词的现在分词形式。根据句中的内容 to prison 推测,所填词可能是要表示"判刑"的含义。sentencing 意为"判刑"。

(42) <u>overcrowded</u>. Each prison has a local Board of Visitors who make reports about (43) <u>conditions</u> and also deal with serious bad behavior. (44) <u>An offence in prison may be punished by the loss of some days of remission</u>. There are several kinds of prisons, (45) <u>including open ones, and some prisoners go out to work in groups outside</u>. Prisoners who want to study for examination are helped to do so, and there are training courses in prison. (46) <u>But in practice some spend very little time outside their cells, and they must stay in the cells most of the time</u>.

41. 空前的介词 in 和空后的介词 to 提示所填词应为名词。proportion 意为"比例"。

42. 空前的系动词 are 和副词 still 提示所填词应为形容词或动词的被动形式。空前提到英国建造了很多监狱，由 but 推测下句表达监狱里的人还是很多的意思，故所填词很可能表达"拥挤的"的含义。overcrowded 意为"过于拥挤的"。

43. 空前的名词 reports 和介词 about 提示所填词应为名词。conditions 意为"状况"。

44. 【Main Points】An offence in prison may be punished by **losing some days' remission**

45. 【Main Points】including open **prisons**, and some prisoners **go to** work **outside** in groups

46. 【Main Points】But **practically** some spend little time outside their cells, and they must stay in **their** cells **most time**

Exercise 3

【听力原文】

　　The tobacco industry has been large and important to America's economy ever since colonial farmers grew tobacco for export 300 years ago. Even today tobacco is grown in large (36) <u>quantities</u> along America's Eastern Coast.

　　Since the 1800's the most (37) <u>common</u> form of smoking tobacco is in cigarettes. Men and women of all (38) <u>ages</u> smoke cigarettes and there are dozens of (39) <u>brands</u> sold in the U. S. Pipe smoking has some (40) <u>popularity</u> and cigars are usually only smoked by older men. Over the past (41) <u>fifteen</u> years, many people have stopped smoking.

【答案解析】

36. 空前的形容词 large 和空后的介词 along 提示所填词应为名词。空前提到 300 年前美国主要种植烟草，由后面的 Even today 推测美国现在种植的烟草也很多，故所填词很可能表达"数量"的含义。quantities 意为"数量"。

37. 空前的形容词最高级 most 和空后的名词 form 提示所填词应为形容词。根据常识，吸香烟是 smoking tobacco 最常见的一种形式，故所填词很可能表达"普通的，平常的"的含义。common 意为"平常的"。

38. 空前的形容词 all 和空后的动词 smoke 提示所填词应为名词的复数形式。ages 意为"年龄"。

39. 空前的名词短语 dozens of 提示所填词应为复数可数名词。brands 意为"品牌"。

This (42) <u>movement</u> away from cigarettes began when lung cancer and other (43) <u>ailments</u> were linked to smoking. In the 1970's, when taxes on cigarettes were greatly incr-eased, cigarette smoking became much more expensive. (44) <u>Since the late 1970's physical fitness has become a major aim of millions of Americans.</u> These three factors have been the major causes for many people to stop smoking.

Today in the U. S. cigarette smoking is restricted in many ways. (45) <u>When smokers are in restaurants, on trains and in public buildings, they may smoke only in designated areas.</u> When they are on public buses, in theaters and in classrooms, they may not smoke at all. Cigarettes are not advertised on television or radio. (46) <u>A notice is on every package of cigarettes sold in America warning that smoking is dangerous to health.</u>

40. 空前的泛指形容词 some 提示所填词应为名词。popularity 意为"流行"。

41. 空前的形容词 past 和空后的名词 years 提示所填词应为形容词，根据句中 over 和 years 推测，所填词应为数词。fifteen 意为"十五"。

42. 空前的指示形容词 this 提示所填词应为名词的单数形式。movement 意为"运动"。

43. 空前的形容词 other 和空后的系动词 were 提示所填词应为名词的复数形式。根据 lung cancer 和 and other 推测此处可能是要表示肺癌和其他疾病与吸烟有联系，故所填词可能是要表示"疾病"的含义。ailments 意为"疾病"。

44. 〖Main Points〗Since the late 1970's physical **health** has become a **main** aim of millions of Americans

45. 〖Main Points〗**When being** in resta-urants, on trains and in public buildings, **smokers** may smoke only in **special** areas

46. 〖Main Points〗In America on every package of cigarettes sold **there is a notice** warning that smoking is **a danger** to health

高分模拟

本篇严格按照六级新题型考试听力试题的难度、特点和出题思路,精心设计了 8 套模拟试题,考生可以通过自测学习,对前面的复习进行巩固,熟悉并适应考试环境,提高应试能力。

Model Test 1

Section A

Directions: *In this section, you will hear 8 short conversations and 2 long conversations. At the end of each conversation, one or more questions will be asked about what was said. Both the conversation and the questions will be spoken only once. After each question there will be a pause. During the pause, you must read the four choices marked [A], [B], [C] and [D], and decide which is the best answer. Then mark the corresponding letter on **Answer Sheet 2** with a single line through the centre.*

11. [A] He decided not to go to New York.

   [B] He won an award recently.

   [C] He is going to organize a dinner.

   [D] No one expected him to move.

12. [A] Joe bought Fred's car.

   [B] The man is joking.

   [C] Fred's car is not good.

   [D] The man wants Jack's car.

13. [A] Repair the other door.　　[B] Visit some ruins.

   [C] Have an outdoor party.　　[D] Catch a Saturday train.

14. [A] $150.　[B] $175.　[C] $200.　[D] $225.

15. [A] The man shouldn't expect her to go along.

   [B] She doesn't think she has enough money.

   [C] She'll go even though the movie is over.

   [D] The man should count the number of people going.

16. [A] He should look for a battery at the drugstore.

   [B] The drugstore may not be open at this hour.

   [C] He should have tried the radio earlier.

   [D] She doesn't know how to open the radio.

17. [A] Moving into a different office in the department.

   [B] Taking a day off from studying.

[C] Joining the other students in the department.

[D] Finding more students to help with the move.

18. [A] He will no longer ask for their help.

[B] He will regret not having their help.

[C] He still needs their help.

[D] He has to manage without their help.

Questions 19 to 21 are based on the conversation you have just heard.

19. [A] Confident. [B] Hesitant. [C] Determined. [D] Doubtful.

20. [A] An export salesman working overseas.

[B] A trainee working through every branch.

[C] A production manager in a branch.

[D] A policy maker in the company.

21. [A] Trainees are required to sign contracts initially.

[B] Trainees' performance is evaluated occasionally.

[C] Trainees' starting salary is 870 pounds.

[D] Trainees cannot quit the management scheme at will.

Questions 22 to 25 are based on the conversation you have just heard.

22. [A] She needs some information.

[B] She wants packing materials.

[C] She is checking her package.

[D] She is moving to California.

23. [A] Fresh fruit.   [B] A gift certificate.

[C] Homemade candy.   [D] A wedding present.

24. [A] The next day.   [B] On Saturday.

[C] In three days.   [D] In one week.

25. [A] Regular service.   [B] Overnight express.

[C] Same day delivery.   [D] Priority service.

Section B

Directions: *In this section, you will hear 3 short passages. At the end of each passage, you will hear some questions. Both the passage and the questions will be spoken only once. After you hear a question, you must choose the best answer from the four choices marked [A], [B], [C] and [D]. Then mark the corresponding letter on **Answer Sheet 2** with a single line through the centre.*

边听边记

Passage One

边听边记

Questions 26 to 28 are based on the passage you have just heard.

26. [A] Canada and New Mexico. [B] Canada and Mexico.

　　[C] Alaska and Hawaii. 　　[D] India and England.

27. [A] In the northern part.

　　[B] In the eastern part.

　　[C] In the eastern part of the American continent.

　　[D] In the eastern part of the North American continent.

28. [A] Because all the Americans are from England.

　　[B] Because all the Americans like English very much.

　　[C] Because the earliest settlers were mostly from England.

　　[D] Because English is a world language.

Passage Two

Questions 29 to 31 are based on the passage you have just heard.

29. [A] A person is doing a job which he likes very much.

　　[B] A person is doing a job which he doesn't like.

　　[C] A person is doing a job which he is not suited tor.

　　[D] A person is doing a job which he thinks very important.

30. [A] Because it will make a person earn a lot of money.

　　[B] Because many people in the world don't want to be square pegs.

　　[C] Because good jobs make them happy.

　　[D] Because it will make full use of their talents.

31. [A] Businessmen, managers and accountants.

　　[B] Chemists, physicists and biologists.

　　[C] Governors, doctors and teachers.

　　[D] Engineers, public servants and news reporters.

Passage Three

Questions 32 to 35 are based on the passage you have just heard.

32. [A] Geography and Land Features.

　　[B] The Importance of a Good Climate.

　　[C] Different Physical Characteristics.

　　[D] The Importance of Lakes and Rivers.

33. [A] The climate varies a little in the United States.

　　[B] The climate varies a lot in the United States.

　　[C] There is no variation in climate in the United States.

　　[D] The climate is very pleasant all the year round.

34. [A] The United States is full of wide plains and high mountains.
 [B] The United States is full of lakes and rivers.
 [C] The United States is full of cool forests and hot deserts.
 [D] The United States has a great variety of different land features.

35. [A] They provide us plenty of fresh water.
 [B] They provide us plenty of fisheries products.
 [C] They made possible the easy irrigation of fields.
 [D] They made possible the easy transportation of people and all the things people need.

Section C

Directions: *In this section, you will hear a passage three times. When the passage is read for the first time, you should listen carefully for its general idea. When the passage is read for the second time, you are required to fill in the blanks numbered from 36 to 43 with the exact words you have just heard. For blanks numbered from 44 to 46 you are required to fill in the missing information. For these blanks, you can either use the exact words you have just heard or write down the main points in your own words. Finally, when the passage is read for the third time, you should check what you have written.*

Chinese students are (36) _____ willing to study very hard for long hours. This is an excellent (37) _____, but it is often an (38) _____ method of study. An efficient student must have enough food, rest and (39) _____. You need to play ball, or sing a song, or go out with friends, see a movie, visit some (40) _____ spots. When you return to your studies, your mind will be (41)_____ and you'll learn more. Shorter, more intense study (42) _____ are more effective than endless hours of (43) _____ over your books.

Finally, be realistic. (44) _____. Psychologists have determined that learning takes place this way: first, you make a lot of progress and you feel very happy. Then your language ability seems to stay the same; (45) _____

_____.

Perhaps we can say that learning English is like taking Chinese medicine. We don't mean that it's bitter. (46) ＿＿＿＿＿＿＿＿
＿＿＿＿＿＿. So, don't give up along the way.

听力原文与答案详解

Section A & Section B

11	D	12	A	13	C	14	B	15	A	16	A	17	D	18	D	19	B
20	A	21	C	22	A	23	C	24	B	25	D	26	B	27	D	28	C
29	C	30	D	31	B	32	A	33	D	34	D	35	D				

Section C

36. generally　　37. characteristic　　38. inefficient　　39. relaxation
40. scenic　　41. refreshed　　42. sessions　　43. nodding
44. If you set impossible goals for yourself you can only be disappointed in your progress
45. this period can last for days or even weeks, but you mustn't be discouraged
46. We mean that, like Chinese medicine, the effects of your study come slowly but surely

Section A

11.

[A] He decided not to go to New York.	M: I didn't know till recently that Mike was going to move to New York.
[B] He won an award recently.	
[C] He is going to organize a dinner.	W: That took us all by surprise.
[D] No one expected him to move.	Q: What does the woman say about Mike?

【解析】观点态度题。男士说他最近才知道 Mike 打算搬到 New York,女士说 That took us all by surprise(这让我们大家都很吃惊),由此可知没有人想到 Mike 会搬家。

12.

[A] Joe bought Fred's car.	M: I heard that Jack bought Fred's old car.
[B] The man is joking.	W: That's funny. I heard that Joe did.
[C] Fred's car is not good.	Q: What does the woman think?
[D] The man wants Jack's car.	

【解析】事实状况题。男士说他听说 Jack 买了 Fred 的旧车,女士则说她听说 Joe did,言外之意是她认为是 Joe 买了 Fred 的旧车。

13.

[A] Repair the other door.	M: If it rains on Saturday, the party will be ruined.
[B] Visit some ruins.	W: What does it matter? We can always hold it indo-
[C] Have an outdoor party.	ors.
[D] Catch a Saturday train.	Q: What are the man and the woman hoping to do?

【解析】行为活动题。男士说如果周六下雨就不能举行 party 了,女士则说他们还能 hold … indoors,由此可知他们原本打算 have an outdoor party。

14.

[A] $150.	M: How much is the rent?
[B] $175.	W: It's a hundred and fifty dollars a month unfurnished or two hundred
[C] $200.	dollars a month furnished. Utilities are twenty-five dollars extra.
[D] $225.	Q: How much will it cost the man to rent an unfurnished apartment
	including utilities?

【解析】事实状况题。女士说未装修的公寓每月租金为 150 美元,utilities(用品设施)另加 25 美元,因此共计 175 美元。

15.

[A] The man shouldn't expect her to go along.	M: It would be funny to see the new movie downtown.
[B] She doesn't think she has enough money.	W: Count me out. I heard it isn't wo-
[C] She'll go even though the movie is over.	rth the money.
[D] The man should count the number of people going.	Q: What does the woman mean?

【解析】观点态度题。男士建议女士去看电影,女士说别算上她,因为她听说这部电影 isn't worth the money,由此可知她不会陪男士去看那场电影。

16.

[A] He should look for a battery at the drugstore.	M: Where can I find batteries for my radio at this time of the night?
[B] The drugstore may not be open at this hour.	W: Why don't you try the drugstore? It's closed late.
[C] He should have tried the radio earlier.	
[D] She doesn't know how to open the radio.	Q: What does the woman mean?

【解析】事实状况题。男士不知道这么晚哪里还可以买到 batteries(电池),女士建议他去 drugstore(杂货店)看看,没准他能买到电池。

17.

[A] Moving into a different office in the department.	W: I'm moving to a new place tomorrow, could you possibly give me a hand?
[B] Taking a day off from studying.	M: Sure, why not ask around the department to see if some of the other students will be free too?
[C] Joining the other students in the department.	Q: What does the man suggest?
[D] Finding more students to help with the move.	

【解析】行为活动题。女士说她要搬家，请男士帮忙，男士表示同意并建议她看看是否 some of the other students will be free，那样她可以多找些学生来帮忙。give sb a hand 意为"帮某人的忙"。

18.

[A] He will no longer ask for their help.	W: Though we cared for Mike for a while, now he must care for himself.
[B] He will regret not having their help.	M: Yes, he can live on his own now.
[C] He still needs their help.	Q: What does the woman think of Mike?
[D] He has to manage without their help.	

【解析】观点态度题。女士说我们照看 Mike 有一段时间了，他现在必须 care for himself(自己照顾自己了)，由此可知女士认为 Mike 必须要在没有别人的帮助下生活了。

Conversation One

【听力原文】	【答案解析】
W: Now I've got your background, let's talk about the management trainee scheme. What exactly do you think a manager does?	19. How does Mr. Smith sound when asked what a manager's role is?
M: I don't know a great deal about the work.	【解析】选 [B]。推断题。当被问到经理的确切职责是什么时，男士回答说他对这个工作了解不多，在女士的一再要求下，男士才支支吾吾地说经理要做许多 policy-making(决策)，还要知道如何处理
W: But have you got any ideas about it? You must have thought about it.	
M: [19] Well, er, I suppose he has a lot of, er, what is called, policy-making to do. And, mm, he'd have to know how to work with people and all about the company.	
W: Mm.	
M: Yes, I, er, should think a manager must know, er, something about all aspects of the work.	

【听力原文】	【答案解析】
W: Yes, that's right. We like our executive staff to undergo a thorough training. Young men on our trainee scheme have to work through every branch in the company. M: Well, if I had to do it, I suppose. But I was thinking that my French and German would mean that I could specialize in overseas work. [20] I'd like to be some sort of an export salesman and travel abroad. W: You know the charm of traveling abroad disappears when you've got to work hard. It's not all fun and game. M: Oh, yes, I realize that. It's just that my knowledge of languages would be useful. W: Now, Mr. Smith, is there anything you want to ask me? M: Well, there's one or two things. I'd like to know if I'd have to sign a contract, what the salary is and what the prospects are. W: With our scheme, Mr. Smith, [21①] there is no contract involved. Your progress is kept under constant review. If we, at any time, decide we don't like you, then that's that! [21②] We reserve the right to dismiss you. Of course, you have the same choice about us. As for salary, you'd be on our fixed scale starting at 870 pounds. For the successful trainee, the prospects are very good.	公司的人和事,并由男士话中的多个er可推断出,男士回答这个问题时非常犹豫,没有把握。 20. What does Mr. Smith say he would like to be? 【解析】选[A]。细节题。男士说他想做一名export salesman(出口业务员),这样可以travel abroad。 21. What can we learn about the management trainee scheme? 【解析】选[C]。细节题。对话结尾处,女士说there is no contract(没有合同),双方可以随时解除合同,工资是on … fixed scale(按固定的级别标准),起点是870英镑。

Conversation Two

【听力原文】	【答案解析】
M: Hello, National Express Courier Company, Customer Service Department. W: Hello, [22] I have some questions about a package I'm going to send, can you help me? M: Yes, ma'am. What would you like to know? W: [23] I have a box of homemade candy. And I want to send it to my sister, it's a birthday present. Do you have any special rules about delivering	22. Why is the woman calling the delivery company? 【解析】选[A]。细节题。女士打电话说她想询问some questions about a package(一些关于邮寄包裹的相关事宜),由此可知

food?

M: No, not in this case, ma'ma. If you were sending fruit or vegetables, they would have to be packed specially. But there are no rules about sending candy.

W: OK, I have another question. I'm very concerned about the package reaching my sister on time. Can you make sure that [24]it will be there by her birthday on Saturday?

M: Where does it have to go?

W: California.

M: Hmm. Saturday's only four days away. We have a priority service that would guarantee delivery in three days but it's more expensive than our regular rate.

W: Well, I don't want to waste money, but it's more important that the package be there on time.

M: OK. Bring your package to the office, and [25] we'll send it by priority service.

W: OK. I'll do that.

她给邮递公司打电话是想获得 some information。

23. What is the woman sending to her sister?

【解析】选[C]。细节题。女士明确提到她准备给妹妹邮寄一盒 homemade candy(自制糖果)。

24. When is her sister's birthday?

【解析】选[B]。细节题。女士明确提到她妹妹的生日在 Saturday。

25. Which method will the woman probably use to send her package?

【解析】选[D]。细节题。对话结尾处,男士说他就以 priority service(快件)方式来邮寄女士的包裹。

Section B

Passage One

【听力原文】	【答案解析】

The United States covers a large part of the North American continent. [26]Its neighbors are Canada to the north, and Mexico to the south. Although the United States is a big country, it is not the largest in the world. In 1964, its population was over 185,000,000.

When this land first became a nation, after winning its independence from England, it had thirteen states. Each of the states was represented on the American flag by a star. [27]All these states were in the eastern part of the continent. As the nation grew toward the west, new states were added and new stars appeared on the flag. For a long time, there were 48 states. In 1959, however, two more

26. What countries are neighbors of the United States?

【解析】选[B]。细节题。文章开头说美国的邻国有北面的 Canada(加拿大)和南面的 Mexico(墨西哥)。

27. Where were the earlier states located?

【解析】选[D]。细节题。

stars were added to the flag representing the new states of Alaska and Hawaii.

Indians were the first inhabitants of the land which is now the United States. There are still many thousands of the descendants of these original inhabitants living in all parts of the country. Sometimes it is said that the Indians are " the only real Americans ". Most Americans, however, are descendants of [28]those who came first and in greatest numbers to make their homes on the eastern coast of North America were mostly from England. It is for that reason that the language of the United States is English and that its culture and customs are more like those of England than those of any other country in the world.

文中说早先成立的13个州都位于 the eastern part of the continent（北美洲的东部）。

28. For what reason is it that the language of the United States is English?

【解析】选[C]。文章结尾处说，美国使用的语言为英语是因为最早来美国东部定居的人 mostly from England。

Passage Two

【听力原文】	【答案解析】

Sometimes we say that someone we know is "a square peg in a round hole". [29]This simply means that the person we are talking about is not suited for the job he is doing. He may be a bookkeeper who really wants to be an actor or a mechanic who likes cooking. Unfortunately, many people in the world are "square pegs", they are not doing the kind of work they should be doing, for one reason or another. As a result, they probably are not doing a very good job and certainly they are not happy.

Choosing the right career is very important. [30]Most of us spend a great part of our lives at our jobs. For that reason we should try to find out what our talents are and how we can use them.

We can do this through aptitude tests, interviews with specialists, and study of books in our field of interest.

There are many careers open to each of us. [31]Perhaps we like science, then we might pr-

29. What is implied in "a square peg in a round hole"?

【解析】选[C]。细节题。文中说 a square peg in a round hole 是用来指某个人并不 suited for the job he is doing（适合他所做的工作）。

30. Why is it important to find the right career?

【解析】选[D]。细节题。文中说选择适合的工作很重要，接着说大部分人都把大半生的时间花在工作上，所以只有找到适合的工作，尽可能挖掘 what our talents are（我们的才能是什么），才能很好的利用这些才能，也就是说找到适合的工作能 make full use of ... talents。

31. What are some of the careers found in the scientific world acco-

epare ourselves to be chemists, physicists, or biologists. Maybe our interests take us into the business world and such work as accounting, personnel management or public relations. Many persons find their place in government service. Teaching, newspaper work, medicine, engineering — these and many other fields offer fascinating careers to persons with talent and training.

rding to the passage?
【解析】选[B]。推断题。文中说我们可以选择各种各样的工作,如果有人喜欢 science,那么他们就可以培养自己成为 chemists, physicists 或 biologists,由此可推断 chemists, physicists 和 biologists 这些职业属于 the scientific world。

Passage Three

【听力原文】	【答案解析】
[32①] The geographical location of a country and its physical characteristics are very important to its development and progress. The United States is very fortunate in this respect. First of all, [32②][33] it has a good climate. In almost all sections of the country it is possible to live comfortably during the whole year. It is true that in the south it sometimes gets very hot, and in the north very cold. But the people who live in these regions become accustomed to the climate and never suffer very much when the weather is either very hot or very cold. In a large country there is usually a great variety of different physical characteristics. [32③][34] In the United States, there are wide plains and high mountains, thousands of lakes and rivers of all sizes, cool forests and hot deserts, and a coastline several thousand miles long. Many lakes and rivers, as well as the long coastline, have been of great importance to the development of the country, since	32. What's the main topic of the talk? 【解析】选[A]。主旨题。文章开头就说一个国家的 geographical location (地理位置)和 physical characteristics(自然特征)对它的发展和进步至关重要,接着通过气候和地理位置论证了该论点,由此可知文章是要谈论地理位置和自然特征的重要性。 33. What kind of climate does the United States have? 【解析】选[D]。细节题。文中说美国在地理和自然条件上都占有优势,它有一个 good climate,一年四季人们都可以 live comfortably,由此可知美国全年气候宜人。 34. What are the principal physical characteristics of the United States? 【解析】选[D]。细节题。文中列举了美国各种各样的地形:wide plains、high mountains、lakes and rivers、cool forests、hot deserts、coastline,由此可知美国有着复杂多样的地形特征。 35. What's the role of lakes and rivers

[35] they made possible the easy transportation of people and all the things people need. Transportation by water is still necessary and important. In modern times, however, trains, automobiles, trucks and airplanes are doing much of the work which was formerly done by ships and boats.

according to the passage?

【解析】选[D]。细节题。文中说湖泊和河流对一个国家的发展至关重要，因为这些水域使 the easy transportation of people and all the things people need 成为现实。

Section C

【听力原文】

Chinese students are (36) generally willing to study very hard for long hours. This is an excellent (37) characteristic, but it is often an (38) inefficient method of study. An efficient student must have enough food, rest and (39) relaxation. You need to play ball, or sing a song, or go out with friends, see a movie, visit some (40) scenic spots. When you return to your studies, your mind will be (41) refreshed and you'll learn more. Shorter, more intense study (42) sessions are more effective than endless hours of (43) nodding over your books.

Finally, be realistic. (44) If you set impossible goals for yourself you can only be disappointed in your progress. Psychologists have determined that learning takes place this way: first, you make a lot of progress and you feel very happy. Then your language

【答案解析】

36. 空前的系动词 are 和空后的形容词 willing 提示所填词应为副词。generally 意为"普遍地"。

37. 空前的不定冠词 an 和形容词 excellent 提示所填词应为单数可数名词。由文中的 excellent 和 but 可推断所填词可能表示习惯或特点的含义。characteristic 意为"特点"。

38. 空前的不定冠词 an 和空后的名词 method 提示所填词应为以元音音素开头的形容词。根据下文的 efficient 学生有足够的食品和休息等信息，可推测此处可能是指"没有效率"的学习方法。inefficient 意为"效率低的"。

39. 空前的并列连词 and 提示所填词应为名词，与 food 和 rest 构成并列关系。relaxation 意为"放松，娱乐"。

40. 空前的泛指形容词 some 和空后的名词 spots 提示所填词应为形容词。由句中的 visit 和 spots 推测此处可能表示"名胜古迹"的含义。scenic 意为"风景的"。

41. 空前的系动词 be 提示所填词应为形容词或动词的过去分词形式。refreshed 意为"精神振作的"。

42. 空前的名词 study 和空后的系动词 are 提示所填词应为名词。sessions 意为"会议"。

| ability seems to stay the same; (45) this period can last for days or even weeks, but you mustn't be discouraged.

　　Perhaps we can say that learning English is like taking Chinese medicine. We don't mean that it's bitter. (46) We mean that, like Chinese medicine, the effects of your study come slowly but surely. So, don't give up along the way. | 43. 空前的介词 of 和空后的介词 over 提示所填词应为动词的分词形式。nodding 意为"昏昏欲睡的"。
44.【Main Points】If you set impossible **aims** for yourself you can only be disappointed **at** your progress
45.【Main Points】this period can **maintain** days or even weeks, but you **must be encouraged**
46.【Main Points】We mean that, like Chinese medicine, the **benefits** of your study come slowly but **safely** |

Model Test 2

Section A

边听边记

Directions: *In this section, you will hear 8 short conversations and 2 long conversations. At the end of each conversation, one or more questions will be asked about what was said. Both the conversation and the questions will be spoken only once. After each question there will be a pause. During the pause, you must read the four choices marked [A], [B], [C] and [D], and decide which is the best answer. Then mark the corresponding letter on **Answer Sheet 2** with a single line through the centre.*

11. [A] A thief.　　　　　　　　[B] A soldier.
　　[C] A priest.　　　　　　　　[D] A policewoman.

12. [A] He is going to visit the woman later.
　　[B] He ran in at the woman's home.
　　[C] He saw the woman unexpectedly at the supermarket.
　　[D] He saw the woman at the coffee shop.

13. [A] He has finished the paper.
　　[B] The paper is not important.
　　[C] He always does things just at the deadline.
　　[D] The paper is a secret.

14. [A] Man and wife,　　　　　　[B] Boyfriend and girlfriend.
　　[C] Brother and sister.　　　　[D] Father and daughter.

15. [A] Get off the floor.　　　　　[B] Go out.
　　[C] Stand up.　　　　　　　　[D] Hang up.

16. [A] He was very brave.
　　[B] He's a guide in the forest.
　　[C] He hated the metal.
　　[D] He's quite proud of his medal.

17. [A] Joyful.　[B] Frustrated.　[C] Excited.　[D] Sorrowful.

18. [A] Both the man and the woman were in class on Friday.
　　[B] The man was in class on Friday but the woman was not.

[C] The woman was in class on Friday but the man was not.　　边听边记
[D] Neither the man nor the woman was in class on Friday.

Questions 19 to 21 are based on the conversation you have just heard.

19. [A] Because she hasn't got ready yet.
    [B] Because she is waiting for David.
    [C] Because she is waiting for a taxi to pick her up.
    [D] Because it is raining very hard and she doesn't have an umbrella.

20. [A] They are going to see film downtown.
    [B] They are going to call on the Johnsons'.
    [C] They are packing and going on their holiday.
    [D] They are going to buy an umbrella since it is raining very hard.

21. [A] It was left in David's office.
    [B] It was left in Kate's office.
    [C] It was lost in the train some day.
    [D] It was left in the Johnsons'.

Questions 22 to 25 are based on the conversation you have just heard.

22. [A] The definition of eccentricity.
    [B] Essentiality.
    [C] How to keep pets.
    [D] How to enjoy special food.

23. [A] Person being unusual and strange.
    [B] Person being charming and special.
    [C] Person being aggressive and hardworking.
    [D] Person being common and usual.

24. [A] A poor British man.　　[B] A rich American.
    [C] A rich British man.　　[D] A poor American.

25. [A] The Victorian surgeon lived at Buckland.
    [B] Howard was always a hermit.
    [C] A hermit is a person who enjoys communicating with others.
    [D] Howard Hughes became a recluse because he was tired of high living.

Section B

Directions: *In this section, you will hear 3 short passages. At the end*

of each passage, you will hear some questions. Both the
passage and the questions will be spoken only once.
After you hear a question, you must choose the best
answer from the four choices marked [A], [B], [C] and
[D]. Then mark the corresponding letter on Answer
Sheet 2 with a single line through the centre.

Passage One

Questions 26 to 28 are based on the passage you have just heard.

26. [A] A solution to man's food problem.

    [B] A solution to the population problem.

    [C] Advantages of soybean.

    [D] How to develop good eating habits.

27. [A] Because people have to spend too much time and energy to produce it.

    [B] Because too much grain protein is needed to produce it.

    [C] Because it contains too much fat and protein.

    [D] Because it is not good to the health.

28. [A] It is similar to real meat in appearance but not in taste.

    [B] It is similar to real meat neither in appearance nor in taste.

    [C] It is similar to real meat both in appearance and in taste.

    [D] It is similar to real meat in taste, but not in appearance.

Passage Two

Questions 29 to 31 are based on the passage you have just heard.

29. [A] An examination of farmers in northern Japan.

    [B] Tests given on a thousand old people.

    [C] Examining the brain volumes of different people.

    [D] Using computer technology.

30. [A] Our brain contracts as we grow old.

    [B] One part of the brain does not contract.

    [C] Sixty-year olds have better brains than thirty-year olds.

    [D] Some people's brains have contracted earlier than other people's.

31. [A] Most of us should take more exercise.

    [B] It's better to live in the town.

    [C] The brain contracts if it is not used.

    [D] The more one uses his brain, the sooner he becomes old.

Passage Three

Questions 32 to 35 are based on the passage you have just heard.

32. [A] Because he knew he would be paid more than what was usual.

[B] Because Robin was just over 20.

[C] Because he felt sorry for the handsome young man.

[D] Because the boat could only carry one passenger.

33. [A] In spring.   [B] In summer.

[C] In autumn.   [D] In winter.

34. [A] In the morning.   [B] In the afternoon.

[C] At noon.   [D] At night.

35. [A] He used to live in London or Madrid.

[B] He was in poor health.

[C] He had never been to any city.

[D] He was going to find a job in London.

Section C

Directions: *In this section, you will hear a passage three times. When the passage is read for the first time, you should listen carefully for its general idea. When the passage is read for the second time, you are required to fill in the blanks numbered from 36 to 43 with the exact words you have just heard. For blanks numbered from 44 to 46 you are required to fill in the missing information. For these blanks, you can either use the exact words you have just heard or write down the main points in your own words. Finally, when the passage is read for the third time, you should check what you have written.*

Humans are (36) _____ animals. They live in groups all over the world. As these groups of people live, apart from each other groups, over the years and (37) _____, they develop their own habits and ideas, (38) _____ different cultures. One important (39) _____ side of every culture is how its people deal with time.

Time is not very important in non-industrial societies. The Nuer people of East Africa, for example, do not even have the word time that is in (40) _____ with the abstract thing we call time. The

daily lives of the people of such non-industrial societies are likely to 边听边记
be (41) _____ around their physical needs and natural events
rather than around a time (42) _____ based on the clock.
They cook and eat when they are hungry and sleep when the sun goes
down. (43) _____, such a society measures days in terms of
" sleep" or longer in terms of "moon".

　　(44) _____. This is because
industrialized societies require the helpful efforts of many people in
order to work. For a factory to work efficiently, for example, all of
the workers must work at the same time. (45) _____
_____. Passengers must know the exact time that an
airplane will arrive or depart. Stores must open on time in order to
serve their customers. Complicated societies need clocks and
calendars. (46) _____.

听力原文与答案详解

Section A & Section B																	
11	D	12	B	13	C	14	B	15	D	16	A	17	B	18	D	19	D
20	B	21	C	22	A	23	A	24	B	25	D	26	A	27	B	28	C
29	C	30	D	31	C	32	A	33	D	34	A	35	C						

Section C

36. social　　　37. centuries　　　38. forming　　　39. particular
40. agreement　41. patterned　　42. schedule　　43. Frequently
44. In contrast, exact correct measurement of time is very important to modern,
　　industrialized societies
45. Therefore, they must know what time to start work in the morning and what
　　time they may go home in the afternoon
46. Thus, we can see that if each person worked according to his or her own
　　timetable, a complicated society could hardly work at all

Section A

11.

[A] A thief.	W: When you saw the thieves, did you imme-
[B] A soldier.	diately ring the alarm?
[C] A priest.	M: No, officer. I'm afraid that for a few min-
[D] A policewoman.	utes I was too shocked to do anything.
	Q: Who is the woman likely to be?

【解析】身份关系题。女士问男士当他看到 thieves 的时候是否立即报了警,男士称女士为 officer(警官),并回答女士提出的问题,由此可知女士是一个正在调查案件的 policewoman。

12.

[A] He is going to visit the woman later.	M: Hello, Susan. I was in the neighborhood so I thought I'd drop by.
[B] He ran in at the woman's home.	W: What a pleasant surprise! Make yourself at home; I'll put some coffee on.
[C] He saw the woman unexpectedly at the supermarket.	Q: What do we learn about the man in this conversation?
[D] He saw the woman at the coffee shop.	

【解析】行为活动题。男士对女士说他碰巧在附近,所以 drop by(顺便来看望)她一下,女士让男士 make yourself at home(就像在自己的家里一样),由此可知男士是来到女士的家里看望她。run in ≈ drop by。

13.

[A] He has finished the paper.	W: Bill, have you finished the research paper for anthropology?
[B] The paper is not important.	
[C] He always does things just at the deadline.	M: Not yet. I always seem to put things off until the last minute.
[D] The paper is a secret.	Q: What does the man mean?

【解析】事实状况题。女士问男士是否写完了人类学的研究论文,男士回答说他似乎总是 put things off until the last minute(不到最后一刻不会去做),由此可知男士总是在最后期限的时候才开始做一件事。

14.

[A] Man and wife.	M: You've been seeing Tom again, haven't you? I don't know how you can stand him.
[B] Boyfriend and girlfriend.	
[C] Brother and sister.	W: No, I haven't. You know perfectly well I'm not going out with him. You're too jealous.
[D] Father and daughter.	
	Q: What's the probable relationship between these two people?

【解析】身份关系题。男士问女士是不是又去见 Tom 了,女士回答说没有,并且说男士太 jealous,由此可知他们是恋爱中的男女朋友的关系。

15.

[A] Get off the floor.	W: Can you get off the phone? I have to make
[B] Go out.	a call.
[C] Stand up.	M: Just a minute. I'm talking to my sister.
[D] Hang up.	Q: What does the woman want the man to do?

【解析】行为活动题。女士说她要打个电话,请求男士 get off the phone(挂断电话)。get off the phone ≈ hang up。

16.

[A] He was very brave.	M: Peter was given a medal for helping to
[B] He was a guide in the forest.	put out the forest fire.
[C] He hated the medal.	W: He certainly showed a lot of courage.
[D] He was quite proud of his medal.	Q: What did the woman say about Peter?

【解析】观点态度题。男士说 Peter 因为扑灭森林大火而获得奖章,女士说 Peter 确实 showed a lot of courage(表现得很勇敢),由此可知女士认为男士很勇敢。

17.

[A] Joyful.	M: Have you filled out your tax forms yet?
[B] Frustrated.	W: Don't remind me of them! They're so confusing
[C] Excited.	that I'm discouraged before I start.
[D] Sorrowful.	Q: How does the woman feel?

【解析】事实状况题。男士问女士是否填好了纳税申请表,女士回答说她非常的 confusing,并且感到 discouraged(沮丧),由此可知女士感到很 frustrated(受挫)。

18.

[A] Both the man and the woman were in class on Friday.	W: Weren't you in class on Friday either?
[B] The man was in class on Friday but the woman was not.	M: No. I had to take my brother to the airport. He went back to New York.
[C] The woman was in class on Friday but the man was not.	Q: What do we learn about the two students in this conversation?
[D] Neither the man nor the woman was in class on Friday.	

【解析】事实状况题。女士问男士周五是不是也没有去上课,男士回答说他没去上课,either 说明女士周五也没有去上课,由此可知男士和女士周五都没有去上课。

Conversation One

【听力原文】	【答案解析】
M: Hurry up, Kate. We'll be late. W: I am hurrying. I can't move any faster. M: It's always the same. We can never get anywhere on time. W: Right! I'm ready. Really, David, if you gave me some help around the house, we'd never have to hurry like this. I can't do everything, you know. M: Well, we'd better be off. We're late already. W: Oh, no! [19①] It's absolutely pouring. We can't go out in that. We'll be soaked. M: Nonsense! Come on. It's only a shower. It won't last long. W: A shower? That! It's set in for the night. I'm not going out in that. M: Well, you've got your umbrella, haven't you? Use that. [20] And anyway, it's only five minutes to the Johnsons' house. W: It might just as well be five miles in that rain. [19②] And I haven't got my umbrella. I left it in the office. M: That wasn't very clever of you, was it? W: Well, we could use your umbrella, I suppose. M: We can't. [21] I left it on the train six weeks ago. W: Oh, David. Really, you are impossible. M: Well, we can't stand here all night. We're late enough as it is. Let's go. W: I'm not going out in that. And that's final. M: I'd better ring for a taxi then. W: Yes. You'd better, hadn't you?	19. Why does Kate refuse to leave the house then? 【解析】选[D]。细节题。女士即 Kate 说 It's absolutely pouring（外面下起了大雨），没法出去了，出去的话身上会淋湿的，而且她把雨伞落在了办公室，所以她也没有 umbrella，所以 Kate 不想离开这间屋子。 20. Where are Kate and David going? 【解析】选[B]。细节题。男士即 David 说他们可以打伞出去，毕竟 it's only five minutes to the Johnsons' house（去 Johnson 家只要五分钟时间），由此可知他们要去拜访 Johnson 一家。 21. What happened to David's umbrella? 【解析】选[C]。细节题。男士即 David 说六周前，他把雨伞 left ... on the train（落在火车上了）。

Conversation Two

【听力原文】	【答案解析】
W: [22] Dr. Jones, how exactly would you define eccentricity?	22. What did Mary want to talk to Dr. Jones about?
M: Well, we all have our own particular habits which others find irritating or amusing, but [23] an eccentric is someone who behaves in a totally different manner from those in the society in which he lives.	【解析】选 [A]。细节题。对话一开头,女士即 Mary 问 Dr. Jones 如何准确定义 eccentricity(怪癖),接
W: When you talk about eccentricity, are you referring mainly to matters of appearance?	下来两人围绕这一话题展开讨论,由此可知 Mary 想和 Dr. Jones 讨
M: Not specifically. There are many other ways in which eccentricity is displayed. For instance, some individuals like to leave their marks on this earth with strange buildings. Others have the craziest desires which influence their whole way of life.	论的就是 the definition of eccentricity。 23. According to the dialogue, what's an eccentric?
W: Can you give me an example?	【解析】选 [A]。细节
M: Certainly. One that immediately springs to mind was a Victorian surgeon by the name of Buckland. Being a great animal lover he used to share his house openly with the strangest creatures, including snakes, bears, rats, monkeys and eagles.	题。男士说有怪癖的人与其他人比起来 behaves in a totally different manner(行为举止大不相同),也就
W: That must have been quite dangerous at times. Does one of these stand out in your mind at all?	是说 an eccentric 就是一个 unusual and
M: Yes, I suppose this century has produced one of the most famous ones: [24] the American billionaire, Howard Hughes.	strange person。 24. Who is Howard Hughes?
W: But he wasn't a recluse all his life, was he?	【解析】选 [B]。细节
M: That's correct. In fact, he was just the opposite in his younger days. He was a rich young man who loved the Hollywood society of his day. [25] But he began to disappear for long periods when he grew tired of high living. Finally, nobody was allowed to touch his food and he would wrap his hand in a tissue before picking anything up. He didn't even allow a barber to go near him too often and his hair and beard grew down to his waist.	题。男士明确提到 Howard Hughes 是 the American billionaire(美国的亿万富翁)。 25. Which of the following statements is co-

W: Did he live completely alone?

M: No, that was the strangest thing. He always stayed in luxury hotels with a group of servants to take care of him. He used to spend his days locked up in a penthouse suite watching adventure films over and over again and often eating nothing but ice cream and chocolate bars.

W: It sounds a very sad story.

M: It does. But, as you said earlier, life wouldn't be the same without characters like him, would it?

rrect according to your comprehension of this dialogue?

【解析】选[D]。细节题。男士说 Howard Hughes 因为厌倦了 high living（奢侈阔绰的生活），所以隐居了很长一段时间。

Section B

Passage One

【听力原文】	【答案解析】

In the year 2000, the world is going to have a population of about 8 billion. Most scientists agree that [26①] the most severe problem is food supply.

Who is going to feed all those people? Where is the food going to come from? Are you going to have enough food? Are we going to produce more artificial food? [26②] One way of improving the situation is for people to eat less meat. Why? [27] Because it takes four kilos of grain protein to produce half a kilo of meat protein. Clearly, there is not going to be sufficient meat protein for 8 billion people. Therefore, it will also be necessary to change eating habits because meat is the main part of many people's food today.

[26③] A possible solution to this latter problem is the soybean. The soybean plant produces beans which have a very high fat and protein content. [28] Scientists can now make these look and taste like real meat. They can also make many other artificial products such as soybean milk, for example, which has a taste of milk and can be used in cooking in very much the same ways as cow's milk. In fact, one wo-

26. What is the main subject of the passage?

【解析】选[A]。主旨题。文章开头揭示目前人类面临的最严重的问题是 food supply，接着下文围绕如何改善和解决这个问题而展开，由此可知短文的主题是 a solution to man's food problem。

27. Why will meat completely disappear in the future according to the passage?

【解析】选[B]。细节题。文中说 4 千克的 grain protein（植物蛋白）才能产出 0.5 千克的 meat protein（动物蛋白），所以食用的肉类将来会消失主要是因为要用大量的植物蛋白才能产出少量的动物蛋白。

28. What do we know about

man in the United States fed her family only on soybeans for a year! She gave them soybean beef, soybean chicken, soybean milk, and sometimes just soybeans. Possibly, we are all going to eat soybeans in the future and finally give up meat completely from our tables.

soybean meat?

【解析】选[C]。细节题。文中说现在科学家们可以把soybean(黄豆)制成在 look and taste like real meat(口感和外形上类似真正的肉)。

Passage Two

【听力原文】

If you want to stay young, sit down and have a good think. This is the research finding of a team of Japanese doctors, who say that most of our brains are not getting enough exercise—and as a result, we are growing old unnecessarily soon. Professor Taiju Matsuzawa wanted to find out why quite healthy farmers in northern Japan appeared to be losing their ability to think and reason at a rather early age, and how the speed of getting old could be slowed down.

With a team of researchers at Tokyo National University, he set about [29] measuring brain volumes of a thousand people of different jobs.

Computer technology helped the researchers to get most measurements of the volume of the front and side parts of the brains, which have something to do with intellect and feelings, and decide the human character. As we all know, the back part of the brain, which controls tasks like eating and breathing, does not contract with age.

Contraction of the front and side parts—as cells die off—was seen in some people in their thirties, but it was still not found in some sixty and seventy years olds.

[31] Matsuzawa concluded from his tests that there is a simple way to prevent the contraction—using the head.

[30] The findings show that contraction of the brain begins sooner in people in the country than in the towns.

Those with least possibility, says Matsuzawa, are

【答案解析】

29. What are the research findings of Tokyo National University based on?

【解析】选[C]。细节题。文中说东京国立大学的研究员开始着手 measuring brains volumes of a thousand people of different jobs(测量一千个不同的人的大脑容量),而这正是研究结果的依据。

30. What do the doctors' tests show?

【解析】选[D]。推断题。文中说测试结果显示,农村人要比城市里的人早出现 contraction of the brain(大脑萎缩)这一现象,由此可知一些人出现脑萎缩要早于另一些人。

31. What is the most possible conclusion of the passage?

【解析】选[C]。推断题。Matsuzawa 得出结论说,

| lawyers, followed by university professors and doctors. White collar workers doing the same work day after day in government offices are, however, as possible to have contracting brains as the farm worker, bus drivers and shop assistant. | 防止脑萎缩最简单的办法就是 using the head（多动脑筋），由此可知，要是不经常用脑，大脑就容易萎缩。 |

Passage Three

【听力原文】	【答案解析】
[34]It was not yet eleven o'clock when a boat crossed the river with [32] a single passenger, who had promised to pay an extra fare. While the youth stood on the landing place searching in his pockets for money, the boatman got close to him and, with the help of the moonlight, took a careful look at the stranger—a young man of just 18 years, obviously country bred, and now, as it seemed, [35]on his first visit to town . He was wearing a rough gray coat, which was in good shape. [33①]The clothes under his coat were well made of leather, and fitted tightly to a pair of fat legs; [33②]his blue cotton stockings must have been the work of his mother or sister, and on his head was a three-cornered hat. In his left hand was a walking stick, which hung on his strong shoulders, with two leather bags on both ends of the stick. The youth, whose name was Robin, paid the boatman, and then walked forward into the town with light steps, as if he had not already traveled more than 30 miles that day. As he walked along, [35] he looked about his surroundings as eagerly as if he were entering London or Madrid, instead of the little town.	32. Why was the boatman willing to take Robin across the river? 【解析】选[A]。细节题。文中说 Robin 承诺要 pay an extra fare（付额外的费用），船夫才愿意载他的。 33. What time of the year did the story most probably take place? 【解析】选[D]。推断题。文中没有直接提到有关季节的信息，但从 Robin 的穿着：coat made of leather（皮衣）和 cotton stockings（棉袜）可以推断出，故事可能发生在冬天。 34. At what time of the day did Robin cross the river? 【解析】选[A]。细节题。文章开头说船过河的时候还不到 eleven o'clock（11 点），由此可知 Robin 应该是早上过河的。 35. What do we know from the context about Robin? 【解析】选[C]。推断题。文章结尾处提到 Robin 第一次 visit to town，他环顾四周，渴望的眼神犹如身处 London 或 Madrid（马德里）这样的大城市，由此可知他还没有去过任何一个 city。

Section C

【听力原文】	【答案解析】
Humans are (36) <u>social</u> animals. They live in groups all over the world. As these groups of people live, apart from each other groups, over the years and (37) <u>centuries</u>, they develop their own habits and ideas, (38) <u>forming</u> different cultures. One important (39) <u>particular</u> side of every culture is how its people deal with time. Time is not very important in non-industrial societies. The Nuer people of East Africa, for example, do not even have the word time that is in (40) <u>agreement</u> with the abstract thing we call time. The daily lives of the people of such non-industrial societies are likely to be (41) <u>patterned</u> around their physical needs and natural events rather than around a time (42) <u>schedule</u> based on the clock. They cook and eat when they are hungry and sleep when the sun goes down. (43) <u>Frequently</u>, such a society measures days in terms of "sleep" or longer in terms of "moon". (44) <u>In contrast, exact correct measurement of time is very important to modern, industrialized societies.</u> This is because industrialized societies require the helpful efforts of many people in order to work. For a factory to work efficiently, for example, all of the workers must work at the same time. (45) <u>Therefore, they must know what time to start work in the</u>	36. 空前的系动词 are 和空后的名词 animals 提示所填词应为名词或形容词。social 意为"社会性的"。 37. 空前的并列连词 and 提示所填词应为名词的复数形式, 与 years 构成并列关系。根据 over the years and … 推测所填词应是一个表示年份的词。centuries 意为"世纪"。 38. 根据所填词在句子中的位置及空后的名词短语 different cultures 推测所填词应为动词的现在分词形式, 在句中作伴随状语。根据空前的 develop their own habits and ideas 和空后的 different cultures 推测, 所填词很可能是要表达"形成"的含义。forming 意为"形成"。 39. 空前的形容词 important 和空后的名词 idea 提示所填词应为形容词或名词。particular 意为"独特的"。 40. 空前的介词 in 和空后的介词 with 提示所填词应为名词, 且能与介词 with 搭配。agreement 意为"同意"。 41. 空前的短语 be likely to 和系动词 be 提示所填词应为动词的过去分词形式。patterned 意为"模式化的"。 42. 空前的不定冠词 a 和名词 time 提示所填词应为单数可数名词。schedule 意为"时间表"。 43. 根据所填词的位置推测所填词应为副词, 在句中作状语。frequently 意为"经常地"。 44. 【Main Points】**Contrarily**, exact correct measurement of time is very **signi-**

morning and what time they may go home in the afternoon. Passengers must know the exact time that an airplane will arrive or depart. Stores must open on time in order to serve their customers. Complicated societies need clocks and calendars. (46) Thus, we can see that if each person worked according to his or her own timetable, a complicated society could hardly work at all.

ficant to modern, industrialized socities

45. 【Main Points】 Thus, they must know what time to **begin** work in the morning and what time they may go home in the afternoon

46. 【Main Points】 Thus, we can see that if each person worked **following** his or her own timetable, a complicated society could **barely** work at all

Model Test 3

Section A

∩ 边听边记

Directions: *In this section, you will hear 8 short conversations and 2 long conversations. At the end of each conversation, one or more questions will be asked about what was said. Both the conversation and the questions will be spoken only once. After each question there will be a pause. During the pause, you must read the four choices marked [A], [B], [C] and [D], and decide which is the best answer. Then mark the corresponding letter on **Answer Sheet 2** with a single line through the centre.*

11. [A] It was given away.   [B] It was made smaller.
    [C] It was put on display.   [D] It was taken to the cleaner's.

12. [A] To save 150 dollars.   [B] To spend 200 dollars.
    [C] To buy a new car.   [D] To repair the old car.

13. [A] At four-forty.   [B] At five-forty.
    [C] At four o'clock.   [D] At five o'clock.

14. [A] It is likely to rain on the way to the airport.
    [B] He forgot to put the umbrella in his bag.
    [C] The umbrella was too long to fit in his bag.
    [D] His bag was too full.

15. [A] The light hurts his eyes. [B] He can't see.
    [C] His ears hurt.   [D] He can't hear.

16. [A] Boss and secretary.   [B] Professor and student.
    [C] Father and son.   [D] Lawyer and client.

17. [A] A bank saving.   [B] An insurance claim.
    [C] A loan.   [D] An income tax return.

18. [A] At a supermarket.   [B] At a bar.
    [C] At a dormitory.   [D] At a library.

Questions 19 to 21 are based on the conversation you have just heard.

19. [A] 3:40 p.m.   [B] 4:15 p.m.
    [C] 4:30 p.m.   [D] 4:45 p.m.

20. [A] One that is relatively inexpensive.

   [B] One that is not very crowded.

   [C] One that offers large servings.

   [D] One that is situated close to her hotel.

21. [A] By taxi.   [B] By bus.

   [C] By subway.   [D] On foot.

Questions 22 to 25 are based on the conversation you have just heard.

22. [A] He arrested a robber.

   [B] He was hurt by a robber.

   [C] He committed a robbery.

   [D] He did nothing.

23. [A] He spent 3 days.   [B] He spent 13 days.

   [C] He spent 3 hours.   [D] He spent 30 days.

24. [A] The robber didn't use his own car.

   [B] The robber didn't wear gloves.

   [C] The robber wore a mask.

   [D] The robber hided money under the mattress.

25. [A] The officer is too stupid.

   [B] The officer should not do anything for police because she and the robber are friends.

   [C] The officer should be a scientist because she is so clever.

   [D] If the officer took burglary, she could have made a fortune.

Section B

Directions: *In this section, you will hear 3 short passages. At the end of each passage, you will hear some questions. Both the passage and the questions will be spoken only once. After you hear a question, you must choose the best answer from the four choices marked [A], [B], [C] and [D]. Then mark the corresponding letter on Answer Sheet 2 with a single line through the centre.*

Passage One

Questions 26 to 28 are based on the passage you have just heard.

26. [A] The pilot.   [B] The lorry-driver.

   [C] The airport controller.   [D] Nobody.

27. [A] The driver brought some goods to the airport.

[B] The driver wanted to help the pilot.

[C] The driver came to get some goods.

[D] The driver wanted to help the fireman.

28. [A] He landed safely.

[B] The pilot controller managed to land safely.

[C] The plane didn't damage the lorry.

[D] He wasn't asked to pay for the damage to the lorry.

Passage Two

Questions 29 to 31 are based on the passage you have just heard.

29. [A] Health food.　　　　　[B] The processing of bread.

[C] Organic gardens.　　　[D] Poisons.

30. [A] Refined foods.　　　　[B] Natural foods.

[C] Organic foods.　　　　[D] Unprocessed foods.

31. [A] The ultimate content remains the same.

[B] Vitamin information is not available after processing.

[C] Vitamins are added to the food.

[D] The vitamin content is reduced.

Passage Three

Questions 32 to 35 are based on the passage you have just heard.

32. [A] In 1968.　[B] In 1926.　[C] In 1948.　[D] In 1929.

33. [A] The old editor retired.

[B] He wrote a good story.

[C] Another reporter quit.

[D] He was interested in financial news.

34. [A] His wife.　　　　　　[B] His editor.

[C] Another writer.　　　　[D] Himself.

35. [A] From cancer.　　　　[B] From a heart attack.

[C] In a car accident.　　　[D] In a plane crash.

Section C

Directions: *In this section, you will hear a passage three times. When the passage is read for the first time, you should listen carefully for its general idea. When the passage is read for the second time, you are required to fill in the blanks numbered from 36 to 43 with the exact words you have just heard. For blanks numbered from 44 to 46 you are required to fill in the missing information. For these* *blanks, you can either use the exact words you have just heard or write down the main points in your own words. Finally, when the passage is read for the third time, you should check what you have written.*

A fire is always (36) _____ and dangerous. People crowd around to watch the smoke, the flames and fire fighters, who risk their lives to save others'lives. Fire fighters are in danger of burns and smoke injuries. Nevertheless, they save thousands of lives and (37) _____ of dollars of property every year.

Fighting fires is not just risky. It is also very (38) _____. Fire fighters do their jobs in rain or shine, whether it's 100 °F or 20° F below zero. At a fire, they carry heavy gear up and down stairs or (39) _____. They search for (40) _____ people. They hack holes in the roof to (41) _____ smoke and gas. They hold hoses on the fire. The hoses are heavy, and the water in them shoots out under great (42) _____. In fact, it usually takes two fire fighters to hold one hose.

Fire fighters also have many other duties. Sometimes they have to give first aid, and their (43) _____ must be kept in order. They must visit factories and public buildings to check fire dangers.

(44) _____. Fighting fires is an important job. That means there will always be jobs for fire fighters. (45) _____. Beginning fire fighters make between $10,000 and $12,000, and they generally receive regular raises.

A person has to pass certain tests in order to be hired as a fire fighter. Among these are tests of intelligence and strength. (46) _____. Applicants must also be at least 18 years old. After they are hired, new fire fighters spend a few weeks in a training school.

听力原文与答案详解

Section A & Section B																
11	B	12	C	13	A	14	A	15	D	16	B	17	B	18	D	19	C
20	A	21	C	22	C	23	A	24	B	25	D	26	C	27	C	28	A		
29	A'	30	B	31	D	32	B	33	B	34	B	35	A						
Section C																

36. exciting   37. millions   38. demanding   39. ladders
40. trapped   41. release   42. pressure   43. equipment
44. Fire fighters are hired by local governments, and some small cities and towns use volunteer fire fighters
45. However, the number of jobs available and the rate of pay depend upon the budget
46. The tests are given to men and women who meet the height and weight standards and have high school degrees

Section A

11.

[A] It was given away.	M: Your grey jacket looks better now.
[B] It was made smaller.	W: Thanks. I had a tailor take it in.
[C] It was put on display.	Q: What was done to the jacket?
[D] It was taken to the cleaner's.	

【解析】事实状况题。男士对女士说她的灰夹克现在看起来合适多了,女士说她让裁缝 take it in(把它改小了),由此可知这件夹克 was made smaller。

12.

[A] To save 150 dollars.	W: The mechanic said it cost 50 dollars to have the car repaired.
[B] To spend 200 dollars.	M: We might as well spend 150 dollars more to buy a new one.
[C] To buy a new car.	Q: What does the man intend to do?
[D] To repair the old car.	

【解析】行为活动题。女士说修车要花 50 美元,男士认为还不如再多花 150 美元 to buy a new one(买一辆新车)。

13.

[A] At four-forty.	M: Oh, it's five o'clock already and I haven't finished typing these letters.
[B] At five-forty.	W: Don't worry. That clock is 20 minutes fast. You will have time to do them.
[C] At four o'clock.	Q: When does this conversation take place?
[D] At five o'clock.	

【解析】数字信息题。男士说现在已经 5 点钟了,女士则说那块表是 20 minutes fast(快 20 分钟),由此可知现在时刻是四点四十分。

14.

[A] It is likely to rain on the way to the airport.	W: Why didn't you put that umbrella into your bag? Now we'll have to carry it on the plane with us.
[B] He forgot to put the umbrella in his bag.	M: The bag isn't too full, but I kept it out. It looks like it might rain on the way to the airport.
[C] The umbrella was too long to fit in his bag.	Q: Why isn't the umbrella in the man's bag?
[D] His bag was too full.	

【解析】事实状况题。女士问男士刚才为什么没把雨伞放到包里,男士回答说他认为 it might rain on the way to the airport,所以才没把雨伞放进包里。

15.

[A] The light hurts his eyes.	M: Please turn down the television. I can't under-stand anything my friend is saying on the phone.
[B] He can't see.	W: Hurry up and finish your call. I don't like standing so close. The light hurts my eyes.
[C] His ears hurt.	Q: Why is the man upset?
[D] He can't hear.	

【解析】事实状况题。男士要求女士把电视机的声音调小,因为他正在打电话,电视机声音太大使他 can't understand anything…friend is saying on the phone(听不清对方在讲什么),所以他才 upset。

16.

[A] Boss and secretary.	M: The essays you have done this term have been weak, and your attendance at the lecture has been poor.
[B] Professor and student.	W: I'm sorry; I've been busy with my union acti-vities.
[C] Father and son.	Q: What is the probable relationship between the two speakers?
[D] Lawyer and client.	

【解析】身份关系题。男士对女士说她这学期的论文做得很差,attendance(出勤)at the lecture 也很少,女士表示抱歉,并且说她最近在忙于 union activities(学生会活动),由此可知他们是师生关系。

17.

| [A] A bank saving. | M: Have you received the check from the company to cover the damage to your car? |
| [B] An insurance claim. | |

| [C] A loan.
[D] An income tax return. | W: No, not yet, but I expect to get it within the next few days.
Q: What is the most likely subject of this conversation? |

【解析】谈论话题题。男士问女士是否收到(保险)公司 cover the damage to …car(赔偿她车辆损失)的 check(支票),由此可知他们是在谈论保险索赔。

18.

| [A] At a supermarket.
[B] At a bar.
[C] At a dormitory.
[D] At a library. | M: I'd like to check those three out and return these two.
W: OK. But they are overdue. I'll have to charge you for two days.
Q: Where did this conversation most likely take place? |

【解析】地点场景题。由对话中的关键词 check out(借出),return(归还)和 overdue(过期)可以推断出,对话可能发生在图书馆。

Conversation One

【听力原文】	【答案解析】
W: Hey Taxi! Ah great. Thanks for pulling over. M: Where to? W: Well, I'm going to the National Museum of Art, and … M: Sure. Hop in. No problem. W: Uh. Excuse me. How long does it take to get there? M: Well, that all depends on the traffic, but it shouldn't take more than twenty minutes for the average driver. And I'm not average. We should be able to get there in less than twelve minutes. W: Okay. Uh, sorry for asking, but do you have any idea how much the fare will be? M: Oh, it shouldn't be more than 18 dollars … not including a … uh-hum … a tip of course. W: Oh, and by the way, do you know what time the museum closes? M: Well, I would guess around 6:00 o'clock.	19. What is the current time in the conversation? 【解析】选[C]。细节题。女士问男士现在几点了,男士明确回答说 It's half past four,由此可知对话发生的时间是 4:30p. m.。 20. What sort of restaurant is the woman looking for? 【解析】选[A]。细节题。女士想让男士给她推荐一些 good restaurants downtown that offer meals at a reasonable price(市区里好吃又不贵的餐馆),由此可知女士是想找一家价格相对便宜一点的餐馆。 21. According to the driver,

W: Uh, do you have the time?

M: Yeah. [19] It's half past four. Uh, this is your first time to the city, right?

W: Yeah. How did you know?

M: Well, you can tell tourists from a mile away in this city because they walk down the street looking straight up at the skyscrapers.

W: Was it that obvious?

M: Well …

W: Oh, before I forget, [20] can you recommend any good restaurants downtown that offer meals at a reasonable price?

M: Um… Well, the Mexican restaurant, La Fajita, is fantastic. It's not as expensive as other places I know, but the furnishing is very authentic, and the portions are larger than most places I've been to.

W: Sounds great! How do I get there from the museum?

M: Well, [21] you can catch the subway right outside the museum. There are buses that run that way, but you would have to transfer a couple of times. And there are taxis too, but they don't run by the museum that often.

W: Okay. Thanks.

how should the passenger go to the restaurant?

【解析】选[C]。细节题。女士问男士她从博物馆怎么去那个餐馆,男士即出租车司机提供了三种去博物馆的乘车方式,但是他认为在博物馆外面 catch the subway(乘坐地铁)是最好的方式,另外两种方式都不太方便。

Conversation Two

【听力原文】	【答案解析】
M: Me, officer? You're joking! I'm not the one you are looking for. I am very cute and innocent. So do not call me please. I'm just a common citizen in a common place. W: Come off it, Mulligan. Don't pretend to be naive and innocent. Tell me something about what you are doing right now. [22①][23] For a start, you spent three days watching the house.	22. What did Mulligan do? 【解析】选[C]。推断题。女士说男士即 Mulligan 花三天时间观察一处住所,并且 on the day of the robbery 男士开着自己的车到了案发地,男士最后说 My God! You know everything! 由此可知

You shouldn't have done that, you know. The neighbors got suspicious and phoned the police …

M: But I was only looking, officer. I did nothing. I just walked around. Is it guilty for me to walk around?

W: … and [22②] on the day of the robbery, you really shouldn't have used your own car. We got your number. And if you'd worn a mask, you wouldn't have been recognized.

M: I didn't go inside! I told you I did nothing. I am innocent. Please believe me, OK?

W: Ah, there's another thing. [24] You should have worn gloves, Mulligan. If you had, you wouldn't have left your fingerprints all over the house. We found your fingerprints on the jewels, too.

M: You mean … , you've found the jewels? Oh, my god!

W: Oh yes. Where you, er … "hid" them. Under your mattress. Is that true?

M: [22③] My God! You know everything! I'll tell you something, officer, you shouldn't have joined the police force. [25] If you'd taken up burglary, you'd have made a fortune!

Mulligan 确实 committed a robbery。

23. How many days did the robber watch the house?
【解析】选［A］。细节题。女警官说男士 spent three days watching the house（花了三天时间观察案发地的房子）。

24. Which of the following statement is mentioned in the dialogue?
【解析】选［B］。推断题。女警官说男士即 Mulligan 应该 have worn gloves（戴上手套），这样就不会满屋子都留下指纹，由此可知，Mulligan 作案时没有戴手套。

25. What does the sentence "officer, you shouldn't have joined the police force" mean?
【解析】选［D］。细节题。窃贼最后对女警官说她不应该选择警察这行，如果她 take up burglary（作窃贼），肯定会 make a fortune（发大财）。

Section B

Passage One

【听力原文】	【答案解析】
A few months ago, the pilot of a small plane had an unusual adventure. He took off from an airport runway on a training flight. A strong wind blew the plane sideways, and it touched the top of a tree. Both wheels of the plane were knocked off but the plane did not crash. The pilot sent a radio message to the airport. He	26. Who probably told the fireman to borrow an open lorry? 【解析】选［C］。细节题。文中提到 The airport controller（机场管理员）答应帮助飞行员，他给机场的

did not know how to land without wheels. [26] The airport controller promised to help the pilot . He telephoned the airport firemen and told them what to do.

　　A fireman borrowed a long, open lorry. [27] It was waiting at the airport building to collect some goods. The fireman borrowed it and drove to one end of the airport runway. Then he turned around and waited for the plane to come. The airport controller sent a radio message to the pilot. He told him to try to land on top of the lorry. [28] The fireman drove quickly along the runway and the pilot flew down to land. Luckily, he managed to land on the lorry. Part of the lorry was damaged and the tail of the plane was broken but nobody was injured. The fireman slowed the lorry down and then stopped.

　　The pilot was very grateful. He gladly agreed to pay for the damage to the lorry.

消防人员打电话，并告诉他们 what to do，由此可知是机场管理员告诉消防员这么做的。

27. Why did the lorry come to the airport?
【解析】选［C］。细节题。文中说当时卡车停在机场大楼是要准备 collect some goods。

28. Why was the pilot grateful?
【解析】选［A］。推断题。文中提到经过消防人员的帮助，飞行员成功地 land on the lorry（在货车上着陆），保住了性命而且没有人受伤，所以飞行员是对此表示非常感激。

Passage Two

【听力原文】	【答案解析】

[29] Health food is a general term applied to all kinds of foods that are considered more healthy than the types of foods widely sold in supermarkets. For example, whole grains, dried beans, and corn oil are health foods. [30] A narrower classification of health food is natural food. This term is used to distinguish between types of the same food. Raw honey is a natural sweetener, whereas refined sugar is not. Fresh fruit is a natural food, but canned fruit, with sugars and other additives, is not. The most precise term of all and the narrowest classification within health foods is organic food. This term is used to describe food that has been grown in gardens that are treated only with organic fertilizers, that are not sprayed with poisonous insecticides; and that are not refined after harvest. Meats,

29. What is the main idea of this talk?
【解析】选［A］。主旨题。文章开头就点题说 health food 是各种健康食品的通用术语，而且文章接下来都是围绕 health food 展开的，由此可知短文的主题就是 health food。

30. Which term is used to distinguish between types of the same food?
【解析】选［B］。细节题。文中说 natural food（天然食品）是 health food 狭义

fish, dairy and poultry products from animals that are fed only organically-grown feed and that are not injected with hormones are organic foods.

In choosing the type of food you eat, then, you have basically two choices: inorganic, processed foods, or organic, unprocessed foods. A wise decision should include investigation of the allegations that processed foods contain chemicals, some of which are proven to be toxic, and that [31] vitamin content is greatly reduced in processed foods.

上的分类,用来区分同类食品的类型。

31. What happens to food when it is processed?
【解析】选[D]。细节题。文章结尾处说加工过的食品中的 vitamin content(维生素含量)会大大减少。

Passage Three

【听力原文】

Bill Grant was a famous newspaper editor in the United States. [32]He worked for the same newspaper from 1926 to 1968. He started as a clerk but by 1948 he had become the editor. That was the position he held until he retired.

Bill wrote his first story for the paper the day the New York Stock Market crashed in 1929. Two of the paper's writers were thirty miles from town checking on an airplane crash. The other one was in San Francisco writing a story about China Town.

[33①]When the first news of the stock market crash came into the office, Bill immediately sat down and wrote up the story. The editor liked it so much that he used the story. And he didn't make any changes in it. [33②]After that the editor decided Bill should be a writer. He felt he was not using his ability working as a clerk.

After the first story Bill became especially interested in financial news. But he wrote stories on just about everything. In 1945 he spent 5 months in Europe. His editor had decided he should write about the end of WWII. His paper was the smallest one with a writer in Europe.

【答案解析】

32. When did Bill begin working for the paper?
【解析】选[B]。细节题。文中说 Bill 从 1926 年到 1968 年从事报纸这行的,由此可知 Bill 从 1926 年开始在这家报社工作。

33. What made him a writer for the paper?
【解析】选[B]。细节题。文中说当股市下跌的消息一传到办公室,Bill 就立即 worte up the story(写成文章),主编非常喜欢他这篇文章,因此决定让他做 writer。

34. Whom did Bill give all his credit to for his award?
【解析】选[B]。细节题。文中说 Bill 撰写的关于二战的文章获得大奖,但他把所有的荣誉都归功于 his editor。

One of Bill's greatest moments came in 1946. [34] A story he had written on war won the National Newspaper's Award. Bill took the prize but he gave all the credit to his editor.

It was just before Christmas in 1967 that [35] he learned that he had cancer. Six months later he was dead. But he never stopped his work as an editor. The day before he died he had spent a full day at the office.

35. How did Bill die?

【解析】选［A］。细节题。文中结尾处提到 Bill 在 1967 年得知自己患了 cancer，六个月之后就过世了，由此可知，他死于癌症。

Section C

【听力原文】	【答案解析】
A fire is always (36) exciting and dangerous. People crowd around to watch the smoke, the flames and fire fighters, who risk their lives to save others' lives. Fire fighters are in danger of burns and smoke injuries. Nevertheless, they save thousands of lives and (37) millions of dollars of property every year. Fighting fires is not just risky. It is also very (38) demanding. Fire fighters do their jobs in rain or shine, whether it's 100°F or 20°F below zero. At a fire, they carry heavy gear up and down stairs or (39) ladders. They search for (40) trapped people. They hack holes in the roof to (41) release smoke and gas. They hold hoses on the fire. The hoses are heavy, and the water in them shoots out under great (42) pressure. In fact, it usually takes two fire fighters to hold one hose. Fire fighters also have many other	36. 空前的系动词 is 和空后的并列连词 and 提示所填词应为形容词，与 dangerous 构成并列结构。exciting 意为"令人兴奋的"。 37. 空前的并列连词 and 和空后的介词 of 提示所填词应为表达数量的名词复数，与 thousands 并列。millions 意为"数百万"。 38. 空前的系动词 is 与副词 very 提示所填词应为形容词。后面提到消防工作的工作环境艰苦、需要高度的耐性，并且工作强度很大，由此可推测所填词很可能是要表示"繁重的"或"苛求的"含义。demanding 意为"苛求的"。 39. 空前的并列连词 or 提示所填词应为名词的复数形式，与 stairs 构成并列结构。ladders 意为"梯子"。 40. 空前的介词 for 和空后的名词 people 提示所填词应为形容词。根据常识，消防员搜寻的应该是被大火困住的人们，故所填词很可能表达"困住的"的含义。trapped 意为"被困住的"。 41. 空前的不定式 to 与空后的名词短语

duties. Sometimes they have to give first aid, and their (43) equipment must be kept in order. They must visit factories and public buildings to check fire dangers.

(44) Fire fighters are hired by local governments, and some small cities and towns use volunteer fire fighters. Fighting fires is an important job. That means there will always be jobs for fire fighters. (45) However, the number of jobs available and the rate of pay depend upon the budget. Beginning fire fighters make between $10, 000 and $12, 000, and they generally receive regular raises.

A person has to pass certain tests in order to be hired as a fire fighter. Among these are tests of intelligence and strength. (46) The tests are given to men and women who meet the height and weight standards and have high school degrees. Applicants must also be at least 18 years old. After they are hired, new fire fighters spend a few weeks in a training school.

smoke and gas 提示所填词应为动词原形。根据空前的 hole 和空后的 smoke and gas 推测所填词很可能要表达"释放"的含义。release 意为"释放"。

42. 空前的形容词 great 提示所填词应为名词。根据常识,水在压力足够大的情况下才会喷出来,由此可推测所填词很可能要表达"压力"的含义。pressure 意为"压力"。

43. 空前的形容词性物主代词 their 提示所填词应为名词。equipment 意为"设备"。

44. [Main Points] Fire fighters are **employed** by local governments, and **several** small cities and towns use volunteer fire fighters

45. [Main Points] However, the number of jobs available and the **pay rate** depend **on** the budget

46. [Main Points] The tests are given to men and women **meeting** the height and weight standards and **having** high school degrees

Model Test 4

Section A

Directions: *In this section, you will hear 8 short conversations and 2 long conversations. At the end of each conversation, one or more questions will be asked about what was said. Both the conversation and the questions will be spoken only once. After each question there will be a pause. During the pause, you must read the four choices marked [A], [B], [C] and [D], and decide which is the best answer. Then mark the corresponding letter on **Answer Sheet 2** with a single line through the centre.*

11. [A] At 7:00.   [B] At 6:30.
   [C] At 7:30.   [D] At 8:00.

12. [A] The weather is terrible.
   [B] The TV set has to be cleared.
   [C] The weather will be fine.
   [D] The umbrella should be fetched.

13. [A] 500,000.   [B] 550,000.
   [C] 510,000.   [D] 450,000.

14. [A] In the bookstore.   [B] In the library.
   [C] In the office.   [D] In the classroom.

15. [A] Maths.   [B] Business administration.
   [C] English.   [D] Microbiology.

16. [A] John was always against the man in the discussion.
   [B] John and the man had a quarrel.
   [C] John never came to the point.
   [D] John didn't attend the discussion because he was busy with gardening.

17. [A] He went to Hongkong and Macao.
   [B] He went to Macao.
   [C] He stayed at home.
   [D] He is still planning on it.

18. [A] Mrs. Smith is carrying a bag.

　　[B] The man agrees with the woman's words.

　　[C] The woman likes Mrs. Smith.

　　[D] The man doesn't want to talk about Mrs. Smith.

Questions 19 to 21 are based on the conversation you have just heard.

19. [A] The room has not been checked before she moves in.

　　[B] The room is too dirty.

　　[C] There is no water in the toilet.

　　[D] The dish tastes too bad.

20. [A] The air-conditioning does not work very well.

　　[B] There's not hot water in the room.

　　[C] There is an ugly pillow in her room.

　　[D] There's not soap in the toilet.

21. [A] Replace the air-conditioner for a new one.

　　[B] Send someone along right away to look at the toilet and shower.

　　[C] Try to find another room for the woman.

　　[D] Offer more delicious food.

Questions 22 to 25 are based on the conversation you have just heard.

22. [A] She is from a radio station.

　　[B] She is a common employee in advertising company.

　　[C] She is working with a lot of women.

　　[D] She is the Head of Pushet Advertising.

23. [A] She is single.

　　[B] She is married.

　　[C] She is divorced.

　　[D] Her marriage status is not clear.

24. [A] Her husband is a manager.

　　[B] Her husband is laid off.

　　[C] Her husband enjoys running the house.

　　[D] Not clear.

25. [A] Most her employees are women.

　　[B] The male employees mind having a female boss.

　　[C] Her husband like a career woman.

　　[D] She is right at the top of the profession in advertising.

Section B

Directions: *In this section, you will hear 3 short passages. At the end of each passage, you will hear some questions. Both the passage and the questions will be spoken only once. After you hear a question, you must choose the best answer from the four choices marked [A], [B], [C] and [D], Then mark the corresponding letter on **Answer Sheet 2** with a single line through the centre.*

边听边记

Passage One

Questions 26 to 28 are based on the passage you have just heard.

26. [A] A buyer will get something useful free of charge.

[B] A buyer will get what he pays for.

[C] A buyer will gain more than he loses.

[D] A buyer will not get what he wants for free.

27. [A] Package is often a successful advertisement.

[B] Children are often made to buy a product by its package with attractive pictures.

[C] A buyer is usually attracted by the size of the container.

[D] Compared to a well-designed container, a buyer often values what is inside it.

28. [A] Do not buy the product which is sold in a glass or dish.

[B] The quality of a container has nothing to do with the quality of the product.

[C] A buyer should get what he needs most.

[D] The best choice for a buyer is to get a product in a package.

Passage Two

Questions 29 to 31 are based on the passage you have just heard.

29. [A] Americans life-style.　　[B] Me-books.

[C] Do-it-yourself.　　[D] Mind your own business.

30. [A] It publishes books with aid of computers.

[B] It only publishes children's books.

[C] It personalizes the books by having the computer make the reader the leading character in the story.

[D] It publishes books written by oneself.

31. [A] To tell children how to learn to read.

[B] To love animals.

[C] To love life.

[D] To develop enthusiasm for reading and help a child to learn how to read.

Passage Three

Questions 32 to 35 are based on the passage you have just heard.

32. [A] The story of Hollanders.

[B] The story of the word "Yankee".

[C] The story of the Scots.

[D] The story of the English.

33. [A] Scotland.　　　　　　[B] Germany.

[C] Holland.　　　　　　[D] England.

34. [A] The New England colonists.

[B] The Americans.

[C] Hollanders.

[D] The soldiers in the northern states.

35. [A] An American.　　　　[B] A European.

[C] A person of the Allied Nations. [D] Another American.

Section C

Directions: *In this section, you will hear a passage three times. When the passage is read for the first time, you should listen carefully for its general idea. When the passage is read for the second time, you are required to fill in the blanks numbered from 36 to 43 with the exact words you have just heard. For blanks numbered from 44 to 46 you are required to fill in the missing information. For these blanks, you can either use the exact words you have just heard or write down the main points in your own words. Finally, when the passage is read for the third time, you should check what you have written.*

Faster is better. This should be the (36) _____ of every person and every business. The pace and (37) _____ of our world reward those who can get it done and get it done quickly. And we should all know that a slow response is no response. Whether we're talking about fixing a problem or (38) _____ an opportunity, the turtle wins the race in fairy tales.

One of the reasons for an increased (39)＿＿＿＿＿＿ on speed 🎧 边听边记
has to do with today's lifestyles. We're getting pretty used to (40)
＿＿＿＿＿＿＿ service today, and anything less is a loser. We live
atthe speed of light: pushing a few buttons on our phones and
talking to someone in London, pushing a key on a word (41)
＿＿＿＿＿＿ and getting immediate printouts. Waiting is not (42)
＿＿＿＿＿＿ into much of what we do. Neither is it part of human
nature to wait. (43)＿＿＿＿＿＿ does not come naturally. The
people you deal with every day come from this world. (44)
＿＿＿＿＿＿＿＿＿＿＿＿＿＿. They get extremely frustrated
when they push your button and get a "please hold" reaction.

　　(45)＿＿＿＿＿＿＿＿＿＿＿＿＿. Here's the secret to fast
response: You don't have to reach closure in a nanosecond—just
signal that your disk drives are spinning, that you're actively going
after the result. (46)＿＿＿＿＿＿＿＿＿＿＿＿＿＿＿.
Tell them that you felt your button being pushed, that you "heard"
their request.

听力原文与答案详解

Section A & Section B

11	A	12	C	13	D	14	B	15	B	16	C	17	C	18	D	19	A
20	A	21	B	22	D	23	B	24	D	25	D	26	D	27	B	28	B
29	B	30	C	31	D	32	B	33	C	34	D	35	A				

Section C

36. motto　　　37. intensity　　　38. exploiting　　　39. premium

40. instantaneous 41. processor　　　42. programmed　　43. Patience

44. They get their doctor's visits in ten minutes at a roadside medical center and they
get their microwave food in a flash

45. It's not that you have to operate at the speed of light or that you have to compete
with computers or robots

46. Send that signal early: you'll give yourself plenty of time to act on it

Section A

11.

[A] At 7:00.	W: Could you tell me the timetable of No. 16 bus?
[B] At 6:30.	M: Well, the bus leaves here for the city centre every　half　hour
[C] At 7:30.	from 7 a.m., but on weekends it starts half an hour earlier.

[D] At 8:00.　Q: When does the second bus leave on Sunday?

【解析】数字信息题。开往市中心的 16 路车从早上 7 点开始，每隔半小时一趟，而在 weekends 出发时间会提前 half an hour，由此可知，Sunday 的第二班公共汽车 7 点出发。

12.

[A] The weather is terrible.	W: What terrible weather! I have to go back to fetch an umbrella.
[B] The TV set has to be cleared.	M: Take it easy, the TV said it would clear up in the afternoon.
[C] The weather will be fine.	Q: What does the man mean?
[D] The umbrella should be fetched.	

【解析】事实状况题。女士准备回去取伞，男士说电视上预报了今天下午天气会 clear up(放晴)。

13.

[A] 500,000.	W: Can you describe the change of the population in recent years in the city?
[B] 550,000.	M: The population rose to 500,000 in 1990 with an addition of 50,000 over the previous 3 years. No rapid increase was made until 1998 and now the total has reached 510,000.
[C] 510,000.	Q: What was the population in the city in 1987?
[D] 450,000.	

【解析】数字信息题。对话中说 1990 年该城市人口已达到 500,000，比三年前增加了 50,000，两数相减便可得出 1987 年该城市的人口数量为 450,000。

14.

[A] In the bookstore.	W: Please show me how to find books in the stacks here?
[B] In the library.	M: With pleasure. First, did you see the "card catalogues" in alphabetical order?
[C] In the office.	Q: Where does the conversation take place?
[D] In the classroom.	

【解析】地点场景题。由对话中的 show me how to find books, stacks(书架)和 card catalogues(卡片目录)可以推测出，对话发生在图书馆。

15.

[A] Maths.	W: What courses did you take at college?
[B] Business administration.	M: In addition to the basic courses such as English and computer, I studied accounting, economics and statistics.
[C] English.	Q: What does the man probably major in?
[D] Microbiology.	

【解析】事实状况题。男士说他除了学习一些基础课程外,还要学 accounting(会计学),economics(经济学)和 statistics(统计学),由此可知,男士的专业是 business administration(工商管理)。

16.

[A] John was always against the man in the discussion. [B] John and the man had a quarrel. [C] John never came to the point. [D] John didn't attend the discussion because he was busy with gardening.	W: How was your discussion with John yesterday? M: We didn't reach any agreement. He kept beating around the bush. Q: What does the man mean?

【解析】事实状况题。男士说 John 总是 beating around the bush(兜圈子),所以他们没有达成一致,由此可知,John 说话总是不切题。

17.

[A] He went to Hongkong and Macao. [B] He went to Macao. [C] He stayed at home. [D] He is still planning on it.	W: Where did you spend your summer vacation? M: I had intended to go to Hongkong and Macao, but I couldn't afford it, then I chose home to be my vacation spot. Q: How did the man spend his vacation?

【解析】事实状况题。男士说他本打算去香港和澳门度假,但是他 couldn't afford it,所以还是选择在家过假期。

18.

[A] Mrs. Smith is carrying a bag. [B] The man agrees with the woman's words. [C] The woman likes Mrs. Smith. [D] The man doesn't want to talk about Mrs. Smith.	W: Mrs. Smith is an old bag. Don't you think so? M: It's quite delightful to walk on such a fine day, isn't it? Q: What can you conclude from the conversation?

【解析】事实状况题。女士说 Mrs. Smith 是一个 old bag(令人讨厌的人),男士却说起了另外的话题——天气,由此可知,男士不想说关于 Mrs. Smith 的话题。

Conversation One

【听力原文】	【答案解析】
W: Could I see the Manager, please? I have a complaint. I have to see him. M: Can I help you, madam? W: Yes. [19] Did you have this room checked before we moved in? There's not a scrap of lavatory paper and the toilet doesn't flush properly, the water doesn't run away in the shower and I would like an extra pillow. What have you to say to that? M: I'm extremely sorry to hear that. I'll attend to it right away. The housekeeper usually checks every room before new guests move in. We have been extremely busy with a large conference. W: That's no way to run a hotel. One doesn't expect this sort of thing in a well-run hotel. M: No, madam. I really feel sorry about it. Here I'm really want to apologize for some disorder here. It's the most unusual. We do try to check the rooms as thoroughly as possible. Just the one pillow, was it? Is there anything else? W: Well, [20] your thermostatically-controlled air-conditioning doesn't seem to be working too well. It's as hot as hell up there. I really can't bear it. M: OK, do not worry about it. I'll just adjust the regulator for you and I think you'll find it a little cooler in a short time. [21] I'll also send someone along right away to look at the toilet and shower. Here I want to apologize to you again for the troubles we have brought to you.	19. What is the woman complaining about? 【解析】选[A]。细节题。女士问旅店经理她的房间在入住之前是否检查过?并且抱怨卫生间没有lavatory paper(卫生纸),也不能flush properly(正常冲水),并且shower(淋浴器)没有水,由此可知,女士投诉旅店在她入住之前没有检查过她住的房间。 20. Which of the following is the problem mentioned by the woman? 【解析】选[A]。细节题。女士说旅店的thermostatically-controlled air-conditioning(恒温控制的空调)似乎也出问题了。 21. Which of the following is the measure taken by the hotel? 【解析】选[B]。细节题。男士说旅店会尽快派人look at the toilet and shower(检查厕所和淋浴),并且向女士道歉。

Conversation Two

【听力原文】	【答案解析】
M: Now I'd like to introduce [22] Miss Barbara Pream, the Head of Pushet Advertising Agency.	22. Who is Miss Pream? 【解析】选[D]。细节题。

So, here you are, Miss Pream, [25] right at the top of the profession in advertising. I suppose you have quite a lot of men working under you, don't you?

W: Yes, I do. Most of my employees are men, in fact. It is not so common for a company to have so many female employees and there are few female bosses in the company.

M: I see. And they don't mind having a woman boss? Do you feel very comfortable to be a boss in such a male dominating society?

W: No. Why should they? I'm good at my job. I can manage my job as well as they can.

M: Yes, of course. But, tell me, Miss Pream, have you never thought …, about getting married? I mean, most women do think about it from time to time. Have you thought about it a lot?

W: [23]But, I am married.

M: I'm sorry. I didn't realize, Mrs …

W: I prefer not to use my married name in the office.

M: And your husband, how does he like being married to a career woman?

W: He has nothing to complain about.

M: No, of course not. By the way, what does he do?

W: [24] Well , he prefers to stay at home and run the house . He enjoys doing that as a matter of fact.

对话开头处便介绍 Miss Pream 是 the Head of Pushet Advertising Agency (Pushet 广告公司的总裁)。

23. What's Miss Pream's marriage status?
【解析】选[B]。细节题。对话中男士问女士有没有考虑过结婚,女士说她已经 married 了。

24. What's Miss Pream's husband's job?
【解析】选[D]。推断题。男士问女士的丈夫是做什么的,女士只说她丈夫喜欢 stay at home and run the house(呆在家里, 做些家务),并没有提到丈夫的工作,所以我们对女士的丈夫的工作 not clear。

25. Which statement below is true?
【解析】选[D]。细节题。对话开始男士便介绍女士正处于 the top of the profession in advertising (广告界职业生涯的高峰)。

Section B

Passage One

【听力原文】	【答案解析】
Packaging is an important form of advertising. A package can sometimes motivate someone to buy a product. For example, a small child might ask for a breakfast food that comes in a box with a picture of a	26. What does "A buyer will get something for nothing" most probably mean? 【解析】选[D]。推断题。文

TV character. The child is more interested in the picture than in breakfast food. [27] Pictures for children to colour or cut out, games printed on a package, or small gifts inside a box also motivate many children to buy products —or to ask their parents for them.

Some packages suggest that a buyer will get something for nothing. Food products sold in reusable containers are examples of this. [26] Although a similar product in a plain container might cost less, people often prefer to buy the product in a reusable glass or dish, because they believe the container is free. However, the cost of the container is added to the cost of the product.

The size of a package also motivates a buyer. Maybe the package has "Economy Size" or "Family Size" printed on it. This suggests that the large size has the most product for the least money, but that is not always true. To find out, a buyer has to know how the product is sold and the price of the basic unit.

The information on the package should provide some answers. But the important thing for any buyer to remember is that a package is often an advertisement. [28] The words and pictures do not tell the whole story. Only the product inside can do that.

中说有的食品用很漂亮的盒子包装, 很多消费者以为 the container is free, 也就是说 get something for nothing, 其实盒子的费用已经附加在产品的价值上了, 由此可推断, 这句话真正想表达的是消费者并没有免费得到他们希望得到的。

27. Which of the following statements is mentioned in the passage?
【解析】选[B]。细节题。文中说孩子们常常是因为包装的图片或是包装内的小礼物才想去购买某种产品, 由此可知, 答案为[B]。

28. What suggestion does the author give in the passage?
【解析】选[B]。推断题。文中说无论是文字还是图片都不能 tell the whole story (说明一切), 只有 product inside 才能决定产品的好坏, 由此可推断, 产品包装的好坏与产品本身的好坏是没有关联的。

Passage Two

【听力原文】	【答案解析】
In America, where labor costs are so high, "do-it-yourself" is a way of life. Many people repair their own cars, build their own garages, even remodel their own houses. Soon they may also be writing their own books. In Hollywood there is a company that publishes children's books with the aid of computers. Although other book companies also publish that way,	29. What is the subject of the passage? 【解析】选[B]。主旨题。文中介绍了一种不同寻常的书, 该书就是 Me-books, 并通过例子描述了该书的制作过程, 阐述了该书的影响, 即

this particular company is very unusual. [29①][30] It " personalizes " the books by having the computer make the reader the leading character in the story. Here is how they do it. Let us say your child is named Jenny. She lives on Oak Drive in St. Louis, has a dog named Spot, a cat named Tabby, and three playmates whose names are Betsy, Sandy and Jody. The computer uses this information to fill out a story that has already been prepared and illustrated. The story is then printed with standard equipment as a hardcover book. A child who receives such a book might say. "This book is about me"; the company therefore calls itself the "Me-books Publishing Company".

[29②]Children like the Me-books because they like to see in print their own names and the names of their friends and their pets. But more important, [31]"personalization" has been found to be an important tool in developing enthusiasm for reading. Me-books are thus helping a child to learn how to read by appealing to that natural desire to see his own name in print.

整篇文章都是围绕儿童读物 Me-books 展开的，由此可知，文章的主题应该是 Me-books。

30. What characteristics does the company have?
【解析】选 [C]。细节题。文中提到，这个出版公司通过使读者自己成为故事中的 leading character(主角)把书 personalizes(人性化)了，这就是他们的特色。

31. What's the purpose of the Me-books?
【解析】选 [D]。细节题。文章结尾处提到，人性化的出版物对于培养孩子的 enthusiasm for reading(读书兴趣)很有帮助，并且还可以帮助孩子 to learn how to read，由此可知 Me-books 的目的就是教孩子如何读书。

Passage Three

【听力原文】	【答案解析】
[32]Every word has its own story. So does the word "Yankee". Where did the word come from? What does it mean? And how did it get into the language? A number of people believe that the word "Yankee" comes from a Scottish word, meaning sharp and clever. [33]But most experts agree that the word comes from Holland. Many years ago the Hollanders who made cheese were called "John Cheese" by the Germans. Then some of these Hollanders came to America in the early 1600s. They settled near the New England colonists. The Hollanders were great farmers and they laughed at the	32. What did the speaker tell us? 【解析】选 [B]。主旨题。文章开头说每个单词都有一个故事，Yankee 也不例外，接着提到了 Yankee 这个词的由来，变化以及现在的含义，由此可知，作者讲了 Yankee 这个单词的故事。 33. According to most experts, where did the word "Yankee" come from?

colonists in the north who tried to build farms in the mountain rocks. And so the Hollanders gave their own nickname "John Cheese" to the New England colonists. In Dutch "John Cheese" was spelt J-A-N-J-E-E-S and pronounced "Yankees". [34] During the American Civil War, that name "Yankee" took on a wider meaning. The soldiers in the northern states were called "Yankees" by the men of the southern army. During World War I, the nickname "Yankee" spread to Europe. The word "Yankee" was shortened to "Yank", and the words "The Yanks are coming" brought tears and joy to the people of the Allied Nations. [35] Today, the word "Yankee" is known throughout the world as another name for an American.

【解析】选[C]。细节题。文中说大多数的专家都认为"Yankee"这个词来自Holland(荷兰)。

34. What did the word "Yankees" refer to during the American Civil War?

【解析】选[D]。细节题。文中说美国内战期间,soldiers in the northern states 被南方军队称为"Yankees"。

35. What does the word "Yankee" mean today?

【解析】选[A]。细节题。今天全世界的人都知道"Yankee"已经成为美国人的别称。

Section C

【听力原文】	【答案解析】

Faster is better. This should be the (36) <u>motto</u> of every person and every business. The pace and (37) <u>intensity</u> of our world reward those who can get it done and get it done quickly. And we should all know that a slow response is no response. Whether we're talking about fixing a problem or (38) <u>exploiting</u> an opportunity, the turtle wins the race in fairy tales.

One of the reasons for an increased (39) <u>premium</u> on speed has to do with today's lifestyles. We're getting pretty used to (40) <u>instantaneous</u> service today, and anything less is a loser. We live at the speed of light: pushing a few

36. 空前的定冠词 the 和空后的介词 of 提示所填词应为名词。根据 faster is better(越快越好)推测,此处很有可能是要表达这应当是每个人以及各行业的至理名言,故所填词可能表达"格言"的含义。motto 意为"格言"。

37. 空前的并列连词 and 和空后的介词 of 提示所填词应为名词,与 pace 并列。intensity 意为"强度"。

38. 空前的并列连词 or 及空后的名词短语 an opportunity 提示所填词应为动名词,与 fixing 并列。根据 fixing a problem 与空后的 an opportunity 推测所填词很可能表达"寻找"的含义。exploiting 意为"寻找"。

39. 空前的不定冠词 an 与形容词 increased

buttons on our phones and talking to someone in London, pushing a key on a word (41) processor and getting immediate printouts. Waiting is not (42) programmed into much of what we do. Neither is it part of human nature to wait. (43) Patience does not come naturally.

The people you deal with every day come from this world. (44) They get their doctor's visits in ten minutes at a roadside medical center and they get their microwave food in a flash. They get extremely frustrated when they push your button and get a "please hold" reaction.

(45) It's not that you have to operate at the speed of light or that you have to compete with computers or robots. Here's the secret to fast response: You don't have to reach closure in a nanosecond—just signal that your disk drives are spinning, that you're actively going after the result. (46) Send that signal early: you'll give yourself plenty of time to act on it. Tell them that you felt your button being pushed, that you "heard" their request.

提示所填词应为单数可数名词, 且能与介词 on 搭配。premium 意为"超额"。

40. 空前的动词短语 get used to 和空后的名词 service 提示所填词应为形容词。根据前面的 speed 与后面的 the speed of light 推测人们很可能已习惯于快速服务, 故所填词应表达"速度很快"的含义。instantaneous 意为"立刻的"。

41. 空前的不定冠词 a 提示所填词应为单数可数名词。由后面的 printouts 推测所填词很可能表达"文字处理器"的含义。processor 意为"处理器"。

42. 空前的系动词 is 与空后的介词短语 into much of what we do 提示所填词应为动词的被动形式, 且能与介词 into 搭配。programmed 意为"被编入"。

43. 分析句子结构可知, 句子缺少主语, 再根据空后的助动词 does 推测所填词应为单数名词。patience 意为"耐性, 忍耐"。

44. 【Main Points】They get their doctor's visits in ten minutes at a roadside medical center **and their** microwave food **very quickly**

45. 【Main Points】It's not that you **must** operate at **light's speed** or that you have to compete with computers or robots

46. 【Main Points】Send that signal early: you'll give yourself **a lot of** time to **operate it**

Model Test 5

本套题录音在网上
www.sinoexam.cn

Section A ──────────────────────────── 🎧 边听边记

Directions: *In this section, you will hear 8 short conversations and 2 long conversations. At the end of each conversation, one or more questions will be asked about what was said. Both the conversation and the questions will be spoken only once. After each question there will be a pause. During the pause, you must read the four choices marked [A], [B], [C] and [D], and decide which is the best answer. Then mark the corresponding letter on **Answer Sheet 2** with a single line through the centre.*

11. [A] At a drugstore.　　　　　[B] At a grocery.
　　[C] At a stationary shop.　　[D] At a clothing store.

12. [A] Tom is a professional football player.
　　[B] Tom will never be a professional football player although he practises every day.
　　[C] Tom will never be a professional football player since he doesn't practise.
　　[D] Tom doesn't want to be a professional football player because he has interest in law.

13. [A] He will type it up next week.
　　[B] He would rather work on it than do nothing.
　　[C] It took him an entire week to type it up.
　　[D] He still isn't quite finished with it.

14. [A] He was an adopted child.
　　[B] He is a photographer.
　　[C] He wants to learn about wildlife in the mountains.
　　[D] He is used to outdoor activities.

15. [A] The homework was very easy.
　　[B] The woman should go to class.
　　[C] The woman should sit in the back of the classroom.

[D] He is further behind in his work than the woman is.

边听边记

16. [A] 10:00.   [B] 10:30.

    [C] 10:45.   [D] 9:30.

17. [A] Jane.   [B] Joe.

    [C] Peter.   [D] John.

18. [A] $90.   [B] $100.

    [C] $110.   [D] $99.

Questions 19 to 21 are based on the conversation you have just heard.

19. [A] Five years old, eleven inches tall.

    [B] Five and a half years old, thirteen inches tall.

    [C] Six and a half years old, thirteen inches tall.

    [D] Six and a haft years old, eleven inches tall.

20. [A] Poodle breed, dark brown, a spot on the forehead.

    [B] Poodle breed, pure white.

    [C] Poodle breed, two little white rings on the back feet.

    [D] Poodle breed, dark brown, a spot on the back.

21. [A] A cat.   [B] A kid.

    [C] A dog.   [D] A pig.

Questions 22 to 25 are based on the conversation you have just heard.

22. [A] Some cigarettes.   [B] His flashlight.

    [C] A cigarette lighter.   [D] A leave.

23. [A] She didn't have a light.

    [B] She forgot to bring a light to Tony.

    [C] She had a light but forgets to offer it to Tony.

    [D] She burned Tony's finger.

24. [A] He was on duty.

    [B] He was taking a walk.

    [C] He was taking a break between classes.

    [D] He was taking exercises.

25. [A] Mary tried to persuade Tony to go off so that she could have a good time with Jill.

    [B] Mary said she would find a person to take Tony's place.

    [C] Mary was really friendly to Tony.

    [D] Mary did not really want to help Tony.

Section B

Directions: *In this section, you will hear 3 short passages. At the end of each passage, you will hear some questions. Both the passage and the questions will be spoken only once. After you hear a question, you must choose the best answer from the four choices marked [A], [B], [C] and [D]. Then mark the corresponding letter on **Answer Sheet 2** with a single line through the centre.*

边听边记

Passage One

Questions 26 to 28 are based on the passage you have just heard.

26. [A] In the 16th century.　　　[B] In the 17th century.
　　[C] In the 18th century.　　　[D] During the Middle-ages.

27. [A] The development of capitalism, the Renaissance and the religious reform movement.
　　[B] The development of capitalism and the Renaissance.
　　[C] The Renaissance and the religious reformation.
　　[D] The gap between the poor and the rich and the religious reformation.

28. [A] The English permanent settlements in North America.
　　[B] The pushing social forces.
　　[C] The emergence of bourgeoisie.
　　[D] The changing outlook on life.

Passage Two

Questions 29 to 31 are based on the passage you have just heard.

29. [A] 9 percent.　　　[B] 15 percent.
　　[C] 90 percent.　　　[D] 150 percent.

30. [A] They must pay more than out-of-state students.
　　[B] Only a few are accepted.
　　[C] They are not eligible for scholarships at state universities.
　　[D] Their scholarships are very small.

31. [A] Not as good as it was in 1960.
　　[B] Better than it was last year.
　　[C] Especially good for graduates in liberal arts.
　　[D] Not very good for recent graduates.

Passage Three

Questions 32 to 35 are based on the passage you have just heard.

32. [A] Supermarkets provide cheaper foods.
    [B] There is less delay in choosing in supermarkets.
    [C] Food and meat are more clean and more tasty.
    [D] Air-conditioning is at different temperature.

33. [A] How to properly display the foods.
    [B] How to keep perishable food frozen.
    [C] How to keep the shelves rotating.
    [D] How to make the adjustable shelves.

34. [A] Zero degree.   [B] 40-50 degrees Fahrenheit.
    [C] 28-32 degrees Fahrenheit. [D] 32-28 degrees below Zero.

35. [A] It's not popular.   [B] It's very new.
    [C] It's catching on.   [D] It's on the decline.

Section C

Directions: *In this section, you will hear a passage three times. When the passage is read for the first time, you should listen carefully for its general idea. When the passage is read for the second time, you are required to fill in the blanks numbered from 36 to 43 with the exact words you have just heard. For blanks numbered from 44 to 46 you are required to fill in the missing information. For these blanks, you can either use the exact words you have just heard or write down the main points in your own words. Finally, when the passage is read for the third time, you should check what you have written.*

Sport is not only physically challenging, but it can also be mentally challenging. Criticism from coaches, parents, and other teammates, as well as pressure to win can create an (36) _____ amount of anxiety or stress for young athletes. Stress can be physical, emotional, or psychological, and research has (37) _____ that it can lead to burnout. Burnout has been (38) _____ as dropping or (39) _____ of an activity that was at one time enjoyable.

   The early years of (40) _____ are critical years for learning about oneself. The sport setting is one where valuable (41) _____ can take place. Young athletes can, for example, learn how to (42) _____ with others, make friends, and gain

other social skills that will be used throughout their lives. Coaches 边听边记
and parents should be aware, at all times, that their (43)
_____ to youngsters can greatly affect their children.
(44) _____.

Coaches and parents should also be cautious that youth sport
participation does not become work for children. (45) _____.
In today's youth sport setting, young athletes may be worrying more about
who will win instead of enjoying themselves and the sport. Following a
game, many parents and coaches focus on the outcome and find fault with
youngsters'performances. Positive reinforcement should be provided
regardless of the outcome. (46) _____. Again,
criticism can create high levels of stress, which can lead to burnout.

听力原文与答案详解

Section A & Section B																
11	B	12	C	13	C	14	D	15	B	16	B	17	D	18	C	19	D
20	A	21	C	22	C	23	C	24	A	25	D	26	B	27	A	28	B
29	A	30	C	31	B	32	A	33	A	34	B	35	C						

Section C

36. excessive   37. indicated   38. described   39. quitting

40. development   41. experiences   42. cooperate   43. feedback

44. Youngsters may take their parents'and coaches'criticisms to heart and find a flaw
in themselves

45. The outcome of the game should not be more important than the process of
learning the sport and other life lessons

46. Research indicates that positive reinforcement motivates and has a greater effect
on learning than criticism

Section A

11.

[A] At a drugstore.	W: I need some aspirin and one eyebrow pencil.
[B] At a grocery.	M: The prescriptions are on the corner and the
[C] At a stationary shop.	cosmetic counter is in the back.
[D] At a clothing store.	Q: Where does the conversation probably take place?

【解析】地点场景题。由对话中的关键词 aspirin(阿司匹林),eyebrow pencil(眉笔),prescriptions(药方)和 cosmetic counter(化妆品专柜)可以推测出,对话很可能发生在 a grocery(杂货店)。

12.

[A] Tom is a professional football player.	W: What do you think of Tom's career?
[B] Tom will never be a professional football player although he practices every day.	M: He has the potential to be a professional football player, but he is too lazy to practise.
[C] Tom will never be a professional football player since he doesn't practise.	Q: What does the man mean?
[D] Tom doesn't want to be a professional football player because he has interest in law.	

【解析】观点态度题。男士说 Tom 很有潜力成为 a professional football player（职业球员），但是 Tom 太懒了不去练习，言外之意就是 Tom 会因此成不了大器。

13.

[A] He will type it up next week.	W: Have you finished with your report?
[B] He would rather work on it than doing nothing.	M: Finally. I've done nothing else this whole week but type it up.
[C] It took him an entire week to type it up.	Q: What does the man say about the report?
[D] He still isn't quite finished with it.	

【解析】事实状况题。女士问男士是否把报告完成了，男士回答说他这周除了 type it up，其它什么也没做，由此可知，男士花了 an entire week 把报告打了出来。

14.

[A] He was an adopted child.	W: I never pictured you as the outdoors type.
[B] He is a photographer.	M: When you live in the mountains you learn to adapt.
[C] He wants to learn about wildlife in the mountains.	Q: What is true about the man?
[D] He is used to outdoor activities.	

【解析】事实状况题。女士说她从没把男士 picture... as the outdoors type（看作是户外型的人），男士回应说要是住在山里就得学会适应，由此可知，他已经习惯了户外活动。

15.

[A] The homework was very easy.	W: Since I didn't even begin my project, I might not go to class today.
[B] The woman should go to class.	M: Are you kidding? That would only put you further behind.
[C] The woman should sit in the back of the classroom.	Q: What is the man's opinion?
[D] He is further behind in his work than the woman is.	

【解析】观点态度题。女士说她今天可能不去上课了，男士说 Are you kidding?（没开玩笑吧），那样她会落下很多课，由此可知，男士认为女士应该 go to class。

16.

[A] 10:00.	M: The bus was scheduled to leave at 10:00 and it's already
[B] 10:30.	half an hour late. How long will we have to wait?
[C] 10:45.	W: The longest time I know it's been delayed is three
[D] 9:30.	quarters of an hour.
	Q: What time is it now?

【解析】数字信息题。对话中提到公交车计划 10:00 出发，但是现在已经 half an hour late（晚了半小时了），由此可知，现在是 10:30。

17.

[A] Jane.	W: I'm a bit worried about John, Peter. He looks very
[B] Joe.	pale, so I'm going to visit him with Jane and Joe.
[C] Peter.	M: Good idea. He does look a big run-down.
[D] John.	Q: Who is the woman going to visit?

【解析】事实状况题。女士说她有点担心 John，所以打算和 Jane 与 Joe 去看望他，听音时注意不要把这三个名字混淆。

18.

[A] $90.	W: Can you tell me why you charged me $11 on a $10
[B] $100.	purchase? Did you make a mistake?
[C] $110.	M: No. Madam, that's the 10% sales tax. Maybe you are new
[D] $99.	in town and don't know about it.
	Q: How much will the woman have to pay when making a
	$100 purchase?

【解析】数字信息题。女士问男士为何 10 美元的东西要付 11 美元，男士说其中有 10% 的 sales tax（营业税），由此可知，女士要购买 100 美元的商品，就得付 110 美元。

Conversation One

【听力原文】	【答案解析】
M: Good morning, madam. Can I help you?	19. How old and
W: Oh, something dreadful has happened.	how tall is Harold?
M: Well, tell me.	【解析】选[D]。
W: I lost my little Harold.	细节题。男士也

【听力原文】	【答案解析】
M: Oh. Let me just fill in this form, madam. Here we are. Now, the name is Harold Trott. Right? W: That's right, little Harold Trott. M: And when did you last see Harold, Mrs. Trott? W: Early this morning. In the park. M: And had there been any quarrel? W: Well, he'd been a very naughty boy so I hit him with a stick and he tried to bite me and I'm afraid he got very angry and just ran away. M: Yes, madam. Now, what time exactly did you go to the park with Harold? W: Oh, eight o'clock. We go for a nice stroll in the park each morning. M: Eight o'clock. W: Yes, I take him out to do his job. M: Oh. How old is Harold, madam? W: [19①] He must be six and a half now. M: And you have to take him into the park to do his… W: Yes. He loves it. M: What's his height? W: Oh, [19②] he could be more than eleven inches tall. M: Eleven… er… we are talking about a little boy, madam? W: A boy? No! It's my Harold, my little Harold. M: Dog or cat, madam? W: [21] Dog. M: What breed? W: [20] Poodle. He's a dark brown with lovely velvet fur and has two little white rings on his front feet and a dear little spot on his forehead. Oh, constable, you'll do everything you can to find him for me, won't you?	就是警官问女士 Harold 有多大了, 身高是多少, 女士回答说 Harold 有 six and a half(六岁半)了, 并且 more than eleven inches tall(11 英尺多高)。 20. What are the features of Harold? 【解析】选［A］。细节题。当警官问 Harold 的品种时, 女士回答说 Harold 是 Poodle(贵宾犬), 皮毛的颜色是 dark brown(咖啡色), 并且它的前额有 a dear little spot(一个可爱的小斑点)。 21. Who is Harold? 【解析】选［C］。细节题。男士即警察原以为 Harold 是一个 boy, 后经询问, 才得知 Harold 原来是一只 dog。

Conversation Two

【听力原文】	【答案解析】
W: Cigarette? Do you want some special and good quality cigarette? It will fresh you up. Actually it's very useful for us to use it as something	22. What does the man ask the woman for? 【解析】选［C］。细节题。女

that can cheer us up.

M: Oh… er…thanks, Mary… Um，[22] do you have a light? I don't have a lighter or match on me at the moment.

W: [23] Sorry. Here you are.

M: Thanks. What a good and lovely day. [24] What a big pity I'm on duty today.

W: [25①] I'll stand in for you if you like. I've got nothing else to do. Maybe we can spend this lovely and good day together and this special and good quality cigarette together, right?

M: Oh no, I couldn't possibly…

W: Go on. Go off and have a good time. Here you can have the Mini if you like.

M: But… are you sure, Mary?

W: Of course I am. Take Jill up the mountains, or something.

M: That's ever so good of you, Mary. Oh, you …, er… you won't tell anyone, will you… I mean，I am on duty. You know, if someone knows I am doing something else while I am on duty, something horrible may happen to me!

W: Of course, I will keep this secret for you. Not a word. Bye, Tony—enjoy yourself.

M: [25②] Thanks, Mary. I won't forget this…

W: [25③] Damned right you won't, you poor fool！Go to hell！

士递给男士一根香烟，男士问女士是否有火，他没带 lighter（打火机），由此可知，男士想要 a cigarette lighter。

23. Why did the woman say "sorry"?

【解析】选[C]。推断题。男士向女士借打火机，女士说 Here you are 表明她带打火机了，只是刚才忘了给男士，所以才说 sorry。

24. What was the man doing in the conversation?

【解析】选[A]。细节题。男士说这么好的天，可惜他还得 on duty（值班），由此可知，男士在值班。

25. Which of the following statements is true according to the conversation?

【解析】选[D]。推断题。女士（Mary）提出愿意替男士（Tony）值班，当男士表示感谢时，而女士却说 Damned right you won't, you poor fool！，由此可推断，Mary 只是说说而已，并没有真的打算帮 Tony。

Section B

Passage One

【听力原文】	【答案解析】
[26] The English permanent settlements in North America began in the 17th century when Western Europe was undergoing great changes. During the Middle-Ages, Europe was under the single spiritual authority of the Roman Catholic Church. The peasants were tied to the	26. When did the British immigrants begin to permanently settle in North America? 【解析】选[B]。细节题。

soil and worked in the fields for their lords. Merchants and craftsmen were handicapped by the social disorders. Art and learning were controlled by the Church. By the 16th century, some new and powerful social forces began to emerge which led to the awakening of Europe and the discovery of America.

[27①][28①]The first new force was the development of capitalism. The growth of capitalism produced two new classes—the bourgeois class and the working class. With the fast development of commerce and trade, the bourgeoisie became increasingly powerful in politics as well as in economy. They wanted to share power with feudal lords and in some countries such as England they wanted to have more power from the king so that they could have free development. The English Revolution was the result of this growth of capitalism.

[27②][28②]The second major force that brought about the modern development of Europe was the Renaissance, which was marked by a changing outlook on life. The God-centered world was challenged by the great progress in natural and social science. Many challenged the authority of the Bible and were willing to observe, experiment and test truths for themselves. This attitude pushed the development of technology.

[27③][28③]The third influence force was the Religious Reformation, a religious reform movement that started from Germany.

文章开头便说英国移民在北美的 permanent settlements(永久居住)始于 the 17th century。

27. Which are the forces led to the awakening of Europe and the discovery of America mentioned in the passage?

【解析】选[A]。细节题。文中分别提到三个因素 led to the awakening of Europe and the discovery of America(促使欧洲剧变和美洲大陆的发现),它们是 the development of capitalism(资本主义的发展),the Renaissance(文艺复兴)与 the Religious Reformation(宗教改革)。

28. Which is the best title for the passage?

【解析】选[B]。主旨题。文章主要说的就是促使欧洲剧变和美洲大陆新发现的几个 pushing forces(推动因素)。

Passage Two

【听力原文】	【答案解析】

The cost is going up for just about everything, and college tuition is no exception. According to a nationwide survey published by the College Board's Scholarship Service, [29] tuition at most American universities will be on average of 9 percent higher this

29. What is the average increase in tuition expenses at American universities this year over last?

【解析】选[A]。细节题。

year over last.

The biggest increase will occur at private colleges. Public colleges, heavily subsidized by tax funds, will also increase their tuition, but the increase will be a few percentages points lower than their privately-sponsored neighbors.

As a follow up, the United Press International did their own study at Massachusetts Institute of Technology. At M. I. T., advisors recommended that students have $8,900 available for one year's expenses, including $5,300 for tuition, $2,685 for room and board, $630 for personal expenses, and $285 for books and supplies. Ten years ago, the tuition was only $2,150. To put that another way, the cost has climbed 150 percent in the last decade.

An additional burden is placed on out-of-state students who must pay extra charges ranging from $200 to $2,000, and [30] foreign students who are not eligible for scholarships at state-funded universities.

On the brighter side, the survey revealed that college graduates are entering the best job market since the middle 1960s. [31]Job offers are up 16 percent from last year, and salaries are good, at least for graduates in technical fields. For example, a recent graduate in petroleum engineering can expect to make as much as $20,000 per year. A student with a liberal arts degree might expect to make about half that salary.

文中说今年美国大多数大学的学费较去年 will be on average of 9 percent higher（平均高出9个百分点）。

30. According to the reporter, what is the problem for foreign students at state universities?
【解析】选［C］。细节题。文中说对外国学生来说，他们 are not eligible for scholarships at state-funded universities（没有资格在州立大学申请奖学金）。

31. What is the job market like for college graduates?
【解析】选［B］。推断题。文中说与去年相比，毕业生就业市场提供的工作数量 up 16 percent（增长16%），并且 salaries are good（薪金也不错），由此可知，就业市场今年好过去年。

Passage Three

【听力原文】

[35]During the last few years, there has been an enormous increase in the number of shops, stores and supermarkets which provide facilities for self-service. Their general purpose is to provide goods of every description attractively and cleanly and in perfect condition, so that the customer can serve herself, and

【答案解析】

32. Which statement is true?
【解析】选［A］。文章结尾处说自选超市这种购物形式更加便捷与 economical（节省金钱）。

33. What is the problem to the

then pay for the goods with the minimum of delay.

The organizers of a self-service store have their difficulties. [33] They must display a great number of goods in a minimum space without coveting up anything. They must deal with perishable foodstuffs requiring different ranges of temperature; and they must arrange a speedy flow of customers past the cash registers without overtaxing the operators.

For the purposes of display, many devices are used such as long lengths of adjustable shelves to take various sizes of packs, rotating circular shelves, islands of display stands, racks for tubed foods, and multi-tiered mobile stalls.

Perishable foodstuffs and quick frozen fruit, vegetables and meat are kept in refrigerated self-service cabinets, which keep goods at the required temperatures. These are at zero Fahrenheit for frozen food, 28-32 degrees for meat and fish, and [34] 40-50 degrees for dairy produce and provisions.

Some of the advantages of self-service seem to be that there is no waiting to be served; there is a wide variety of choice, and it is claimed that prepacked meat and vegetables are hygienic. [32] Shopping is said to be more "stream-lined" and more economical. Nevertheless many people still prefer to be served by a small shopkeeper who knows them personally and will deliver goods to their homes.

organizers in supermarkets?

【解析】选[A]。推断题。文中说自选超市的管理员要 display a great number of goods in a minimum space, (在很小的空间里摆放大量的商品),由此可知,他们的问题就是需要合理摆放这些商品。

34. What is the required temperature to keep milk in the self-service store?

【解析】选[B]。细节题。文中说对于 dairy produce (乳制品)来说,保存温度应该在40-50度。

35. What can we infer from the passage about the self-service nowadays?

【解析】选[C]。推断题。文章开头便说,最近几年 an enormous increase in the number of shops, stores and supermarkets(超市的数量大大增加),给顾客带来很多便利,由此可知,自选超市这种形式 is catching on (很流行)。

Section C

【听力原文】	【答案解析】
Sport is not only physically challenging, but it can also be mentally challenging. Criticism from coaches, parents, and other teammates, as well as pressure to win can create an (36) excessive	36. 空前的不定冠词 an 和空后的名词 amount 提示所填词应为以元音音素开头的形容词。由 pressure、create 和 anxiety 推测此处很可能表达压力会造成过度的焦虑,故所填词很可能表达"大量的、过

amount of anxiety or stress for young athletes. Stress can be physical, emotional, or psychological, and research has (37) indicated that it can lead to burnout. Burnout has been (38) described as dropping or (39) quitting of an activity that was at one time enjoyable.

The early years of (40) development are critical years for learning about oneself. The sport setting is one where valuable (41) experiences can take place. Young athletes can, for example, learn how to (42) cooperate with others, make friends, and gain other social skills that will be used throughout their lives. Coaches and parents should be aware, at all times, that their (43) feedback to youngsters can greatly affect their children. (44) Youngsters may take their parents' and coaches' criticisms to heart and find a flaw in themselves.

Coaches and parents should also be cautious that youth sport participation does not become work for children. (45) The outcome of the game should not be more important than the process of learning the sport and other life lessons. In today's youth sport setting, young athletes may be worrying more about who will win instead of enjoying themselves and the sport. Following a game, many parents and coaches focus on the outcome and find fault with youngsters' performances. Positive reinforcement should be provided regardless of the outcome. (46) Research

量的"的含义。excessive 意为"过量的"。

37. 空前的助动词 has 提示所填词应为动词的过去分词。根据主语 research 与宾语从句内容的关系可推测所填词很可能要表达"显示、表明"的含义。indicated 意为"指出"。

38. 空前的 has been 提示所填词应为动词的被动式，且能与介词 as 搭配。described 意为"描述"。

39. 空前的并列连词 or 提示所填词应为动名词，与 dropping 并列，且意义与dropping 相近。quitting 意为"放弃"。

40. 空前的介词 of 和空后的系动词 are 提示所填词应为名词。development 意为"发展"。

41. 空前的形容词 valuable 提示所填词应为名词。根据后面提到的学习内容可推测运动场是一个人获得宝贵经验的地方，故所填词很可能要表达"经验"的含义。experiences 意为"经验"。

42. 空前的 how to 提示所填词应为动词原形，且能与介词 with 搭配。根据 sport，with others，make friends 推测此处很可能要表达如何与他人合作,故所填词很可能表达"合作"的含义。cooperate 意为"合作"。

43. 空前的形容词性物主代词 their 提示所填词应为名词,且能与介词 to 搭配。根据上文的 Criticism from coaches, parents, and other teammates 会给孩子造成压力，而它们都是家长与教练对孩子的反馈,故所填词很可能表达"反应"的含义。feedback 意为"反馈"。

44. 【Main Points】Youngsters may take their parents' and coaches' criticisms **into**

indicates that positive reinforcement motivates and has a greater effect on learning than criticism. Again, criticism can create high levels of stress, which can lead to burnout.

heart and find a **defect** in themselves

45. 【Main Points】The **result** of the game should **be less important** than the process of learning the sport and other life lessons

46. 【Main Points】Research **shows** that positive reinforcement motivates and has a **larger influence** on learning than criticism

Model Test 6

本套题录音在网上
www. sinoexam. en

Section A

🎧 边听边记

Directions: *In this section, you will hear 8 short conversations and 2 long conversations. At the end of each conversation, one or more questions will be asked about what was said. Both the conversation and the questions will be spoken only once. After each question there will be a pause. During the pause, you must read the four choices marked [A], [B], [C], and [D], and decide which is the best answer. Then mark the corresponding letter on **Answer Sheet 2** with a single line through the centre.*

11. [A] Teacher and student.　　[B] Husband and wife.
　　[C] Classmates.　　[D] Boss and secretary.

12. [A] Clean up her room.
　　[B] Get her report back.
　　[C] Not wait for him past noon.
　　[D] Not worry about her raincoat.

13. [A] Seven hours.　　[B] Two hours and a half.
　　[C] Four hours.　　[D] Three hours.

14. [A] The noise in the library.　　[B] The heat inside.
　　[C] The late hour.　　[D] The crowded room.

15. [A] At an art gallery.　　[B] At a travel agency.
　　[C] At a bookstore.　　[D] At a history lecture.

16. [A] 11:00 p.m..　　[B] 10:00 p.m..
　　[C] 12:00 p.m..　　[D] 12:00 a.m..

17. [A] Politics.　　[B] Statistics.
　　[C] Political science.　　[D] Statistics and politics.

18. [A] $14.　　[B] $40.　　[C] $46.　　[D] $48.

Questions 19 to 21 are based on the conversation you have just heard.

19. [A] In a police station.　　[B] In a lost property office.
　　[C] In a bank.　　[D] In a restaurant.

20. [A] She left her handbag in the restaurant and couldn't find it

🎧 边听边记

back.

[B] She was robbed.

[C] Someone stole her handbag.

[D] She forgot to take her handbag when she rushed off the train at her destination.

21. [A] Thirty pounds, driving licence, keys, a ticket.

[B] Three hundred and thirty pounds, driving licence, keys, a ticket.

[C] Thirty pounds, ID, keys, a ticket.

[D] Thirty pounds, ID, keys, driving licence.

Questions 22 to 25 are based on the conversation you have just heard.

22. [A] In a supermarket.　　　[B] In a bank.

[C] In a restaurant.　　　[D] In a prison.

23. [A] She follows the robber's order right now.

[B] She is too scared to move.

[C] She tells the robber to wait for his turn.

[D] She faints.

24. [A] His doctor and the customer.

[B] His doctor and his probation officer.

[C] His doctor arid himself.

[D] Only the customer.

25. [A] Next week.　　　[B] This week.

[C] Right now.　　　[D] Next month

Section B

Directions: *In this section, you will hear 3 short passages. At the end of each passage, you will hear some questions. Both the passage and the questions will be spoken only once. After you hear a question, you must choose the best answer from the four choices marked [A], [B], [C], and [D]. Then mark the corresponding letter on **Answer Sheet 2** with a single line through the centre.*

Passage One

Questions 26 to 28 are based on the passage you have just heard.

26. [A] One fourth of their income .

[B] Two fifths of their income.

[C] Half of their income.

[D] Two thirds of their income.

27. [A] Borrow money from their relatives.

[B] Get a mortgage.

[C] Use a credit card.

[D] Pay cash.

28. [A] It is near big cities.

[B] It is cheaper.

[C] It is easier to get repairs.

[D] It is cheaper and easier to get repairs.

Passage Two

Questions 29 to 31 are based on the passage you have just heard.

29. [A] Threaten to organize a strike.

[B] Negotiate with management.

[C] Get higher wages and better work situations.

[D] Gain effectiveness.

30. [A] 100 years ago.　　　　　[B] By the 1950's.

[C] By 1915.　　　　　　　[D] By now.

31. [A] Discuss with business management

[B] Train workers for jobs, give unemployed members money
and pay retirement pensions.

[C] Hold on a strike.　　　　[D] Hold conferences.

Passage Three

Questions 32 to 35 are based on the passage you have just heard.

32. [A] The benefits of manageable stress.

[B] How to avoid stressful situations.

[C] How to cope with stress effectively.

[D] The effects of stress hormones on memory.

33. [A] People under stress tend to have a poor memory.

[B] People who can't get their job done experience more stress.

[C] Doing challenging work may be good for one's health.

[D] Stress will weaken the body's defense against germs.

34. [A] They experienced a decline in the antibody.

[B] They controlled the outcome successfully.

[C] Their memory level had an increase.

[D] They felt no pressure while watching the video.

35. [A] A person's memory is determined by the level of hormones
in his body.

[B] Stress hormones have lasting positive effects on the brain.

[C] Short bursts of stress hormones enhance memory function.

[D] A person's memory improves with continued experience of stress.

Section C

Directions: *In this section, you will hear a passage three times. When the passage is read for the first time, you should listen carefully for its general idea. When the passage is read for the second time, you are required to fill in the blanks numbered from 36 to 43 with the exact words you have just heard. For blanks numbered from 44 to 46 you are required to fill in the missing information. For these blanks, you can either use the exact words you have just heard or write down the main points in your own words. Finally, when the passage is read for the third time, you should check what you have written.*

Some of the most (36) _____ lessons coming out of research in (37) _____ are the area of memory. People ask, why can't I remember the time the (38) _____ book is due?

Of a lot of people, memory may be weak, because they don't use it enough. It's like the (39) _____ . If you don't (40) _____ it, it won't get strong. That's why it's (41) _____ to keep our mind active, to keep on (42) _____ through our life. We can do this by reading, playing memory games and so on.

It's my guess though that the lack of (43) _____ isn't a problem for students like you. (44) _____. Later on I will discuss how information is recorded from memory. But, first, the information needs to be recorded, in other words, learned, and for busy people like you and me, that will be the real problem. If we are distracted, or we are trying to think what we are going to do next, the incoming message just might not be getting recorded effectively, and (45) _____. Give your full attention to the information you hope to retain. (46) _____ , perhaps to make a mental picture, even a wild ridiculous one, so the new fact will stick in memory.

听力原文与答案详解

Section A & Section B

11	B	12	D	13	D	14	B	15	A	16	B	17	B	18	C	19	B
20	D	21	A	22	B	23	D	24	C	25	A	26	A	27	B	28	D
29	C	30	B	31	B	32	A	33	C	34	A	35	C								

Section C

36. practical　　　37. psychology　　　38. library　　　39. muscle

40. exercise　　　41. important　　　42. learning　　　43. stimulation

44. More likely, the life is so busy and stimulating that it itself may sometimes interfere with learning

45. that leads to the first tip for students who want to improve their memories

46. Research clearly shows the advantages of this, and also of active learning, of consciously trying to visualize a new fact

Section A

11.

[A] Teacher and student.	M: Being an efficient secretary, you should finish your
[B] Husband and wife.	work at the office, not do it now at home.
[C] Classmates.	W: I know that. But I've been very busy and I couldn't
[D] Boss and secretary.	finish it before the end of the office hours.
	Q: What's the probable relationship between the two
	speakers?

【解析】身份关系题。男士认为女士作为一个高效率的秘书,应该把所有的工作在办公室做完,而不应该 do it now at home,由此推断,此对话发生在家里,[B]选项最为可能。

12.

[A] Clean up her room.	W: I left my raincoat in my room. Wait
[B] Get her report back.	while I go back to get it.
[C] Not wait for him past noon.	M: Don't bother, the weather report said it
[D] Not go back to get her raincoat.	would clear up by noon.
	Q: What does the man advise the woman
	to do?

【解析】行为活动题。女士想回去取雨衣,男士说不必担心,预报说到中午天气就会 clear up(放晴),由此可知,男士的言外之意就是劝女士不必回去取雨衣。

13.

[A] Seven hours.	M: It only takes seven hours from here to San
[B] Two hours and a half.	Francisco, but you'll have three-hour layover bet-
[C] Four hours.	ween the flights.
[D] Three hours.	W: It doesn't matter. I would like to spend two and a
	half hours doing some shopping in San Francisco.
	Q: How long will the woman stay in San Francisco?

【解析】数字信息题。男士说女士在 San Francisco 有 three-hour layover(3 个小时的中途停留),虽然女士说她要花 two and half hours 购物,但这 2 个半小时也包含在 3 小时内,所以女士在 San Fransisco 停留 3 小时。

14.

[A] The noise in the libr-	W: It's so hot today that I can't work. I wish there
ary.	was fan in this library.
[B] The heat inside.	M: So do I. I'll fall asleep if I don't get out of the
[C] The late hour.	stuffy room soon.
[D] The crowded room.	Q: What are these people complaining about?

【解析】事实状况题。由对话中的 hot, fan 和 fall asleep 可以推测出,它们是在谈论图书馆里太热,让他们待不下去。

15.

[A] At an art gallery.	W: Excuse me. Do you know the name of this sculpture?
[B] At a travel agency.	M: I'm not sure what it's called, but I think it's a carving
[C] At a bookstore.	from Alaska. You can look it up in the catalog.
[D] At a history lecture.	Q: Where does the conversation probably take place?

【解析】地点场景题。由对话中的关键词 sculpture(雕刻品),carving(雕刻品)和 catalog(目录)可以推断出,对话很可能发生在 an art gallery(美术馆)。

16.

[A] 11:00 p.m.	W: When do you usually go to bed?
[B] 10:00 p.m.	M: Around 10:00, but recently I have been busy doing my
[C] 12:00 p.m.	research paper, so I haven't been able to go to bed until 11:
[D] 12:00 a.m.	00 or 12:00.
	Q: What time does the man usually go to bed?

【解析】数字信息题。女士问男士通常什么时候睡觉,男士回答说 around 10:00,由此可知,男士通常是在 10 点睡觉。

17.

[A] Politics. [B] Statistics. [C] Political science. [D] Statistics and politics.	W: Mike got an A in statistics and only a B in political science. M: Well, I still say that political science is a bit less complicated than statistics. Q: Which subject is more difficult according to the man?

【解析】事实状况题。男士说他还是认为 political science（政治学）没有 statistics（统计学）复杂，由此可知，男士认为 statistics 要难一些。

18.

[A] $ 14. [B] $ 40. [C] $ 46. [D] $ 48.	M: Operator, I want to make a call to Paris, France. How much is it? W: It's $10 for the first three minutes and $4 for each additional minute. Q: How much would a twelve-minute call cost?

【解析】数字信息题。女士说打电话头三分钟收费为 10 美元，$4 for each additional minute（每加一分钟收费 4 美元），由此可推算出，打 12 分钟电话，要付 46（10 + （12 −3）×4 =46）美元。

Conversation One

【听力原文】	【答案解析】
W: Can you help me, please? Look, I'm desperate. [19] Are you responsible for lost property? M: Yes, I am. What is it you've lost? W: I've lost my handbag. M: Where did you lose it, madam? W: I've just come off the tube, the last train, from Paddington. M: Yes, the last train tonight. There isn't another one. W: On the circle line, on the circle line. M: Yes, yes. W: Oh, it's terrible. We haven't got much time, I mean I have got so many valuable things in that bag. M: Will you please explain… W: [20] I was asleep on the train. I must have dropped off. I woke up, almost missed my station, so I rushed	19. Where is the woman? 【解析】选[B]。推断题。女开头就请男士帮忙，并且问男士是不是 responsible for lost property（负责丢失物品）的，接着男士便问女士丢了什么东西，知道是手提包之后，又对手提包内的东西进行了询问并登记，由此可推断，女士在 a lost property office（失物招领处）。

off the train and then I realized my handbag was still on it.

M: Yes?

W: By that time the doors were shut and it was too late.

M: So your handbag is still on the train.

W: It's on the train traveling…

M: Now, can you tell me exactly what was in the handbag?

W: Well, [21①] there was money…

M: How much?

W: [21②] Nearly thirty pounds. I had my driving licence…

M: So, thirty pounds; driving licence, yes…

W: I had [21③] my keys, and I had [21④] the office keys, they'll kill me when I go to work tomorrow, and I'd just been to the travel agent, I had [21⑤] my ticket to Athens…

M: Just one moment. House and office keys, ticket to Athens.

W: Yes, hurry please. You've got to phone the next station…

M: Yes, just a moment. Anything else?

W: I had [21⑥] my season ticket.

M: Your season ticket for travelling on the tube.

W: And [21⑦] a very expensive bottle of perfume, and…

M: Yes, well, I'll get the guard to look in… the train…

20. Why did the woman lose her handbag?
【解析】选 [D]。细节题。女士说因为她 was a sleep on the train（在车上睡着了），醒的时候发现到站了，rushed off the train（匆匆忙忙下了火车）之后，才想起 handbag was still on it（包落在车上了）。

21. What does the woman have in her handbag?
【解析】选 [A]。细节题。女士说包里有将近 thirty pounds（30 英镑）的钱，driving licence（驾驶执照），keys（钥匙），ticket to Athens（去雅典的票），season ticket（季票），还有 a very expensive bottle of perfume（一瓶很贵的香水）。

Conversation Two

【听力原文】	【答案解析】
M: This is a hold-up! Hands up! Hand over the money or I'll shoot. W: Just a minute. [23] Would you mind waiting your turn? This lady was before you. Now. What can I do for you? M: I've just told you. This is a hold-up and I want some money. W: Well, I'm afraid it's not that easy. If you want me to give you some money, you'll have to [22①]	**22.** Where does the story take place? 【解析】选 [B]。推断题。由对话中的 open account（开账户），references（担保人）和 fill in these forms 等可推测，对话应该发生在银行。 **23.** When the clerk is

open account first.

M: Do you mean that if I open an account, then you'll give me some money?

W: That would be the first step.

M: OK, I'll open an account. Hand over the form. Quickly.

W: Here we are. Just fill it in and sign at the bottom.

M: OK, Thanks. Now hand over the money. Quickly.

W: I'm sorry, but before we can open the account you'll need [22②] references.

M: [24①] What about my doctor?

W: [24②] Yes, that'll be fine for one. And the other?

M: (thinks hard) [24③] Would my probation officer do?

W: Yes, I should think so. Would you like to ask him to [22③] fill in these forms and then bring them back next week?

M: [25①] So, if I bring back these forms next week, you'll give me some money?

W: Well, we'll see what we can do.

M: (holds up forms and puts gun away) [25②] Right, then, I'll see you next week. Thanks for being so helpful.

W: It's all part of the service. Good bye.

asked to hand over the money, what does she do?

【解析】选[D]。细节题。当女职员被要求举起手来的时候,她让男士 waiting…turn(排队等候),因为在他前面还有一位女士。

24. Who will be the robber's references?

【解析】选[C]。细节题。女士说开账户需要两个 references(担保人),男士即 robber 提到他的 doctor 和 probation officer(缓刑监督官)可以做他的担保人。

25. When does the robber think he can get the money?

【解析】选[A]。推断题。男士即 robber 问女士是否 next week 把表格带来就可以拿到钱,女士说到时候你就知道了,男士接着说 see…next week,由此可推断,他认为下周可以拿到钱。

Section B

Passage One

【听力原文】	【答案解析】
In western countries today, the cost of housing is very high. [26] It is common to pay one fourth or one third of a family's income on a place to live. The price of a house depends on its size and location. Big houses are more expensive than smaller ones, and houses closer to the center of big cities are more expensive than one in the suburbs or in small towns. Regardless of the cost, it is usual for people	26. How much do most westerners pay for a place to live in? 【解析】选[A]。细节题。文中明确提到,在西方国家住房花费特别高,人们通常将 one fourth or one third of a family's income(家庭收入

to buy their houses over a period of time. [27] When a family buys a house, it is necessary to borrow money from a bank to pay for it. Then they repay the bank in regular payments. This kind of bank loan is called a mortgage. Families can take 30 years to pay off the mortgage. Without a mortgage it would be impossible for most people to buy their houses.

Many people don't own their homes. They pay landlords to live in their homes. The money they pay for this is called rent. [28] Usually, it is cheaper to rent than it is to buy and to pay a mortgage. Also, when something needs to be repaired, it is easy for the renter to ask the landlord to fix it. Some people rent houses, but most renters live in apartments. Apartment buildings are located in cities where it is too costly to build houses.

Recently it has become common for renters to buy their apartments. When this happens, the cost usually increases but the money goes to pay off the mortgage. Apartments bought this way are called condominiums.

的 1/4 到 1/3）用来支付住房的费用。

27. How do most people pay for a house?

【解析】选[B]。细节题。文中提到，当一个家庭决定要买房，通常是 borrow money from a bank 来付款，然后他们 repay the bank in regular payments（再向银行交纳定期的付款），这种银行贷款的方式叫做 mortgage（按揭），也就是说他们是通过 mortgage 来买房的。

28. What is the advantage of renting an apartment?

【解析】选[D]。细节题。文中说通常情况下，租房要比买房或贷款 cheaper，而且，当房子需要修理时，可以 ask the renter to fix it，这样也很方便。

Passage Two

【听力原文】	【答案解析】

[29] Nearly 100 years ago, America's working people began to join together to improve their wages and their working conditions. They formed unions. The unions presented a united position among workers in discussions with owners of businesses and factories. This idea became known as collective bargaining. Unions were started at separate local factories. Slowly unions in several factories started to join together. As they gained size, the unions wereable to gain strength and effectiveness. [30] By the 1950's unions were successfully representing their members in most American industries.

29. Why do American workers join unions?

【解析】选[C]。细节题。文章开头便提到，差不多 100 年前，美国工人联合在一起组成 unions（工会）to improve ... wages and ... working conditions（以改善他们的工资和工作环境）。

30. When were the unions successfully representing their members in most American industries?

Unions began as organizations for factory workers. Later skilled workers such as electricians and plumbers organized into unions. Recently professional people have also begun to form unions. Many teachers and nurses, for example, belong to unions.

Today the largest unions have several million members. [31]The unions not only represent the workers in discussions with business management. They also train workers for jobs, give members money if they lose their jobs, and pay workers pensions when they retire. In many situations, a person is not allowed to take a job unless he belongs to the unions.

Unions have become established institutions of American industry. Unions and management have learned to work for the benefit of both workers and owners.

【解析】选[B]。细节题。文中明确提到 by the 1950(到 20 世纪 50 年代),工会已经 successfully representing their members in most A merican industries(成功地代表了大多数美国工业成员)。

31. What do unions do nowadays?

【解析】选[B]。细节题。文中说在今天,工会还会 train workers for jobs(培训工人上岗),如果工人失业了,会 give members money,并且他们退休了,还会 pay workers pensions(支付退休金)。

Passage Three

【听力原文】

"Humans should not try to avoid stress any more than they would shun food, love or exercise." said Dr. Hans Selye, the first physician to document the effects of stress on the body. While there's no question that continuous stress is harmful, several studies suggest that [32①]challenging situations in which you're able to rise to the occasion can be good for you.

In a 2001 study of 158 hospital nurses, those who [33]coped with the challenging work were more likely to say they were in good health than those who felt they couldn't get the job done.

Stress that you can manage may also boost immune function. In a study at the Academic Center for Dentistry in Amsterdam, researchers put volunteers through two stressful experiences. In the

【答案解析】

32. What is this passage mainly about?

【解析】选[A]。主旨题。文章的开头和结尾都揭示了本文的主题是关于 stress。由关键词语 be good for(对⋯友好处)和 protective(起保护作用的)即可推知本文主要是讲述了压力的 benefits(好处)。[D]只是压力的好处之一,不能概括全文的主旨。

33. What can we conclude from the study of the 158 nurses in 2001?

【解析】选[C]。细节题。文

first, a timed task that required memorizing a list followed by a short test, subjects believed they had control over the outcome. In the second, they weren't in control: They had to sit through a bloody video on surgical procedures. Those who did go on the memory test had an increase in levels of immunoglobulin A, an antibody that's the body's first line of defense against germs.[34]The videowatchers experienced a decrease in the antibody.

Stress prompts the body to produce certain stress hormones.[35]In short bursts these hormones have a positive effect, including improved memory function. But in the long run these hormones can have a harmful effect on the body and brain.

Sustained stress is not good for you, but[32②]it's the occasional burst of stress or brief exposure to stress that could be protective.

中提到，能够妥善应付挑战工作的人 are more likely to...in good health（会处于更加健康的状态），由此可知从事具有挑战性的工作 may be good for one's health。

34. In the second stressful experiments, what happened to the video-watchers?

【解析】选[A]。细节题。文中提到，在第二个压力实验中，实验对象观看了一个 bloody video，他们对所面临的压力没有控制能力，因而导致他们体内的 a decrease in the antibody（抗体有所下降）。decrease ≈ decline。

35. What can we learn from the passage about stress hormones?

【解析】选[C]。细节题。文中提到在压力产生的瞬间，体内分泌的 hormones（荷尔蒙）会产生积极的效果，包括 improved memory function，也就是说短暂的荷尔蒙分泌能够 enhance memory function，但从长远角度来看，对身体会有害。

Section C

【听力原文】	【答案解析】
Some of the most (36) practical lessons coming out of research in (37) psychology are the area of memory. People ask, why can't I remember the time the (38) library book is due? Of a lot of people, memory may be weak, because they don't use it enough. It's like the (39) muscle. If you don't (40) exercise it, it won't get strong. That's why it's (41) important to keep our mind active,	36. 空前的形容词最高级 the most 及空后的名词 lessons 提示所填词应为形容词。practical 意为"实际的"。 37. 空前的介词 in 和空后的系动词 are 提示所填词应为名词。前面的 research 提示所填词应为表达某一学科或领域的词。psychology 意为"心理学、心理"。 38. 空前的定冠词 the 和空后的名词 book 提示所填词可能为名词或形容词，

to keep on (42) learning through our life. We can do this by reading, playing memory games and so on.

It's my guess though that the lack of (43) stimulation isn't a problem for students like you. (44) More likely, the life is so busy and stimulating that it itself may sometimes interfere with learning. Later on I will discuss how information is recorded from memory. But, first, the information needs to be recorded, in other words, learned, and for busy people like you and me, that will be the real problem. If we are distracted, or we are trying to think what we are going to do next, the incoming message just might not be getting recorded effectively, and (45) that leads to the first tip for students who want to improve their memories. Give your full attention to the information you hope to retain. (46) Research clearly shows the advantages of this, and also of active learning, of consciously trying to visualize a new fact, perhaps to make a mental picture, even a wild ridiculous one, so the new fact will stick in memory.

由 the time the ＿＿＿＿ book is due(还书的时间)推测所填词很可能表达"图书馆"的含义。library 意为"图书馆"。

39. 空前的介词 like 与定冠词 the 提示所填词应为名词。由后面的 it won't get strong 推测所填词可能表达"身体或肌肉"的含义。muscle 意为"肌肉"。

40. 空前的助动词 do 提示所填词应为动词原形。前面提到人经常不用脑，记忆力会下降，由此推测此处可能表达不"锻炼"身体或肌肉也不会变强壮，故所填词很可能表达"锻炼"的含义。exercise 意为"锻炼"。

41. 空前的 It's 与空后的动词不定式 to keep 提示所填词应为形容词。根据动词不定式的内容"to keep our mind active"推测，所填词很可能是要表示"重要的"的含义。important 意为"重要的"。

42. 空前的动词短语 keep on 和空后的介词 through 提示所填词应为动名词。根据空后的内容"through our life"与"reading"推测所填词很可能表达"学习"的含义。learning 意为"学习"。

43. 空前的介词 of 与空后的系动词 is 提示所填词应为名词。stimulation 意为"鼓励"。

44. 〖Main Points〗More **possibly**, the life is so busy and stimulating that it itself may **at times** interfere with learning

45. 〖Main Points〗that **shows** the first tip **to** students **hoping** to improve their memories

46. 〖Main Points〗Research clearly shows the **strong points** of this, and also of active learning, of trying to visualize a new fact **with consciousness**

Model Test 7

本套题录音在网上
www.sinoexam.cn

Section A
边听边记

Directions: *In this section, you will hear 8 short conversations and 2 long conversations. At the end of each conversation, one or more questions will be asked about what was said. Both the conversation and the questions will be spoken only once. After each question there will be a pause. During the pause, you must read the four choices marked [A], [B], [C], and [D], and decide which is the best answer. Then mark the corresponding letter on* **Answer Sheet** *2* with a single line through the centre.

11. [A] Make the shoes smaller.
    [B] Exchange the shoes for a larger pair.
    [C] Sell the shoes for men.
    [D] Work as a shoemaker at this shop.

12. [A] At home.   [B] In the countryside.
    [C] In hospital.   [D] At work.

13. [A] Planting something.   [B] Looking for something.
    [C] Looking for water.   [D] Getting dirt.

14. [A] Half an hour.   [B] A quarter of an hour.
    [C] Three quarters.   [D] Ten minutes.

15. [A] Jim's new truck.   [B] The weather.
    [C] Their exercise for the day. [D] A new business.

16. [A] A good citizen should be an expert in politics.
    [B] A good citizen should know a lot of curren affairs.
    [C] A citizen has no relationship with current affairs.
    [D] A good citizen needn't know too much about current affairs.

17. [A] The man and his brother's girlfriend.
    [B] The man and his classmate Jane.
    [C] The man, his brother and Jane.
    [D] The man, his brother John, his brother's girlfriend and the man's classmate Jane.

18. [A] Washington, D. C.   [B] Chicago.

     [C] New York City.   [D] Boston.

边听边记

Questions 19 to 21 are based on the conversation you have just heard.

19. [A] He is a supporter of Women's Liberation Movement.

     [B] He has strong prejudice against women.

     [C] He is not afraid to tell his firm belief to anyone.

     [D] He believes women can do men's jobs.

20. [A] She doesn't support the Women's Liberation Movement.

     [B] She is articulate and can express herself forcefully.

     [C] She doesn't think that women are intellectually inferior to men.

     [D] She convinces the man.

21. [A] The man and the woman are husband and wife.

     [B] The man and the woman are cousins.

     [C] The woman's name is Maggie.

     [D] The woman is cleverer than the man.

Questions 22 to 25 are based on the conversation you have just heard.

22. [A] Every day.   [B] Every other day.

     [C] Every week.   [D] Every month.

23. [A] The building site where an underground railroad was being built.

     [B] The building site where an underground garage was being built.

     [C] The building site where an underground department store was being built.

     [D] The building site where an underground walkway was being built.

24. [A] Plastic pail.   [B] Some plastic boxes.

     [C] Some plastic bags.   [D] A spade.

25. [A] Back home.   [B] To the market.

     [C] To the pond.   [D] To the police station.

Section B

Directions: *In this section, you will hear 3 short passages. At the end of each passage, you will hear some questions. Both the passage and the questions will be spoken only once. After you hear a question, you must choose the best* *answer from the four choices marked [A], [B], [C], and [D]. Then mark the corresponding letter on **Answer Sheet 2** with a single line through the centre.*

边听边记

Passage One

Questions 26 to 28 are based on the passage you have just heard.

26. [A] Extremely anxious.   [B] Very afraid of the trip.
    [C] With high expectations.   [D] Very excited.

27. [A] To go through the security.
    [B] To go to the shops and restaurants.
    [C] To check in.
    [D] To look around at the airport.

28. [A] Because the flight is going to an end.
    [B] Because people can see the city high from the sky.
    [C] Because people are high in the sky.
    [D] Because people are going to arrive safely.

Passage Two

Questions 29 to 31 are based on the passage you have just heard.

29. [A] To protect the children from smoking.
    [B] To make streets and schools safer for the children.
    [C] To give the children something positive to do after school.
    [D] To teach the children that drugs are dangerous, illegal and wrong.

30. [A] To forbid the teenagers to buy cigarettes.
    [B] To reduce their access to tobacco products.
    [C] To forbid tobacco advertisements.
    [D] To reduce the output of cigarettes.

31. [A] The Danger of Smoking.
    [B] The Fight against Youth Smoking.
    [C] The Education to Children.
    [D] Adolescent Problems.

Passage Three

Questions 32 to 35 are based on the passage you have just heard.

32. [A] Reasons for increased productivity.
    [B] How wristwatches are manufactured.
    [C] The industrialization of the United States.
    [D] The development of individual timepieces.

33. [A] They were common in the United States but not in Europe. 🎧 边听边记

　　[B] Only a few people had them.

　　[C] People considered them essential.

　　[D] They were not very accurate.

34. [A] They were a sign of wealth.

　　[B] It was important to be on time.

　　[C] It was fashionable to wear them.

　　[D] They were inexpensive.

35. [A] Watches were of higher quality than ever before.

　　[B] More clocks were manufactured than watches.

　　[C] The availability of watches increased.

　　[D] Watches became less important because factories had clocks.

Section C

Directions: *In this section, you will hear a passage three times. When the passage is read for the first time, you should listen carefully for its general idea. When the passage is read for the second time, you are required to fill in the blanks numbered from 36 to 43 with the exact words you have just heard. For blanks numbered from 44 to 46 you are required to fill in the missing information. For these blanks, you can either use the exact words you have just heard or write down the main points in your own words. Finally, when the passage is read for the third time, you should check what you have written.*

Have you ever felt that you are not (36) _____ , or worse have you been told this (37) _____ message? Many people (38) _____ with what is called time management. It is a skill that is rarely taught in school, however, its importance affects all of us.

All of us have had homework in school or (39) _____ around the house. Sometimes most of us if we were honest would admit to not completing a reading (40) _____ or two on time. Usually when the homework was not completed in the (41) _____ time, it had nothing to do with us lacking time, but how we (42) _____ our time. We lacked a solid time management plan.

Why should such a plan be important? There are twenty four

hours in any day. It is your job to (43) _____ all of the tasks 边听边记
assigned to you in a manageable time flame. (44)
_____. Some people prefer to write their
daily schedule down, in order to enforce what needs to be done at a
particular time. (45) _____.

It is up to the individual to implement a time management plan.
Working smarter is a result of having good time management skills.
(46) _____.

听力原文与答案详解

Section A & Section B

11	B	12	C	13	A	14	B	15	C	16	B	17	C	18	C	19	B
20	C	21	C	22	A	23	B	24	C	25	C	26	D	27	C	28	B
29	A	30	B	31	B	32	D	33	B	34	A	35	C						

Section C

36. productive   37. painful   38. struggle   39. chores
40. assignment   41. required   42. prioritized   43. accomplish
44. We all have deadlines, whether it is taking the kids to soccer practice, or a ten-page marketing plan due Friday at work
45. While others like myself, who are more liberal, do not write hour by hour what needs to be done, but what must be done on a certain day
46. You know specifically what needs to be done, and most importantly you won't forget that project at work that is due on Friday

Section A

11.

[A] Make the shoes smaller.	W: This pair of shoes is too small for
[B] Exchange the shoes for a larger pair.	my husband, so I have brought
[C] Sell the shoes for men.	them back for a larger pair.
[D] Work as a shoemaker at this shop.	M: Certainly, madam. Did you bring
	the receipt with you?
	Q: What does the woman want to do?

【解析】行为活动题。女士说这双鞋丈夫穿着有点小,所以把它带来想换 a larger pair(一双大一些的鞋)。

12.

[A] At home. [B] In the country- 　　side. [C] In hospital. [D] At work.	W: I heard that your brother Tom was injured in the accident 　　on his way to the countryside. M: Yes, he broke his leg, but he is much better now. In a 　　few days he should be coming home. The doctor said he 　　would recover in no time. Q: Where is Tom now?

【解析】地点场景题。由对话中的 injured, doctor 和 recover, 以及男士说过几天 Tom 就可以回家了可以推断出, Tom 现在在医院里。

13.

[A] Planting something. [B] Looking for something. [C] Looking for water. [D] Getting dirt.	W: May I watch what you are doing? M: Sure. You dig a hole, put in the seed, cover it 　　with dirt, and then water it. Q: What is the man doing?

【解析】行为活动题。男士说先 dig a hole(挖洞), 放入 seed(种子), 用土填好, 然后再浇水, 由此可知, 他正在植树。

14.

[A] Half an hour. [B] A quarter of an hour. [C] Three quarters. [D] Ten minutes.	W: Hurry up. We're not going to make it to the airport 　　on time. It is already 10:45. M: Take it easy. It only takes half an hour to get to the 　　airport and the plane won't leave until 11:30. I thi- 　　nk we'll make it all right if we leave immediately. Q: How much time will be left when the couple gets to 　　the airport?

【解析】数字信息题。女士说现在已经 10:45 了, 男士说没关系, 半个小时就到机场了, 飞机 11:30 才起飞, 由此可知, 他们到达机场还有 15 分钟的富余时间。

15.

[A] Jim's new truck. [B] The weather. [C] Their exercise for the day. [D] A new business.	W: Let's try out the new track in the gym. M: OK. But I'll need to warm up a little before 　　I start running. Q: What are the two speakers talking about?

【解析】谈论话题题。由对话中的关键词 track(跑道), gym(体育馆), warm up (热身)和 running 可以推断出, 他们在谈论 exercise。

16.

[A] A good citizen should be an expert in politics. [B] A good citizen should know a lot of curren affairs. [C] A citizen has no relationship with current affairs. [D] A good citizen needn't know too much about current affairs.	W: I have no interest in political affairs at all. M: A good citizen should be aware of current affairs even if he doesn't want to be an expert in politics. Q: What does the man mean?

【解析】观点态度题。女士说他对国家大事不感兴趣,男士则说一个好的公民应该了解 current affairs(时事),即使他并不想成为政治专家,由此可知,男士认为一个好公民应该知道 a lot of current affairs。

17.

[A] The man and his brother's girlfriend. [B] The man and his classmate Jane. [C] The man, his brother and Jane. [D] The man, his brother John, his brother's girlfriend and the man's classmate Jane.	W: Who's that girl between you and your brother John in the picture? M: She's John's girlfriend, my classmate Jane. Q: Who is in the picture?

【解析】事实状况题。女士问男士照片中男士和他哥哥中间的那个女孩是谁,男士回答说是他的同学、也是他哥哥的 girlfriend Jane,由此可知,照片中有男士、他的哥哥以及他哥哥的女朋友。

18.

[A] Washington, D. C.. [B] Chicago. [C] New York City. [D] Boston.	W: Go to bed as early as possible, Tom. Tomorrow, we'll see the Empire State Building and the Statue of Liberty. M: Wonderful. I also want to see the United Nations Building tomorrow. Q: Which city are the two speakers visiting?

【解析】事实状况题。由关键词 the Empire State Building(帝国大厦)和 the Statue of Liberty(自由女神像)可知,两个说话者在纽约。

Conversation One

【听力原文】	【答案解析】
M: I see that dreadful women's liberation group was out in Trafalgar Square yesterday. Hmm. In my	19. What can we learn according to the man's saying

opinion, they all talk rubbish. Maybe you won't agree with me.

W: But you can't really believe they all talk rubbish. You don't know the real condition. You can't judge it by that.

M: Of course, I can. I consider that it is unfeminine to protest.

W: But you can't really believe it's unfeminine to protest.

M: [19①] Women should be seen and not heard. That's really my way to think about it.

W: But you can't really believe that women should be seen and not heard.

M: Certainly. [19②] It's my belief that a woman's place is in the home. It's the only place they should belong to.

W: But you can't really believe that a woman's place is in the home.

M: Yes. And she should stay there. Women should look after men. Yes, they should and must look after men.

W: But you can't really believe women should look after men.

M: Created to feed and support them. That's what they were. [19③] I'm certain that women are intellectually inferior to men.

W: [20] But you can't really believe women are intellectually inferior to men.

M: Not only inferior, but I know they can't do a man's job.

W: But you can't really believe they can't do a man's job.

M: [21] Yes, Maggie. That's my firm belief. But don't tell your mother I said that.

"they all talk rubbish"?

【解析】选[B]。推断题。男士说他昨天看见追求妇女解放运动的人员外出示威,并且认为"they all talk rubbish"(他们在胡说八道),之后还多次说出轻视女性的言语,由此可推断,"they all talk rubbish"表现出他对妇女的轻视和偏见。

20. Which of the following statements is true of the woman?

【解析】选[C]。细节题。每次男士说出轻视女士的话时,女士都不同意他的观点,并加以反驳,当提到智力问题时,女士明确指出 women are (not) intellectually inferior to men(在智力方面,女人不比男人差)。

21. What can we infer from the conversation?

【解析】选[C]。细节题。男士在对话结尾处称女士 Maggie,而他们之间的关系,对话中并没有体现出来。

Conversation Two

【听力原文】	【答案解析】
W: A funny thing happened to me the other night.	22. How often does the woman take a walk?
M: Oh?	【解析】选［A］。细节
W: Well, you know ［22］I usually go out for a walk every night just after dark. Well, I was out the other night taking my usual walk and ［23］I heard a funny noise coming out of the building site down the road, the one where they dug a big hole lately, going to make it into an underground garage.	题。女士说她通常 go out for a walk every night(每晚都要外出散步)，由此可知,女士散步的频率是 every day。
M: Yes, I know it, go on.	23. Where did the funny noise come from?
W: I thought it must be some dog or cat that had got itself trapped or something.	【解析】选［B］。细节
M: So, what did you do?	题。女士说她散步的
W: Well, I went down there to investigate. Well, when I got down there I found the hole was full of frogs.	时候，听到 a funny noise (一个有趣的声音)从路边的工地传
M: Frogs?	来,这儿将要建成 an
W: Yes. So I thought what are they going to do when the bulldozers come to work tomorrow? So I climbed back out, ［24］went home and got some plastic bags, big ones, like you use for the rubbish.	underground garage (地下停车场)。
M: What for?	24. What did the woman go back home to get?
W: I went back and started collecting the frogs and putting them into the plastic bags. ［25］I thought I'd take them to the pond in the park. Next thing I know there are sirens screaming and bright lights everywhere.	【解析】选［C］。细节 题。女士说她回家取了一些 plastic bags (塑料袋)，来装青蛙。
M: What was going on then?	25. Where did the woman want to take the frogs to?
W: It was the police. Somebody had reported seeing me going into the building site and thought I was a burglar.	【解析】选［C］。细节
M: Well, what happened?	题。女士说她把青蛙装
W: They put me in one of the cars and took me down to the Station. Luckily I still had one of the bags on me full of frogs. The inspector turned out to be a bit of an animal-lover himself and he sent the two cars back to the building site and told his men to help me collect all the frogs.	入塑料袋,再把这些青蛙放入 the pond in the park(公园的池塘里)。

Section B

Passage One

【听力原文】	【答案解析】
[26]Many people get very excited when they go flying for the first time. Their reactions can vary from extreme anxiety to high expectations. Flying is very different from taking a train, bus or car. First time flyers experience many new things when they go on their first flight. [27]The process for checking in at the airport is much more complicated than when you get onto a bus or train. They will notice that security is much stricter. Very busy airports often have lots of shops and restaurants to entertain people while they are waiting. Once the passengers get onto the airplane, they find their seats and wait for the take-off. Before take-off, the flight attendant will go over what to do in case of an emergency. This can cause some fear in those who are nervous about flying, since it reminds them of the worst case. Next comes the take-off, which is very exciting because one can look out of the window and see the ground gradually disappear from view. Flights can vary from very short, an hour or so, or very long, up to 10 and 12 hours. Meals and movies are usually provided for the longer flights in all classes. Last, [28]the landing is once again another exciting moment, because you can see the city you are flying into high from the sky.	26. What is the reaction of people when they go flying for the first time? 【解析】选[D]。细节题。文章开始就说第一次坐飞机的人会 get very excited（感到非常激动）。 27. What is the first new thing for the-first-time flyers to experience? 【解析】选[C]。细节题。文中说对于第一次乘飞机的人来说，许多经历都是新的，文中依次提到了 checking in at the airport（办理登机手续），通过安检等，而办理登机手续是第一件要经历的事。 28. Why is landing so exciting to the first-time flyers? 【解析】选[B]。细节题。文中最后说飞机着陆时飞机乘客可以 see the city…high from the sky（从高空俯瞰城市），所以第一次乘坐飞机的人在飞机降落时会感觉很兴奋。

Passage Two

【听力原文】	【答案解析】
Since I took office I've done everything in my power to protect our children from harm. We've worked to make their streets and their schools safer, to give them something positive to do after school and	29. According to the speaker, what is the more important thing we have to do for the children?

and before their parents get home. We've worked to teach our children that drugs are dangerous, illegal and wrong.

Today, [29][31] I want to talk to you about the historic opportunity we now have to protect our nation's children from an even more deadly threat: smoking. Smoking kills more people every day than AIDS, alcohol, car accidents, murders, suicides, drugs and fires combined. Nearly 90 percent of those smokers lit their first cigarette before they turned 18. Consider this: 3,000 children start to smoke every day illegally, and 1,000 of them will die sooner because of it.

This is a national tragedy that every American should be honor-bound to help prevent. For more than five years we've worked to stop our children from smoking before they start, [30] launching a nationwide campaign to educate them about the dangers of smoking, to reduce their access to tobacco products, and to severely restrict tobacco companies from advertising to young people. If we do these, we'll cut teen smoking by almost half over the next five years. That means if we act now, we have it in our power to stop three million children from smoking—and to save a million lives as a result.

【解析】选[A]。细节题。短文在开头提出人们已经尽力为青少年提供了更健康的生活环境，接着讲话人说现在更重要的是应该保护我们国家的孩子们远离 more deadly threat（更加致命的威胁）：smoking，由此可知，防止青少年吸烟是目前最重要的事情。

30. Which of the four choices has been done to stop the children from smoking?

【解析】选[B]。细节题。文中说，为了阻止青少年吸烟，采取了一系列的措施：educate them about the dangers of smoking（宣传吸烟危害），reduce their access to tobacco products（减少青少年接近烟草产品的机会），禁止针对青少年的 advertising，。

31. Which is the best title for this passage?

【解析】选[B]。主旨题。本文主要谈论的就是青少年吸烟问题，并且谈到了为解决这个问题所采取的措施，所以短文的标题应该是 the danger of smoking。

Passage Three

【听力原文】	【答案解析】
I'm sure almost every one of you looked at your watch or at a clock before you came to class today. Watches and clocks seem as much a part of our life as breathing or eating. [33] And yet did you know that [32①] watches and clocks were scarce in the United States until the 1850's? In the late 1700's, people didn't know the exact time unless they were	32. What does the speaker mainly discuss? 【解析】选[D]。主旨题。根据文中不断出现的年代以及不同年代里 watch 的情况可知，本文主要谈论的是钟表是如何一步步走入普通人

near a clock. Those delightful clocks in the squares of European towns were built for the public. After all, most citizens simply couldn't afford a personal timepiece. [34]In the 1800's in Europe and the United States, the main purpose of a watch, which by the way was attached to a gold chain, was to show others how wealthy you were. The ' word [32②] "wrist watch" didn't even enter the English language until nearly 1900. By then the rapid pace of the industrialization in the United States meant that measuring time had become essential. How could the factory worker get to work on time unless he or she knew exactly what time it was? Since the efficiency was now measured by how fast the job was done, everyone was interested in time. [35]And since industrialization made possible the manufacture of large quantities of goods, [32③] watches became fairly inexpensive. Furthermore, electric light kept factories going around the clock. Being "on time" had entered the language and life of every citizen.

生活并得到普及的。

33. What was true about watches before the 1850's?

【解析】选[B]。细节题。文中说在 1850 年之前钟表还是很 scarce (稀少)的东西,由此可知,在那之前只有很少一部分人拥有钟表。

34. According to the passage, why did some people wear watches in the 1800's?

【解析】选[A]。细节题。文中说在 19 世纪手表的主要用途是 show others how wealthy …were (显示手表拥有者的富有)。选项[A]是原文的同义转述。

35. What effect did industrialization have on watch-making?

【解析】选[C]。推断题。文章最后说工业化使手表的产量增加,价格 became fairly inexpensive(降低了),由此可推断,工业化使手表的使用者增加了。

Section C

【听力原文】	【答案解析】
Have you ever felt that you are not (36) **productive**, or worse have you been told this (37) **painful** message? Many people (38) **struggle** with what is called time management. It is a skill that is rarely taught in school, however, its importance affects all of us. All of us have had homework in school or (39) **chores** around the house. Sometimes most of us if we	36. 空前的系动词 are 提示所填词应为形容词或动词的被动形式。productive 意为"多产的"。 37. 空前的指示代词 this 和空后的名词 message 提示所填词应为形容词。根据前面的 worse 推测此处应是指不好的消息。painful 意为"痛苦的"。 38. 分析句子结构可知,句子缺少谓语成分,主语 many people 与上下文时态提示所填词应为动词原形,且能与介词 with 搭配。struggle 意为"斗争"。

were honest would admit to not completing a reading (40) assignment or two on time. Usually when the homework was not completed in the (41) required time, it had nothing to do with us lacking time, but how we (42) prioritized our time. We lacked a solid time management plan.

Why should such a plan be important? There are twenty four hours in any day. It is your job to (43) accomplish all of the tasks assigned to you in a manageable time flame. (44) We all have deadlines, whether it is taking the kids to soccer practice, or a ten-page marketing plan due Friday at work. Some people prefer to write their daily schedule down, in order to enforce what needs to be done at a particular time. (45) While others like myself, who are more liberal, do not write hour by hour what needs to be done, but what must be done on a certain day.

It is up to the individual to implement a time management plan. Working smarter is a result of having good time management skills. (46) You know specifically what needs to be done, and most importantly you won't forget that project at work that is due on Friday.

39. 并列连词 or 提示所填词应为名词，与 homework 构成并列结构。由 homework in school 和空后的 around the house 推测所填词很可能表达"家务"的含义。chores 意为"家务活"。

40. 空前的不定冠词 a 及名词 reading 提示所填词应为单数可数名词。由后面的 homework 推测所填词很可能是要表示"任务"的含义。assignment 意为"任务"。

41. 空前的定冠词 the 和空后的名词 time 提示所填词应为形容词。根据下文中出现的 in a manageable time 推测，此处应表达在规定的时间内，与 manageable 为近义复现，故所填词很可能表达"规定的、要求的"的含义。required 意为"需要的"。

42. 分析句子结构可知，句子缺少谓语成分，故所填词为动词，根据本段上下文的时态推测，所填词应为动词的过去式。prioritized 意为"优先考虑"。

43. 空前的不定词 to 与空后的名词短语 all of the tasks 提示所填词应为动词原形。根据句子后面的 tasks assigned to you 推测所填词可能是要表达"完成"的含义。accomplish 意为"完成"。

44.【Main Points】We all have deadlines, whether it is taking the **children** to soccer practice, or marketing plan **of ten pages** due Friday at work

45.【Main Points】While others like myself, who are more **free**, do not write hour by hour what **should** be done, but what must be done on a certain day

46.【Main Points】You know **certainly** what needs to be done, and most importantly you won't forget that project at work that is due on Friday

Model Test 8

Section A

Directions: *In this section, you will hear 8 short conversations and 2 long conversations. At the end of each conversation, one or more questions will be asked about what was said. Both the conversation and the questions will be spoken only once. After each question there will be a pause. During the pause, you must read the four choices marked [A], [B], [C], and [D], and decide which is the best answer. Then mark the corresponding letter on **Answer Sheet** 2 with a single line through the centre.*

11. [A] She can't give more without doctor's orders.
    [B] She has no more of what he wants.
    [C] She can give a new prescription.
    [D] She can't recommend a doctor to him.

12. [A] He has just begun taking music lessons.
    [B] He gives music lessons.
    [C] He plays the violin very well.
    [D] He is very proud of his violin.

13. [A] She likes ice cream best.
    [B] She likes hamburgers best.
    [C] She likes nothing.
    [D] She likes both hamburgers and ice cream.

14. [A] John will be late for two or three minutes.
    [B] They should call John now to find out what happened.
    [C] They should not wait for John.
    [D] John will be here in no time.

15. [A] Because she is ill.
    [B] Becauseshe has to do the research paper.
    [C] Because she doesn't want to.
    [D] Because she has to look after her mother.

16. [A] Boss and secretary.

〔B〕Doctor and nurse.

〔C〕Patient and dentist.

〔D〕Patient and receptionist.

17. 〔A〕A letter from Mark and a thank-you note for taking the picture.

〔B〕A letter from Mark, a bill for bread and butter and a picture.

〔C〕Two letters and a picture of Carlos.

〔D〕A letter from Mark, a thank-you note from Carlos and a picture.

18. 〔A〕At home. 〔B〕On a plane.

〔C〕In his office. 〔D〕On a bus.

Questions 19 to 21 are based on the conversation you have just heard.

19. 〔A〕Father and daughter. 〔B〕Brother and sister.

〔C〕Husband and wife. 〔D〕Mother and son.

20. 〔A〕The woman has no patience in filling in the questionnaire.

〔B〕The woman is interested in filling in the questionnaire.

〔C〕The woman is enthusiastic about filling in the question-naire.

〔D〕The woman is worried about filling in the questionnaire.

21. 〔A〕The cat didn't touch it. 〔B〕The cat enjoyed eating it.

〔C〕The cat became ill. 〔D〕The cat was dead.

Questions 22 to 25 are based on the conversation you have just heard.

22. 〔A〕Walking around the streets and looking for signs or looking in the paper.

〔B〕Looking in the map.

〔C〕Going to city ball and signing his name in the office.

〔D〕Asking the local police station.

23. 〔A〕Small hostels. 〔B〕Youth hostels.

〔C〕Old Hostels. 〔D〕Large hostels.

24. 〔A〕Call in advance.

〔B〕Become a member.

〔C〕Work in the hostels for some time instead of paying.

〔D〕Make reservations.

25. 〔A〕Angry. 〔B〕Enthusiastic.

〔C〕Hysterical. 〔D〕Arrogant.

Section B

Directions: *In this section, you will hear 3 short passages. At the end of each passage, you will hear some questions. Both the passage and the questions will be spoken only once. After you hear a question, you must choose the best answer from the four choices marked [A], [B], [C], and [D]. Then mark the corresponding letter on* **Answer Sheet 2** *with a single line through the centre.*

Passage One

Questions 26 to 28 are based on the passage you have just heard.

26. [A] They work to earn a master's degree.

　　[B] They work to earn a master's or a doctorate.

　　[C] They work to earn a bachelor's degree.

　　[D] They work to earn a doctorate.

27. [A] Because they hope to learn more important things.

　　[B] Because they hope to earn higher degrees.

　　[C] Because they hope to get better jobs with their degrees.

　　[D] Because they hope to become experts after they graduate.

28. [A] Because of changes and new developments in all fields.

　　[B] Because of the attraction of good living.

　　[C] Because of their regret of not owning a higher degree.

　　[D] Because of the high paying they may receive after graduation.

Passage Two

Questions 29 to 31 are based on the passage you have just heard.

29. [A] Holding food. 　　　　　　[B] Jumping and fighting.

　　[C] Eating food. 　　　　　　　[D] Finding food.

30. [A] It climbs into its mother's pouch.

　　[B] It's born in the pouch.

　　[C] It's put into the pouch by a nurse.

　　[D] The mother kangaroo puts the baby in the pouch.

31. [A] A few weeks after it is born.

　　[B] Many weeks after it is born.

　　[C] Thirty or forty days after it is born.

　　[D] Six months after it is born.

Passage Three

边听边记

Questions 32 to 35 are based on the passage you have just heard.

32. ［A］18 American undergraduates.
　　［B］18 American postgraduates.
　　［C］18 overseas undergraduates.
　　［D］18 overseas postgraduates.

33. ［A］Family relations.　　　［B］Social problems.
　　［C］Family planning.　　　［D］Personal matters.

34. ［A］Red.　［B］Blue.　［C］Green.　［D］Purple.

35. ［A］The five questions were not well designed.
　　［B］Not all the questionnaires were returned.
　　［C］Only a small number of students were surveyed.
　　［D］Some of the answers to the questionnaire were not valid.

Section C

Directions: *In this section，you will hear a passage three times. When the passage is read for the first time，you should listen carefully for its general idea. When the passage is read for the second time，you are required to fill in the blanks numbered from 36 to 43 with the exact words you have just heard. For blanks numbered from 44 to 46 you are required to fill in the missing information. For these blanks，you can either use the exact words you have just heard or write down the main points in your own words. Finally，when the passage is read for the third time，you should check what you have written.*

　　Advertisers can use numerous media，or means，to deliver their sales messages. The (36) _____ media are newspapers，magazines，television，radio，(37) _____ mail，outdoor signs，and point-of-sale or (38) _____ advertising. Which single medium or (39) _____ of media is used depends on the product，the market area in which the company (40) _____，the income group to which the product appeals，and other (41) _____.

　　Newspapers are the oldest advertising medium in the United States. The newspaper，with its fresh stream of news and features，(42) _____ a high degree of reader interest every day.

Housewives often buy papers for the advertisements as much as for 边听边记
the（43）＿＿＿＿＿ content. They use the retail ads as shopping
guides.（44）＿＿＿＿＿＿＿＿＿＿＿＿＿＿＿＿. Newspapers
are useful for both local and national advertising.

　　Magazines are another important medium for advertisers.（45）
＿＿＿＿＿＿＿＿＿＿＿＿＿＿＿＿＿＿＿＿＿. Mass-circulation
magazines, such as *Times*, *Newsweek*, *Playboy*, *and Reader's
Digest*,（46）＿＿＿＿＿＿＿＿＿＿＿＿＿＿＿＿＿＿.

听力原文与答案详解

Section A & Section B

11	A	12	C	13	B	14	D	15	D	16	D	17	D	18	B	19	C
20	A	21	C	22	A	23	B	24	B	25	B	26	B	27	C	28	A
29	B	30	A	31	D	32	D	33	D	34	B	35	C				

Section C

36. principal　　37. direct　　　　38. point-of-purchase　　39. combination
40. operates　　41. considerations　　42. stimulates　　　43. editorial
44. Classified ads provide an important service for readers, who are seeking a job,
　　an apartment or a house or a special service
45. Many magazines are printed on high-quality paper, which makes it possible to
　　run unusually attractive ads in color
46. reach millions of readers and are used mainly by national advertisers

Section A

11.

［A］She can't give more without doctor's orders. ［B］She has no more of what he wants. ［C］She can give a new prescription. ［D］She can't recommend a doctor to him.	M: May I please get this prescription refilled? W: I'm sorry we can't give you a refill on that, sir, and you will have to get a new prescription from your doctor. Q: What did the woman mean?

【解析】事实状况题。男士问女士是否可以 get this prescription refilled（按处方再开一份药），女士回答说他必须 get a new prescription from...doctor，由此可知女士的言外之意就是没有医生的吩咐她不能再卖药给男士。

12.

［A］He has just begun taking music lessons.	W: I was very surprised to hear Thomas play the violin. From what he said, I thought

[B] He gives music lessons.	he had just started his lessons.
[C] He plays the violin very well.	M: No, that's the way he always talks.
[D] He is very proud of his violin.	Q: What can we learn from the conversation?

【解析】事实状况题。女士说听了 Thomas 演奏小提琴,她很震惊,原来还以为真像 Thomas 说的那样他只是 started…lessons(刚刚开始学),由此可知 Thomas 不是刚开始学小提琴,而是演奏得非常好。

13.

[A] She likes ice cream best.	W: What can I buy for your little sister?
[B] She likes hamburgers best.	M: Except for hamburgers, there is nothing
[C] She likes nothing.	Kitty likes better than ice cream.
[D] She likes both hamburgers and ice cream.	Q: What does Kitty like best?

【解析】事实状况题。男士说除了 hamburgers,Kitty 最喜欢的是 ice cream,由此可知 Kitty 最喜欢 hamburgers。

14.

[A] John will be late for two or three minutes.	M: John was supposed to meet us here at 8: 30. How come he still hasn't shown up till now?
[B] They should call John now to find out what happened.	W: I just got a call from John. He said the traffic was backed up but he would try to
[C] They should not wait for John.	be here in two or three minutes.
[D] John will be here in no time.	Q: What does the woman mean?

【解析】行为活动题。女士说 John 说路上堵车了,但他尽力 be here in two or three minutes,也就是说 John 立刻就到。in no time 意为"马上,立刻"。

15.

[A] Because she is ill.	M: Mary won't attend the birthday party
[B] Because she has to do the research paper.	because she has to do her research paper.
[C] Because she doesn't want to.	W: Tom has a bad cold and Kitty has to look after her sick mother. So they'll both stay
[D] Because she has to look after her mother.	at home.
	Q: Why won't Kitty go to the party?

【解析】事实状况题。女士说 Kitty 必须要去 look after her sick mother,所以也不能来参加聚会。

16.

[A] Boss and secretary.	M: I'd like to have Dr. Smith look at my teeth.
[B] Doctor and nurse.	W: Let's see. I can arrange for you to see the doctor
[C] Patient and dentist.	five days from now.
[D] Patient and receptionist.	Q: What is the probable relationship between the two
	speakers?

【解析】身份关系题。男士说他想让 Dr. Smith 给他看牙,女士说那她只能给男士安排到五天以后了,由此可知他们是患者和接待员的关系。

17.

[A] A letter from Mark and a thank-you note for taking the picture.	W: What a thick letter!
[B] A letter from Mark, a bill for bread and butter and a picture.	M: Yes. Inside the envelope was a letter from Mark, a bread-and-butter letter from Carlos and a picture of all the graduates.
[C] Two letters and a picture of Carlos.	
[D] A letter from Mark, a thank - you note from Carlos and a picture.	Q: What's inside the envelope?

【解析】事实状况题。男士说信中有 a letter from Mark, a bread-and-butter letter (感谢信) from Carlos 和 a picture。

18.

[A] At home.	W: Where were you last Boxing Day?
[B] On a plane.	M: I was a passenger on Air American Liner a year ago today. At that time I'd just left my home for my office in London.
[C] In his office.	
[D] On a bus.	Q: Where was the man last Boxing Day?

【解析】事实状况题。女士问男士上一个 Boxing Day(节礼日)他在什么地方,男士回答说那时他是 Air American Liner(美国空中客机)上的一名乘客,由此可知男士当时正在飞机上。

Conversation One

【听力原文】	【答案解析】
M: [19] Good morning, love.	19. What is the possible relationship between the two speakers?
W: Morning.	
M: Sleep well? I've made some tea; there you are.	
W: Thanks. Any post?	

M: Not really. There's a postcard from Aunt Lily and there's a questionnaire to fill in from the company which gave us the free samples of tinned meat to try out for them.	【解析】选[C]。推断题。对话一开头，男士称女士 love，由此可推断他们是夫妻关系。
W: [20] They've got a nerve!	
M: But we did say we'd return the questionnaire when we took the samples.	20. Which of the following statements is true?
W: What do they want to know?	
M: If we liked it.	【解析】选[A]。推断题。男士告诉女士这还有一个 questionnaire（调查问卷）需要填，女士说 They've got a nerve!（他们还好意思问!），由此可推断她很不耐烦。
W: If we liked it? Are they joking? You're not filling it in now, are you? What for?	
M: We did promise and if I do it now I can post it on my way to work.	
W: Well, write "we didn't like it."	
M: I'll put "not much". That sounds nicer. Then it says "If not, why?"	
W: No flavor. Too much fat.	
M: "How did you cook it?" is next.	21. For "Guests' comments", what is the woman's answer?
W: Fried it like they said, didn't I? Took a mouthful and gave it to the cat.	
M: [21] "Guests' comments, if any!"	【解析】选[C]。细节题。女士把灌装肉喂了猫，所以当男士问女士 Guests' comments（顾客评价）这一栏填什么时，女士回答说猫 became ill，更糟的是，它的毛都变绿了。
W: The cat became ill. Poor thing, her fur went all green.	
M: "Did guests ask for the brand name?"	
W: Tell them that our cat can't speak.	
M: "Will you be buying our product regularly?"	
W: Certainly not! They must be out of their minds.	
M: "Did you find the tin attractive?"	
W: Cut myself opening it. Nearly lost my thumb. Couldn't use it for a week. I thought it was infected.	
M: "Any other comments?"	
W: Well, tell them we're too polite to answer that.	

Conversation Two

【听力原文】	【答案解析】
M: Excuse me, Madame. Will you be so kind to tell me something? Actually, could you tell me where can I stay in this town, please?	22. How can the visitor find bed and breakfast places?
	【解析】选[A]。细节题。女

W: Of course, it's my honor. You must be a stranger here.

M: Yes, I am here for a tour and I am a visitor.

W: OK, I see. That's why you are carrying a lot of things. There are lots of hotels, but they tend to be fairly expensive. And then there are bed and breakfast places, which are much cheaper, and [22] you can find out about them through looking in the paper, or else just walking around the streets, and they have signs in thewindow saying "Bed & Breakfast".

M: Are there any other hostels? For example, are there [23①] any cheap hostels?

W: [23②] Oh, yes, of course there are some youth hostels.

M: What are the youth hostels like? Is it expensive or cheap?

W: The youth hostels are OK. All you get is a bed, but they do tend to be very cheap.

M: [24①] Do I have to become a member?

W: [24②] Yes, you do, in fact. But it's very easy to join, and there's an office along the road, where you can go and sign on.

M: [25] It's really very kind of you to tell me so much about it. Thank you very much.

W: Don't mention it. Every resident here is very kind. You will know it later.

士说男士(visitor)可以通过 looking in the paper 的方式,或 通过 walking around the streets 寻找挂着 Bed & Breakfast 牌子 的方式找到提供食宿的地方。

23. Besides bed and breakfast places, where can the visitors find cheap accommodations?

【解析】选[B]。细节题。男士 问这里还有没有其他 cheap hostels(便宜些的招待所),女 士回答说,还有 youth hostels (青年招待所)。

24. To live in youth hostels, what do visitors have to do?

【解析】选[B]。男士问女士他 要入住青年招待所,是否需要 成为 a member(会员),女士回 答说是这样的,由此可知旅客 想要入住青年招待所就得 become a member。

25. What's the woman's attitude towards the stranger?

【解析】选[B]。推断题。男士 提出的每个问题女士都详尽回答, 男士说她 really very kind,并对 她表示非常感谢,由此可知,女士 对待这个陌生人是非常热情的。

Section B

Passage One

【听力原文】	【答案解析】
After graduation, many American students postpone finding jobs. They stay at the university and work for a higher degree. Other students take a job for a few years. They then quit and resume	26. What degree do graduate students work to earn? 【解析】选[B]。细节题。文 中提到许多大学生毕业后继

studying at the university. [26] These students work to earn higher degrees: a master's or a doctorate. They are called graduate students. Graduate students specialize in a particular field of study. They study to become experts in this field and to learn new advances in their fields while they earn an M. A. or Ph. D. [27] They hope that when they earn their graduate degrees they will succeed in finding important jobs that are interesting and high paying.

The life of a graduate student is often difficult. They are usually too busy studying to make a good living. Often they have to pay high tuition fees for their education.

In today's world, most graduate students don't regret spending time with their studies. [28] They find that things are changing very fast. New developments are occurring in all fields. For many, graduate study has become a necessity.

续努力学习以获得更高的学位，如 a master's（硕士学位）或 a doctorate（博士学位）。

27. Why do people go to the graduate school?

【解析】选[C]。细节题。文中提到人们希望拿到更高的学历之后可以找到更 interesting（有趣）而且 high paying（待遇好）的工作。

28. Why has graduate study become necessary for many people nowadays?

【解析】选[A]。细节题。文章结尾提到，许多研究生并不后悔花费时间去学习，因为他们觉得所有事物都在不断 changing，各行各业都有 new development，所以对于许多人来说，研究生教育已经成为一件必要的事。

Passage Two

【听力原文】

Australia is the home of the kangaroo. In most parts of the world, a person must go to a zoo to see a kangaroo. In Australia, kangaroos move about in freedom in the forests and on the plains. Long ago, kangaroos were giants. They were almost ten feet tall. Today, kangaroos are about the size of a man. They are five to six feet tall and weigh about 150 pounds. [29] Kangaroos stand on their large hind legs. They use these hind legs for jumping and, if necessary, for fighting. Close to the kangaroo's bodies are small front legs. These are for finding and holding food.

A kangaroo has a pouch. A baby kangaroo lives inside its mother for only thirty to forty days. At birth, the baby is only about one inch long and it is not fully formed. Its eyes and ears are closed, it has no fur, and

【答案解析】

29. What do kangaroos use their hind legs for?

【解析】选[B]。细节题。文中提到袋鼠后腿的作用是 jumping（跳跃）和 fighting（格斗）。

30. How does the baby kangaroo get into its mother's pouch?

【解析】选[A]。文中提到小袋鼠是 climbs up（爬到）妈妈身上，然后钻进妈妈的 pouch（袋子）里。

31. At what age can a baby kangaroo live outside

its hind legs are not developed. [30] This small baby climbs up its mother's body and into her pouch. It takes hold of a nipple and stays there for many weeks, nursing and developing. Soon, its eyes open and its ears form. It grows fur. Finally the baby kangaroo lets go of the nipple and looks outside. Soon, it climbs in and out of the pouch easily. [31] At six months of age, the young kangaroo leaves the pouch. Now it's called a joey.

its mother's pouch?

【解析】选 [D]。细节题。文中提到小袋鼠 at six months of age(在六个月大的时候)就可以离开妈妈的 pouch（育儿袋）了。

Passage Three

【听力原文】

On 15th, Feb, 1989, [32] an instant survey was carried out among 18 overseas postgraduate students, 11 students were male and 7 were female. [33] The purpose of the survey was to discover the views of the students on a number of matters of personal concern. The survey was conducted by means of a questionnaire given to the students to complete. There were five questions. The first question concerned favorite color and the second favorite number. The next 3 questions were all concerned with aspects of marriage. No. 3 looked at the ideal age to get married, No. 4 examined the qualities looked for in a partner and No. 5 asked about the ideal number of children. The main findings were as follows. [34] Blue was the most popular color. This was followed by Green and Purple. There was no real significance in the choice of lucky number. About one third of the students said that they had none. Sixty-one percent of the students selected the age group 26 to 30 years as ideal for marriage, followed by 21 to 25 years. Looking at the most important qualities in an ideal partner, someone hoped the person to be "intelligent", others chose "natural", and still others indicated "attractive" and "honest". The ideal number of chi-

【答案解析】

32. Who were involved in this instant survey?

【解析】选 [D]。细节题。文中提到，18 overseas postgraduate students（国外的研究生）参与了这项调查。

33. What do the five questions in the survey focus on?

【解析】选 [D]。细节题。文中提到调查的重点放在学生们的 personal concern（私人问题方面）。personal matters ≈ matters of personal concern。

34. What color was chosen as the most popular in the survey?

【解析】选 [B]。细节题。文中提到调查结果显示，Blue was the most popular color（蓝色最受欢迎）。

35. Why is it difficult to reach any definite conclusions from the survey?

【解析】选 [C]。文章结尾

ldren was 2, followed by 3. [35] It is not easy to reach any definite conclusions based upon such a small sample of students from such widely different backgrounds. However, it is clear that majority favorite of 26 to 30 is the ideal age to get married with an intelligent partner, and producing 2 children.	处提到,因为 based upon such a small sample of students(学生样本的数量太少),而且学生的背景因素又各不相同,所以此次调查很难得出明确的结论。

Section C

【听力原文】	【答案解析】
Advertisers can use numerous media, or means, to deliver their sales messages. The (36) <u>principal</u> media are newspapers, magazines, television, radio, (37) <u>direct</u> mail, outdoor signs, and point-of-sale or (38) <u>point-of-purchase</u> advertising. Which single medium or (39) <u>combination</u> of media is used depends on the product, the market area in which the company (40) <u>operates</u>, the income group to which the product appeals, and other (41) <u>considerations</u>. Newspapers are the oldest advertising medium in the United States. The newspaper, with its fresh stream of news and features, (42) <u>stimulates</u> a high degree of reader interest every day. Housewives often buy papers for the advertisements as much as for the (43) <u>editorial</u> content. They use the retail ads as shopping guides. (44) <u>Classified ads provide an important service for readers, who are seeking a job, an apartment or a house or a</u>	36. 空前的定冠词 the 和空后的名词 media 提示所填词应为形容词。由前面提到的 numerous media 和空后的 newspapers, magazines, television, radio… 推测,此处可能是要表达报纸、杂志等是"主要的"媒介的含义。principal 意为"主要的"。 37. 空后的名词 mail 提示所填词应为名词或形容词。direct 意为"直接的"。 38. 空前的并列连词 or 和空后的名词 advertising 提示所填词应为形容词或名词与 point-of-sale 并列,修饰 advertising。point-of-purchase 意为"购买点"。 39. 空前的并列连词 or 和空后的介词 of 提示所填词应为名词,与 single medium 并列。combination 意为"组合"。 40. 分析句子结构可知,所填词应在从句中作谓语,再根据本段的时态推测,所填词应为动词的第三人称单数形式。operates 意为"操作"。 41. 空前的并列连词 and 和形容词 other 提示所填词应为名词的复数形式,与前面的 market 和 income 并列。前面提到了影响广告的多种考虑,再根据 other 推测所填词可能表达其他"考虑"的含义。considerations 意为"考虑"。 42. 分析句子结构可知,所填词应在句子中作谓语,再根据本段时态和主语 the newspa-

special service. Newspapers are useful for both local and national advertising.

Magazines are another important medium for advertisers. (45) Many magazines are printed on high-quality paper, which makes it possible to run unusually attractive ads in color. Mass-circulation magazines, such as *Times*, *Newsweek*, *Playboy*, *and Reader's Digest*, (46) reach millions of readers and are used mainly by national advertisers.

per 推测,所填词应为动词的第三人称单数形式。由句子内容和空后的 reader interest 推测所填词可能要表示"激发"的含义。stimulates 意为"激发"。

43.空前的定冠词 the 和空后的名词 content 提示所填词应为形容词。editorial 意为"编辑的"。

44. [Main Points] Classified ads **offer** an important service for readers **looking for** a job, an apartment or a house or a special service

45. [Main Points] Many magazines are printed on high-quality paper, which makes it **likely** to run unusually attractive **colorful** ads

46. [Main Points] **have** millions of readers and are used **mostly** by national advertisers